Ian Rankin

The Impossible Dead

First published in Great Britain in 2011 by Orion Books,
an imprint of The Orion Publishing Group Ltd
Orion House, 5 Upper Saint Martin's Lane,
London WC2H 9EA

An Hachette UK Company

A CIP catalogue record for this book
is available from the British Library.

Typeset by Deltatype Ltd, Birkenhead, Merseyside

Printed in Great Britain by Clays Ltd, St Ives plc

The Orion Publishing Group's policy is to use papers
that are natural, renewable and recyclable products and
made from wood grown in sustainable forests. The logging
and manufacturing processes are expected to conform to
the environmental regulations of the country of origin.

www.orionbooks.co.uk

One

1

'He's not here,' the desk sergeant said.

'So where is he?'

'Out on a call.'

Fox stared hard at the man, knowing it wouldn't do any good. The sergeant was one of those old-timers who reckoned they'd seen it all and faced most of it down. Fox glanced at the next name on his list.

'Haldane?'

'Sick leave.'

'Michaelson?'

'Out on the call with DI Scholes.'

Tony Kaye was standing just behind Fox's left shoulder. An instant before the words were out of his mouth, Fox knew what his colleague was going to say.

'This is taking the piss.'

Fox turned to give Kaye a look. News would now travel through the station: job done. The Complaints had come to town, found no one home, and had let their annoyance show. The desk sergeant shifted his weight from one foot to the other, trying not to seem too satisfied at this turn of events.

Fox took a moment to study his surroundings. The notices pinned to the walls were the usual stuff. It was a modern police station, meaning it could just as easily have been the reception area of a doctors' surgery or DSS office, as long as you disregarded the sign warning that the Alert Status had been lifted from LOW to MODERATE. Nothing to do with Fox and his men: there'd been reports of a blast in woodland outside Lockerbie. Kids, probably,

3

and a good long way from Kirkcaldy. Nevertheless, every police station in the country would have been notified.

The button on the counter had a hand written sign next to it saying Press For Attention – which was what Fox had done three or four minutes ago. There was a two-way mirror behind the counter, and the desk sergeant had almost certainly been watching the three arrivals – Inspector Malcolm Fox, Sergeant Tony Kaye and Constable Joe Naysmith. The station had been told they were coming. Interviews had been arranged with DI Scholes, and DSs Haldane and Michaelson.

'Think this is the first time we've had this stunt pulled on us?' Kaye was asking the desk sergeant. 'Maybe we'll start the interviews with you instead.'

Fox flipped to the second sheet of paper in his folder. 'How about your boss – Superintendent Pitkethly?'

'She's not in yet.'

Kaye made a show of checking his watch.

'Meeting at HQ,' the desk sergeant explained. Joe Naysmith, standing to Fox's right, seemed more interested in the leaflets on the counter. Fox liked that: it spoke of easy confidence, the confidence that these officers *would* be interviewed, that delaying tactics were nothing new to the Complaints.

The Complaints: the term was already outdated, even though Fox and his team couldn't help using it, at least among themselves. Complaints and Conduct had been their official title until recently. Now they were supposed to be Professional Ethics and Standards. Next year they'd be something else again: the name Standards and Values had been mooted, to nobody's liking. They were The Complaints, the cops who investigated other cops. Which was why those other cops were never happy to see them.

And seldom entirely cooperative.

'HQ means Glenrothes?' Fox checked with the desk sergeant.

'That's right.'

'How long to drive there – twenty minutes?'

'Provided you don't get lost.'

The phone on the desk behind the sergeant started to ring. 'You can always wait,' he said, turning to lift the receiver, keeping his back to Fox as he started a muffled conversation.

Joe Naysmith was holding a pamphlet about home security. He plonked himself on one of the chairs by the window and started reading. Fox and Kaye shared a look.

4

'What do you reckon?' Kaye asked at last. 'Whole town's out there waiting to be explored ...'

Kirkcaldy: a coastal town in Fife. Kaye had driven them there in his car. Forty minutes from Edinburgh, most of them spent in the outside lane. As they had crossed the Forth Road Bridge, they'd discussed the long queue of traffic on the opposite carriageway, heading into the capital at the start of another working day.

'Coming over here, stealing our jobs,' Kaye had joked, sounding his horn and giving a wave. Naysmith seemed to be the one with the local knowledge.

'Linoleum,' he'd said. 'Used to be what Kirkcaldy was famous for. And Adam Smith.'

'Who did he play for?' Kaye had asked.

'He was an economist.'

'What about Gordon Brown?' Fox had added.

'Kirkcaldy,' Naysmith had confirmed, nodding slowly.

Now, standing in the police station's reception area, Fox weighed up his options. They could sit and wait, growing restless. Or he could phone his boss in Edinburgh with a complaint of his own. His boss would then call Fife HQ and eventually something would happen – the equivalent of a wee boy running to his daddy when the big kid's done something.

Or ...

Fox looked at Kaye again. Kaye smiled and batted Naysmith's leaflet with the back of his hand.

'Break out the pith helmets, young Joe,' he said. 'We're heading into the wild.'

They parked the car on the seafront and stood for a few moments staring out across the Firth of Forth towards Edinburgh.

'Looks sunny over there,' Kaye complained, buttoning his coat. 'Bet you wish you'd worn more than a donkey jacket.'

Joe Naysmith had become inured to comments about his latest designer buy, but he did turn the collar up. There was a fierce wind blowing in from the North Sea. The water was choppy, and puddles along the promenade offered evidence that the tide was prone to break over the sea wall. The gulls overhead looked to be working hard at staying airborne. There was something odd about the design of this waterfront: almost no use had been made of it. Buildings tended to face away from the view and towards the

5

town centre. Fox had noted this elsewhere in Scotland: from Fort William to Dundee, the planners seemed to deny the existence of any shoreline. He'd never understood it, but doubted Kaye and Naysmith would be able to help.

Joe Naysmith's suggestion had been a beach walk, but Tony Kaye was already heading for one of the wynds leading uphill towards Kirkcaldy's shops and cafés, leaving Naysmith to dig out eighty-five pence in change for the parking. The narrow main street had roadworks on it. Kaye crossed to the other side and kept climbing.

'Where's he going?' Naysmith complained.

'Tony has a nose,' Fox explained. 'Not just any old café will do.'

Kaye had stopped at a doorway, made sure they could see him, then headed inside. The Pancake Place was light and spacious and not too busy. They took a corner table and tried to look like regulars. Fox often wondered if it was true that cops the world over tended to act the same. He liked corner tables, where he could see everything that was happening or might be about to happen. Naysmith hadn't quite learned that lesson yet and seemed happy enough to sit with his back to the door. Fox had squeezed in next to Kaye, eyes scanning the room, finding only women intent on their conversations, past being interested in the three new arrivals. They studied their menus in silence, placed an order, and waited a few minutes for the waitress to return with a tray.

'Good-looking scone,' Naysmith commented, getting to work with his knife and the pat of low-fat spread.

Fox had brought the folder with him. 'Don't want you getting too comfortable,' he said, emptying its contents on to the table. 'While the tea's cooling, you can be refreshing your memories.'

'Is it worth the risk?' Tony Kaye asked.

'What risk?'

'A smear of butter on the cover sheet. Won't look exactly professional when we're doing the interviews.'

'I'm feeling reckless today,' Fox countered. 'I'll take a chance ...'

With a sigh from Kaye, the three men started reading.

Paul Carter was the reason they'd come to Fife. Carter held the rank of detective constable and had been a cop for fifteen years. He was thirty-eight years old and came from a family of cops – both his father and an uncle had served in Fife Constabulary. The uncle, Alan Carter, had actually made the original complaint

6

against his nephew. It involved a drug addict, sexual favours, and turning a blind eye. Two other women then came forward to say that Paul Carter had arrested them for drunken behaviour, but offered to drop any charges if they would be 'accommodating'.

'Does anybody actually ever say "accommodating"?' Kaye muttered, halfway down a page.

'Courtroom and newspapers,' Naysmith replied, brushing crumbs from his own copy of the case notes.

Malcolm Fox had some of those newspaper reports in front of him. There were photos of Paul Carter leaving court at the end of a day's testimony. Pudding-bowl haircut; face pitted by acne. Giving the photographer a hard stare.

It was four days since the guilty verdict had been delivered, along with the sheriff's comment that Detective Constable Carter's own colleagues seemed 'either wilfully stupid or wilfully complicit'. Meaning: they'd known for years Carter was a bad cop, but they'd protected him, lied for him, maybe even attempted to falsify witness statements and put pressure on witnesses not to come forward.

All of which had brought the Complaints to town. Fife Constabulary needed to know, and in order to reassure the public (and more importantly, the media) that the investigation would be rigorous, they had asked a neighbouring force to run the inquiry. Fox had been given a copy of Fife Constabulary's Suspension Policy and Suspension Process Considerations, along with the Chief Constable's written report outlining why the three officers under investigation were still at work, this being 'in the best interests of the force'.

Fox took a sip of tea and skimmed another page of notes. Almost every sentence had been underlined or highlighted. The margins were filled with his own scribbled queries, concerns and exclamation marks. He knew most of it by heart, could stand up and recite it to the café's customers. Maybe they were gossiping about it anyway. In a town this size, sides would have been taken, opinions rigidly formed. Carter was a slimeball, a sleazebag, a predator. Or he'd been stitched up by a low-life junkie and a couple of cheap dates. Where was the harm in anything he'd done? And what had he done anyway?

Not much, except bring his police force into disrepute.

'Reminds me a bit of Colin Balfour,' Tony Kaye said. 'Remember him?'

Fox nodded. Edinburgh cop who liked to visit the cells if women were being held overnight. The prosecution against him had faltered, but an internal inquiry had seen him kicked off the force anyway.

'Interesting that the uncle's the one who spoke up,' Naysmith commented, drawing them back to the current case.

'But only after he retired from the force,' Fox added.

'Even so ... Must have stirred up the family a bit.'

'Could be some history there,' Kaye offered. 'Bad blood.'

'Could be,' Naysmith agreed.

Kaye slapped a hand down on the pile of papers in front of him. 'So where does any of this get us? How many days are we going to be shuttling backwards and forwards?'

'As many as it takes. Might only be a week or two.'

Kaye rolled his eyes. 'Just so Fife Constabulary can say they've got one bad apple and not a whole cider factory?'

'Do they make cider in factories?' Naysmith asked.

'Where do you think they make it?'

Fox didn't bother joining in. He was wondering again about the main player, Paul Carter. There was no use trying to interview the man, even though he was available. He'd been found guilty, held in custody, but had yet to receive a sentence. The sheriff was 'deliberating'. Fox reckoned Carter would go to jail. Couple of years and maybe a listing on the Sex Offenders Register. He was almost certainly talking to his lawyers about an appeal.

Yes, he'd talk to his legal team, but not to the Complaints. The man had nothing to gain by grassing up his mates at the station, the ones who'd stood by him. Fox couldn't offer him any kind of deal. The most they could hope for was that he would let something slip. If he talked at all.

Which he wouldn't.

Fox doubted anyone would talk. Or rather, they'd talk but say nothing worth hearing. They'd had plenty of warning this day was coming. Scholes. Haldane. Michaelson. The sheriff had singled them out for their conflicting or confused testimony, their muddying of the water, their memory lapses. Their immediate boss in CID, Detective Chief Inspector Laird, had escaped criticism, as had a detective constable called Forrester.

'Forrester's the one we should be talking to,' Kaye said suddenly, breaking off from his argument with Naysmith.

'Why?'

'Because her first name's Cheryl. My years of experience tell me that makes her a woman.'

'And?'

'And if one of her colleagues was a sex pest, surely she'd have had an inkling. Surrounded by blokes circling the wagons when the rumours start flying ... She's got to know something.' Kaye rose to his feet. 'Who's for a refill?'

'Let me check first.' Fox took out his phone and found the number for the station. 'Maybe Scholes is back from his wee jaunt.' He punched in the number and waited, while Kaye flicked the back of Naysmith's head with a finger and offered his services as a barber.

'Hello?' It was a woman's voice.

'DI Scholes, please.'

'Who's calling?'

Fox looked around the café. 'I'm from the Pancake Place. He was in earlier and we think he left something.'

'Hold on, I'll put you through.'

'Thank you.' Fox ended the call and started gathering up all the paperwork.

'Nicely played,' Tony Kaye said. Then, to Naysmith: 'Back into your donkey jacket, Joe. Let's get that jackhammer started ...'

2

Detective Inspector Ray Scholes ran a hand through his short black hair. He was seated in the station's only interview room. Fox had offered him any location he liked, as long as it had a table and four chairs.

'And a socket,' Joe Naysmith had added. The socket was for the electrical adaptor. Naysmith had set up the video camera and was now just about finished with the audio recorder. There were two microphones, one pointed at Scholes and one centred between Fox and Tony Kaye. Kaye had his arms folded, a scowl on his face. He'd already told Scholes how much they'd enjoyed his little ruse.

'I don't call official police business a "ruse",' Scholes had shot back at him. 'On the other hand, *this* almost certainly qualifies as a waste of time.'

'Only "almost"?' Malcolm Fox had responded, busying himself with the paperwork.

'All set,' Naysmith was now telling them.

'Happy to start?' Fox asked Scholes.

Scholes was nodding when his phone sounded. He answered it by identifying himself as 'Ray Scholes, public enemy number one.' Sounded like his girlfriend on the other end, asking him to pick up something for dinner. But she knew about the Complaints.

'Yeah, they're here,' Scholes drawled, eyes on Fox. Fox drew a finger across his throat, but Scholes was in no hurry. When he eventually ended the call, Fox asked if the phone could be switched off. Scholes shook his head.

'Never know when something *important*'s going to crop up.'

'How long before it rings again?' Fox asked. 'Will it be her every

10

time, or have you split the task between your friends?' Fox looked towards Tony Kaye. 'What is it usually – five minutes or ten?'

'Ten,' Kaye stated definitively.

Fox turned his attention back to Ray Scholes. 'I doubt there's anything you can do that hasn't been tried a hundred times. So why not just switch the phone off?'

Scholes managed a bit of a smile as he complied, Fox thanking him with a nod.

'Was DC Carter a good cop, in your opinion?' Fox then asked.

'Still is.'

'We both know he's not coming back.'

'How come you hate cops so much?'

Fox stared at the man across the desk. Scholes was in his mid-thirties but looked younger. A freckled face and milky-blue eyes. An odd image flashed up in Fox's memory: a big bag of marbles he'd owned as a boy. His favourite had been a pale-blue one, its flaws only visible when you peered at it, turning it slowly between your fingers ...

'That's an original question,' Tony Kaye was answering Scholes. 'I doubt we're asked that more than a few dozen times a month.'

'I just don't know why you'd want to punish everyone who's ever worked with Paul.'

'Not everyone,' Fox corrected him. 'Just the names mentioned by the sheriff.'

Scholes snorted. 'Call that a sheriff? Ask anyone on the force – Colin Cardonald's just the man to stick the knife in. Number of cases where he's tried everything possible to swing it the defendant's way ...'

'There's always one,' Kaye conceded.

'Was there any history between Sheriff Cardonald and DC Carter?' Fox asked.

'A bit.'

'And between the judge and yourself?' Fox waited, but no answer came. 'Are you saying that Sheriff Cardonald singled out certain names because of a grudge?'

'No comment.'

'A complaint was made about Paul Carter almost a year back, wasn't it? His own uncle said Carter had admitted taking advantage of a woman. The claim was investigated ...' Fox made show of looking for the relevant page in his notes.

'Nothing ever came of it,' Scholes stated.

'Not straight away, not until Teresa Collins decided she'd had enough ...' Fox paused. 'Did you know Carter's uncle?'

'He was a cop.'

'That's a yes, then. Why do you think he said what he said?'

Scholes shrugged.

'Yet another grudge? And the three women – the original complainant plus the two who came forward later – more grudges? Lot of grudges piling up against your friend, the "good cop" Paul Carter.' Fox leaned back in his chair, feigning interest in some of the pages of text. The newspaper cuttings were in full view on the desk. Kaye and Naysmith knew that silence was useful sometimes, and that when Fox leaned back like that it wasn't because he'd run out of questions. Naysmith checked the equipment; Kaye studied his wristwatch.

'Is that the starters finished, then?' Scholes asked eventually. 'Are we moving on to the meat and veg?'

'Meat and veg?'

'Where you try taking me down with Paul. Where you make out I lied in court, tried putting the fear on the witnesses ...'

'Teresa Collins states that you were in the car with Carter when he pulled up beside her and told her he'd be coming to her house later that day for sex.'

'I wasn't.'

'When she made her complaint, you phoned her and tried to get her to withdraw it.'

'No.'

'Her mobile phone had your number in it. Date, time and duration of call.'

'As I said in court, it was a mistake. How long did the call last?'

'Eighteen seconds.'

'Right – soon as I realised, I hung up.'

'Why did you have her number?'

'It was on a bit of paper on one of the desks in the office.'

'You got curious, so you called the mystery number?'

'That's it.'

Tony Kaye was shaking his head slowly, making evident his disbelief.

'So you deny telling her to ...' Fox glanced at his notes again, '"back the fuck off"?'

'Yes.'

'Did you spend time with Carter when the two of you were off duty?'

'Few beers now and then.'

'And clubs ... away days to Edinburgh and Glasgow.'

'It's no secret.'

'That's right. It all came out in court.'

Scholes snorted. 'Cops stick together and like a drink now and then – hold the front page.'

'Carter was a DC, you're a DI.'

'So?'

'So he'd never been promoted. Lowest rank in CID, and he'd been a cop as long as you.'

'Not everybody wants promotion.'

'Not everybody merits it,' Fox stated. 'Which was it with Paul Carter?'

Scholes was opening his mouth to answer when the interview room door opened. There was a uniformed woman there.

'Sorry to interrupt,' she said, not looking sorry at all. 'Thought I'd better say hello.' She saw that Naysmith was switching off the recorders. Reaching the desk, she introduced herself as Superintendent Isabel Pitkethly. Fox stood up with a certain reluctance and offered his hand for her to shake.

'Inspector Malcolm Fox,' he stated.

'Everything all right?' Pitkethly looked around the room. 'Got everything you need?'

'We're fine.'

She was almost a foot shorter than Fox but much the same age – early forties. Collar-length brown hair, blue eyes glinting behind her spectacles. She wore a regulation white blouse with epaulettes at the shoulders. Dark skirt falling to just above her knees.

'Ray behaving himself?' She gave a nervous laugh, and Fox could see that the past few weeks had left their mark on her. She probably saw herself as captain of a tight ship, and now the structure had been damaged from within.

'We were only just getting started,' Tony Kaye said, not bothering to disguise the complaint.

'Funny, I thought we were on to cheese and biscuits,' Scholes countered.

'DI Scholes does actually have to be at another meeting in five minutes,' Pitkethly said. 'Procurator Fiscal has a case to prepare ...'

Scholes wasted no time getting to his feet. 'Gentlemen, it's been a pleasure.'

'How soon can we have him back?' Fox asked Pitkethly.

'Mid-afternoon, probably.'

'Unless the Fiscal has other ideas.' Scholes had switched his phone back on and was checking for messages.

'Couple of missed calls?'

Scholes looked at Fox and smiled. 'How did you guess?'

Pitkethly seemed to be wondering the same thing. 'Can I have a word in my office, Inspector Fox?'

'I was about to suggest it,' Fox answered.

A minute later, Kaye and Naysmith were alone together in the interview room.

'Do I pack it all up?' Naysmith asked, his hand resting on the tripod.

'Better had. Can't trust Scholes and his crew not to come in here and wipe their cocks over everything ...'

'Sit down,' Pitkethly instructed from behind her desk. Fox stayed standing. The desk was empty. There was another at a right angle to it, and this second desk boasted a computer and busy-looking in-tray. The window had a view on to the car park outside. There were no knick-knacks on the sill; no photos of loved ones. The walls were bare except for a No Smoking sign and a year-planner.

'Been here long?' Fox asked.

'Few months.'

'And before that?'

He could see she was annoyed: somehow he was the one getting to ask the questions. But politeness demanded an answer.

'Glenrothes.'

'HQ?'

'Wouldn't it be quicker just to look at my file?'

Fox raised both hands by way of apology, and when she nodded towards the chair he decided not to refuse a second time.

'I'm sorry I wasn't here this morning,' she began. 'I was hoping the two of us might have had this discussion before your work began.' It sounded like a prepared speech, because that was what it was. Pitkethly probably had friends at HQ in Glenrothes, and had gone there for a bit of advice on dealing with the Complaints. Fox could have written the script for her. Most cases, someone up the chain of command would invite him to their office and tell him the same thing.

This is a good crew here.

We've got work to do.

It's in nobody's interest that officers are kept back from their duties.

Naturally, no one wants a whitewash.

But all the same ...

'So if any concerns could be brought to me in the first instance ...' Colour had risen to Pitkethly's cheeks. Fox wondered how elated she'd been when promotion had come, when she'd been offered her own station to run. And now this.

She'd been told what to say, but hadn't had time for a rehearsal. Her voice drifted off and she started to clear her throat, almost bringing on a fit of coughing. Fox liked her all the better for this apparent awkwardness. He realised she'd maybe called in no favours, but had been summoned to Glenrothes.

Here's what you have to get through to him, Superintendent ...

'Can I get you a drink?' he asked. 'Some water?' But she waved the offer away. He leaned forward a little in his chair. 'For what it's worth,' he said, 'we'll try to be discreet. And quick. That doesn't mean we'll be cutting corners – I promise you we'll be thorough. And we can't give you any tip-offs. Our report goes to your Chief Constable. It's up to him what he does with it.'

She had managed to compose herself. She was nodding, her eyes focused on his.

'We're not in the business of making waves,' he went on. This, too, was a speech he'd made many times, in rooms much like this. 'We just want the truth. We want to know procedures were followed and no one thinks they're somehow above the law. If you can help us get that message across to your officers, that would be great. If there's a room we could use as a base, so much the better. It needs to be lockable, and I'll need all the keys. I'm hoping we'll be out of your hair in a week.'

He decided not to add 'or two'.

'A week,' she echoed. He couldn't decide if this was coming as good or bad news to her.

'I was told this morning that DS Haldane's on sick leave ...'

'Flu,' she confirmed.

'Flu, palsy or plague, we need him for interview.'

She nodded again. 'I'll make sure he knows.'

15

'A bit of local knowledge might be useful, too – just where we can get a decent lunch or sandwich. But nowhere your officers would go.'

'I'll have a think.' She was getting to her feet, signalling the end of the meeting. Fox stayed in his seat.

'Did you ever have an inkling about DC Carter?'

It took her a few moments to decide whether she was going to answer, at the end of which she shook her head.

'None of the women working here ...?' he pressed.

'What?'

'Gossip in the toilets ... warnings of wandering hands ...'

'Nothing,' she stated.

'Never any doubts?'

'None,' she said firmly, crossing to the door and holding it open for him. Fox took his time; gave her a little smile as he passed her. Kaye and Naysmith were waiting for him at the end of the corridor.

'Well?' Kaye asked.

'Much as expected.'

'Michaelson might be around – want him next?'

Fox shook his head. 'Let's go back into town, grab a bite, drive around a bit.'

'Just to get a feel for the place?' Kaye guessed.

'Just to get a feel for the place,' Fox confirmed.

3

Kirkcaldy boasted a railway station, a football club, a museum and art gallery, and a college named after Adam Smith. There were streets of solid, prosperous-looking Victorian villas, some of which had been turned into offices and businesses. Further out were housing schemes, some of them so recent there were still plots waiting to be sold. A couple of parks, at least two high schools, and some 1960s high-rises. The dialect was not impenetrable, and shoppers stopped to talk to each other outside the bakeries and newsagents.

'I'm nodding off here,' Tony Kaye commented at one point. He was in his own car's passenger seat, Joe Naysmith driving and Fox in the back. Lunch had comprised filled rolls and packets of crisps. Fox had called their boss in Edinburgh to make an initial report. The call had lasted no more than three minutes.

'So?' Kaye asked, turning in his seat to make eye contact with Fox.

'I like it,' Fox answered, staring at the passing scene.

'Shall I tell you what I see, Foxy? I see people who should be at work this time of day. Scroungers and the walking wounded, coffin-dodgers, jakeys and ASBOs.'

Joe Naysmith had started humming the tune to 'What a Wonderful World'.

'Every car we've passed,' Kaye went on, undeterred, 'the driver's either a drug dealer or he's hot-wired it. The pavements need hosing down and so do half the kids. It tells you all you need to know about a place when the biggest shop seems to be called Rejects.' He paused for effect. 'And you're telling me you *like* it?'

'You're seeing what you want to see, Tony, and then letting your imagination run riot.'

Kaye turned to Naysmith. 'And as for you, you weren't even born when that song came out, so you can shut it.'

'My mum had the record. Well, the cassette anyway. Or maybe the CD.'

Kaye was looking at Fox again. 'Can we please go back and ask our questions, get whatever answers they want to dump on us, and then vamoose the hell out of here?'

'When did CDs start appearing? Naysmith asked.

Kaye punched him on the shoulder.

'What's that for?'

'Cruelty to my gearbox. Have you ever even driven a car before?'

'Okay,' Fox said. 'You win. Joe, take us back to the station.'

'Left or right at the next junction?'

'Enough's enough,' Tony Kaye said, making to open the glove box. 'I'm plugging in the satnav.'

Detective Sergeant Gary Michaelson had grown up in Greenock but lived in Fife since the age of eighteen. He'd attended Adam Smith College, then done his police training at Tulliallan. He was three years younger than Ray Scholes, married, and had two daughters.

'Schools here good?' Fox had asked him.

'Not bad.'

Michaelson was happy to talk about Fife and Greenock and family, but when the subject turned to Detective Constable Paul Carter, he offered as little as Scholes before him.

'If I didn't know better,' Fox commented at one point, 'I'd say you'd been put through your paces.'

'How do you mean?'

'Coached in what not to say – coached by DI Scholes, maybe ...'

'Not true,' Michaelson had insisted.

It was also untrue that he had altered or deleted notes he had taken during an interview conducted both at the home of Teresa Collins and in the very same interview room where they were now seated. Fox recited part of Teresa Collins's testimony:

'*You can charge me with anything you like, Paul. Just don't think you're putting your hands on me again.* She didn't say that?'

18

'No.'

'Verdict suggests otherwise.'

'Not much I can do about that.'

'But there was a bit of personal history between Carter and Ms Collins. You can't have been unaware of it.'

'*She* says there was a history.'

'Neighbours saw him coming and going.'

'Half of them known to us, by the way.'

'You're saying they're liars?'

'What do you think?'

'Doesn't really matter what I think. How about the missing page from your notebook?'

'Spilled coffee on it.'

'Pages underneath seem fine.'

'Not much I can do about that.'

'So you keep saying ...'

Throughout the interview, Fox knew better than to make eye contact with Tony Kaye. Kaye's infrequent contributions to the questioning showed his growing irritation. They were getting nowhere and would almost certainly continue to get nowhere. Scholes, Michaelson and the allegedly flu-ridden Haldane had not only had plenty of time to choreograph their answers, they'd also already premiered the routine in the courtroom.

Teresa Collins was lying.

The other two complainants were chancers.

The judge had helped the prosecution at every available turn.

'Thing is,' Fox said, slowly and quietly, making sure he had Michaelson's attention, 'when your own force's Professional Standards team looked into the allegations, they reckoned there might be something to them. And don't forget: it wasn't Ms Collins who started the whole process ...'

He let that sink in for a moment. Michaelson's focus remained fixed to a portion of the wall over Fox's left shoulder. He was wiry and prematurely bald and his nose had been broken at some point in his life. Plus there was an inch-long scar running across his chin. Fox wondered if he'd done any amateur boxing.

'It was another police officer,' he continued, 'Paul Carter's uncle. Are you calling him a liar too?'

'He's not a cop, he's an ex-cop.'

'What difference does it make?'

Michaelson offered a shrug and folded his arms.

'Battery change,' Naysmith broke in, switching off the camera. Michaelson stretched his back. Fox heard the clicking of vertebrae. Tony Kaye was on his feet, shaking each leg as if trying to get the circulation going.

'Much longer?' Michaelson asked.

'That's up to you,' Fox told him.

'Well we all still get paid at the end of the day, eh?'

'Not in a rush to get back to your desk?'

'Doesn't really matter, does it? You tidy up one crime, another two or three are just around the corner.'

Fox saw that Joe Naysmith was going through the pockets of the equipment bag. Naysmith knew he was being watched, looked up, and had the good sense to look contrite.

'The spare's still charging,' he said.

'Where?' Tony Kaye asked.

'The office.' Naysmith paused. 'In Edinburgh.'

'Meaning we're done?' Gary Michaelson's eyes were on Malcolm Fox.

'So it would seem,' Fox answered, grudgingly. 'For now ...'

'What a complete and utter waste of a day,' said Tony Kaye, not for the first time. They had retraced their route back to Edinburgh, still mainly in the outside lane. This time, the bulk of the traffic was heading into Fife, the bottleneck on the Edinburgh side of the Forth Road Bridge. Their destination was Police HQ on Fettes Avenue. Chief Inspector Bob McEwan was still in the office. He pointed to the battery charger next to the kettle and mugs.

'Wondered about that,' he said.

'Wonder no more,' Fox replied.

The room wasn't large, because Counter Corruption comprised a small team. Most Complaints officers worked in a larger office along the corridor where Professional Ethics and Standards handled the meat-and-potatoes workload. This year, McEwan seemed to be spending most of his time in meetings to do with restructuring the whole department.

'Basically, writing myself out of a job,' as he had put it himself. 'Not that you should worry your pretty little heads ...'

Kaye had thrown his coat over the back of his chair and was seated at his desk, while Naysmith busied himself switching the batteries in the charger.

'Two interviews conducted,' Fox told McEwan. 'Both somewhat curtailed.'

'I take it there was a bit of resistance.'

Fox gave a twitch of his mouth. 'Tony thinks we're talking to the wrong people anyway. I'm beginning to agree with him.'

'Nobody's expecting miracles, Malcolm. The Deputy Chief Constable phoned me earlier. It takes as long as it takes.'

'Any longer than a week and I might run a hose from my car exhaust,' Kaye muttered.

'It takes as long as it takes,' McEwan repeated for his benefit.

Eventually they settled down to review the recordings. Halfway through, McEwan checked his watch and said that he had to be elsewhere. Then Kaye received a text.

'Urgent appointment with the wife and a bottle of wine,' he explained, patting Fox's shoulder. 'Let me know how it turns out, eh?'

For the next five minutes, Fox could sense Naysmith fidgeting. It was gone five anyway, so he told his young colleague to bugger off.

'You sure?'

Fox gestured towards the door, and soon he was alone in the office, thinking that maybe he should have praised Naysmith for his work behind the camera. Both picture and sound were sharp. There was a notepad on Fox's lap, but it was blank apart from spirals, stars and other assorted doodles. He thought back to something Scholes had said, about the Complaints wanting to drag everyone else down with Paul Carter. Carter was history. What reason was there to suppose Scholes and the others would keep breaking the rules? Of course they'd look out for each other, stick up for each other, but maybe a lesson had been learned. Fox knew he could put the investigation into cruise control, could ask the questions, log the responses and come to no great conclusions. That might be the outcome anyway. So what was the point of busting a gut? This, he felt, was the subtext of the whole day, the thing Tony Kaye had been bursting to say. The three officers had been named and shamed in court. Now they were the subject of an internal inquiry. Did all that not comprise punishment enough?

In the Pancake Place, Kaye had mentioned Colin Balfour. The Complaints had put together just about enough of a case to see him drummed out of the force, but they'd stopped short of implicating two or three other officers who had attempted a cover-up. Those officers were still working; never a hint of trouble.

No complaints, as the saying went.

Fox used the remote to switch off the recording. All it proved was that they were doing what was expected of them. He very much doubted the bosses at Fife Constabulary HQ required further bad news; they just wanted to be able to say that the judge's comments had not been ignored. Scholes, Haldane and Michaelson needed only to go on denying everything. And that meant Tony Kaye was right. It was the other CID officers they should be talking to – if they wanted to be thorough. And what about Carter's uncle? Shouldn't they also get his side of the story? Fox was intrigued about the man's motive. His evidence in court had been brief but effective. The way he told it, his nephew had paid him a visit one afternoon after a few drinks. He'd been garrulous, talking about the ways in which policing had changed since his uncle's day. Not so many corners could be cut, and there were fewer fringe benefits.

But there's one perk I get that maybe you and my dad never did ...

Fox was reminded that he hadn't spoken to his own father in a couple of days. His sister and he took it in turns to visit. She was probably at the care home right now. The staff liked you to avoid mealtimes, and by mid-evening a lot of the 'clients' (as staff insisted on calling them) were being readied for bed. He walked over to the windows and stared out at the darkening city. Was Edinburgh ten times the size of Kirkcaldy? Bigger, surely. Back at his desk, he switched on his computer and sat down to do a search.

Just under an hour later, he was in his car and heading for his home in Oxgangs. There was a supermarket almost on his doorstep, and he stopped long enough to grab a microwave curry and a bottle of Appletiser, plus the evening paper. The story on the front page concerned a drug dealer who had just been found guilty and sent to jail. Fox knew the detective who had led the inquiry – he'd been the subject of a Complaints investigation two years back. Now he was smiling for the cameras, job done.

How come you hate cops so much? The question Scholes had asked. Time was, CID could cut corners and be sure of getting away with it. Fox's task was to stop them doing that. Not for ever and a day – in a year or two he would be back in CID himself, rubbing shoulders with those he had scrutinised; trying to put drug dealers behind bars without bending the rules, fearful of the

Complaints and coming to despise them. He had begun to wonder if he could do that – work with officers who knew his past; work what everyone regarded as 'proper' cases …

He stuffed the newspaper into the bottom of his basket, covered by his other purchases.

The bungalow was in darkness. He'd thought of buying one of those timers that brought a light on at dusk, but knew this was no real deterrent to housebreakers. He had little enough worth stealing: TV and computer, after which they'd be looking around in vain. A couple of homes near him had been broken into in the past month. He'd even had a police constable on his doorstep, asking if he'd seen or heard anything. Fox hadn't bothered identifying himself as a fellow officer. He'd just shaken his head and the constable had nodded and headed elsewhere.

Going through the motions.

Six minutes, the curry took. Fox found a news channel on the TV and turned the sound up. The world seemed to be filled with war, famine and natural disasters. An earthquake here, a tornado there. A climate-change expert was being interviewed. He was warning that viewers needed to get used to these phenomena, to floods and droughts and heatwaves. The interviewer managed somehow to hand back to the studio with a smile. Maybe once he was off air, he would start running around pulling out clumps of his hair and screaming, but Fox doubted it. He pressed the interactive button on the remote and scanned the Scottish headlines. There was nothing new on the explosion outside Lockerbie; the Alert Status at Fettes had been MODERATE, same as at Kirkcaldy. Lockerbie: as if that benighted spot hadn't seen enough in its history … Fox flipped to a sports channel and watched the darts as he ate the remainder of his meal.

He was just finishing when his phone started ringing. It was his sister Jude.

'What's up?' he asked her. They took it in turns to call. It was his turn, not hers.

'I've just been to see Dad.' He heard her sniff back a tear.

'Is he okay?'

'He keeps forgetting things.'

'I know.'

'One of the carers told me he didn't make it to the toilet in time this morning. They've put him in a *pad*.'

Fox closed his eyes.

'And sometimes he forgets my name or what year it is.'

'He has good days too, Jude.'

'How would *you* know? Just because you pick up the bills doesn't mean you can walk away!'

'Who's walking away?'

'I never see you there.'

'You know that's not true. I visit when I can.'

'Not nearly enough.'

'We can't all lead lives of leisure, Jude.'

'You think I'm not looking for a job?'

Fox squeezed his eyes shut again: *walked into that one, Malc.* 'That's not what I meant.'

'It's *exactly* what you meant!'

'Let's not get into this, eh?'

There was silence on the line for a few moments. Jude sighed and began speaking again. 'I took him a box of photographs today. Thought maybe the pair of us could go through them. But they just seemed to upset him. He kept saying, "They're all dead. How can everyone be dead?"'

'I'll go see him, Jude. Don't worry about it. Maybe the thing to do is phone ahead, and if the staff don't think it's worth a visit that day—'

'That's not what I'm saying!' Her voice rose again. 'You think I *mind* visiting him? He's our *dad*.'

'I know that. I was just …' He paused, then asked the question he felt was expected of him. 'Do you want me to come over?'

'It's not me you need to go see.'

'You're right.'

'So you'll do it?'

'Of course.'

'Even though you're busy?'

'Soon as I'm off the phone,' Fox assured her.

'And you'll get back to me? Tell me what you think?'

'I'm sure he's fine, Jude.'

'You *want* him to be – that way he's not on your conscience.'

'I'm putting the phone down now, Jude. I'm putting the phone down and heading out to see Dad …'

24

4

The staff of Lauder Lodge, however, had other ideas.

It was past nine when Fox got there. He could hear a TV blaring in the lounge. Lots of people coming and going – looked like a shift changeover.

'Your father's in bed,' Fox was told. 'He'll be asleep.'

'Then I won't wake him. I just want to see him for a minute.'

'We try not to disturb clients once they're in bed.'

'Didn't he used to stay up for the ten o'clock news?'

'That was then.'

'Is he on any new medication? Anything I don't know about?'

The woman took a moment to weigh up whether an accusation was being made, then gave a resigned sigh. 'Just a minute, you say?'

Fox nodded, and she nodded back. Anything for a quiet life ...

Mitch Fox's room was in a new annexe to the side of the original Victorian property. Fox walked past a room that had, until a couple of months back, been home to Mrs Sanderson. Mrs Sanderson and Fox's father had become firm friends during their time in Lauder Lodge. Fox had helped Mitch attend her funeral, no more than a dozen people in the crematorium chapel. No one had come from her family, because no family had been traced. There was a new name next to the door of her old room: D. Nesbitt. Fox got the feeling that if he peeled away that sticker, there'd be another underneath bearing Mrs Sanderson's name, and maybe another beneath that.

He didn't bother knocking on his father's door, just turned the handle and crept in. The curtains were closed and the light was off, but there was a good amount of illumination from the street

25

lamp outside. Fox could make out his father's form under the duvet. He had almost reached the bedside chair when a dry voice asked what time it was.

'Twenty past,' Fox told his father.

'Twenty past what?'

'Nine.'

'So what brings you here, then?' Mitch Fox turned on the lamp and started to sit up. His son moved forward to help him. 'Has something happened?'

'Jude was a bit worried.' Fox saw that the shoebox full of old family photos was on the chair. He lifted it and sat down, resting it on his knees. His father's hair, wispy, almost like a baby's, had a yellowish tinge. His face was thinner than ever, the skin resembling parchment. But the eyes seemed clear and untroubled.

'We both know your sister likes her little dramas. What's she been telling you?'

'Just that your memory's not what it was.'

'Whose is?' Mitch nodded towards the shoebox. 'Because I couldn't tell her the exact spot where some photo was taken fifty-odd years ago?'

Fox opened the lid of the box and lifted out a handful of snaps. Some had writing on the back: names, dates, places. But there were question marks, too. Lots of question marks ... and something that looked like a tear stain. Fox rubbed a finger across it, then turned the photo over. His mother dandled a child on either knee. She was seated on the edge of a rockery.

'This one only goes back thirty years,' Fox said, holding the photo up for his father to see. Mitch peered at it.

'Blackpool maybe,' he said. 'You and Jude ...'

'And Mum.'

Mitch Fox nodded slowly. 'Any water there?' he asked. Fox looked, but there was no jug on the bedside cabinet. 'Get me some, will you?'

Fox went into the adjoining bathroom. The jug was there, along with a plastic tumbler. He reckoned the staff didn't want Mitchell Fox guzzling water at night, not if it meant trouble in the morning. The pack of incontinence pads sat in full view next to the sink. Fox filled jug and tumbler both and took them through.

'Good lad,' his father said. A few drops dribbled from his chin as he drank, but he needed no help placing the drained tumbler next to him by the bed. 'You'll tell Jude not to worry?'

26

'Sure.' Fox sat down again.

'And you'll manage to do it without falling out?'

'I'll try my best.'

'Takes two to make an argument.'

'You sure about that? I think Jude could have a pretty good go in an empty room.'

'Maybe so, but you don't always help.'

'Is this you and me arguing now?' Fox watched his father give a tired smile. 'Want me to go so you can get back to sleep?'

'I don't sleep. I just lie here, waiting.'

Fox knew what the answer to his next question would be, so he didn't ask it. Instead, he told his father that he'd just spent a fruitless day over in Fife.

'You used to love it there,' Mitch told him.

'Where?'

'Fife.'

'When was I ever in Fife?'

'My cousin Chris – we used to visit him.'

'Where did he live?'

'Burntisland. The beach, the outdoor pool, the links ...'

'How old was I?'

'Chris died young. Take a look, he should be in there somewhere.'

Fox realised that his father meant the shoebox. So they lifted out the contents on to the bed. Some of the photos were loose, others in packets along with their negatives. A mixture of colour and black-and-white, including some wedding photos. (Fox ignored the ones of him and Elaine – their marriage hadn't lasted long.) There were blurry snaps of holidays, Christmases, birthdays, works outings. Until eventually Mitch was handing a particular shot to him.

'That's Chris there. He's got Jude on his shoulders. Big, tall, strapping chap.'

'Would this be Burntisland then?' Fox studied the photograph. Jude's gap-toothed mouth was wide open. Hard to tell if it was laughter or terror at being so high off the ground. Chris was grinning for the camera. Fox tried to remember him, but failed.

'Might be his back garden,' Mitch Fox was saying.

'How did he die?'

'Motorbike, daft laddie. Look at them all.' Mitch waved a hand

27

across the strewn photographs. 'Dead and buried and mostly forgotten.'

'Some of us are still here, though,' Fox said. 'And that's the way I like it.'

Mitch patted the back of his son's hand.

'Did I really love it in Fife?'

'There was a park up near St Andrews. We went there one day. It had a train we all sat on. There might be a photo if we look hard enough. Lots of beaches, too – and a market in Kirkcaldy once a year ...'

'Kirkcaldy? That's where I've just been. How come I don't remember it?'

'You won a goldfish there once. Poor thing was dead inside a day.' Mitch fixed his son with a look. 'You'll put Jude's mind at rest?'

Fox nodded, and his father patted his hand again before lying back against the pillows. Fox sat with him for another hour and a half, looking at photographs. He switched the lamp off just before he left.

Two

5

'This is a joke, right?'

'It's what's on offer,' the desk sergeant said. He looked every bit as pleased with this morning's outcome as he had done the day before when informing them that none of their interviewees were available. 'The door locks, and the key's yours if you want it.'

'It's a storeroom,' Joe Naysmith stated, switching on the light.

'Forty-watt bulb,' Tony Kaye said. 'We might as well bring torches.'

Someone had placed three rickety-looking chairs in the centre of the small room, leaving no space for a desk of any kind. The shelves were filled with boxes – old cases identified by a code number and year – plus broken and superannuated office equipment.

'Any chance of a word with Superintendent Pitkethly?' Fox asked the sergeant.

'She's in Glenrothes.'

'Now there's a surprise.'

The sergeant was dangling the key from his finger.

'It's somewhere to park the gear, if nothing else,' Naysmith reasoned.

Fox gave a loud exhalation through his nostrils and snatched the key from the sergeant.

While Naysmith brought the equipment bag in from the car, Fox and Kaye stayed in the corridor, eyeing the interior of the storeroom. The corridor was suddenly busy with uniforms and civilian staff, all passing through and stifling smirks.

'No way I'm parking myself in there,' Kaye said with a slow shake of the head. 'I'd look like the bloody janitor.'

'Joe's right, though – it's somewhere to store the gear between interviews.'

'Any way we can speed the process, Malcolm?'

'How do you mean?'

'You and me – we could take an interview each, be done in half the time. The only people we need on tape are Scholes, Haldane and Michaelson. The others are just chats, aren't they?'

Fox nodded. 'But there's only one interview room.'

'Not everyone we're talking to is based at the station ...'

Fox stared at Kaye. 'You really *do* want this over and done with.'

'Basic time management,' Kaye said with a glint in his eye. 'Better value for the hard-pressed taxpayer.'

'So how do we split it?' Fox folded his arms.

'Got any favourites?'

'I fancy a word with the uncle.'

Kaye considered this, then nodded slowly. 'Take my car. I'll try Cheryl Forrester.'

'Fair enough. What do we do with Joe?'

They turned to watch as Joe Naysmith pushed open the door at the end of the corridor, the heavy black bag slung over one shoulder.

'We toss a coin,' Kaye said, holding out a fifty-pence piece. 'Loser keeps him.'

A few minutes later, Malcolm Fox was heading out to Kaye's Ford Mondeo, minus Naysmith. He adjusted the driver's seat and reached into the glove box for the satnav, plugging it in and fixing it to the dashboard. Alan Carter's postcode was in the file, and he found it after a bit of hunting. The satnav did a quick search before pointing him in the right direction. He soon found himself on the coast road, heading south towards a place called Kinghorn. Signposts told him the next town after this was Burntisland. He thought again of his father's cousin Chris. Maybe the motorbike had crashed on this very stretch. It was the kind of drive he reck-oned bikers would relish, winding gently and with the sea to one side, steep hillside to the other. Was that a seal's head bobbing in the water? He slowed the car a little. The driver behind flashed his lights, then overtook with a blast of his horn.

'Yeah, yeah,' Fox muttered, glancing at the satnav. His destina-tion was close by. He passed a caravan site and signalled to take the next road on the right. It was a steep track, rutted and throwing up clouds of dust behind him. He knew he daren't ding Kaye's pride and joy, so ended up in first gear, doing five miles an hour. The climb continued. According to the satnav, he was nowhere, had passed his destination. Fox stopped the car and got out. He had a fine view down towards the shoreline, rows of caravans to his left and a hotel to his right. He looked at the address he had for Alan Carter: Gallowhill Cottage. The road was about to disappear into woodland. Something caught Fox's eye: a wisp of smoke from above the treeline. He got back behind the steering wheel and eased the gear lever forward.

The cottage sat near the top of the rise, just as the track came to an end at a gate leading to fields. A few sheep were scattered around. Noiseless crows glided between the trees. The wind was biting, though the sun had broken from behind a bank of cloud.

Smoke continued to drift up from the cottage's chimney. There was an olive-green Land Rover parked off to one side, next to a large, neat pile of split logs. The door of the cottage rattled open. The man who filled the doorway was almost a parody of the big, jolly policeman. Alan Carter's face was ruddy, cheeks and nose criss-crossed with thin red veins. His eyes sparkled and his pale yellow cardigan was stretched to the limit of its buttons. The check shirt beneath was open at the collar, allowing copious grey chest hair to breathe. Though almost completely bald, he retained bushy sideburns, which almost met at one of his chins.

'I knew I'd be getting a visit,' Carter bellowed, one pudgy hand resting on the door frame. 'Should've made an appointment, though. I seem to be busier these days than ever.' Fox was standing in front of him now, and the two men shook hands.

'You're not in the Craft, then?' Carter asked.

'No.'

'Time was, most coppers you met were Masons. In you come then, lad ...'

The hallway was short and narrow, most of the space taken up with bookshelves, coat rack and a selection of wellington boots. The living room was small and sweltering, courtesy of a fire piled high with logs.

'Need to keep it warm for Jimmy Nicholl,' Carter said.

'Who?'

'The dog.'

An ancient-looking Border collie with rheumy eyes blinked in Fox's direction from its basket near the fireplace.

33

'Who's he named for?'

'The Raith manager. Not now, of course, but Jimmy took us into Europe.' Carter broke off and gave Fox a look. 'Not a football fan either?'

'Used to be. My name's Fox, by the way. Inspector Fox.'

'Rubber-Sole Brigade – that what they still call you?'

'That or the Complaints.'

'And doubtless worse things too, behind your back.'

'Or to our faces.'

'Will it be a mug of tea or something stronger?' Carter nodded towards a bottle of whisky on a shelf.

'Tea'll do the job.'

'Bit early in the day for the "cratur", maybe,' Carter agreed. 'I won't be a minute.'

He headed for the kitchen. Fox could hear him pouring water into a kettle. His voice boomed down the hallway. 'When I read Cardonald's summing-up, I knew there'd have to be an inquiry. You're not local, though. A local might've known the name Jimmy Nicholl. On top of which, your car's from Edinburgh ...'

Carter was back in the room now, looking pleased with himself.

'The registration?' Fox guessed.

'The dealer's sticker in the back window,' Carter corrected him. 'Take a seat, laddie.' He gestured to one of the two armchairs. 'Milk and sugar?'

'Just milk. Are you still in security, Mr Carter?'

'Is this you showing me you've done your research?' Carter smiled. 'The company's still mine.'

'What exactly does the company do?'

'Doormen for bars and clubs ... security guards ... protection for visiting dignitaries.'

'Do a lot of dignitaries pass through Kirkcaldy?'

'They did when Gordon Brown was PM. And they still like to play golf at St Andrews.'

Carter left the room to fetch their drinks, and Fox crossed to the window. There was a dining table there, piled high with paperwork and magazines. The paperwork had been stuffed into folders. A map of Fife lay open, locations circled in black ink. The magazines seemed to date back to the 1980s, and when Fox lifted one of them he saw that there was a newspaper beneath it. The date on the newspaper was Monday, 29 April 1985.

'You'll have me pegged as a hoarder,' Carter said, carrying a tray into the room. He placed it on a corner of the table and poured out tea for the both of them. Half a dozen shortbread fingers had been emptied on to a patterned plate.

'And a bachelor?' Fox guessed.

'Your research has let you down. My wife ran off with somebody two decades back, and the same number of years younger than me at the time.'

'Making her a cradle-snatcher.'

Carter wagged a finger. 'I'm sixty-two. Jessica was forty and the wee shite-bag twenty-one.'

'Nobody else since?'

'Christ, man, is this a Complaints interview or a dating service? She's dead anyway, God rest her. Had a kid with the shite-bag.'

'But none with yourself?' Carter gave a twitch of the mouth. 'Does that rankle?'

'Why should it? Maybe my son or daughter would have turned out as bad as my nephew.'

Carter gestured towards the chairs and the two men sat down with their drinks. There was a slight stinging sensation in Fox's eyes, which he tried blinking away.

'It's the woodsmoke,' Carter explained. 'You can't see it, but it's there.' He reached down and fed Jimmy Nicholl half a shortbread finger. 'His teeth are just about up to it. Come to think of it, mine aren't much better.'

'You've been retired fifteen years?'

'I've been out of the force that long.'

'Your brother was a cop same time as you?'

'A year shy of retirement when his heart gave out.'

'Was that around the time your nephew joined the police?'

Alan Carter nodded. 'Maybe it was *why* he joined up. He never seemed to have a gift for it. What's the word I'm looking for?'

'Vocation?'

'Aye. That's what Paul never had.'

'You weren't keen on him following the family tradition?'

Alan Carter was silent for a moment, then he leaned forward as best he could, resting the mug on one knee.

'Paul was never a good son. He ran his mother ragged until the cancer took her. After that, it was his dad's turn. At the funeral, all he seemed interested in was how much the house was worth, and how much effort it was going to take to get the place emptied.'

'The two of you weren't exactly friendly, then. Yet he came to see you ...'

'I think he'd been partying all night. It was just past noon. How he got the car up here without smashing it ...' Carter stared into the fire. 'He wanted to do a bit of bragging. But he was maudlin, too – you know the way drink can sometimes take us.'

'One of the reasons I don't do it.' Fox took a swig of tea. It was dark and strong, coating his tongue and the back of his throat.

'He came here to show off. Said he was a better cop than any of us. He "owned" Kirkcaldy, and I needn't go thinking *I* did, even if I could hide behind an army of bouncers.'

'I get the feeling this is verbatim.'

'Got to have a good memory. Whenever I was called to give evidence, I always knew it by heart – one way to impress a jury.'

'So eventually he told you about Teresa Collins?'

'Aye.' Carter nodded to himself, still watching the fire spit and crackle. 'Hers was the only name, but he said there'd been others. I thought the force had seen the back of his kind – maybe you're not old enough to remember the way it was.'

'Full of racists and sexists?' Fox paused. 'And Masons ...'

Carter gave a quiet chuckle.

'It still goes on,' Fox continued. 'Maybe not nearly as widespread as it was, but all the same.'

'Your line of work, I suppose you see it more than most.'

Fox answered with a shrug and placed his empty mug on the floor, declining the offer of a refill. 'The day he came here, did he mention the others: Scholes, Haldane, Michaelson?'

'Only in passing.'

'Nothing about them bending the rules?'

'No.'

'And you hadn't heard rumours to that effect?'

'I'd say you've got your work cut out there.'

'Mmm.' Fox sounded as if he were in complete agreement.

'The force is going to want to move on.'

'I'd think so.' Fox shifted in his chair, hearing it creak beneath him. 'Can I ask you something else about your nephew?'

'Fire away.'

'Well, it's one thing to disapprove of what he said he did ...'

'But quite another to take it further?' Carter pursed his lips. 'I didn't do anything about it ... not straight away. But lying in bed at night, I'd be thinking of Tommy – Paul's dad. A good man;

36

a really good man. And Paul's mum, too; such a lovely woman. I was wondering what they'd be thinking. Then there was Teresa Collins – I didn't know her, but I didn't like the way he'd talked about her. So I had a quiet word.'

'And this quiet word was with …?'

'Superintendent Hendryson. He's not there any more. Retired, I seem to think.'

'It's a woman called Pitkethly nowadays.'

Carter nodded. 'It was Hendryson who really started the ball rolling.'

'Nothing happened, though, did it?'

'Teresa Collins wouldn't talk. Not at first. Without her, there was nothing for the Fife Complaints to investigate.'

'Any idea why she changed her mind?'

'Maybe she was tossing and turning, same as me.'

'You've no friends left on the force, Mr Carter?'

'All retired.'

'Superintendent Hendryson?'

'He was after my time, more or less.'

'So you went to Hendryson. He brought in the local Complaints team. They didn't get very far. But then these other two women came forward, and that's when Teresa Collins decided she'd co-operate?'

'That's about the size of it.'

Fox sat for a few moments longer. Alan Carter seemed in no rush to see him go, but he had nothing keeping him there, nothing but the warmth of the fire and companionable silence.

'A long way from Edinburgh, isn't it, Inspector?' Carter said quietly. 'These are the backlands, where things tend to get fixed on the quiet.'

'You regret what's happened to your nephew? All that media exposure?'

'I doubt anything's "happened" to him.' Carter tapped the side of his head. 'Not in here.'

'He's in jail, though. That's tough on the family.'

'*I'm* the family – all that's left of it.' Carter paused. 'Are your folks still with us?'

'My dad is,' Fox conceded.

'Sisters and brothers?'

'Just the one sister.'

'Close, are you?' Fox chose not to answer. 'Luckier than most if

37

you are. Sometimes you have to draw a line between yourself and the ones you're supposed to love.' Carter ran a finger horizontally through the air. 'It might sting for a while, but that doesn't mean you shouldn't do it.'

Fox sat for a further moment or two, then rose to his feet, his host copying him. The man was almost wedged into the chair, but Fox doubted he'd accept any offer of help.

'Macaroni cheese, that's my downfall, eh, Jimmy?'

The dog's ears pricked up at mention of its name. Fox had paused next to the dining table.

'If I was to describe you,' Fox began, 'I'd say you were orderly – coats on the rack; boots laid out in a row. Biscuits need to go on a plate, not served straight from the packet. And that makes me wonder about this ...' He waved his hand across the table. 'It's not just hoarding, is it? There's some sort of pattern to it.'

'A bit of historical research.'

'Nineteen eighty-five?'

'There or thereabouts.'

'Late April maybe?'

'Go on then – tell me what happened.'

'In April '85?' Fox tried to think. In the end, he gave up.

'Dennis Taylor beat Steve Davis at the snooker,' Alan Carter said, leading the way to the door.

6

Detective Constable Cheryl Forrester liked to ask questions. Questions like: How long have you been in the Complaints? Is there a selection process? How many of you work there? Is it for life, or some kind of fixed term? Why is it you're detective grade but not called detectives? What's been your most shocking case? What's the nightlife like in Edinburgh?

'It's only a train ride away, you know,' Joe Naysmith told her.

'Oh, I've been there plenty times.'

'Then you probably know the nightlife better than we do,' Tony Kaye said.

'But I mean the places locals go ...'

'DC Forrester, we're not really here to pass along tourist tips.'

'I like the Voodoo Rooms,' Naysmith interrupted. He saw the look on his colleague's face and swallowed back a further comment.

The problem was, Forrester's enthusiasm was almost infectious. The description 'bubbly' might have been coined for her. She had curly brown hair, tanned skin, and a rounded face with freckles and large brown eyes. She had been in the force for six years, the last two in CID. Right at the start, she'd told them she was too busy for a boyfriend.

'I'm sure plenty have tried,' Kaye had stated, intending to bring Paul Carter's name into play, but she had steered the conversation in another direction by asking Naysmith if the Complaints worked nine-to-five, to which he'd responded by telling her about their surveillance van and how an operation could last anything up to a year.

'A year of your life? Better be a result at the end of it!'

And so it went, until Kaye finally rapped his knuckles against the table. They were in the interview room again, but without the recording equipment. Forrester, sensing she was somehow worthy of censure, set her mouth tight and clasped her hands together in front of her.

'As you know,' Tony Kaye began, 'certain allegations have been levelled at several of your colleagues. Would you care to tell us what you think of them?'

'The allegations or the colleagues?'

'Why not both?'

Forrester puffed out her cheeks. 'I was shocked when I heard. I think everyone was. I'd worked with DC Carter for almost eighteen months and he'd never ... well, never struck me as being like that.'

'You've been out on calls with him?'

'Yes.'

'In the car with him?'

'Yes.'

'And he's never said anything? Never asked you to wait while he popped into a house or a flat?'

'Not like that, no.'

'Police stations are terrible places for gossip ...'

'I can't say I've ever heard anything.' She stared at Kaye with her wide, innocent-seeming eyes.

'Your colleagues in CID – Scholes, Haldane, Michaelson ...'

'What about them?'

'When the Carter investigation started, they must've talked about it.'

'I suppose so.'

'Did anything strike you? Maybe they went into a huddle?'

She gave a look of concentration, then shook her head slowly but with certainty.

'Did you ever feel left out? Maybe they headed off to the pub together ...'

'We have nights at the pub, yes.'

'You must have discussed the case.'

'Yes, but not how to tamper with evidence.'

'The time Michaelson spilled coffee on his notebook – did you see that?'

'No.'

'And you never saw Teresa Collins, never heard Carter on the phone to her?'

'No.'

'How come you weren't called as a witness at the trial? Sounds to me like you could have done Carter a power of good.'

'I don't really know. I mean, all I could have said is what I've just told you.'

'Carter never came on to you?'

There was silence in the room. Forrester looked down at her hands and then up again. 'Never,' she stated.

'And that's the truth, not just something you've been told to say?'

'It's the truth. Bring me a bible and I'll swear on it.'

'If we can't find a bible,' Naysmith interrupted, 'would a cocktail list suffice?'

Cheryl Forrester laughed, showing perfect pearly teeth.

At the end of the interview, Naysmith said he'd walk her back to CID.

'It's not like she's going to get mugged,' Kaye chided his colleague, but Naysmith ignored him. Kaye decided to wander outside for some air. In the car park, a hovering gull just missed him, splattering an MG's windscreen instead. There was no sign of the Mondeo, and no sign of Fox. Kaye took out his mobile and checked for messages. He had three, one of them from Malcolm. Back inside the station, he kept his finger on the bell until the desk sergeant arrived with the same welcoming black look as ever.

'I'll take DCI Laird, if he's around,' Kaye said.

'I'm not sure he is.'

'Okay, never mind.' Kaye headed for the corridor and climbed the stairs to the next floor. CID comprised several offices here. Cheryl Forrester was in one of them, while Naysmith stood in the doorway, arms folded, one foot crossed over the other, talking to her. Kaye gave him a dig in the back as he passed, then pushed open the door to the large open-plan office further on. Scholes and Michaelson looked up from their desks. Scholes was on the phone, Michaelson navigating his computer screen with a mouse. Another man, slightly older than the other two, stood in the centre of the room. He had dispensed with his suit jacket, and his shirtsleeves were rolled up. He had waxy olive skin, hair that was grey at the temples, and bags under his eyes. He was reading from a sheaf of papers.

'Detective Chief Inspector Laird?' Kaye held out his hand. Laird had yet to make eye contact. He added a couple of words to the margin of one sheet, then pocketed his pen.

'You're Fox?' he drawled.

'Sergeant Kaye,' Kaye corrected him, withdrawing his hand. 'Where's Fox?'

'Probably off getting a second opinion on Haldane's flu.'

'Well now ...' Laird deigned to meet Kaye's eyes at last. 'You're a cheeky little bastard, aren't you?'

'Depends on the situation, sir.' Kaye sensed that he was standing in front of a man who believed in the troops under his command and would defend them to the bitter end. Forrester hadn't been helpful because there was nothing for her to be helpful *with*, but Laird was another matter entirely. He would give them nothing because that was all they deserved. It was there in his tone, his manner, his way of standing, feet planted widely apart. Kaye had encountered the type plenty of times. They could be dismantled, but it took time and effort. Weeks of time, unceasing effort.

Fox's message had been 'Ask Laird why Pitkethly was brought in.' It was a reasonable question, and Kaye knew why it was best not to ask Pitkethly herself. Quite simply, she probably wouldn't know. She hadn't known the station at all until she was shipped there. Laird had served under the previous regime. He was an old hand. If there was a story worth telling, Laird might be the one to tell it.

But a few seconds spent in the man's company told Kaye this wasn't going to happen.

'My boss,' he said, 'had something he wanted me to ask you.'

'Spit it out, then.'

But Kaye just shook his head. 'I don't think I will.'

Then he turned and walked away. Halfway down the corridor, he grabbed Naysmith by the back of his collar and took him with him.

7

The Mondeo's parking space had been taken by an idling Astra. In fact, the only bay left was the one marked Superintendent, so that was where Fox ended up. As he made for the station entrance, he gave the Astra's driver a look. The face was familiar.

'About bloody time,' Tony Kaye said, emerging from the station with Naysmith in tow. 'Got your text but I didn't reckon I was going to get any joy from Laird.'

'DC Forrester was nice and helpful, though,' Naysmith added, Kaye shooting him a look.

'Helpful?' he mimicked. 'She gave us the square root of hee-haw.' Then, turning to Fox: 'Tell me you've been having it worse than us. Got lost a few times maybe. Found the uncle but he's doolally … Foxy? You listening?'

Fox's attention was still focused on the Astra.

'That's Paul Carter,' he said.

'What?'

Fox started walking towards the car. It reversed out of its bay and began to exit the car park. Fox jogged after it for a few paces, then stopped. Kaye caught him up, the two men watching as the car shot away, modified exhaust roaring.

'You sure?'

Fox gave him a cold stare.

'Okay,' Kaye conceded. 'You're sure.'

Fox took out his phone and called the Procurator Fiscal's office. He was passed between extensions and offices until he found some-one with the answers he needed. Paul Carter had been released on bail at 8.15 a.m., pending the sheriff's decision on sentencing.

'Cells are jam-packed,' Fox was told. 'Sheriff Cardonald reckoned he was one of the safer bets. Restricted movements – he's not allowed within range of the three women.'

'Who posted the bail?'

'It wasn't a huge amount.'

'And this was the sheriff's idea? Colin Cardonald?'

'I suppose so.'

'The judge who doesn't like cops?'

'Steady on ...'

But Fox had ended the call. 'He's out,' he confirmed, for Kaye and Naysmith's benefit.

'Want to bring him in for a chat?' Naysmith asked.

Fox shook his head.

'Hell was he doing here?' Kaye added.

'Catching up with his pals,' Fox guessed, turning to look at the station's first-floor windows. Ray Scholes stood in one of them, a mug in his hand. He toasted Fox with it before turning away.

'Doesn't change anything,' Tony Kaye stated.

'No,' Fox agreed.

'And you still haven't told us how you got on with the uncle.'

'Good guy.' Fox paused. 'I liked him.'

'Not half as much as Joe here likes DC Forrester.' Kaye looked around the car park. 'Where's my Mondeo?'

'I had to take Pitkethly's spot.'

'Best move it then, eh?' Kaye held out his hand for the key.

'Better still,' Fox said, 'let's jump in and grab a spot of lunch. My shout.'

Kaye stared at him. 'What's the catch?'

Fox's mouth twitched. 'A wee cruise around town first.'

'With an eye to spotting a silver Astra?' Kaye guessed.

Fox handed him the key.

After a fruitless half-hour, they ended up back at the Pancake Place. Since Fox was paying, Kaye ordered soup and the fish mornay pancake. The same table as before was available, so they'd taken it.

'Where does Carter live?' Joe Naysmith asked.

'Dunnikier Estate,' Fox told him. 'We drove through it yesterday.'

'We drove through a lot of estates yesterday.'

'Semis, pebble-dash, and satellite dishes.'

'You're not narrowing it down.'

44

'We could go there,' Kaye suggested. 'See how he likes having us parked outside for an hour or two.'

'To what end?' Fox asked.

'Getting his back up. Could we maybe set up the surveillance van – bug his phone and computer?'

Naysmith looked interested.

'We'd need permission from HQ,' Fox stated. 'And they won't give it.'

'Why not?' Naysmith asked with a frown.

'Because we're here for Scholes, Haldane and Michaelson – Carter's outwith our remit.'

'Well, what about bugging *their* phones?' Naysmith suggested.

Fox looked at him. 'Surveillance is a whole new game, Joe. I doubt anyone at HQ thinks them big enough fish to merit it. Plus, we're not from here. It would have to be a Fife operation – local Complaints.'

Naysmith considered this for a moment, then went back to eating his Scotch broth. Fox's phone started ringing and he answered. It was Superintendent Isabel Pitkethly.

'Paul Carter's no longer in custody,' she told him.

'I know.'

'Seems the sheriff has a little bit of faith in him.'

'Yes.'

'If he decides to appeal, the allegations against my officers may well be challenged in court.'

'Not my concern, Superintendent.'

'What do you mean?'

'I'm not working for the courts or the prosecution. Your bosses in Glenrothes tell me what to do, and so far they've not said anything about dropping the inquiry.' Fox paused. 'Have you spoken with Carter?'

'Of course not.'

'He was outside the station an hour ago.'

'I didn't know that.'

'Scholes knew. Maybe you should ask why he kept it to himself.'

'I'm not long back from HQ.'

'You seem to spend a lot of time there. Updating them in person?'

She ignored this. 'So you've not finished here yet?'

'Not nearly.'

45

'I'll see you later then. And Inspector ...?'

'Yes, Superintendent?'

'Don't ever park that car in my space again.'

The afternoon comprised a wasted session in the interview room with DCI Peter Laird – there was nothing unusual about Superintendent Hendryson's retirement; it had been his time, that was all – and a visit to the home of the sickly DS Haldane. They found Haldane sprawled on the sofa in his living room, a duvet swamping him and a visiting mother doling out tea, cold remedies and seasoned advice.

'Can't this wait till he's better?' she had chided the three intruders. It had eventually been agreed that Haldane would make himself available at the station in a day or two, so that a proper interview could take place.

'What now?' Kaye asked afterwards as they climbed into the car.

'Dunnikier Estate,' Fox said.

Kaye gave a little smile, as if he'd known this answer might be coming. Their destination was on the other side of town, and traffic was slow.

'Schools coming out,' Naysmith commented, watching uniformed pupils tramping along the pavement.

'You're a regular Hercule Poirot,' Kaye muttered.

Eventually they turned in to Carter's street. 'That house there,' Fox stated.

'The one with the silver Astra in the drive?' Kaye commented. 'Hercule Poirot *and* Sherlock Holmes.'

'Whose is the other car?' Naysmith asked.

Fox supplied the answer. 'Belongs to Ray Scholes.'

'You sure?'

'If that's him coming out of the house ...'

And so it was. A brief hug between the two men, Scholes and Carter, and then Carter disappearing inside, closing the door. Scholes clocked the Mondeo but didn't seem surprised or bothered by it. He unlocked his black VW Golf and got in, Fox watching from the rear window of the Mondeo.

'Do we pay our respects?' Kaye asked, as they slowed for a junction.

'No.'

46

'What then?'

'Back to Edinburgh.'

'Now you're talking.'

'And to while away the time, we'll have a little quiz.' Fox leaned forward so his face was between the two front seats. 'What can either of you remember about 1985? Specifically, late April ...'

Kaye's way of insisting that they have a drink at Minter's before going their separate ways was to drive directly to the pub and park outside it.

'My treat,' he said, ordering a pint for himself, a half for Naysmith and a Big Tom for Fox. From experience, the barman knew Naysmith's 'half' was a joke, and began pouring two pints of Caledonian 80. They took their drinks to a table, and Kaye asked Fox how long it had been since he'd allowed himself a proper drink.

'I've stopped counting.'

'Aye, right.' Kaye wiped a line of foam from his top lip.

'You know,' Joe Naysmith commented, 'surveillance isn't a bad idea.'

'Hey,' Kaye warned him with a wagging finger, 'we're off duty here.'

'I'm just saying, it's how we'd normally build a case.'

'I thought I'd already explained ...' Fox began.

Naysmith nodded. 'But – correct me if I'm wrong – we're going to get nowhere otherwise. Say we asked Bob McEwan for permission, set everything up without letting anyone in Fife know. Then, when we get something—'

'*If* we get something,' Fox corrected him.

'Okay, *if* we get something—'

'And it's a big "if",' Kaye added.

'Yes, but what we'd then do is present it to Fife HQ as a fait accompli.'

'The boy's losing me with all these big words,' Kaye complained to Fox.

'What makes you think McEwan would agree to it in the first place?' Fox asked Naysmith.

'We'd ask him nicely.'

Kaye snorted. 'Oh aye, he's a sucker for a kind word.'

'Like I said,' Fox told Naysmith, 'it'd have to be a Fife call.'

'So where's the harm in asking them? You must know somebody on the Complaints over there ...'

Fox hesitated for a moment before nodding. 'I doubt we're in their good books, though. We're working what should be their patch.'

'But you do know somebody?' Naysmith persisted.

'Yes,' Fox conceded, turning to look at Kaye.

Kaye shrugged. 'Can't see it working.'

'Why not?'

'Surveillance operation needs the okay from upstairs. Haven't we been saying all along that Glenrothes doesn't necessarily want us finding anything?'

'But if they deny their own Complaints department,' Naysmith argued, 'that looks bad, too.'

Kaye's eyes were still on Malcolm Fox. 'What do you say, Foxy?'

'It's a protocol minefield.'

'First step might not blow us up, though.'

'Home phones and mobiles,' Naysmith added, 'just to hear what Carter's saying to his pals in CID.'

'I'll have a think about it,' Fox eventually said.

Kaye slapped a hand down on Naysmith's knee. 'That means he's going to do it. Well played, Joseph. And it's your round, by the way ...'

Once home, Fox microwaved another ready-meal and ate it at the table. The TV stayed off. He was lost in thought. After he'd cleaned up, he called his sister and apologised for not getting back to her sooner.

'Don't tell me: you've been busy?'

'It happens to be true.' Fox squeezed the skin at the bridge of his nose.

'But you *did* go see Dad?'

'Last night, as promised. He was back to himself by the time I got there.'

'Oh?'

'We took a look through some of those photographs.'

'They didn't upset him?'

'Not so much, no.'

'Maybe it's me, then – is that what you're getting at? You think I'm overreacting?'

'No, Jude, I'm sure you're not. And I saw the pack of pads in the bathroom.'

'If he starts wetting himself, they're going to kick him out.'

'I doubt that.'

'They'll want him home with one of us.'

'Listen, Jude—'

'It can't be me, Malcolm! How am I supposed to cope?'

'They're not going to get rid of him.'

'Why? Because you keep coughing up for his bed and board? That's fine as long as he's not a bother to them.'

'Would it put your mind at rest if we went to see them?'

'You do it – they hate me.'

'No they don't.'

'They treat me like dirt. You don't see it because you're the one waving the chequebook. That's all right, though, isn't it? *You'll* be the one getting the lion's share of his will. It's you he likes, the one he's always talking about when I'm there. Never me – I just fetch and carry, like one of the fucking staff!'

'Listen to yourself, Jude.'

But instead it was Fox who listened – listened to his sister as her complaints lengthened and intensified. He pictured the photograph of her as a small girl, atop Chris's shoulders, bursting with carefree energy. Now distilled to this.

Sometimes you have to draw a line ...

Fox watched himself lower the telephone receiver back on to its charger. As the connection was made, the line went dead. He drew in his bottom lip, staring at the machine, wondering if it would ring, Jude enraged on the other end.

But it didn't, so he made himself some tea, considering whether there was anything he could have said to her to make things better – offered to visit his father more often; arranged for the three of them to go to lunch some weekend. *It's you he likes ... I just fetch and carry.*

With a sigh, he went over to his computer and switched it on, wondering what his search engine could tell him about 1985, while the stinging memory of the phone call began to melt away.

Three

8

'You're not a ghost, then?'

'Flesh and blood, last time I looked.'

Fox was starting to reach out a hand, but saw she was holding both of hers towards him. He made to grasp them, then realised it was the prelude to a hug. Awkwardly, he hugged her back.

'Has it been three years or four?' she asked. Three years or four since their one-night stand at, of all things, a Standards of Conduct conference at Tulliallan Police College.

'Not quite four. You look just the same.' He took a step back, the better to judge the truth of this. Her name was Evelyn Mills, much the same age as Fox but wearing the years lightly. She'd been married at the time of their fling, and, by the ring on her left hand, she still was. They were standing on the seafront in Kirkcaldy. There had been a heavy shower earlier, but it had blown over. Thick gobbets of cloud glided overhead. There were a couple of cargo ships on the horizon. Fox took it in, while waiting to see if she had any comment to make about his own appearance.

'Still in the Complaints, then?' she asked instead. He stuffed his hands into his pockets and gave a shrug.

'And you, too.'

'Mmm ...' She seemed to be studying him intently. Then she linked arms with him and they started walking in silence.

'Good result for you,' Fox offered eventually. 'Paul Carter, I mean.'

'Wasn't really us, though, was it? It was down to the witnesses. Even then ... different day, different courtroom – it could have swung the other way.'

'All the same,' he persisted.

'All the same ... we're so good at what we do, *you* have to be hauled here from the bustling metropolis.'

'Arm's-length, Evelyn. This way no one can accuse you of looking out for your own.'

'You think we'd do that?'

'It wouldn't be me pointing the finger.' He paused. 'If it's any consolation ...'

'I'm not looking for consolation, Malcolm.' With her free hand she gave his forearm a squeeze, and he knew she was offering herself as ally rather than foe.

'Carter is walking the streets,' Fox said. 'Did you know that?'

She nodded. They were making towards the dock at the Esplanade's northern end. There was a solitary fishing boat moored there, but no sign of life apart from some fierce-looking gulls.

'We're thinking it might be nice to hear what he says to Scholes and the others.'

'Oh?'

'Home and mobile phones.'

'Of four detectives?'

'Three: Carter's appeal – if he starts one – would have a field day if we eavesdropped on him.'

'I'm not sure we can stretch to it, Malcolm.'

'Manpower or resources?'

She exhaled noisily. 'Both, if I'm being honest. Basically, you're looking at Fife's Complaints department. I'm it. I mean, I can always requisition a few bodies in an emergency ...'

'Is that what you did when Alan Carter made the original complaint?'

She nodded, pushing some hair back from her face. 'Scholes is the one Carter's close to. If I was going to look at anybody, it would be him.'

'We saw him leaving Carter's house yesterday.'

'You mean the surveillance is up and running?'

Fox shook his head again. 'We were just passing.'

Her eyes narrowed. 'Passing through the Dunnikier Estate?'

'In a manner of speaking.'

She scrutinised his face, then gave a short laugh. 'God, the things we do,' she said. He wasn't sure if she meant their job or was thinking back to that night in Tulliallan; best, he felt, not to risk asking.

'You know I'd need to go to my boss?' she said after a moment's thought. 'And he'd have to go to *his* boss?'

Fox nodded.

'And I'm allowed to tell them it's your idea?'

He nodded again.

'All this, just to prove whether or not some colleagues stuck up for one of their own?'

'Perjuring themselves in the process,' Fox reminded her.

She ran her finger down the bridge of her nose, a nose Fox suddenly remembered kissing. She'd had a lot to drink at the bar that night. He'd been the sober one, the one who should have seen her only as far as her bedroom door. But she'd had a kettle in her room. And sachets of instant coffee. And a narrow single bed ...

'What do you think?' he asked her now.

'I think it's freezing out here.'

'Whatever your answer is, thanks for meeting with me.'

This time she patted his arm, and they turned to walk back to her car. Having reached it in silence, she asked him where he had parked. He nodded in the vague direction of the town centre. She unlocked her car and got in. It was an Alfa Romeo with a dark-blue interior.

Fox closed the door for her and watched her start the ignition. The window slid downwards and she peered up at him. 'I was at Fettes a few months back, running an errand. I considered knocking on your door.'

'You should have.'

She released the brake, gave him a wave, and was gone. Fox stayed where he was until he couldn't see the car any more, then crossed the street and headed for the café in the Mercat shopping centre. Kaye and Naysmith were waiting there, drinking coffee and reading their chosen newspapers: *Guardian* for Naysmith, *Daily Record* for Kaye.

'Don't order anything,' Kaye warned Fox. 'Not a patch on the other place.'

'Closer to the car, though,' Fox reminded him. Kaye's eyes were fixed on him, awaiting his report.

'It's a "maybe",' he obliged, squeezing into the booth. Kaye's nostrils flared and he leaned over to sniff Fox's coat. 'Chanel Number 5, unless I'm losing my touch. Your contact's not a bloke, then.'

55

'Now who's Hercule Poirot?' Joe Naysmith muttered, not bothering to look up from his reading.

Not the interview room. Teresa Collins had been insistent. In fact, nowhere near 'that stinking place', which was why Fox had suggested her home. It was the upper storey of a maisonette in Gallatown. Gary Michaelson had hinted it might not be the town's most salubrious area. Actually, it looked all right to Fox: there were plenty worse in Edinburgh. Terraced and semi-detached houses, many of them split. Pebble-dashed walls and plenty of satellite dishes. Young mothers, some pregnant again, pushed their baby buggies while talking into their phones. A few teenage lads in baseball caps scowled as the Mondeo drew to a halt kerbside, and made intuitive grunting noises as the three men stepped out. Fox pressed the bell marked 'Collins'.

'It's open!' a voice yelled.

Fox turned the handle and started climbing the steep flight of stairs. Someone on the ground floor was hosting a party.

'Eminem,' Naysmith stated.

'Just sounds like noise to me,' Tony Kaye muttered.

Teresa Collins was seated in an armchair in her uncluttered living room, dangling one leg over the side and with a lit cigarette in her mouth. She wore black Lycra leggings and a purple T-shirt with the words Porn Star picked out in diamanté.

'No need to spruce yourself up on our account,' Kaye told her, examining a 3-D poster of Beyoncé above the fireplace. The music from downstairs was causing the windowpanes to vibrate.

'I forgot to ask,' Collins said. 'Should I maybe have called my lawyer?'

'You're the victim here,' Fox reminded her, introducing himself, Kaye and Naysmith. There was one other armchair, but it was piled high with laundry. When it came to underwear, Teresa Collins seemed to favour the thong.

'Victim is right,' she said, taking another drag on the cigarette. There was a flat-screen TV and Freeview box in one corner of the room. On an otherwise empty bookcase sat the dock and speakers for an MP3 player. The beige carpet had collected an impressive number of ash burns.

'Everybody needs good neighbours, eh?' Kaye announced, thumping the floor with the heel of his shoe.

'They're all right.' The foot hanging over the arm of the chair was keeping time, while Collins's other knee pumped furiously.

'Few uppers to counteract the methadone?' Fox guessed.

'You won't find anything that's not prescribed,' she snapped back.

'We're not looking for anything. As I said on the phone, it's Carter's colleagues we're checking.'

'So you *say*.'

'It'd be nice if you believed me.'

She looked like she was having trouble focusing on him. 'Go ahead, then,' she said at last. 'Ask me the same bloody questions ...'

'DI Carter used to come here?'

'Aye.'

'Some of your neighbours saw him?'

'They said so, didn't they?'

'Wasn't very discreet of him. What about his colleagues – they never came in?'

'Scholes did, one time. But that was early days, when they were wanting me to be a grass.'

'Scholes was never here when Carter was after one of these "favours"?'

She shook her head. 'Might've waited in the car.' She was looking agitated. 'When you lot got wise, it was Scholes who phoned me, tried to warn me off.'

'I know it can't be easy, going back over this.'

'I thought it was done with. Is this what happens now? He's going down, so you lot keep persecuting me till I go off my head or do myself in?'

Fox didn't answer for a moment. 'You know there are charities that can help, numbers you can phone?'

'Rape Crisis? All that lot?' She shook her head determinedly. 'I just want left alone.' She exhaled a plume of smoke and brushed flecks of ash from her T-shirt. 'Now he's inside, that's all I'm asking ...'

'What if he's not inside?' As soon as the words were out of Naysmith's mouth, he knew he'd made a mistake: the combined glower from Fox and Kaye intimated as much.

'You mean he's out?' The pale eyes in the paler face had widened.

'You should have been told,' Fox said quietly.

'He's ...?' Collins got to her feet and padded over to the window, staring down on to the street.

'He's been warned not to come within half a mile of you,' Fox tried to reassure her. 'If he does, he's back inside pronto.'

'Well that's just dandy,' she said, voice heavy with sarcasm. 'Carter's bound to stick to *that*, isn't he? Law-abiding prick like him ...'

She spun away from the window. 'What if I say it's all a lie? I made it up to get him into bother?'

'Then you'll be the one under lock and key,' Fox cautioned her. He placed his business card on the arm of the chair. 'My number's there – any sign of him, call me.'

'You're here to threaten me,' Teresa Collins stated, pointing a trembling finger. 'Three of you – that's intimidation enough. Plus your story about him being out ... This is me being told, isn't it? Scholes and Haldane and Michaelson, and now you three.'

'I can assure you we're—'

'I'll go to the papers! That's what I'll do! I'll scream blue murder.'

'Will you calm down, Teresa?' Fox had his hands held up in a show of surrender. He took a step forwards, but she had spun round again and pulled the window open.

'Help!' she screamed. 'Somebody help me!'

Fox saw that Kaye was looking at him, waiting for a decision.

'I'll call you,' Fox told Collins, raising his voice in the hope she might hear. 'Later, when you've had a chance to ...'

He signalled to Kaye and Naysmith that they were leaving. The neighbours upstairs were looking down at them from the landing.

'She's hysterical,' Fox explained, starting his descent. Nobody from the ground-floor party had heard – or if they had, they couldn't be bothered to do anything about it. But the kids were outside on the pavement, facing Fox and his colleagues as they emerged. Fox had his warrant card out for them to see.

'Back off,' he told them.

'Youse've raped her,' one voice said accusingly.

'She's just upset.'

'Aye, and who did that, eh? Youse did ...'

'For Christ's sake,' Tony Kaye burst out. 'Look at my car!'

The contents of a waste bin had been tipped over the bonnet and windscreen: fast-food cartons, cigarette butts, crushed beer cans, and what looked like the remains of a dead pigeon.

'Car wash down the road, only three quid,' one of the gang suggested.

'Five if you tell them you're a pig,' another added.

There was laughter, for which Fox was grateful. The situation was being defused – and Teresa Collins had stopped yelling and closed her window.

Tony Kaye, however, looked furious. He lunged at the youths, Fox hauling him back by his arm.

'Easy, Tony, easy. Let's just get out of here, eh?'

'But these wee wankers—'

'In the car,' Fox commanded. Kaye waited another couple of beats before complying, using the wipers to brush aside some of the debris, and reversing hard to dislodge more from the bonnet.

'Swear to God I'm coming back here with a bat,' he muttered, as the gang jogged along by the side of the car, giving it the occasional kick or slap. He revved the engine and shot away in first, doing a U-turn that got rid of almost all the remaining rubbish.

'Forget it, Kaye,' Joe Naysmith said. 'It's Gallatown.'

'Think you're funny, eh?' Tony Kaye leaned over and gave him a hard punch to the side of his head. 'Laugh now, ya wee shitebag ...'

9

'That was quick,' Malcolm Fox said into his phone. Evelyn Mills was on the other end of the line. The eavesdropping operation had been given the green light.

'My boss decided we didn't need to refer it upwards,' she explained.

'Why not?'

'My guess is, he reckons it might have been knocked back.'

'I like the sound of your boss.'

'He reminds me a bit of you, actually.'

'Then I'm flattered. How long till you're operational?'

'Need a telephone engineer to help us with the landline.'

'Us?'

'I've got help: two youngsters from CID. Mobile phone will take longer – first things we'll have access to are numbers called and calls received ...' She broke off. 'You know all this already.'

'True.'

He heard her give a short sigh. 'It'll be end of play today for the landline; some time tomorrow for everything else. Unlikely Scholes would bother e-mailing Carter, so I was going to skip the key-stroke surveillance.'

'Fine by me. And thanks again, Evelyn.'

'It's what neglected friends are for, right?'

'Right.'

'Just one thing, though – Scholes isn't an idiot. Might explain why he went to Carter's house. It keeps their conversation private. Could be all we end up with are texts to arrange more meetings.'

'I know.'

She gave another sigh. 'Of course you do. I keep forgetting how much alike we are. Maybe that's why we hit it off that time.'

'Are you sure you want to say any more? This may not be as secure a line as we'd like.'

She was chuckling as Fox wrapped up the call.

'Sounds like a result,' Kaye commented. All three of them were crammed into the storeroom, door slightly ajar, Joe Naysmith keeping watch for spies and dawdlers.

'Everything should be up and running by tomorrow. Home phone could even be tonight.'

'That's efficient. Care to share the secret of your success?'

'No.'

'Just her name, then.'

'Plus,' Naysmith added, turning towards his colleagues, 'whatever it was you thought she shouldn't be saying over a non-secure line.' He jumped as someone thumped on the door, pushing it open. Superintendent Pitkethly stood there, face like thunder.

'Would I be right in thinking the three of you just paid Teresa Collins a visit?'

Fox rose to his feet. 'She's made a complaint?' he guessed.

'In a manner of speaking. They found your name on a business card on her chair – when they went in with the stretcher.'

She saw immediately the effect her words had had, and kept quiet for a moment, the better to savour the discomfort on the three faces.

'A passer-by saw her at her window, smearing blood on it from her wrists. He called the paramedics.'

All three men were standing now, eyes on Pitkethly. Kaye was the first to speak.

'Is she ...?'

'She's in hospital. Wounds don't look too bad. Question is: what drove her to it? From the look of you, I'd say I've got my answer.'

'She was hysterical,' Naysmith blurted out. 'We left her to it ...'

'Having calmed her down first, obviously,' Pitkethly said, twisting the knife. 'I mean, this is a woman who's had a traumatic experience. Fragile enough to begin with, and with a history of drug use. I'm assuming you didn't just walk away?'

'We don't answer to you,' Fox stated, regaining a little of his composure.

'You might have to, though.'

'We'll make our report.'

'And will there be conferring beforehand?' This question came from DCI Peter Laird, who had just arrived at Pitkethly's shoulder. Fox sensed that there were other spectators in the corridor. He pushed past Pitkethly and saw that he was right. Laird wasn't bothering to suppress his pleasure at this turn of events.

'I mean,' Laird went on, folding his arms, 'you'll want to make sure you've got your stories straight.'

'She's going to be all right, though?' Joe Naysmith was asking Pitkethly.

'Bit late to be showing concern,' she answered him. Fox got right into her face.

'Enough,' he said. Then, to Kaye and Naysmith: 'We're out of here.'

'Going so soon?' Laird was waving with the fingers of one hand as they stalked down the corridor.

'I'll need those statements,' Pitkethly called after them.

As Fox pushed open the door to the outside world, he saw Scholes hurrying in from the car park.

'Looks like I missed the fun,' he said with a grin. Fox ignored him, but Kaye gave him a shoulder-charge that almost felled him. Scholes didn't react. His laughter followed them to the Mondeo.

'Where to?' Kaye asked.

'Home,' Fox stated.

They didn't say anything for the first few miles. It was Naysmith who broke the silence. 'Poor woman.'

Kaye just nodded.

'Reckon we should have stayed?'

Kaye looked to Fox, but saw he wasn't going to answer. He was staring out of the passenger-side window, forehead almost touching it.

'I can't see that we did anything wrong,' Kaye announced, trying for more certainty than he felt. 'We were the ones making her frantic, so we left.'

'But it was me, wasn't it? Telling her Carter was out ...'

'Wasn't our job to keep the facts from her, Joe.'

'You sound,' Fox interrupted, 'as if you've already got your report off-pat.'

'It was her way of crying out for help,' Kaye persisted. 'We've all seen them.'

'I haven't,' Naysmith corrected him.

'You know the type, though. If she'd really wanted to top herself, she wouldn't have stood at the window like that, showing all and sundry what she'd done.'

'What if nobody'd been passing, though?'

'Then she'd have phoned herself an ambulance. Like I say, it happens.'

'I can't help thinking—'

'Then don't think!' Kaye snapped at Naysmith. 'Let's just get back to civilisation and write up what happened.' He looked towards Fox again. 'Come on, Malcolm, back me up here. She could have snapped any time, just our bad luck it happened when it did.'

'We could have tried calming her down.'

'In case you've forgotten, she was screaming fit to burst. Two more minutes in there and every nut-job in the neighbourhood would have had us cornered.' Kaye kneaded the steering wheel with both hands. 'I can't see that we did anything wrong,' he repeated.

Fox saw that they were on the M90 again and had already passed Inverkeithing.

'I need you to do me a favour,' he said quietly.

'What?'

'There's a lay-by just before the bridge. Pull in and let me out.'

'You going to be sick?'

Fox shook his head.

'What then?'

'Just pull over.'

Kaye signalled to move into the inside lane, saw the signpost for the lay-by and signalled again. It was an area for large loads to stop, preparatory to being escorted to the other side of the estuary. Fox got out of the car and felt the fast-moving stream of traffic attempting to suck him on to the carriageway. There was a pavement, though, and it led to a walkway that crossed the road bridge.

'You're kidding,' Kaye called out to him.

'I need some air, that's all.'

'What the hell are we supposed to do?'

'Wait for me on the other side, as near to the old tollbooths as you can get.'

'Want me to come with you?' Naysmith asked, but Fox shook

63

his head and slammed shut the door, turning his collar up. He had walked thirty or forty yards before a break in the traffic allowed the Mondeo to pass him with a single toot of its horn. Fox waved at it and kept walking. He had never crossed the Forth Road Bridge like this before. He knew people did it all the time: joggers and tourists. The noise from the carriageway was punishing, and the drop to the Firth of Forth seemed vertiginous, but Fox kept going, drawing in lungfuls of fumy air. There was a dog-walker coming from the opposite direction. She wore a scarf tied tightly over her hair, and offered him a nod and a smile, neither of which he returned with any degree of success. To his left he could see the rail bridge, much of it under wraps for maintenance. There were islands down there, too, and over to the right the port of Rosyth. The wind was ripping at his ears, but he felt it was as much as he deserved. Kaye was right, of course: a cry for help rather than a serious effort. But all the same. They'd dropped a bomb on her with the news of Paul Carter, then simply walked away. No call to social services or whoever else might willingly check on her. A neighbour? A relative in the area? No, they'd cared more for their own skins and that bloody Mondeo.

Fox hadn't encountered too much violence or tragedy during his years on the force. A few drunken fights to break up when he'd been in uniform; a couple of bad murder cases in CID. Part of the appeal of the Complaints had been its focus on rules broken rather than bones, on cops who crossed the line but were not violent men. Did that make him a coward? He didn't think so. Less of a copper? Again, no. But it was in his nature to avoid confrontation, or ensure it didn't well up in the first place – which was why he felt he had failed with Teresa Collins. Every moment of his time with her could have been played differently, and with a better outcome.

Fox rubbed his hands down either side of his face as he walked. His pace was quickening, the wind growing more biting still as he reached the halfway point. He was in the middle of the Firth of Forth now, steel cables holding him aloft. He was depending on them to do their job and not suddenly snap. Without knowing why he was doing it, he broke into a run – jogging at first, but then speeding up. When had he last run anywhere? He couldn't remember. The sprint lasted only a few tens of metres, and he was breathing hard by the end of it. Two proper joggers gave him a lengthy examination as they passed.

'I'm all right,' he told them with a wave of his hand.

Maybe he believed it, too. He took out his phone and snapped the view, just so he wouldn't forget. South Queensferry was below him now, with its blustery yachts and boat trips out to Inchcolm Abbey. He started looking for the Mondeo ahead of him, but couldn't see it. Had they had enough and left him to it? He double-checked the few parked vehicles, then heard a horn behind him and turned to see Kaye pulling in, having just crossed the bridge.

Fox opened the passenger-side door. 'How did you manage that?' he asked.

'Joe here got worried you might be going to jump,' Kaye explained. 'So we went round the roundabout, crossed back over into Fife, did the same at the other end ... and here we are.'

'Nice to know you care.'

'It was Joe, remember – I'd have left you to it.'

Fox smiled, got in and fastened his seat belt. 'Thanks anyway,' he said.

'Nice walk?' Naysmith asked from the back seat.

'Cleared my head a bit.'

'And?' Kaye asked.

'And I'm fine.'

'We could have sworn we saw you jogging.'

Fox gave Tony Kaye a hard stare. 'Do I look the type?'

Kaye smiled with half his mouth. 'Wouldn't have said so.'

'Then I wasn't jogging, was I?'

'That's your version of events, Inspector.' Kaye glanced at Joe Naysmith in the rear-view mirror. 'We'll always have ours. But in the meantime, can I assume we're headed back to base?'

'Unless you want to visit a car-wash first.' Fox watched Kaye shake his head. 'Okay then. Let's see if the news gets to Bob McEwan before we do ...'

65

10

'Well now,' McEwan said, as they walked into the office. He was leaning with the small of his back against Fox's desk, hands in his pockets.

'You've heard, then.'

'Deputy Chief Constable of Fife Constabulary – the very man who asked for our help in the first place.'

'But he's pleased with the rest of our progress?' Kaye commented.

'*Not* the place for wisecracks, Sergeant Kaye,' McEwan snapped back. 'Suppose one of you tells me what in God's name happened.'

'We went to interview her at her home,' Fox began. 'She learned Carter was no longer in custody and threw a wobbly.'

'We decided our presence wasn't helping,' Kaye added. 'Discretion being the better part of valour and all that.'

'What state was she in when you left?'

'She was a bit shaky.' Naysmith decided to answer.

'A bit shaky?' McEwan echoed. 'Not the screaming abdabs neighbours claim to have heard?'

'She did do some shouting,' Fox conceded.

'About police intimidation?'

'She misread the situation, sir.'

'Sounds to me like she wasn't the only one.' McEwan pinched the bridge of his nose, screwing his eyes shut. He spoke without opening them. 'This gives them a bit of ammo – you know that?'

'Does the Deputy want us replaced?'

'I think he's weighing it up.'

'She wouldn't agree to be interviewed at the station, Bob,' Fox explained calmly. 'We had to go to her.'

McEwan opened his eyes again, blinking as if to regain some focus. 'You told her Carter was out?'

'That was my fault,' Naysmith admitted. McEwan gave a little nod of acknowledgement.

'Well,' he said, 'best get your side of the story down on paper and we'll see what Glenrothes thinks. Anything else I should know?'

Fox and Kaye exchanged a look.

'No, sir,' Fox stated.

News of the surveillance operation on Scholes could wait: one little bombshell at a time was probably enough for the boss.

Later, Fox went to the canteen for coffee, and remembered when he got there that he'd not had anything since breakfast. Egg-and-cress sandwiches were all that remained of the lunch offerings, so he added one to his tray, along with a Kit Kat and a Golden Delicious. When his phone rang, he thought about not answering, but checked the display and recognised the caller.

'Hiya, Evelyn,' he said.

'Ouch,' Mills said.

'You've heard, then?'

'Not much else being talked about here. Local press seem to be on to it too. You know how that lot will twist it.'

'They can try.'

'Did she seem suicidal?'

'No more than any of us.' Fox wiped melted chocolate from his fingers on to a napkin. 'Are you still going to be able to help?'

'Will you still be around for me to help?'

'Hopefully.'

'In that case ... we'll see.'

'What does that mean?'

'It means my boss might get cold feet.'

'Buy him some socks.'

There was silence on the line until she asked him how he was feeling.

'I'm okay.'

'You don't exactly sound it.'

'I'll be all right.' He looked down at his tray. Only one bite was missing from the sandwich, but the Kit Kat was history. The coffee had an oily sheen to it, and he didn't feel like starting on the apple.

'All you can do is tell them the truth,' Mills was saying. 'Give your side of the story.'

He could have told her: that was the problem, right there. Every story had a number of sides; *your* version might differ from everyone else's. Back in Collins's flat, had they been pragmatic, cowardly or callous? Others would decide the truth of it – and that might not be the truth at all.

'Malcolm?'

'I'm still here.'

'Do you want someone to talk to? We could meet for a drink.'

'I don't drink.'

'Since when?' She sounded genuinely surprised.

'Long before I met you.'

'I must have forgotten.' She paused. 'We could still meet, though.'

'Another time, eh?' Fox thanked her and ended the call, then started rolling the apple across the table, from left hand to right and back again.

Nobody suggested a trip to Minter's after work. But as they left the office, Naysmith did something out of the ordinary – reached out his hand for Fox and Kaye to shake. Only afterwards did Fox see it as a reinforcement of the notion that they comprised a team. He drove his Volvo out of the car park and headed for home. He'd almost reached Oxgangs when he found himself turning towards the ring road instead. It was rush-hour busy, but he wasn't in a hurry, not now that he had made up his mind. He followed the signs for the Forth Road Bridge.

They had passed the Victoria Hospital on one of their drives around Kirkcaldy. It resembled a building site, because it was one, a shiny new edifice near to completion standing next to the old original complex. Fox showed his ID at reception and gave them Teresa Collins's name. He was told which ward to go to and pointed in the direction of the lifts. He eventually found himself at a nurses' station.

'No visitors,' came the reply when he asked for Teresa, so he showed his ID again.

'I don't want to disturb her if she's awake,' he explained.

The nurse stared at him, wondering, perhaps, what use Teresa would be to him asleep. But eventually she said she would check.

He thanked her and watched her go. Behind him, a row of half a dozen hard plastic chairs sat next to the ward's swing doors. A young man had been sitting there, busy texting with his thumb. He was on his feet now, crossing to the dispenser on the wall opposite and treating himself to some of the antibacterial hand foam.

'Can't be too careful,' he said, rubbing his palms together.

'True,' Fox agreed.

'Police?' the young man guessed.

'And you are ...?'

'You look like police, and I pride myself on knowing most of the CID faces around here. Edinburgh, is it? Professional Standards? Heard you were in town.' He was doing something with his phone's screen. When he held it out in front of him, Fox realised it doubled as a recording device.

The sandy-haired young man in the black anorak was a reporter.

'If you don't mind me asking, were you at Teresa Collins's flat earlier today?'

Fox stood his ground, saying nothing.

'I've got descriptions of three plain-clothes police officers ...' The journalist looked him up and down. 'You're a dead ringer for one of them. Inspector Malcolm Fox?' As hard as he tried, something in Fox's expression must have changed. The journalist gave a lopsided smile. 'It was on a card left on the armchair,' he offered by way of explanation.

'How about a name for you?' Fox asked in an undertone.

'I'm Brian Jamieson.'

'Local paper?'

'Sometimes. Can I ask you what happened in the flat?'

'No.'

'But you *were* there?' He waited a few moments for an answer. 'And now you're here ...'

Fox turned and walked in the direction the nurse had taken. She appeared around a corner.

'Drowsy from the sedative,' she informed him. Fox checked that Jamieson wasn't in earshot, but kept his voice just audible in any case.

'She's all right, though?'

'A few stitches. We'll just keep her the one night. Psychological Services will assess her in the morning.'

After which, Fox knew, she'd either be sent home or transferred elsewhere.

'If you wait twenty minutes,' the nurse added, 'she may well drift off.'

Fox glanced in Jamieson's direction. 'You know he's a reporter?'

She followed his look, then nodded.

'What's he been asking you?'

'I've not told him anything.'

'Can't security kick him off the ward?'

She turned her attention back to Fox. 'He's not being a nuisance.'

'Has he asked to speak to her?'

'He's been told it's not going to happen.'

'So why is he still here?'

The nurse's tone grew cooler. 'Why don't you ask him? Now, if you'll excuse me …' She brushed past him and returned to her desk, where a phone was ringing. Fox stood there a further thirty seconds or so. Jamieson was back in his chair, busy texting. He looked up as Fox approached.

'What are you expecting to get from her?' Fox asked.

'That's the very question I was about to put to you, Inspector.'

'Not another one!' the nurse was complaining into the receiver. When she saw that they were watching her, she turned away, cupping a hand over the handset. Jamieson had been about to push his phone's mic in Fox's direction again, but he lowered his arm instead. Then he turned and started to leave. Fox stayed where he was. The nurse was ending the call, shaking her head slowly.

'What's up?' Fox asked.

'A man's just tried to do away with himself,' she answered. 'Might not pull through.'

'Hopefully not a normal night,' Fox offered. She puffed out her cheeks and exhaled.

'Two a year would be more like it.' She noticed Jamieson's absence. 'Has he gone?'

'I think you did that.'

She rolled her eyes. 'He'll be down at A and E, if I know Brian.'

'Sounds like you *do* know him.'

'Used to go out with a friend of mine.'

'Who does he work for?'

'All sorts. What is it he calls himself ...?'

'A stringer?'

'That's it.' Her phone was ringing again. She made an exasperated sound and picked the receiver up. Fox considered his options, gave a little bow in her direction, and headed for the lifts.

Downstairs, he got a plastic bottle of Irn-Bru from the vending machine. No sugar tomorrow, he promised himself, heading outside. The sky overhead was black. Fox knew there was nothing for him to do now but drive home. He wondered if the budget for the investigation might stretch to a local hotel room. He'd spotted a place behind the railway station, not far from the park and the football ground. It would save the commute next morning – but then what would he do with himself the rest of tonight? Italian restaurant ... maybe a pub ... There were some ambulances parked up outside the hospital entrance. A couple of green-uniformed paramedics were shooing Brian Jamieson away. The reporter held up his hands in surrender and turned away, pressing his phone to his ear.

'All I know is, he tried blowing his brains out. Can't have been much of a shot, because he was still alive on the way here. Not so sure now, though ...' Jamieson saw that he was about to pass Malcolm Fox. 'Hang on a sec,' he said into the phone. It seemed he was about to share the news, but Fox stopped him.

'I heard,' he said.

'Hellish thing.' Jamieson was shaking his head. His eyes were wide and unblinking, brain racing.

'Many guns in Kirkcaldy?' Fox asked.

'Might have been a farmer. They keep guns, don't they?' He saw that Fox was looking at him. 'It was outside town,' he explained. 'Somewhere off the Burntisland road.'

Fox tried to stop himself looking interested. 'Got a name for the victim?'

Jamieson shook his head and glanced back towards the paramedics. 'I'll get one, though.' He offered Fox the same self-confident smile as before. 'Just you watch me.'

Fox did watch him. Watched him make for the doors to the hospital, the phone to his ear again. Only when he had disappeared inside did Fox walk quickly towards his own car.

*

The police cordon was at the junction of the main road and the track to Alan Carter's cottage. Fox felt acid gathering somewhere between his stomach and his throat. He cursed under his breath, pulled in to the side of the road and got out. The parked patrol car had its roof lights on, strobing the night with a cold, electric blue. The solitary uniform was trying to tie crime-scene tape between the posts either side of the track. The wind had whipped one end of the roll from his grasp and he was fighting to control it. Fox already had his warrant card out.

'Inspector Fox,' he told the uniform. Then: 'Before you do that, I need to get past.'

He returned to his car and watched the uniform move the patrol car forward, leaving space for Fox's Volvo to squeeze through. Fox offered a wave and started the slow climb uphill.

There were lights on in the cottage and just the one car outside, Carter's own Land Rover. As Fox closed the door of the Volvo, he heard a voice call out:

'What the hell are you doing here?'

Ray Scholes was standing in the doorway, hands in pockets.

'Is it Alan Carter?' Fox asked.

'What if it is?'

'I was out here yesterday.'

'Regular bloody Jonah, then, aren't you?'

'What happened?' Fox was standing directly in front of Scholes, peering past him into the hallway.

'Had a good go at topping himself.'

'Why would he do that?'

'If I lived out here, I might do the same.' Scholes sniffed the air, looked at Fox again, and relented, turning and heading indoors.

Fox himself hesitated. 'Don't we need ...?' He looked down at Scholes's feet.

'Not a crime scene, is it?' Scholes answered, walking into the living room. 'Cordon's just to stop weirdos drifting up here for a gawp. Thing I'm wondering is, what are we going to do about the dog?'

Fox had reached the doorway of the living room. The fire had been reduced to a few embers. To the left of it, Jimmy Nicholl lay panting in his basket, eyes open just a fraction. Fox crouched down and stroked the old dog's head and back.

'No note,' Scholes commented, popping a strip of chewing gum into his mouth. 'Not that I can see, anyway.' He waved a hand across the dining table. 'Hard to tell with all this mess ...'

Mess.

Papers strewn everywhere, removed from their folders. Crumpled, some torn into strips, others swept to the floor. Those left on the table were spotted with blood, a darker pool where Carter had been seated on his chair.

'Gun?' Fox said quietly, his mouth dry.

Scholes nodded towards the table. It was half-hidden beneath a magazine. Looked to Fox's untrained eye like an old-style revolver.

'How was he when you spoke to him?' Scholes asked.

'He seemed fine.'

'Until you came calling, eh?'

Fox ignored this. 'Who found him?'

'Pal of his. Makes the regular walk from Kinghorn. They neck a few glasses of whisky and off he toddles. Only today he comes waltzing in and finds this. Poor old bastard ...'

Fox wanted to sit down, but couldn't. He didn't know why; it just felt wrong. Scholes's phone rang. He listened for a moment, gave a grunt, then ended the call.

'Died in the ambulance,' he said.

The two men fell silent. The only sound was the dog's laboured breathing.

'The pair of you talked about Paul?' Scholes asked eventually.

Fox ignored the question. 'Where's this pal now?'

'Michaelson's running him home.' Scholes checked his watch. 'Wish he'd hurry up – there's a beer waiting for me in the pub.'

'You knew Alan Carter – doesn't it bother you?'

Scholes continued chewing the gum as he met Fox's eyes. 'It bothers me,' he said. 'What is it you want to see – wailing and gnashing of teeth? Should I be waving my fist at the skies? He was a cop ...' He paused. 'Then he wasn't. And now he's dead. Good luck to him, wherever he is.'

'He was also Paul Carter's uncle.'

'That he was.'

'And the first complainant.'

'Maybe that's why he did it – an overwhelming sense of guilt. We can play the amateur psychology game all night if you like. Except here's my lift.'

Fox heard it too: engine noise as a car approached the cottage.

'What are you going to do?' he asked. 'Just shut the place up?'

'I wasn't planning on bunking down. We've had a look and seen what's to be seen – uniforms can take it from here.'

'And next of kin ...?'

Scholes shrugged. 'Might even be Paul.'

'Have you told him?'

Scholes nodded. 'He'll be here.'

'How did he sound when you told him?'

There was silence in the room as Scholes stared at Fox. 'Why don't you just piss off back to Edinburgh? Because if I were you, I wouldn't be here when Paul arrives.'

'But you're not staying? I thought he was your mate.'

Scholes cocked his head, having obviously just thought of something. 'Hang on a sec – what are *you* doing here in the first place?'

'That's none of your business.'

'Is that right?' Scholes raised an eyebrow. 'I'll make sure to put that in the report.' He paused. 'Underlined. In bold.'

Gary Michaelson was standing on the threshold of the room, glaring at Fox. 'Thought there was a bad smell,' he said. Then, to Scholes: 'What're you doing letting him tramp all over a crime scene?'

'A what?'

'Carter's pal says he'd never have done himself in. Says they'd talked about it, what they'd do if they ever got cancer or something. Carter told the guy he'd cling on for dear life.'

'Something changed his mind,' Scholes speculated.

'And there's another thing – pal says he'd've known if Carter owned a gun. Something else they talked about – shooting the seagulls for the noise they made.' Michaelson looked towards the basket. 'What are we doing about the dog?'

'You want it?' Scholes asked. 'Do we even know its name?'

'Jimmy Nicholl,' Fox said. 'He's called Jimmy Nicholl.'

The dog's ears pricked up.

'Jimmy Nicholl,' Scholes echoed, folding his arms. 'Owner might've done the decent thing and taken you with him, eh, Jimmy?' Then, to Michaelson: 'We ready for the off?'

Fox was torn between staying and going, but Scholes was not going to give him the choice. 'Out, out, out,' he said.

'The dog,' Fox remonstrated.

'You want it?'

'No, but ...'

'Leave it to the professionals, then.'

They emerged to blue flashing lights: another patrol car, with an unmarked van behind it.

'It's all yours,' Scholes called to the driver at the front. But there was manoeuvring to be done: too many vehicles in a tight space. Someone had the idea of unlocking the gate to the neighbouring field. A bit of reversing, a three-point turn, and they were on their way. Scholes and Michaelson had made sure Fox's Volvo was in front. As they approached the main road, the same constable as before undid the cordon to let them through. There was a white scooter parked next to his car. Brian Jamieson sat astride it, one foot on the tarmac for the sake of balance. He was on his phone again, pausing as he recognised the driver of the Volvo. Fox kept his eyes on the road ahead, Scholes and Michaelson tailing him for the first couple of miles, just to make sure.

Four

11

'A right little Jonah.'

Fox gave Tony Kaye a look. 'That's what Scholes said, too.'

It was the following morning and they were back in Kirkcaldy. They'd ruled out ever using the storeroom again, so had commandeered the interview room.

'We'll be needing it all day,' Fox had informed the desk sergeant. The man had put up no resistance, just nodded and gone back to his paperwork.

Fox had wondered about that: no gloating over Teresa Collins? 'No,' he'd said out loud, once seated in the interview room. *The man's in mourning . . .*

'No?' Joe Naysmith had echoed, arriving with a spare chair from the storeroom.

'Never mind,' Fox had said.

Kaye had been out to a café and fetched them cardboard beakers of coffee. Fox had phoned him the previous night to tell him about Alan Carter.

'Coincidence?' Kaye had asked, getting right to the heart of it.

'Got to be coincidence,' Naysmith said now, prising the top from his cup and adding a couple of thimble-sized cartons of milk.

'I don't know,' Fox countered. 'Scholes said something last night about guilt. Maybe he got wind that his nephew was out and might be lodging an appeal.'

'So he went and stuck a pistol to his head?' Kaye said, his tone one of disbelief.

'Revolver,' Fox corrected him.

'Must be more to it than that, Malcolm.'

'Or less,' Naysmith added.

'You didn't tape your interview with him, did you?' Kaye was asking Fox.

'Wasn't as formal as an interview ... but the answer's no.'

'Reckon it might take some heat off? With this to occupy them, maybe Teresa Collins will stop being the headline.'

'Maybe.'

'Nobody's spoken to you?'

Fox shook his head. 'Far as I know, we're still on the case.'

'Such as it is.'

Fox allowed the point with a shrug of his shoulders.

'So what are we doing today?' Naysmith asked.

'Good question.' Kaye scratched his head. 'Foxy?'

'There are two more victims we could talk to.' Fox wasn't managing to sound enthusiastic.

'The drunken lassies?' Kaye sounded keener. 'That's a point.'

'What about the surveillance?' Naysmith added.

'Might be up and running,' Fox conceded.

'Or we just sit in here all day scratching our arses,' Kaye offered. 'I've a pack of cards in the Mondeo somewhere ...'

'There are heaps of questions still to ask DI Scholes,' Naysmith reminded them. 'We'd hardly started when he got called away.'

'That's true.' Fox finished his coffee, trying to locate any flavour at all in the final mouthful.

'And DCI Laird needs another going at,' Kaye added. 'Even if he gives us hee-haw.'

'I hate to mention it,' Naysmith added, 'but we're not really finished with Teresa Collins, either ...'

'Leave her for now,' Fox cautioned.

'Scholes, then?' Kaye was making to rise to his feet. 'Want me to fetch him?'

'I'll do it, Tony. You finish your drink.'

But as he headed for the stairs, Fox saw the unmistakable shape of Ray Scholes walking in the other direction. He was with a stooped elderly man, his hand resting lightly across the man's shoulders. They were headed for reception. Scholes didn't see the visitor out, though, just pointed him in the right direction before turning to head back to his office. He saw Fox and slowed his pace, jutting his chin out.

'I keep thinking you're going to bring me bad luck,' he said.

'Maybe I am. We need you in the interview room.'

Scholes shook his head. 'Not now. Might be a bit of movement on Alan Carter.'

'What sort of movement?' Fox couldn't help asking.

'Never you mind.' Having said which, Scholes headed for the staircase. Fox watched him, then turned and made for reception. The visitor had yet to leave. He was talking with the desk sergeant. They were shaking hands. When he did push open the front door, Fox followed.

'Where you going?' the desk sergeant barked, but Fox ignored him. The elderly man was standing at the bottom of the steps, looking bewildered.

'Needing a lift back to Kinghorn?' Fox asked him. 'I can do it, if you like.'

The man peered at him. Short-sighted, but lacking glasses. What hair he had left was jet black. Fox reckoned it was dyed. His eyes were small and deep-set, his mouth drawn in on itself, as though he'd forgotten to put his teeth in.

'I'm fine walking,' he said, having studied Fox. 'Do I know you?'

'My name's Fox. Sorry, I don't know yours.'

'Teddy Fraser.'

'You're the one who found Mr Carter?'

Fraser nodded solemnly. Fox noticed that he wore a thin black tie with his threadbare shirt. Mourning again. 'A bad, bad thing,' he muttered to himself.

'You've just been seeing DI Scholes?'

'Aye.'

'I only met Mr Carter the one time, but I liked him.'

'He was hard to dislike.'

'Did you walk here this morning, Mr Fraser?'

'I like walking. It's not that far.'

'Busy road, though.'

'There are a few short cuts.'

'Must have been a shock, finding Mr Carter ...'

'A shock?' Fraser gave a short, cold laugh. 'You might say that.'

'What I mean is ... I didn't really know him, but he seemed fine in himself.'

Fraser nodded again. 'There was nothing wrong with him. The DI's saying they're checking his health, in case the doctor had given him bad news. But he'd have told *me*, wouldn't he? No secrets between us.'

'You'd known one another a long time?'

'We were at school together – two years between us, but we were in the team.'

Fox didn't like to say that Fraser looked a lot older. If he were the elder by two years, then he'd be no more than sixty-four. 'Football?' he asked instead.

'Fife champions two years in a row.' Fraser sounded so proud, Fox wondered if anything since had given the man the same satisfaction.

'Where did Mr Carter play?'

'Right up front – a real poacher. Twenty-nine goals one season. That was a school record. If the minister doesn't mention it at the funeral, I'll be on my feet reminding everyone.'

Fox smiled at this. 'What did DI Scholes want?'

'Ach, he was just asking about the gun and stuff. How was Alan positioned when I found him? Had I moved anything?'

'And had you?'

'I picked up the phone and dialled 999.'

'But Mr Carter wasn't dead, was he?'

'As good as.'

'You tried rousing him?'

'He was breathing. Not conscious, though. But a *gun*? Alan never owned a gun. And the door unlocked?' He shook his head vigorously. 'Kept it locked, even if he knew I was expected. If he heard me, he'd be at the door waiting, but otherwise I had to knock and Jimmy Nicholl would start barking.'

'The door wasn't locked?'

'No barking when I knocked. Thought they must be out on a walk, even though the dog could only manage a few yards at a time without its back legs giving way. So I was expecting the door to be locked.' He seemed to remember something. 'In fact, it wasn't even closed properly. That's right ... when I knocked, it opened a wee bit.'

'I suppose,' Fox said, playing devil's advocate, 'if he'd planned to do what he did, he might leave the door open so he could be found.'

Fraser considered this notion, but then dismissed it with a snort. 'You know I'm looking after Jimmy Nicholl? It's the least I could do. Alan doted on that hound – and you're telling me he wouldn't have taken Jimmy to a vet's before doing away with himself?' He screwed up his face.

'Can I ask you something else, Mr Fraser?'

'I'm Teddy, son. Everybody calls me Teddy.'

'I was just wondering what he was working on – all those papers on his table.'

'Ancient history.'

'Nineteen eighty-five's not *that* ancient.'

'To some people it is. I'll prove it to you right here.' Fraser paused, readying himself to gauge Fox's reaction. He clasped his hands together, then mentioned a name.

'You've got me,' Fox conceded after a moment. 'Who's Francis Vernal?'

'You'd do better finding out for yourself.'

'Why was Mr Carter so interested in him?'

'I'm not sure he was – not at first.'

'I don't follow.'

'Alan was a copper back then – that's why he got the job.'

'Someone was paying him to look back at 1985? Was this some case he'd worked on?'

Fraser dug a bony finger into Fox's chest, stabbing out a beat to his next words. 'Better – finding – out – for – yourself.'

Having said which, he gave a little bow, turned, and started walking away at a brisker pace than Fox had foreseen. It actually hurt where the little man had poked him. He rubbed the spot with the heel of his hand. Back inside, the desk sergeant was lying in wait.

'Come here, you,' he said from the other side of the desk. Fox walked up to him. 'You've not been pestering Teddy, I hope?'

'He gave as good as he got. I take it you know him?'

'Donkey's years.'

'And you knew Alan Carter, too?'

'Served with him.' The desk sergeant puffed out his chest. 'One of the old school ...'

'I got the same feeling, the one time we met. I'm sorry.'

The muscles in the sergeant's face twitched.

'I don't even know your name,' Fox apologised further.

'Robinson. Alec Robinson.'

Fox held out his hand, and after the briefest of hesitations Robinson took it.

'Pleased to meet you,' Fox said, causing the man to smile.

83

'Sorry if I seemed to give you such a hard time,' the sergeant responded. 'You know what it's like ...'

'I've had worse, trust me.' Fox paused. 'But can I ask you this – did you see much of Alan Carter in his later years?'

'Not really. Maybe at the football or a reunion ...'

'He liked to keep busy, though, eh?'

'Built that company of his from scratch.' Robinson sounded impressed, so Fox nodded his agreement.

'The day I saw him, he was still busy,' he informed the sergeant.

'Oh?'

'All that work he was doing on Francis Vernal.'

Robinson's face stiffened.

'Care to shed some light?'

'I'm not the one to talk to,' Robinson eventually confided.

'Then who is?'

'These days?' Robinson pondered his answer. 'Probably no one ...'

Back in the interview room, Fox pointed at Joe Naysmith.

'I need you to do something for me. Got a laptop with you?'

'No.'

'Well there must be a spare computer somewhere around here.'

'What is it you need?'

'An internet search.'

'My phone can do that.'

'Can it print, though?' When Naysmith shook his head, Fox told him that only a computer would do.

'What am I searching for?'

'Francis Vernal.'

'You mean the lawyer?' Tony Kaye said. Fox turned towards him. 'Died in a car smash back in the eighties.'

'Go on.'

Kaye gave a shrug. 'I was only a kid ...' He paused. 'Come to think of it, didn't he shoot himself?'

'Before or after he crashed the car?'

Kaye shrugged again, and Fox turned his attention back to Naysmith, who took the hint and started to leave.

'What's this about?' Kaye asked as the door closed behind Naysmith.

'Something Alan Carter was working on.'

'And what's that got to do with us?'

'Maybe nothing ...'

'*Maybe* nothing? I thought you were bringing us back Ray Scholes – Joe got the camera ready and everything.'

Fox noticed the tripod for the first time. The audio recorder was on the table, flanked by microphones.

'He says he's busy.'

'Whoopee for him. Let's all take a holiday until he deigns to grace us with his presence.'

'The two women,' Fox said. 'Why don't you go talk to them?'

'You trying to get rid of me?'

'I thought you were keen?'

'I suppose it beats sitting here watching the cogs whir inside that head of yours.'

'Well then ...'

'But first you need to tell me what's going on.'

'Nothing's going on. A guy died, I liked him, his front room was like a shrine to someone called Francis Vernal.'

'And you want to know why?'

'And I want to know why.' Fox paused, eyes boring into those of his colleague and friend. 'Good enough for you?'

'Anything for a quiet life.' Kaye was rising from his chair, easing his arms back into the sleeves of his suit jacket. 'Do I take Junior with me?'

'If you need him.'

'Isn't he busy on a little job for you?'

'It can wait.'

'And while we're out there on the mean streets, you'll be doing what exactly?'

'Checking on the surveillance ... telling McEwan about the suicide ... trying to pin Ray Scholes down – I won't be slacking.'

'Okay.' Kaye nodded slowly. 'But we'll miss you, you know that. Hell, we might even send you a postcard.'

12

It wasn't Fox's fault that Evelyn Mills wasn't answering her phone. The same was true of Bob McEwan – while Ray Scholes had gone AWOL. Fox found himself back in the police station's reception area, staring at one of the notices on the wall. It was an advert for a local cab company. Five minutes later, he was in the passenger seat of a dented white Hyundai. The driver was keen to learn more about the suicide, but Fox offered him nothing. The cordon had been removed and there was no activity outside the cottage itself. The driver asked if he wanted him to wait.

'Good idea.'

The man turned off the engine. He looked to be readying to get out of the car, but Fox stopped him.

'Nothing to see,' he stated.

So the driver switched the radio on, modern dance music soundtracking Fox as he made for the front door.

It was locked.

He made a circuit around the house, but there was no back door. He peered in through the living-room window. There were flecks of blood on the insides of a couple of the panes. Fox's fingers brushed a small plant pot balanced on the outside ledge. He lifted it and saw a key lying there. Either a spare, or left by the police. He unlocked the door and went inside.

Jimmy Nicholl's basket was no longer in the living room. Fox wondered if he should have asked Teddy Fraser how the dog was doing. Didn't pets often pass away soon after their owners? The room smelled of woodsmoke. The remains of a charred log sat in the grate, a fine layer of ash coating the top of the mantelpiece. Fox started leafing through the paperwork on the table. Sure enough, the news clippings related to the life and death of Francis Vernal. One lengthy story was headlined 'The Inner Turmoil of the Activist Patriot'. It looked to Fox as though the media at the time had soon switched their focus from eulogies to something meatier: the dead man's private life. There was a blurry photo of his attractive wife, and mention of Vernal's 'heavy-drinking lifestyle and string of affairs'. The same photo of the lawyer had been picked up by several newspapers. He was addressing a Scottish National Party rally. It was outside a factory earmarked for closure. Vernal was in full flow, one hand bunched into a fist, mouth open wide, teeth bared. Fox glanced through the window to check that the cab-driver was still in his car. He was whistling and had opened a newspaper.

Francis Vernal had died on the evening of Sunday, 28 April 1985, the same day Dennis Taylor played Steve Davis in the World Snooker final. His car had been spotted by a van driver. It had left the road near Anstruther. A Volvo 244. Must have been travelling at speed. Vernal was in the driver's seat, dead. His body was taken to the Victoria Hospital, at which time the bullet hole in the side of his head was identified as such. A heavy drinker and smoker, he had also been prone to bouts of depression. His beloved Nationalists seemed to have stalled in the polls, and Vernal's dream of a Socialist Scots Republic looked destined to remain unrealised in his lifetime. Fox sifted through the newsprint. Some passages had been underlined. Alan Carter's handwritten notes were almost indecipherable. There were screeds of them. No sign of a computer or laptop, meaning nothing had been typed. Fox was wondering who had given him the job, and why. Suddenly, a photo caught his eye. Another rally, but taken longer ago, Vernal in his early twenties by the look of it. A bit more hair on his head, and slimmer around the chest and stomach, but still with mouth wide open and fist clenched. There was another young man standing next to him, and Fox was stunned to find he recognised him. It was Chris – his father's cousin Chris – looking just the same as in the photo where he was carrying Jude on his shoulders. Fox lifted this picture from the table and stared at it. It had been clipped from the *Fife Free Press*. There was no date, and only a few lines of explanation: an SNP picnic on the links at Burntisland; 'the noted Edinburgh lawyer Francis Vernal gives the speech of the afternoon'. With Chris Fox standing at his side, laughing and leading the applause ...

Fox paced the room a couple of times, the photo still in his hand. Then he folded it into his pocket, looking around him as if fearing someone might have noticed. There was a telephone on a chest of drawers behind the door, and he crossed over to it. An address book sat next to it. It was open and had been turned over. Fox lifted it and saw that it was open at the page for surnames beginning with C. Paul Carter's name was there – home and mobile numbers listed. Fox flipped through the book, not sure what he thought he would find. A few business cards fell out and he stooped to pick them up. One was for an Indian restaurant, another for a garage. But the third belonged to a man called Charles Mangold. He was senior partner in a firm of solicitors called Mangold Bain, with an address in Edinburgh's New Town. Fox jotted the details into his notebook, then tapped his pen against the telephone receiver, and stared at the 'C' page again. Three names there, one with a thick line through it, probably meaning the person was no longer part of Alan Carter's life, or had passed away. Leaving two names.

One of them Paul Carter's ...

Fox lifted the receiver and dialled 1471. The computerised voice informed him that the last number to call the phone had been Paul Carter's mobile. The call had taken place the previous evening, barely an hour before Alan Carter had been found. He put down the receiver and started opening the various drawers in the chest below it. Neat and tidy: Alan Carter had kept his bank statements and utility bills filed away. The phone bills were itemised. There was no sign that Alan had called his nephew at any point in the past six months. No, because they weren't close – hadn't Alan said as much himself? But Paul, soon after his release from custody, had felt the need to phone his uncle. Fox wondered why. He looked around the room again. Where had the mess come from? Had something made Alan Carter angry, so that he swept papers from the table on to the floor? Or had someone else done it?

Fox flinched at the sound of tapping on the window. It was the cab-driver. Fox gave him a nod to let him know he was just coming. The man lingered, taking in the scene. Fox replaced the address book, made sure he was leaving the room as he had found it – the one borrowed photograph aside – and went outside.

His driver was apologising. 'No skin off my nose, but the meter's up to thirty quid ...'

'It's fine,' Fox told him. He locked the front door of the cottage and slid the key under the flowerpot.

'Back to where we started?' the driver asked.

'Back to where we started,' Fox agreed, getting into the passenger seat.

Calls to and from Ray Scholes's home phone were now being logged and recorded. The news came in a text message from Evelyn Mills. The network provider for his mobile phone had also been contacted, and they would soon have access to information about calls made and received – but no access to the actual calls themselves, not without taking their request further and throwing money and manpower at it.

Fox had managed a word with Bob McEwan, letting him know that Alan Carter was dead. McEwan had sounded distracted – he was between budget meetings – and had thanked Fox for his 'input', a word presumably picked up at the earlier meeting.

Fox had told Kaye he'd try to track down Ray Scholes, but he now had another destination, the office of Superintendent Isabel Pitkethly.

'What is it now?' she asked, removing her glasses and rubbing at her eyes.

'It's a bit awkward,' Fox said. She was immediately interested, repositioning her glasses the better to study him. When she gestured for him to sit, he did as he was told, brushing his hands across the knees of his trousers.

'Well?' she prompted, elbows on the desk, palms pressed together.

'Paul Carter's uncle is supposed to have committed suicide.'

'I'm aware of that.'

'It happened soon after he got a call from his nephew ...'

She considered this for a moment. 'What of it?'

'They weren't the best of friends,' Fox pressed on. 'It'd be good to know why Paul made that call.'

She leaned back in her chair. 'Why? What difference does it make?'

'Maybe none,' he conceded.

'And how do you know about this call, anyway?'

'I dialled 1471.'

'From the deceased's home? And what in hell took you there, Inspector?'

Fox didn't really have an answer to that, so he stayed silent.

'This is way past your remit,' Pitkethly said quietly.

There was a rap on the door and DS Michaelson stuck his head into the room. He had his mouth open to say something, but stopped when he saw Pitkethly had company.

'I'll come back,' he offered.

'What is it, Gary?'

Michaelson seemed to be weighing up his options, but he was too excited not to spit it out.

'The thing is, Alan Carter can't be dead, ma'am.'

Pitkethly looked at him. 'What?'

'He can't be dead.'

'Why not?' It was Fox rather than Pitkethly who asked the question.

'Because the gun he used doesn't exist. It hasn't done for twenty-odd years.'

'You're not making any sense.'

Michaelson produced a sheet of paper. Fox couldn't tell if it was a fax or the printout of an e-mail. The detective approached Pitkethly's desk and handed it over. She took her time reading it through. Then she looked at Fox.

'We'll finish our little chat later.' She was rising to her feet. Michaelson accompanied her out of the room, Fox following for the first few steps until she stopped him.

'Not your remit,' was all she said, before continuing in the direction of the CID suite. Michaelson looked over his shoulder, giving Fox a huge, cold smile of satisfaction.

Fox pursed his lips and watched them go. Then he had an idea.

It took Alec Robinson a while to answer the desk buzzer. Fox could guess why.

'Have you heard?' Robinson said.

'Some of it,' Fox hedged. 'I'm surprised how quick it all happened.'

Robinson nodded his agreement. 'Not that many guns in Fife,' he explained. 'The register was put on computer last year. Can't think why they backdated it, but they did.'

Fox still wasn't sure he understood. 'Twenty-odd years ...' he prompted.

'Like I say, we don't take many firearms off the street.'

'No, but when you do ...' Fox was still feeling his way.

'Broken up and melted down – that used to be the way. Once or twice a year, when there were enough to make it worthwhile.'

It was Fox's turn to nod. 'And this gun's on record as having been disposed of?'

Robinson stared at him. 'I thought you knew.'

'Only some of it.' Fox folded his arms. 'So how come it suddenly turns up in Alan Carter's cottage? Could he have swiped it?'

Robinson shrugged. 'Not sure he was ever on the detail. Guns weren't kept here anyway – Glenrothes, I think.'

Fox exhaled noisily. 'It's a mystery,' he said.

'That's what it is,' Robinson agreed. Then, eyes on Fox: 'Don't tell me there'll be another inquiry now. That's all we bloody well need ...'

13

'Very nice girls,' Tony Kaye said.

'Very,' Joe Naysmith agreed.

They were back in the interview room, the three of them seated around the table with beakers of tea.

'Hairdressers.'

'Though Billie's a senior stylist and Bekkah's not quite got there yet.'

'Lucky it was quiet in the salon. We were able to grab twenty minutes in the privacy of the tanning booth. Don't worry, though – it wasn't switched on.'

'Bekkah looked like she'd spent some time in there,' Naysmith added.

'Good figure on her, too – if that's not being sexist.'

Fox could see his two colleagues had enjoyed themselves.

'She'd like to give modelling a try,' Naysmith informed him.

'Cut to the chase,' Fox muttered.

'Well ...' Naysmith began, but Kaye took over the story.

'Night out. Started with the whole team from the salon. Few casualties along the way. Chinese meal, then pubs and a club. It's past midnight and they reckon on walking home. Bekkah's caught short and nips down a side street. Car pulls up. It's Paul Carter. Identifies himself and says he's taking them in. Public indecency or some such. Billie asks if he can't just drop them home instead. He says maybe he can but it'd mean spending a bit of time on the car's back seat. Makes a grab for her crotch. She pushes him away, so then he asks Bekkah if she wants to spend the night in the cells. Same bargain. They tell him where he can go and he heads back to his car and calls it in. Patrol car turns up and they're put in a cell to sober up. Which is when Carter suddenly reappears and repeats the offer – any and all charges dropped if they'll "scratch his back". No dice.'

'Billie told him her boyfriend was a bouncer,' Naysmith got the chance to say.

'As if that would cut any ice with Carter.'

Fox rubbed his chin. 'Carter's uncle ran a security company,' he commented.

'So?'

Fox shrugged. 'Just wondering.'

'We can always visit the girls again and ask.' Kaye glanced at Naysmith, who didn't look entirely opposed to the idea. 'Anyway, that's about it. In the morning they were released without charge – no sign of Carter.'

'But they didn't make a complaint?'

'Not until they read about Teresa Collins.' Kaye paused. 'How is she, by the way? Any news?'

'I've not checked. Been some developments here ...' He filled them in. Naysmith seemed the more interested of the two, asking questions and getting Fox to repeat bits, the better to understand them. Kaye looked glum throughout.

'What?' Fox eventually asked him.

'I hate to side with Pitkethly, but she's got a point – what has any of this to do with us?'

'Paul Carter comes riding back into town and a day later his uncle has topped himself? You don't think there's anything to that?'

'Whether there is or there isn't, we're here to investigate three officers, none of whom happens to be Paul Carter. We report our findings and then we get to go home.'

'So the gun,' Joe Naysmith was saying to himself, 'was meant to be destroyed but obviously wasn't. They must keep records of these things ...'

Kaye stretched out his arms in mock-supplication. 'This is not our case,' he said, laying equal stress on each of the words. 'It just *isn't*.'

'It might *connect* to our case,' Fox told him. 'Little bit of digging, you never know ...'

'Did Alan Carter work on the disposal team?' Naysmith asked.

'I'm sure CID are looking into that,' Kaye said. 'Because

that's the sort of thing CID do. We, on the other hand, are the Complaints.'

The door opened. Fox was about to remonstrate, but saw that it was Superintendent Pitkethly.

'I need a word,' she said, pointing in Fox's direction. Then, to Kaye and Naysmith: 'Either of you two see or speak to Alan Carter before he died?'

'Nor after he died,' Kaye said with a shake of his head. She gave him a hard look.

'Then it's just you,' she told Fox. 'My office ... unless you'd rather do it here?'

Fox told her he preferred her office. She turned away, and he got up to follow.

She was already seated behind her desk when he arrived. She told him to close the door, and when he made to sit down, she ordered him to stay on his feet. She had a pen in her hand, which she studied as she spoke.

'You may just have been the last person who saw Alan Carter alive, Inspector. That means CID would like to ask a few questions.'

'Hardly feasible when I'm running an inquiry into three of them.'

'Which is why I'm asking instead.' She paused. 'Always supposing you've given *me* a clean bill of health?' He didn't answer, causing her to look up at him. She narrowed her eyes and returned her attention to the pen.

'Why did you visit him?'

'He made the original complaint about Paul Carter.'

'That hardly connects him to Scholes, Haldane and Michaelson. Oh, and by the way, Haldane's feeling a lot worse since your little home visit, so thanks for that.' Again, Fox chose not to comment. 'So what did you talk about with Alan Carter? How did he seem?'

'I liked him. He wasn't evasive, was a welcoming host.'

'Troubled in any way?'

'I wouldn't have said so.' Fox paused. 'There's something else, isn't there?'

'Someone in Forensics seems to have been watching *CSI*. She was the one who traced the revolver ...'

'And?'

'And she's got a few concerns about the prints.'

'The prints on the gun?'

94

'Don't get too excited – just a couple of anomalies.'

Fox thought back to the scene: Ray Scholes already there; stuff strewn on the floor; the revolver half-hidden below a magazine ... He remembered Alan Carter moving around the room, making tea, handing him a mug ...

'Carter was right-handed,' he stated.

'What?'

'Why was the gun lying to the left of him? His head was slumped against the table and the gun was to the left, not the right.'

She stared at him.

'Not one of the anomalies?' he guessed.

'No,' Pitkethly conceded, writing a note to herself.

'What then?'

'Alan Carter's prints are on the gun – no one else's. There's a good thumbprint slap-bang in the middle of the grip.'

Fox made show of holding a revolver. His thumb was high up on the grip. He tried bringing it lower down, but it felt awkward.

'And a partial fingerprint halfway along the barrel,' Pitkethly added, tossing the pen on to the desk and folding her arms.

'No prints anywhere else?'

'You're sure he didn't seem worried about anything?'

Fox shook his head. 'But then he probably didn't know at that point that his nephew had been released from custody.'

'Let's not get carried away, Malcolm.' The use of his first name came as a jolt to him. She needed him. She needed him on her side.

'You have to bring Paul Carter in,' he said quietly.

'I can't do that.'

No, not to his own police station, not to be interviewed by his own friends.

'*I* can ask the questions,' Fox offered.

She shook her head. 'You're the Complaints. This is ... this is something else.' When he looked at her, she met his eyes. 'There's no proof Alan Carter didn't pull the trigger,' she said quietly.

'But all the same ...'

'Anomalies,' she repeated. 'Carter ran a security company. He might have made enemies.'

'On top of which, he was doing some research into an old case.'

'Oh?'

'He was surrounded by the paperwork when he died – didn't Scholes tell you?'

95

'He said the place was a bit of a tip ...'

'Tidy enough when I visited. But afterwards, looked like someone had been through it. Scholes and Michaelson were first on the scene. Michaelson gave Teddy Fraser a lift home, leaving Scholes alone in the cottage ...'

Pitkethly closed her eyes, rubbing at her eyebrows with thumb and forefinger. Fox sat down across the desk from her.

'Honeymoon's over,' he told her. 'You've got some big decisions to make. First one should probably be to phone HQ. If you know anyone there, talk to them first.'

She nodded, opening her eyes again. Then she took a couple of deep breaths and picked up the receiver.

'That'll be all, Inspector,' she said, her voice firm. But there was a momentary smile of thanks as he got up to leave.

14

In the car back to Edinburgh, Naysmith asked Fox if he still wanted information on Francis Vernal.

'I can do it at home tonight,' he offered.

'Thanks,' Fox replied.

'And in case you were thinking that Kirkcaldy's boring ...' He took a folded printout from his pocket and handed it over. 'Here's what I already discovered about the place.'

It was a newspaper report about a Yugoslav secret-service agent, sent to Kirkcaldy in 1988 to assassinate a Croatian dissident. The story was back in the news because the assassination had failed, the gunman had been jailed, and he now claimed he had information about the murder of Swedish prime minister Olaf Palme.

Fox read the piece aloud for Tony Kaye's benefit. 'Unbelievable,' was Kaye's only comment, before turning the hi-fi on.

'Alex Harvey again,' Naysmith complained.

'The *Sensational* Alex Harvey,' Kaye corrected him, drumming his fingers against the steering wheel. 'Part and parcel of your musical education, young Joseph.'

'Terrorists and bampots, eh?' Naysmith offered, eyes fixed on Malcolm Fox. 'We never seem to be rid of them.'

'We never do,' Fox agreed, reading the article a second time.

They decided to have one drink at Minter's. It was mid-afternoon and the place was dead. Fox went outside and called the offices of Mangold Bain.

'I'm afraid Mr Mangold's appointments diary is full,' he was told.

'My name's Fox. I'm an inspector with Lothian and Borders

Police. If that doesn't clear me some space today, tell him it concerns Alan Carter.'

He was asked to hold the line. The woman's lilting voice was replaced for a full minute by Vivaldi's *Four Seasons*.

'Six o'clock?' she offered. 'Mr Mangold wonders if the New Club might be acceptable – he has another meeting there at six thirty.'

'It'll have to do, then, won't it?' Fox said, secretly pleased – the New Club was one of those Edinburgh institutions he'd heard about but never been able to visit. He knew it was somewhere on Princes Street and filled with lawyers and bankers escaping their womenfolk.

Back in the bar, Kaye and Naysmith were waiting to hear if they needed to go back to the office or could call it a day. Fox checked his watch – not quite four. He nodded, to let them know they were off the hook.

'That calls for another drink,' Kaye said, draining his glass. 'And it's your shout, Joseph.'

Naysmith rose from the table and asked Fox if he wanted another Big Tom. Fox shook his head.

'Somewhere else to go,' he said, glancing at the TV above the bar. The local newsreader was telling viewers that there was no further information on the explosion in the woods outside Lockerbie.

'Some sick sod's idea of a practical joke,' Kaye muttered. 'Unless you think the Yugoslavs are back, Joe ...'

Half an hour later, Fox was at Lauder Lodge. When he opened the door to his father's room, he saw that Mitch had a visitor. There was a half-bottle of Bell's open on the mantelpiece.

'Hiya, Dad,' Fox said. His father looked sprightly. He was dressed and his eyes sparkled.

'Malcolm,' Mitch said, with a nod towards the visitor, 'you remember Sandy?'

Malcolm shook Sandy Cameron's hand. The three of them had attended Hearts games together when Malcolm had been a boy, his father always keen to remind him that Sandy had almost become a professional, back in the day. Years later, the two men had played indoor bowls for a team in the local league.

'Decent measure,' Fox noted, watching Cameron switch his tumbler to his left hand so he could shake with the right.

'Whisky shandy,' Cameron explained, angling his head towards a bottle of Barr's lemonade on the floor next to the chair.

'Don't know how you can bear to dilute it,' Mitch Fox said, draining his own glass.

'Maybe you should learn, Dad,' Malcolm chided him. He dragged another chair over and joined them. 'How are you, Mr Cameron?'

'Can't complain, son.'

'Sandy was just reminiscing about the ice rink,' Mitch confided. Fox reckoned they'd be stories he had heard half a dozen times or more. 'A hell of a skater you were, Sandy. Could have turned pro.'

'I did love it.' Cameron smiled to himself. 'And the football ...'

But Fox knew he had ended up a draughtsman. Married to Myra. Two kids. A contented life.

'What brings you here?' Mitch was asking his son. 'Thought you were doing something in Fife?'

Fox dug in his pocket and produced the photograph. 'Came across this,' he said, handing it over. His father made show of focusing, holding the cutting as far from him as his arm would allow. Then he fished in his cardigan pocket for his reading glasses.

'That's Francis Vernal,' he stated.

'But who's next to him?'

'Is it Chris?' His father's voice rose a little in surprise. 'It's Chris, isn't it?'

'Looks like,' Fox agreed.

Mitch had handed the photo across to his old friend.

'Francis Vernal,' Cameron confirmed. 'And who did you say the other fellow was?'

'Cousin of mine,' Mitch explained. 'Chris, his name was. Died young in a bike crash.'

'How come he knew Vernal?' Fox asked.

'Chris was a shop steward at the dockyard.'

'And an SNP man?'

'That too.'

'I saw Vernal speak once,' Cameron added. 'At a miners' institute somewhere – Lasswade, maybe. "Firebrand" is the word that springs to mind.'

'I don't really remember him,' Fox admitted. 'I was in my teens when he died.'

'There were rumours at the time,' Cameron went on. 'His wife ...'

'Bloody tittle-tattle,' Mitch said dismissively. 'Selling papers is all it's good for.' He looked at his son. 'Where did you find this?'

99

'There's an ex-cop in Fife, he was interested in Vernal.'

'Why?'

'I'm not sure.' Fox thought for a moment. 'What year did Chris die?'

It was his father's turn to think. 'Seventy-five, seventy-six ... Late on in seventy-five, I think. Crematorium in Kirkcaldy, then a meal at a hotel near the station.' Mitch had retrieved the photo and was staring at it. 'Smashing lad, our Chris.'

'He never married?'

Fox's father shook his head. 'Always told me he liked life free and easy. That way he could just jump on his bike and go exploring.'

'Whereabouts did the crash happen?'

'Why are you so interested all of a sudden?'

Fox gave a shrug.

'Is this you trying some real detective work for a change?' Mitch turned towards Cameron. 'Malcolm here's only got another year or two till he's back in CID.'

'Oh aye? The Complaints isn't for life, then?'

'I think Malcolm would like it better if it was.'

'What's that supposed to mean?' Fox couldn't keep the irritation out of his voice.

'You were never happy there,' his father told him.

'Says who?'

'You'll be a bit rusty, then,' Cameron chipped in, 'when you have to go back to the detective work.'

'What I do now is detective work.'

'It's not the same, though, is it?' his father continued.

'It's *exactly* the same.'

His father just shook his head slowly. Silence descended on the room for a moment.

'Firebrand,' Cameron eventually repeated. He seemed to be thinking back to Francis Vernal's speech. 'The hairs went up on your arms. If he'd been asking you to advance on the enemy lines, you'd have done it, armed or not.'

'I saw him on the James Connolly march one year,' Mitch added. 'Not something I usually paid attention to, but a pal wanted to go to the rally. Leith Links, I think it was. Francis Vernal got up to speak, and you're right, Sandy – he had the gift. Not saying I agreed with him, but I listened.'

'People used to compare him to Jimmy Reid,' Cameron mused.

'I thought he was better. There was none of the "comrades" stuff.'

'It seemed a lost cause back then, though, didn't it?' Fox added, relieved that he was no longer the focus of attention. 'Nationalism, I mean.'

'They were strange times,' Mitch said. 'A lot of anger. Things getting blown up ...' He had poured himself another whisky, the bottle pretty well empty now. 'I was always Labour, but I remember your mum getting on her high horse about the SNP. They used to recruit outside folk concerts.'

'Same thing at the picture house when *Braveheart* was playing,' Cameron added.

'Malcolm was never political, though,' Mitch Fox said. 'Maybe worried about sticking his head above the parapet – or at least above his homework books ...'

Fox was staring at his father's whisky. 'Dash of water with that?' he asked.

'Dash of water be damned.'

The New Club was hard to find. The edifice Fox had always assumed it to be turned out to belong to the Royal Overseas League instead. A woman in reception pointed him back along Princes Street. The evening was turning blustery. A set of tramlines had been laid, but there was now yet another delay as the contractors bickered with the council about payment. Workers were queuing at bus stops, keen to get home. It didn't help Fox's cause that few of the shops on Princes Street had numbers. It was 86 that he was after, but he missed it again and had to retrace his steps. Eventually, next to a cash machine, he saw an anonymous varnished wooden door. There was a small window above it, and he could just about make out the name etched there. He rang the bell and was eventually admitted.

He had been expecting small, stuffy Georgian-style rooms, but the interior was vast and modern. A uniformed porter told him he was expected and led him up a further flight of stairs. A few elderly gentlemen wandered around, or could be glimpsed poring over newspapers in armchairs. Fox had thought his destination would be some lounge or bar, but in fact it was a well-appointed meeting room. Charles Mangold was seated at a large circular table, a carafe of water in front of him.

101

'Thank you, Eddie,' he said to the porter, who bowed and left them to it. Mangold had risen and was shaking Fox's hand.

'Charles Mangold,' he said, introducing himself. 'Inspector Fox, is it?'

'It is.'

'Mind if I see some proof?'

Fox pulled out his warrant card.

'Can't be too careful these days, I'm afraid.' Mangold handed back the wallet and gestured for him to take a seat. 'I forgot to ask Eddie to fetch us some drinks ...'

'Water's fine, sir.'

Mangold poured them a glass apiece while Fox studied him. Portly, early sixties, bald and bespectacled. He wore a dark three-piece suit, pale-lemon shirt with gold cufflinks, and a tie of maroon and blue striped diagonals. His confident air was edging towards smugness. Or maybe 'entitlement' was the word.

'Been here before?' he asked.

'First time.'

'Most other clubs have closed their doors, but somehow this place soldiers on.' He took a sip of water. 'I'm sorry I can't offer you very much time, Inspector. As my secretary may have said ...'

'You have another meeting at half past.'

'Yes,' Mangold said, glancing at his watch.

'Did you know Alan Carter was dead, Mr Mangold?'

The lawyer froze for a second. 'Dead?'

'Put a gun to his head yesterday evening.'

'Good God.' Mangold stared at one of the wood-panelled walls.

'How did you know him?'

'He was doing some work for me.'

'On Francis Vernal?'

'Yes.'

'Had you known Mr Carter long?'

'I barely knew him at all.' Mangold seemed to be considering what to say next. Fox bided his time, sipping from the glass. 'There was a profile of him in the *Scotsman* a while back – focusing on his various business interests. It mentioned that he was an ex-policeman and that he'd played a small role in the original investigation.'

'The Francis Vernal investigation, you mean?'

Mangold nodded. 'Not that there was much of one. Suicide was the story everyone stuck to. There wasn't even an FAI.'

Meaning a Fatal Accident Inquiry. 'Bit odd,' Fox commented.

'Yes,' Mangold agreed.

'You reckon there was a cover-up of some kind?'

'The truth's what I've been after, Inspector.'

'Twenty-five years on? Why the wait?'

Mangold bowed his head a little, as if to acknowledge the acuity of the question. 'Imogen isn't well,' he said.

'Vernal's widow?'

'Six months or a year from now, I doubt she'll be with us – and I know the papers will dredge it up again.'

'The stories that she drove him to it?'

'Yes.'

'You don't think she did?'

'Of course not.'

'Did you work alongside Mr Vernal?'

'For a long time.'

'Friend of his, or friend of his wife?'

Mangold stared hard at Fox. 'I'm not sure I can let that insinuation pass.'

'Then don't.'

'Look, I'm sorry Alan Carter's dead, but what precisely does it have to do with me?'

'You'll be wanting to take charge of all his research material. Might have to get used to a few blood spatters, mind ...' Fox looked to be readying himself to rise from his chair and leave.

'Francis Vernal was murdered,' Mangold blurted out. 'And no one's done anything about it. If I didn't know better, I'd say officers at the time went beyond wilful negligence.'

'Meaning?'

'Meaning they were involved. By the time they found out he'd been shot, his car had been removed from the scene, the scene itself trampled over, obliterating any evidence. Took them a full day to find the gun – did you know that? It was lying on the ground, twenty yards from where the car had stopped.' Mangold was talking rapidly, as if needing to put the words out there. 'Francis didn't own a gun, by the way. Papers from his briefcase strewn around nearby. Car's back window smashed, but not the windscreen. Things missing ...'

'What things?'

'Cigarettes, for one – he smoked forty a day. And a fifty-pound note he always carried – the fee from his first case.' Mangold ran a hand across his head. Then he looked up at Fox. 'You're not what I expected ... not at all.'

'In what way?'

'I thought I was going to be warned off. But you're ... too young to have been part of it. And your warrant card says Professional Standards. That means police corruption, yes?'

'It means complaints against the force.'

Mangold nodded slowly. 'Francis Vernal should be a story, Inspector. So many holes in the original investigation ...'

'Was Carter making any progress?'

'A little.' Mangold thought for a moment. 'Not much,' he conceded. 'A lot of the players are no longer with us. I doubt he would have taken the job if Gavin Willis were still alive.'

'Gavin Willis being ...?'

'Alan's mentor. He was a DI at the time Francis died. And he led the inquiry. Only ten years or so older than Alan, but Alan definitely looked up to him.' Mangold leaned forward a little, as if readying himself to share a confidence. 'Did Alan tell you about the cottage?'

'No.'

'It belonged to Gavin Willis. When he died, Alan bought it – *that's* how close the two men were.'

'In which case,' Fox said, 'Carter was hardly going to blacken Willis's name.'

'I'm not so sure. People like to get to the bottom of things, Inspector, don't you find?'

'So what will you do, now that you've lost your researcher?'

'Find another one,' Mangold stated, staring intently at Fox. There was a tap on the door, and the porter, Eddie, announced that the first of Mangold's guests had arrived downstairs. Mangold got to his feet and walked around the table, shaking Fox's hand and thanking him for coming: 'Just a pity the circumstances couldn't have been different ...'

Fox gave the slightest of nods and allowed Eddie to show him back down the staircase.

Just inside the front door, a new arrival was handing his overcoat to a porter while discussing the weather. He glanced towards Fox as if to check whether he warranted some greeting. In the end, the curtest of nods was all Fox got.

'Will you be in your usual spot, Sheriff Cardonald?' the porter was asking. 'I'll bring you your drink.'

'Usual spot,' Cardonald agreed.

Fox paused to watch him head for the stairs. Sheriff Colin Cardonald, the man whose decision had put Paul Carter back on the streets ...

He hadn't felt like another takeaway or microwave meal, so had treated himself to a restaurant in Morningside – an Italian place with plenty of fresh fish on the menu. The evening paper kept him occupied for about ten minutes, after which he tried not to look as if he was interested in the other diners. Really, he was thinking. Trying not to, but thinking all the same.

About Ray Scholes and Paul Carter.

About Paul Carter and his uncle.

About Alan Carter and Charles Mangold.

Charles Mangold and Francis Vernal.

Vernal and Chris Fox.

Chris and Mitch.

Mitch and Fox himself.

Bringing him right back to Scholes and Carter again. No wonder his head was spinning; there was a dance going on in there, an eightsome reel with too many couples and not enough floor space. When his waiter came over, looking concerned and asking if everything was okay, Fox realised he'd hardly touched his main course.

'It's fine,' he said, scooping up another forkful of monkfish.

You were never happy there ...

You'll be a bit rusty then ...

Should he have offered a stronger argument? Defended himself against the charge? Two old men with a couple of drinks under their belts – what was the point? He thought back to his time on the force prior to the Complaints. He had been diligent and scrupulous, never a shirker. He had put in the hours, been commended for his error-free paperwork and ability to lead a team: no egos and no heroes. He hadn't been *un*happy. He had learned much and kept out of trouble. If a problem arose, he either dealt with it or ensured it was moved elsewhere.

Ideally suited to Complaints and Conduct, his reviews eventually started concluding. But was that altogether a good thing, or was it CID's way of telling him he didn't fit in there?

Too scrupulous.

Too willing to sidestep problems.

When he caught his waiter's eye, he told him he was finished.

'Not as hungry as I thought,' he offered by way of apology.

Back at the house, he switched on the TV and found multiple channels of dross. The news was focusing on a royal engagement and not much else. Fox lasted ten minutes, then went in search of his computer. He knew he could wait until morning: Joe Naysmith would stick to his word. But all the same, he typed Francis Vernal's name into the search engine and clicked on the first of 17,250 links.

Half an hour later, a text came in from Tony Kaye.

Copycat blast – Peebles this time. Bloody kids!

Fox couldn't think how to reply, so turned his attention back to the computer screen instead.

Copycat ... Bloody kids ...

As usual, Tony Kaye was seeing what he wanted to see. Fox wasn't so sure.

Five

15

There was a lay-by near the spot where Francis Vernal's car had left the road. A small cairn had been erected, with a plaque on it commemorating 'A Patriot'. Someone had even left a bouquet of flowers. The flowers were shrivelled – could be they dated back to the anniversary of the crash. Mangold's work maybe, on behalf of himself and Vernal's widow.

Fox had brought his own car over to Fife this morning, leaving the M90 and skirting Glenrothes, heading for what was known as the 'East Neuk': little fishing villages popular with landscape painters and caravanners. Lundin Links and Elie, St Monans and Pittenweem, then Anstruther – pronounced 'Ainster' by locals. Francis Vernal had died on a stretch of the B9131, north of Anstruther. He didn't play golf, but had a weekend place on the outskirts of St Andrews. Nobody was sure why he hadn't stuck to the A915 – a quicker route. The only theory was a picturesque detour. Once you headed away from the coast, it was all farmland and forestry. No way to tell which particular tree his car had collided with. Another theory: mud left on the roadway by tractors had caused the car to skid. Fine, Fox could accept that. But something had happened afterwards. Not everyone who smashed their car then felt compelled to reach for a handgun. Had Vernal's lifestyle caught up with him? Stress, a rocky marriage, too much drink. The drink makes him swerve off the road – maybe he wants to end it all. But he's still alive afterwards, so he reaches into the glove box for the revolver.

A revolver: same sort of gun used by Alan Carter.

By him – or on him.

Fox ran his fingers over the memorial. Kids down the years had scratched their names into it. A couple of souped-up cars had flown past him a few miles back, stereos blaring, maybe driven by 'Cambo' or 'Ali', 'Desi' or 'Pug'. Straightening up, he breathed deeply. Not a bad spot: peaceful. The drone of distant farm machinery, the half-hearted cawing of a few crows. He could smell freshly turned earth. A trudge around the vicinity provided no further clues. No one had left a bouquet resting against any of the trees. None of the news reports had been able to provide a photo of the car *in situ*, and even the few monochrome pictures of the site were speculative, apparently. Mangold was right: the Volvo had been removed and taken to a local junkyard before any forensics could be done. The early newspaper reports didn't even mention suicide. It was a 'tragic accident', robbing the country of 'a bright political talent'. The obituaries had been plentiful, but sticking to the same anodyne script. A book had been published a few years later, and half a chapter had been dedicated to the 'mystery death' of 'political activist Francis Vernal'. The book had been a short compendium of unsolved Scottish crimes, but it produced no new evidence. Instead, its author had posed questions, the same questions Fox had been asking himself throughout his online reading of the previous evening. He'd printed out quite a lot of it, finishing one ink cartridge and replacing it with a spare. Back at his car, he lifted the heavy folder from the passenger seat and considered opening it. But then his phone buzzed, meaning he had a text message. It was from Tony Kaye.

Summat's up.

Fox called Kaye's number but he wasn't answering. He turned the ignition key, did a three-point turn, and headed back towards Kirkcaldy.

The cop-shop car park was full, so he parked on the street outside. Single yellow line, so he had to hope he wouldn't get a ticket. The sign next to the front desk stated that the Alert Status had been raised from MODERATE to SUBSTANTIAL. The storeroom was unlocked and empty, so he made for the interview room. Opening the door, he saw Paul Carter slumped in a chair. On the other side of the table sat Isabel Pitkethly.

'Out,' Pitkethly ordered.

Fox muttered an apology and closed the door again. Kaye and Naysmith were coming along the corridor towards him.

'Might have warned me,' Fox growled.

'I just did,' Kaye responded. Sure enough, Fox had another text message.

IR a no-no!

'Thanks,' Fox said, stuffing the phone back into his pocket. 'So what's going on?'

'You should see CID,' Naysmith interrupted. 'They're going mental.'

'It would be nice if someone told me why.'

'Some spotty little reporter,' Tony Kaye obliged. 'There's a petrol station on Kinghorn Road and he went there to fill up his putt-putt—'

'And,' Naysmith butted in again, 'he asks the attendant if he saw anything the night Alan Carter died. Turns out the guy did.'

'Paul Carter,' Kaye added. 'He saw Paul Carter.'

'Looking agitated.'

'Stopped his car at the pumps, got out but didn't do anything about filling it.'

'Pacing up and down.'

'Looking at his phone.'

'Punching the buttons but not seeming to get an answer ...'

'We already know Paul Carter phoned his uncle,' Fox felt it necessary to state.

'But he was heading for the cottage,' Naysmith stressed.

'So half an hour ago it was a clear case of suicide, and now the nephew's a murder suspect?' Fox's stare moved from Kaye to Naysmith and back again.

'He's going to go to jail,' Kaye argued, 'in no small part because of his uncle ...'

'If nothing else,' Naysmith added, 'it probably means he went to the cottage. Whatever they talked about, it ended with a gunshot and a corpse.'

They heard footsteps. Two men and a woman had come through the swing doors, led by Sergeant Alec Robinson. Robinson was stony-faced. The new arrivals took the measure of Fox, Kaye and Naysmith, then knocked on the interview-room door and went in. Robinson avoided eye contact with Fox as he headed back to his desk.

'Glenrothes?' Kaye speculated.

'Aye,' Fox said.

A minute later, the same three officers were leading Paul Carter out. He saw Fox and his colleagues and came to a stop.

111

'I'm being stitched up here,' he snarled. 'I never did nothing!'

The two male officers gripped him by either forearm and led him away.

'Hands off me!'

The woman offered a glance back in Fox's direction as she followed them.

'Know her?' Kaye asked, his mouth close to Fox's left ear.

'Name's Evelyn Mills,' Fox admitted. 'She's Complaints, same as us.'

'And she wears Chanel.'

Pitkethly was standing in the doorway of the interview room. The look she gave Fox told him it had been her decision to bring Glenrothes in. He nodded to let her know he'd have done the same.

'What does he say?' he asked.

'Got a call from his uncle's number. Caller hung up. Another call, same thing happened.' She folded her arms. 'Wondered what was going on, decided to go ask him in person, but got halfway and changed his mind.'

'Maybe that's what happened, then.'

'Maybe.'

'You don't sound convinced.'

She glowered at him and decided against answering. Fox, Kaye and Naysmith watched her stride down the corridor away from them.

'Home sweet home,' Kaye said, making to enter the interview room. Fox saw that Naysmith was lifting a heavy-looking shoulder bag from the floor at his feet.

'That stuff you wanted,' the young man explained. 'Took me half the night, a ream of paper and a change of printer cartridges.' He made to hand the contents of the bag to Fox. 'You'll never guess how many hits there were on Francis Vernal's name.'

He looked stunned when Fox got it exactly right.

It was over an hour before Mills had the chance to call Fox. He hesitated a moment before answering.

'Your girlfriend?' Kaye guessed.

'Yes, Inspector Mills?' Fox said into the phone, letting her know he had company.

112

'I'm not sure what this means for the surveillance,' she told him.

'Me neither.'

'If we catch Carter talking to Scholes and owning up to something ...'

'Might be inadmissible,' Fox concurred.

'I've got the Procurator Fiscal's office working on the pros and cons, but knowing them, it'll take a while.' She paused. 'Might be safer just to pull the plug.'

'On the other hand,' Fox reasoned, 'the tap is on Scholes's phone, not Carter's. And Scholes isn't the one CID have in their sights.' It was Fox's turn to pause. 'How's it looking for Carter?'

'His superintendent tells us you were the one who came up with the left-hand/right-hand thing on the revolver.'

'That's true.'

'It's all circumstantial, of course ...'

'Of course,' he agreed.

'But it might add up to something.'

'Foul play?'

'Yes.'

'A murder inquiry?'

'Quite possibly.'

'Based here?' Fox looked around the small room.

'It's the nearest station. We'd have to send in our own team, naturally.'

'Naturally. CID and the Complaints working together?'

'If that's what the bosses decree.'

'Scholes, Michaelson, Haldane ...?'

'Sidelined.'

'Sounds as if it's going to be pretty hectic around here.'

'You plan to stay put?'

'Until told otherwise.'

'Malcolm ... you realise you're a witness? We'll need to ask you about Alan Carter.'

'No problem.'

'Scholes is already stirring things.'

'Oh?'

'Says you were on the scene pretty fast.'

'Not half as fast as him and Michaelson.'

'Difference is, *they'd* been called to the cottage.'

'I'm happy to answer any questions, Inspector Mills.'

113

'See you soon, then,' she said, ending the call.

Fox relayed everything to Kaye and Naysmith, then told them he was stepping outside for a breath of air. Across the other side of the car park, Brian Jamieson was standing next to his scooter. There was a woman alongside him with some sort of recorder slung over one shoulder and headphones clamped to her ears. She was holding a microphone in front of Jamieson.

Local radio was interviewing local stringer.

Fox walked over. Jamieson had already spotted him and was telling the woman who he was. The microphone swung towards him.

'I need a word,' Fox told Jamieson.

'Inspector,' the young woman said, 'can I just ask you for a comment on the arrest of Paul Carter?'

Fox shook his head and then angled it into the car park, knowing Jamieson would follow. That way, he would look important, and Fox got the feeling he'd want to look important in front of his colleague-cum-competitor.

'We saw him being lifted,' Jamieson was saying as he caught up with Fox. 'Is that him off to Glenrothes?'

'What made you go into the petrol station?'

'Pit stop. After you left the scene, I was there the best part of two hours. Needed a caffeine hit.'

'The attendant knew Paul Carter?'

Jamieson shook his head. 'It was the car he described, rather than the man.'

'So you can't be sure it actually was Carter?'

Jamieson stared at him. 'The forecourt's covered by CCTV. I had to wait for the garage owner to okay me seeing the playback. That's why I didn't come forward sooner. No doubt about it, Inspector – it's Paul Carter caught on camera.'

'And he drives off afterwards?'

'Yes.'

'Still heading towards the cottage?'

'Is he saying it's coincidence?'

'He's saying he did a U-turn.'

Jamieson was thoughtful. 'Camera only covers the pumps.' He had moved ahead of Fox so he was facing him. 'Funny, isn't it?'

'What?'

'Paul Carter ... so close by his uncle's place the night the uncle decides to do away with himself. And who are the first two officers on the scene? Paul Carter's best buddies.'

114

Fox kept his face a blank. 'What made you think to ask the attendant if he'd seen anything suspicious?'

Jamieson gave a twitch of the mouth. 'Maybe a hunch. Hunches have got me where I am today.'

'You're a regular Quasimodo,' Fox agreed, heading for the police station's back door. Waiting for him on the other side stood Ray Scholes, hands in pockets, feet apart.

'You know who he is?' Scholes cautioned.

Fox agreed that he did.

'Are you giving him anything?'

'No.'

'Best keep it like that.'

Fox made to move past, but found his way blocked.

'I need to show you something,' Scholes said. It was the screen of his phone. Fox took it from his hand and peered at the message. It was from Paul Carter.

Get Fox for me. Five minutes.

The phone started vibrating. Fox looked at Scholes.

'That'll be for you,' Scholes told him.

'I don't want it.' Scholes said nothing, and wouldn't take the phone back when Fox offered it to him. The call ended, the two men staring at one another. It rang again immediately.

'Point made,' Scholes said. 'You can answer it now.'

'Hello?' said Fox.

'It's Carter.'

'I know.'

'Listen, I've pulled a few stunts in my time – I admit that. But not this. Never this.'

'What do you want me to do about it?'

'Fuck's sake, Fox. I'm a cop, aren't I?'

'You were.'

'And someone's trying to frame me.'

'So?'

'So somebody's got to be on my side!' There was anger in the voice, but fear too.

'Tell that to Teresa Collins.' Fox's eyes were boring into Scholes's.

'You want me to own up?' Paul Carter was saying. 'Every time I crossed the line or even thought about it?'

'Why did Alan Carter die?'

'How should I know?'

115

'You didn't go to see him?' Fox's voice hardened. 'If you try lying to me, I can't help you.'

'I swear I didn't.'

'Did you send anyone else?' He was still looking at Scholes, who stiffened and bunched his fists.

'No.'

'Any idea why he phoned you?'

'I'm telling you, I don't know *anything*!'

'So what am I supposed to do?'

'Ray can't exactly go snooping, can he?'

'Wouldn't look good,' Fox conceded.

'But he tells me you talked to my uncle ...' The sound that came from Carter's throat was somewhere between a sigh and a wail. 'Maybe you can do something ... anything.'

'Why should I?'

'I don't know,' Carter admitted. 'I really don't know ...'

Wherever Carter was, Fox could hear new noises, muffled voices. He was no longer free to talk. The phone went dead and Fox checked the screen before handing it back to Scholes.

'Well?' Scholes asked.

Fox seemed to be weighing up his options. Then he shook his head, squeezed past Scholes, and headed for the interview room. But Scholes wasn't giving up.

'Alan Carter had enemies,' he said. 'Some he made on the force, others afterwards. The Shafiqs – they own a string of shops and businesses. Had a run-in with some of Carter's boys. Bad blood there.'

Fox stopped and held up a hand. 'You can't just go throwing names around.'

'Bombs going off in Lockerbie and Peebles – we could play the anti-terrorism card, keep them in custody till they talk.' Scholes saw the look on Fox's face. 'Oh aye,' he said with a sneer. 'I forgot – it's racist to lock up anyone with a funny name.'

Fox shook his head and moved off again. This time, Scholes didn't bother following. He called after him instead.

'When he texted me wanting to speak to you, I sent a message straight back, told him he was wasting his time. A *real* cop's what he needs, and that's not you, Fox. That's nothing like you.' His voice dropped just a fraction. 'A real cop's what he needs,' he repeated, as Fox shoved open the swing doors.

16

'Anyone else we should be talking to?' Tony Kaye asked.

The three of them were perched on the sea wall, eating fish and chips from the wrappings. Across the water, a ray of sun picked out Berwick Law. Far to the right, they could make out Arthur's Seat and the Edinburgh skyline. Tankers and cargo vessels sat at rest in the estuary. It was lunchtime, and the gulls were flapping around, looking interested.

'Haldane might be worth another shot,' Fox suggested.

'Really?' Kaye asked.

'What do you think?'

'I think a murder inquiry might be about to happen, and we'd be better off elsewhere. Last thing Fife Constabulary is going to need is us running around, trying not to barge into their murder team.'

'True,' Fox admitted.

'Yet I can't help noticing we're still here.' Kaye tossed a morsel of batter into the air, watching a gull swoop and snatch it, its friends readying to gang up against it. 'So tell me what else we could add to the sum of our knowledge.'

'There's the surveillance,' Fox offered.

'But that's not our operation.'

'Scholes, Haldane and Michaelson – we've hardly scratched the surface with them ...'

'You're clutching at straws, Malcolm.' This time a salted chip spun into the sky, dropping to the ground and being pounced on by four of the gulls.

'All right, I give in.' Fox turned towards Naysmith. 'Joe, tell the man why we can't go home just yet.'

117

'Francis Vernal,' Naysmith said, on cue. It had been evident to Fox from first thing: Naysmith had been reading the same online articles, rumours and suppositions as Fox – and he was hooked. 'Taken for granted at the time that it was suicide. Media hardly touched it – no rolling news or internet back then. But Vernal had told friends he thought he was being watched, that his office and house had been broken into – nothing taken, just stuff put back in the wrong place.'

'So who was watching him?' Kaye asked.

'Spooks, I suppose.'

'And why would they be interested in him?'

'I hadn't realised how wild things were in the mid-eighties,' Naysmith said, licking vinegar from his fingers. 'You had CND demos, Star Wars summits—'

'Star Wars?'

'Not the film – it was a missile defence thing; Reagan and Gorbachev. Cruise missiles were on their way to Britain. The Clyde was being picketed because of Polaris. Friends of the Earth were protesting about acid rain. Animal rights ... Hilda Murrell ...' Naysmith paused. 'You remember her, right?'

'Let's pretend I don't,' Kaye said.

'Pensioner, but also an activist. Tam Dalyell ...' Naysmith broke off.

'The MP,' Kaye stated. 'I'm not completely glaikit.'

'Well, he had a theory she'd been killed by MI5. They'd been paying a private eye to keep tabs on her ...'

'I'm not hearing anything about Francis Vernal.' Kaye was scrunching the greasy wrappings into a ball.

'Early eighties was also a hotbed of nationalism,' Fox informed him. 'Isn't that right, Joe?'

Naysmith nodded. 'SNP weren't doing well in the polls, and that led some nationalists to look towards Ireland for inspiration. They reckoned a few explosions might focus London's attention.'

'Explosions?'

'Letter bombs were sent to Mrs Thatcher and the Queen. Plus Woolwich Arsenal, the Ministry of Defence and Glasgow City Chambers – that last one on a day Princess Di was visiting. All these splinter groups: Seed of the Gael, SNLA ...'

'Scottish National Liberation Army,' Fox explained for Kaye's benefit.

'Scottish Citizen Army ... Dark Harvest Commando. That last

one, they took a wee trip to Gruinard.' Naysmith paused again.

'Enlighten me,' Kaye muttered.

'It's an island off the west coast. Infected with anthrax in World War Two.'

'Germans?' Kaye speculated.

Naysmith shook his head. 'We did it ourselves. Planned to drop anthrax over Germany but wanted to test it first.'

'After which Gruinard was uninhabitable,' Fox added. 'They took it off the maps to stop people finding it.'

'But the Dark Harvest Commando went there and lifted some of the soil, then started sending it to various government agencies.'

'Francis Vernal was involved?' Kaye speculated.

'Few years after he died, one reporter filed a piece. He said Vernal had been paymaster for the Dark Harvest Commando.'

'Did he have proof?'

'Information was harder to come by back then. Remember that book *Spycatcher*? These days it would be on the net, no way a government could stop people reading it.'

Naysmith looked up at Fox, and Fox nodded to let him know he'd done well. Naysmith smiled and pushed a hand through his hair.

'I really got into it,' he said, sounding almost embarrassed at his own enthusiasm. 'Even found some clips of a TV show – *Edge of Darkness*.'

'I remember that,' Kaye broke in. 'Big American CIA guy with a golf bag full of guns ...'

'It was about the nuclear industry,' Naysmith elucidated. 'Catches the paranoia of the time.' He shrugged. 'Seems to me, anyway.'

'How much did you find about Dark Harvest Commando?' Fox asked him.

'Virtually nothing.'

'Same here.'

'For one thing, almost nobody ended up in court. For another, it just seemed to fade away.'

Fox nodded slowly.

'Polaris and acid rain,' Kaye mused. 'Seems like ancient history.' He slid from the sea wall and held the ball of rubbish above a bin. 'See what I'm doing here?' He tossed it in. 'That's what we should be doing with all of this.' He brushed his hands together.

'You really think so?' Fox asked.

'I know so. We're not CID, Malcolm. None of this adds up to anything we should be part of.'

'I'm not so sure.'

Kaye rolled his eyes.

'Did Alan Carter kill himself?' Fox asked quietly.

'Maybe,' Kaye stated after a moment.

'If he was murdered ...'

'His nephew's looking good for it.'

'Paul's adamant it wasn't him.'

'And nor is he a sleazebag who tries coercing women into giving him blow jobs.'

'Oh, he's a sleazebag all right. Doesn't mean we should let them hang him out to dry.'

'Let *who* hang him out to dry?'

'That's what I want us to find out.'

Kaye had moved towards Fox until their faces were a couple of inches apart. 'We're the Complaints, Malcolm. We're not *Mission: Impossible*.'

'I know that.'

'Loved that show when I was a kid,' Naysmith commented. Both men turned to look at him, then Kaye smiled a wan smile and shook his head.

'All right then,' he said, knowing he was beaten. 'What do we do?'

'*You* keep the investigation going – second interviews with the main players. That gives us our reason for being here.'

'While you go snooping?'

'Just for a day or two.'

'A day or two?'

'Scout's honour,' Fox said, pressing two fingers together and holding them up.

17

The cordon had been moved further up the track. It comprised the usual length of crime-scene ribbon guarded by a bored-looking uniform. Fox and Naysmith showed their ID.

'CID must have arrived,' Fox explained to Naysmith as the uniform lifted the tape so their car could pass under it.

The gate to the field was open, the field itself emptied of livestock and now useful as a temporary car park. Two unmarked cars, one patrol car, and two white vans.

A suited, shaven-headed veteran was talking into his phone beside one of the unmarked cars. His eyes were on the new arrivals as they parked and got out. Fox offered him a nod and started walking towards the cottage. He could see figures moving around inside. At least two of them were Scene of Crime – dressed in regulation hooded white overalls, hands and feet covered so they wouldn't contaminate the locus.

'Bit late for that,' Fox muttered, thinking of the number of people who had traipsed in and out since the body had been found.

'Hey, you!'

The man with the phone was approaching from the field. He had a loping gait, which caused him to slip on some mud and nearly lose his footing. From the look on his face, Fox surmised this wasn't the first time it had happened.

'It's treacherous,' Fox commented.

The man ignored him, using his phone as a pointer. 'Who are you?'

'My name's Fox.' Fox reached for his warrant card again. 'Inspector, Lothian and Borders.'

'So what brings you here?'

'How about some ID first? Can't be too careful.'

The man gave him a hard stare, but eventually relented. His name was Brendan Young. He was a detective sergeant.

'Glenrothes?' Fox guessed.

'Dunfermline.'

'You in charge?'

'DI's inside.'

'Not now, he isn't.' The man who stepped from the cottage was six foot three and as broad as a rugby player. Jet-black hair combed straight forward, and small, piercing eyes.

'I'm DI Cash.'

'They're Lothian and Borders,' Young informed him.

'Bit lost, gentlemen?' Cash asked.

'I was out here a few days ago,' Fox began to explain, 'interviewing Alan Carter about his nephew.'

'You're the Complaints?'

Fox sensed a hardening of tone. Doubtless Young's face was hardening too. Normal enough reactions.

'We are,' he concurred.

'Then I was right first time – you *are* a bit fucking lost.' Cash smiled at Young, and Young smiled back. 'This is a suspicious death—'

'Not murder yet, then?' Fox interrupted. But Cash wasn't going to give him the satisfaction of an answer.

'Why don't you just go back to strip-searching your own kind to see if they've pocketed any paper clips from the stationery cupboard?'

Fox managed a twitch of the mouth. 'Thanks for the advice, but I'm here for fingerprints.'

Cash stared at him. 'Fingerprints?'

'Mine,' Fox explained. Then, patiently, as if to a child: 'I was in the living room and hallway. Might have left prints. If I give them to Scene of Crime, they can be verified and eliminated.'

'Up to us to decide that,' Cash stated.

'Of course,' Fox accepted. Cash's eyes stayed on him for a moment, then moved to Young.

'Go fetch someone.'

Young headed into the house. Fox saw that the door jamb was splintered. A crowbar had been used to open it. He walked over to the window ledge, lifted the flowerpot, and showed Cash the key.

'Kirkcaldy CID didn't tell you?' he guessed.

'They didn't.'

'Well, you know what it's like: this is their patch. Don't expect any favours.'

'I might say the same thing.'

Fox gave another twitch of the mouth, nearing a smile this time.

'You'll give us a statement about the deceased?' Cash asked.

'Whenever you're ready for it.'

'How often did you meet him?'

'Just the once.'

'What did you think? Good guy?'

Fox nodded. 'Wouldn't want to get on the wrong side of him, though.'

'Oh?'

'Seems to me he didn't suffer fools – or family – gladly. Plus he ran a security firm.' Fox slipped his hands into his pockets. 'I was here again afterwards,' he went on. 'Not long after the body was discovered. The papers on the table had been disturbed; strewn about the place.'

'Anything taken?'

'Couldn't say.' He paused. 'You know what Carter was working on?'

'I get the feeling you're about to tell me.'

'Lawyer called Francis Vernal. Died in suspicious circumstances. Gunshot. Reckoned suicide at the time. About thirty miles from here …'

'Francis Vernal? That was back in the eighties.'

Fox shrugged. One of the overalled figures was emerging from the cottage. She removed her hood and overshoes.

'Which one of you?' she asked.

'Me,' Malcolm Fox replied.

He followed her to one of the vans. She climbed into the back and found everything she needed. The portable scanner, however, refused to work.

'Flat battery?' Fox guessed.

She had to resort to the back-up of ink and paper. The result was signed by both of them, after which she handed Fox a wet-wipe for his fingers. This was followed by a DNA swab of the inside of his cheek, and the plucking of a couple of hairs from his head.

'I can't afford many,' Fox complained.

'Need to get the root,' she explained. After everything was sealed into pouches, she locked the van.

'Sorry about that,' she said, heading back to the cottage.

'When was the last time you had your prints taken?' Naysmith asked.

'Been a while.' Fox saw Cash watching them from the living room. The DI gave a little wave, as if granting them permission to leave. Naysmith, however, had started walking in the direction of the Land Rover.

'Bit of quality,' he said, peering in through the driver's-side window.

'Mind you don't leave any prints,' Fox warned him.

Naysmith took a step back and looked around. 'Question for you,' he said. 'Why leave your car out here when you've got a garage?'

Fox looked in the direction he was pointing. A track led up the slope behind the cottage, ending at a ramshackle building.

'Afraid it might collapse?' Fox guessed. But all the same, he started trudging uphill, Naysmith a couple of steps behind him.

The garage was padlocked. The lock looked old. The doors comprised vertical slats of wood, weathered and warped by the elements.

'There's a window here,' Naysmith said. By the time Fox reached him, he had wiped at it with a handkerchief, without helping them gain much impression of what was inside.

'Tarpaulin, I think ...'

They walked around the garage, even gave it a kick in a couple of spots, but there was no easy way in.

'Give me a sec,' Fox said, walking back down the slope again. There was no one in the hallway of the cottage, so he moved briskly past the living-room door and found the small kitchen. Keys hung from a row of hooks to the left of the sink. He ran an eye along them and chose the likeliest candidates. As he was turning to leave, he saw Cash emerge from the living room.

'What are you doing there?'

'Looking for you.' Fox slipped the keys into the inside pocket of his jacket, removing a business card at the same time.

'So you can reach me to arrange that interview,' he explained, handing it to Cash. Cash looked at it, then back at Fox.

'I know you're all excited,' he said in an undertone, 'not normally getting to play with the big boys and all that, but I need you to bugger off now.'

'Understood,' Fox said, managing his best to look and sound humbled in the presence of a Murder Squad detective. Cash escorted him to the front door and looked to left and right.

'Where's that work-experience kid of yours?'

'Call of nature,' Fox explained, nodding in the direction of the trees. He walked towards his car, opened it and got in. Cash was at the window again, watching. But after a couple of moments he turned away, and Fox got out of the car, heading back to the garage.

The second key unlocked the padlock, and they were in. Naysmith had been right. A tarpaulin was draped over what looked like another vehicle. There was dust everywhere. A workbench boasted rusty tools. Home-made shelves had buckled under the weight of old paint cans. There was an electric lawnmower for the patches of grass to the front and rear of the cottage. Along with the rolled-up extension cable, it was the newest thing visible.

Naysmith had lifted a corner of the tarp. 'Not exactly roadworthy,' he commented. 'More what you'd call a write-off.'

Fox went to the other end of the vehicle and lifted another corner. The car was a maroon Volvo 244. It seemed fine until he lifted the cover further. There was no glass in the rear window.

'Give me a hand,' he said. Together they pulled back the tarpaulin. The front of the car was wrecked, its engine exposed, grille and bonnet missing.

'Tell me it isn't,' Naysmith said in a voice just above a whisper.

But Fox was in no doubt at all. Vernal's car, the one that had been taken to the scrapyard. Fox tried the passenger-side door, but it was jammed shut from the force of impact. The car's interior didn't look as though it had been touched in quarter of a century. There were bits of broken glass on the back seat, but not much else. Naysmith couldn't get the driver's door to open either.

'How come it's here?' he asked quietly.

'No idea,' Fox said. But then he remembered. 'Cottage used to be owned by a cop called Gavin Willis. He ran the original inquiry.'

'So he could have kept the car for himself? Still doesn't explain why.'

'No, it doesn't.' Fox paused. 'Reckon you can get in through that window?'

He meant the gaping rear windscreen. Naysmith removed his expensive jacket, handed it to Fox for safe-keeping, then hauled himself up, squeezing through the gap.

'What now?' he asked from the back seat.

'Is there anything that might interest us?'

Naysmith felt beneath the front seats, then stretched between them and opened the glove box. He found the paperwork for the car and handed it to Fox, who stuffed it into his pocket.

'Half a set of spare bulbs and a few sweet-wrappers,' Naysmith reported. 'But that's about it.'

Fox could hear voices down at the cottage. They'd be wondering why his car was still there while he wasn't. 'Out you come, then,' he said.

He helped pull Naysmith through the opening. They were standing side by side, Naysmith slipping his jacket back on, when the garage door shuddered open. Cash and Young were standing there.

'What do you think you're doing?'

'Francis Vernal's car,' Fox stated.

Cash stared at the Volvo, then at Fox again. 'How do you know?'

'Make, model, colour,' Fox explained.

'And damage,' Naysmith added, pointing to the engine casing.

'I want the pair of you out of here,' Cash growled, pointing a finger of his own.

'Just leaving,' Fox told him.

Cash and Young stayed with them until they'd reached their own car, then watched as they did a three-point turn and drove slowly back down the hill, Cash following on foot, just so he could be sure. They paused while the cordon was lifted, and waved to the uniform as they trundled towards the main road.

'What now?' Joe Naysmith asked.

'This is where you get to show off your detective skills, Joe,' Fox told him. 'Kirkcaldy Library – find a phone book for 1985 and make a note of every scrapyard in the area. If we track down where the car went, we've half a chance of finding out why it left there again.'

Naysmith nodded. 'Might not mean anything, of course.'

'Every chance,' Fox agreed. 'But at least we'll give it a shot, eh?

18

Having dropped Naysmith outside the library, Fox headed for the police station. Rain had started gusting against the windscreen. He turned on the wipers. The drops were huge, sounding like sparks from a fire. He thought back to that day in Alan Carter's cottage, the two of them seated either side of the fireplace, mugs of tea and an old dog for company. What could have been cosier or more domestic? Yet Carter was a man who had built up a security company from nothing: that spoke to Fox of an inner toughness, maybe even ruthlessness. Then there was the evidence of his old friend Teddy Fraser: the cottage door kept locked at all times – why? What had the jovial old chap to fear? Maybe nothing. Maybe it was the sharp businessman who had to keep his wits about him – to the extent of having a gun nearby ...

If the gun was his to begin with; Teddy Fraser thought otherwise.

There was no sign of Jamieson or the woman reporter outside the car park. Fox spotted Tony Kaye's Mondeo. Pitkethly's space was free again, but she had warned him against taking it. Looked like the Volvo was going to have to sit on the street again and risk a ticket. Francis Vernal, too, had driven a Volvo. A safe, steady choice, so the adverts would have you believe – Kaye had teased Fox often enough about that. The roadway either side of the crash site boasted a few curves and bends, but nothing serious. Fox thought of the speeding cars that had passed him near the memorial. Were there petrolheads back then? Nothing else for the local youths to do of a rural evening? Could someone have driven Vernal off the road?

Having parked, and looked around for traffic wardens in the vicinity, Fox got out and locked the car. He felt something in the pocket of his coat: the logbook from Vernal's Volvo. Its edges were brown with age, warped by damp. Some of the pages were stuck together. At the back were sections to be filled out after each regular service. The lawyer had owned the car from new, by the look of things. Three years he'd been driving it, prior to the crash. Eight and a half thousand miles on the clock at the time of its last trip to the garage. The service centre's stamp was from a dealership on Seafield Road in Edinburgh, long since relocated. There were some loose folded sheets in a clear plastic pocket attached to the inside back cover of the book, dealing with work done to the car and parts replaced. Fox unlocked the driver's-side door, tossed the logbook on to the passenger seat, and headed towards the station. He was halfway across the car park when his phone rang. It was Bob McEwan.

'Sir,' Fox said by way of introduction.

'Malcolm ...' McEwan's tone caused Fox to slow his pace.

'What have I done this time?'

'I've had Fife on the phone – the Deputy Chief.'

'He wants to pull us out?'

'He wants to pull *you* out.' Fox stopped walking. 'Kaye and Naysmith can keep doing their interviews and prepare their report.'

'But Bob—'

'CID called his office, apparently furious with you.'

'Because I told them their job?'

'Because you went barging into a potential crime scene. Because instead of leaving when told, you found somewhere else to stick your nose in ...'

'I went there to assist.'

McEwan was silent for a moment. 'Would you swear to that in court, Malcolm?' Fox didn't answer. 'And would you have Joe Naysmith back you up?'

'All right,' Fox relented. 'It's a fair point.'

'You know better than anyone – we *have* to stick to the rules.'

'Yes, sir.'

'And that's why you're coming home.'

'Is that an order or a request, Bob?'

'It's an order.'

'Do I get to kiss the children goodbye first?'

128

'They're not children, Malcolm. They'll do fine without you.'

Fox was staring at the station's back door.

'I'll let them know what's happened,' McEwan was saying. 'You'll be back here in an hour, yes?'

Fox switched his gaze to the sky above. The shower had passed, but another was on its way.

'Yes,' he told Bob McEwan. 'I will, yes.'

When Fox walked into the Complaints office, there was a note waiting for him from Bob McEwan.

Another bloody meeting. Keep your nose clean …

Fox noticed a couple of supermarket carrier bags sitting on the floor next to his desk. They were heavy. He lifted a box file from one and opened it. A photograph of Francis Vernal in full oratorical flow stared up at him. Below it lay a sequence of stapled sheets, some half-covered in scribbled Post-it notes. The second box file seemed to comprise more of the same. There was no covering letter. Fox phoned down to reception and quizzed the officer there.

'Gentleman dropped them in,' he was told.

'Give me a description.'

There was a thoughtful pause. 'Just a gentleman.'

'And he gave my name?'

'He gave your name.'

Fox ended the call and made another – to Mangold Bain. The secretary put him through to Charles Mangold.

'I'm just heading out,' Mangold warned him.

'I got your little present.'

'Good. It's everything Alan Carter passed on to me before his death.'

'I'm not sure what you think I can do with it …'

'Take a look at it, maybe? Then give me your reaction. That's as much as I can hope for. Now I really need to be on my way.'

Fox ended the call and stared at the two large boxes. Not here: Bob McEwan would have too many questions. He crossed to his boss's desk and left a note of his own.

Knocked off early. At home if you need me. Phone the house if you're sceptical.

Then he drove to Oxgangs, and placed the two boxes on the table in his living room. As he came back through from the kitchen with a glass of Appletiser, he realised how similar the two scenes might eventually be – Alan Carter's table, piled high with paperwork, and now his.

With a tightening of the mouth, he got down to business.

Alan Carter had, on the face of it, done a lot of work. He had sourced copies of the *Scotsman* for the whole of April and May 1985, really to prove only that almost no attention had been paid to the lawyer's death. Fox found himself lost in these newspapers. There was an advert for a computer shop he remembered visiting. The advert was for an ICL personal computer with a price tag of almost four thousand pounds, this at a time when a brand-new Renault 5 – with radio/cassette thrown in – could be had for six. In the Situations Vacant column, one company was seeking security guards at seventy-five quid a week. A flat in Viewforth was on sale at offers over £35,000.

News stories flew at him: bombs in Northern Ireland; a CND demo at Loch Long; 'Soviet Missiles Freeze Snubbed by Washington' ... There were protesters at a proposed cruise missile base in Cambridgeshire. Companies were being advised to protect 'sensitive electronic information' from the effects of a nuclear detonation. The Princess of Wales, on a visit to Scotland Yard, was shown the oven and bath used by serial killer Dennis Nilsen ...

Alex Ferguson was the boss of Aberdeen FC, and they topped the league throughout April. Petrol was going up five pence to just over two pounds a gallon, and Princess Michael of Kent professed herself 'shocked' to find out that her father had been in the SS. Fox found himself reaching for his mug of tea without remembering getting up to make it. Animal-rights protests and acid-rain protests and teachers warned by their employers against wearing CND badges in the classroom. Neil Kinnock was leader of the Labour Party, and Prime Minister Margaret Thatcher was on a Middle East tour. A poll showed support for the SNP stubbornly fixed at fifteen per cent of the Scottish population. A flooded colliery was to be closed, and there were fears the Trustee Savings Bank might move its HQ south of the border.

Joe Naysmith had mentioned Hilda Murrell, and though she had died the previous year, she made it into the newspaper too. The MP Tam Dalyell was insisting she had been killed by British Intelligence, and Home Secretary Leon Brittan was to be quizzed on the matter.

Fox was surprised by how little of this he remembered. He

would have been in his Highers year at Boroughmuir, confident that a university or college place awaited him. Jude had been more interested in politics than him – she'd gone out canvassing for the Labour Party one time. Fox, meanwhile, had turned his bedroom into a sanctum where he could concentrate on his Sinclair Spectrum computer, losing patience as yet another game failed to load because he couldn't find the sweet spot on his cassette-player's volume knob. Hearts games with his dad on a Saturday, but only if he could prove all his homework was done. He was fine with schoolwork, but never watched the news or read a paper – just *2000 AD* and the sports pages.

Francis Vernal had died on the evening of Sunday, 28 April. That night, a large chunk of the population – Fox included – had been glued to their TV sets as Dennis Taylor faced Steve Davis in the final of the World Snooker Championship. Taylor, eight frames down at one stage, had staged the fightback of his career. When he potted the final black of the final frame, to take the match 18–17, it was the first time he'd been ahead in the entire contest. For the few days afterwards, his face was all over the papers. Vernal's death rated not a mention, until his obituary appeared, including, on one line, a misprint of his name as Vernel.

'Couldn't happen today,' Fox mused out loud. No internet back then, as Naysmith had said. Rumours could be contained. Even *news* could be contained. Few enough Woodwards and Bernsteins in the Scottish media at the best of times. Fox could imagine a newspaper editor baulking at reporting details of a suicide: there was the family to consider, and maybe you'd liked the guy, respected him. What good did it do tarnishing his name by letting strangers know how he'd died?

A patriot.

Opening the second box, Fox felt his eyebrows raise a little. Photocopies of the original police notes on the case, along with autopsy details and pictures. Someone had been into the vaults to retrieve this lot, which Alan Carter had then copied and sent to his employer. Had money changed hands, or did Carter still have friends on the force? Where did Fife Constabulary store its old case-work? In Edinburgh, they used a warehouse on an industrial estate. He checked his watch. It would take him a few hours to go through everything. He knew he should take a break. The sound of a message arriving on his phone was timely. Tony Kaye and Joe Naysmith were having a drink at Minter's.

POETS Day, remember!
Fox smiled to himself: Piss Off Early, Tomorrow's Saturday.
It was all the invitation he needed.

19

'I have to tell you,' Kaye said as Fox approached the table, 'you're in danger of becoming a local hero in Kirkcaldy.'

'How's that?' Fox asked, settling into his seat.

'They don't like the Murder Squad muscling in, and so far you're the only one who's managed to put those particular noses out of joint.'

'Is it a murder yet?'

Kaye shook his head as he took a sip of beer. 'Suspicious death,' he confirmed. Joe Naysmith returned from the bar with Fox's spiced tomato juice.

'Thanks, Joe,' Fox said. 'How did you get on at the library?'

'Eight scrapyards in Fife, six of them still going.'

'Did you manage to call all six?'

'Yes.'

'Get lucky?'

'Not exactly. One guy I spoke with reckons the job would've gone to Barron's Wrecking.'

'Can I assume that's one of the two firms no longer in business?'

Naysmith nodded. 'The scrapyard's now a housing estate.'

'And Mr Barron?'

'That's the good news – when he sold up, he got one of the new-builds as part of the deal.'

'He lives on the estate?'

'It's not really an estate – six "executive homes".'

'He's still there?'

'I've not managed to speak to him yet, but I will.'

'Good lad.' Fox realised Kaye was giving him a look not too far removed from pity.

'Wild goose chase,' Kaye duly commented.

'How about you, Tony – anything to report?'

Kaye considered his response while he swilled another mouthful of beer. Then he smacked his lips and said: 'Not much.' Fox waited for more, and Kaye obliged. 'Incident room's been set up in the main CID office, meaning Scholes and Michaelson have been shunted out.'

'Haldane's still off sick?'

Kaye nodded. 'DCI Laird has decided that CID should take up residence in the interview room, leaving Joe and me homeless.'

'Have you talked to Pitkethly about it?'

'She wasn't exactly sympathetic.' Kaye paused. 'There *is* one thing ...'

'What?' Fox asked.

'The surveillance,' Kaye replied. 'With you kicked into touch, shouldn't you hook me up with Coco Chanel? Joe and me need to know what she's hearing from those phone taps.'

'I'll check with her,' Fox said.

Kaye nodded slowly. 'And what about you, Foxy? Got enough to keep you busy?'

'I'll manage.'

'I don't doubt it.' Kaye had finished his drink and was rising to fetch another. Fox shook his head, and Naysmith said he'd just have a half to top up his own pint. Once Kaye had gone to the bar, Naysmith leaned over towards Fox.

'Do you need me for anything?'

'Just keep doing what you're doing.'

Naysmith nodded. 'I was thinking about the gun,' he added.

'Whose gun?'

'The one used to kill Francis Vernal.'

'What about it?'

'Where did it come from?'

'I've been wondering that myself.'

'How outrageous would it be if ...?'

Fox finished the sentence for Naysmith: 'It turned out to be the same gun?' Fox considered this. 'Pretty outrageous,' he decided.

'Any way to find out?'

'Maybe.'

'Want me to ...?'

Fox shook his head. 'You're doing fine as it is.'

'The car's the other thing.' The words were tumbling from Joe Naysmith; Fox had seldom known him so excited. Maybe the youngster was more suited to CID than Complaints. 'I mean, it was never given a forensic check, was it? And the technology these days is way ahead of what they had back then. If we got it to a lab, who knows what they could find ...'

'Up to and including your prints on the interior,' Fox reminded him. 'Which would give you a few awkward questions to answer.'

This reminded Naysmith of something. 'The stuff I got from the glove box ...?'

Fox shrugged. 'Service history.'

Naysmith looked disappointed, then perked up. 'Am I right though – about forensics?'

Fox nodded slowly. 'Let's see if there's a case first, though, eh?'

'The internet has his widow as a prime candidate. Nice-looking woman. Bit younger than him. Came from a rich family.' Naysmith paused. 'Still alive?'

'For now.'

'Worth talking to?'

'Maybe.' Fox wasn't sure Charles Mangold would like that, but all the same ... Kaye was returning with the drinks. Naysmith moved back to his original position.

'Look at the pair of you,' Kaye chided them. 'Like kids plotting something and not wanting the grown-ups to know.' He placed the fresh glasses on the table. 'What do you reckon – should we make a night of it, it being Friday?'

'I'm heading back,' Fox demurred.

'Me too,' Naysmith added.

Kaye sighed, shook his head more in sorrow than in anger, and lifted the pint to his mouth. 'Pair of sodding kids,' he muttered to himself. 'Off you go, then, and remember to do your homework.'

'We will,' Naysmith said with a smile.

'One last thing, though,' Kaye added with a wag of his finger. 'Don't bother to wait up for Daddy.'

Once home, Fox sent a text to Evelyn Mills and sat down at the table again. There was some unopened mail on the windowsill. He hadn't opened it because it comprised a bank statement and a

135

credit-card bill, and neither would be good news. Fees at the care home had risen twice in the past year. Fox didn't begrudge them ... Well, maybe just a bit. More than once he'd considered asking Jude if she couldn't look after their dad. It wasn't as if she had a job. He could pay her, make it worth her while, and he'd still be better off. He wasn't sure why he kept chickening out. Plenty of hints for her to take ... or she could always make the offer herself. Instead, she just nagged at him and said she'd be happy to pay her share if she ever had the money.

You could always take him in ...

'So could you, Malcolm,' he said to himself. Pay a home help to do a lunchtime meal and a bit of cleaning. It would be manageable. Just about manageable. Not really, though. No, Fox couldn't imagine it. He was too set in his ways, liked things just so. It wouldn't work ...

It was almost a relief when his phone rang. He answered: it was Mills.

'Why a text rather than calling me yourself?' she immediately asked. 'Are you cheap or what?'

'I just thought ...' He paused for a second. 'Doesn't it look suspicious, me phoning you of an evening?'

She snorted. 'I get calls all the time – Freddie's used to it.' Freddie: her husband, presumably. 'A mysterious text, on the other hand ...'

'I should have thought of that.'

'Anyway, I'm here now, so what can I do for you?'

'Wondered how the surveillance is going.'

'Nothing to report.' She paused. 'Who *do* I report to anyway?'

'You've heard, then?'

'DI Cash can be like that.'

'You know him?'

'By reputation.'

'Tell me he's on your radar.'

She gave a little laugh. 'He's never crossed the line, Malcolm – not yet, at any rate.'

'Pity.' Fox rubbed a hand across his forehead. 'To answer your question, I suppose Tony Kaye is your contact now. Let me give you his number.' He did so, then asked if it was okay to give Kaye her name and number.

'Sure,' she said.

'How's the Alan Carter inquiry shaping up?'

'Slow going. Kirkcaldy hasn't exactly thrown a welcome party.'

'Evelyn ... I need to ask you another favour.'

'You want me to put in a word? See if they'll let you back?'

'Not that, no. But I'm interested in the gun.'

'Oh?'

'So I'm wondering if I can talk to someone about it.'

'And you want me to arrange it? You don't ask much, do you, Malcolm?'

'I'm sorry. A name and maybe a contact number – that's all.'

'And what do I get in return?' She sounded almost coquettish. Fox stared at the paperwork in front of him.

'What do you mean?'

'Just my little joke.' She laughed again. 'You needn't sound so scared.'

'It's not that, Evelyn.'

'What then?'

'Nothing.'

'Did you really have that bad a time at Tulliallan?'

'I had a great time at Tulliallan.'

'Mmm, I wish I could remember more of it.' She paused, as if waiting for him to say something. When he didn't, she said she would text him if she got anywhere with the gun.

'Thanks again.'

'Can you tell me *why* you're so interested in it, though?'

'Not really, no.' He paused. 'It might be nothing.'

'Need to let that brain of yours ease off. I can hear it working from here. Take the weekend off, Inspector. Let your hair down.'

'You're probably right.' He managed a smile. 'Good night, Evelyn.'

'Sweet dreams, Malcolm. Do you still snore ...?'

His mouth was hanging open, wondering how to answer, but she had already ended the call.

Six

20

'It's not the same gun, I promise you that.'

Her name was Fiona McFadzean and she was, as Mills's text had put it, 'Fife's ballistics person'. She was based at the Constabulary HQ in Glenrothes. It had taken Fox a while to find the place: too many roundabouts and a shortage of signposts. McFadzean didn't work in the main building. Fox had been directed to a squat brick structure behind the petrol pumps. A uniformed officer was filling the tank of his squad car.

'Aye, that's Fiona's lair,' he assured Fox.

McFadzean had to come and unlock the door for him. She wasn't wearing a white coat and seemed quite happy in her windowless space. Against one wall stood an array of building materials, from brick to wood, pockmarked with bullet holes. A glass-fronted cubicle contained a white-painted wall, speckled pink. McFadzean had explained to Fox that they used it to confirm blood spray from a gunshot.

'And what exactly is it that you shoot?' Fox asked.

'Anything from watermelons to pigs' heads. My uncle's a butcher, which is handy.'

She was a young, vibrant woman, and she took him on a quick tour of her domain. An assistant sat at a computer. She introduced him as Paul, and he waved a greeting without looking up from the screen.

'Much gun crime in Fife?' Fox asked.

'Not really. We were set up as a kind of experiment. Carpet's always about to be pulled from under us – budgets getting squeezed, et cetera.'

141

McFadzean had no desk as such. She seemed content to perch on a stool at a narrow counter which ran the length of one wall. There was a coffee pot, and she poured for both of them, while Fox tried to make himself comfortable on the spare stool, before deciding to stand instead.

'Thanks again for seeing me,' he said.

She nodded her head once and lifted the mug to her lips, cupping it in both hands.

'How can you be so sure about the guns?' Fox then asked. The coffee was too bitter, but he took another sip anyway, so as not to give offence.

'Serial numbers for a start,' she said. 'Paul had some free time last year, so he computerised all the old records.' She showed Fox the printout. 'This is the gun Francis Vernal used. Four-inch barrel rather than six-inch. Same-calibre bullet, but six chambers rather than five.' A second printed sheet was passed to Fox. 'The revolver used to kill Mr Carter ...'

Fox studied the details. 'Different gun,' he agreed. 'It says here the gun from the Vernal shooting was destroyed.'

She nodded. 'Happens to all the weapons we confiscate.' She handed him a third sheet. It was a detailed list of weapons from Fife and Tayside Constabularies sent to be melted down. There weren't many. The revolver found on Alan Carter's table should have been destroyed in October 1984. The one found near Vernal's car had suffered the same fate a year later.

'Have you got a history for both guns?' Fox asked.

'We can do only so much,' McFadzean apologised, blowing across the surface of her coffee.

'Be in a file somewhere,' Paul called out. 'Probably at the National Ballistics Lab in Glasgow. Buried deep in the archives.'

'So you don't know where they came from in the first place?'

McFadzean shook her head.

'The revolver found in Alan Carter's cottage ... how do you think it got there?'

'Somewhere between the lock-up and the furnace, it took a walk.'

Fox nodded his agreement. 'Has that happened before?'

'Guidelines are pretty strict – lots of checks and balances.'

'Not a regular occurrence, then?' Fox studied the sheets again. 'Someone pocketed it,' he guessed.

'Seems likely. I mean, it could have been dropped or mislaid ...'

She saw the look on his face. 'Okay, *that's* not so likely,' she admitted.

'Do we know who was on the detail? Whose job it was to dispose of the weapons?'

'Over the page,' she said, motioning for him to flip to the final sheet.

'Ah,' he said, because there was a name there he recognised.

Detective Inspector Gavin Willis.

'Yes?' McFadzean prompted.

Fox tapped a finger against the paper. 'DI Willis,' he explained. 'Alan Carter worked under him. Bought his house when Willis died.'

'Might explain it,' Paul said, swivelling round in his chair to face them. 'Gun was in the house. Carter found it and kept it ...'

'Making it more likely that he took his own life,' McFadzean added.

'Or at least that the revolver was lying around for someone else to use,' Fox argued. 'Wasn't it you who noticed the fingerprints weren't right?'

She nodded. 'First thing we do,' she explained, 'is check any firearm for trace evidence. After that we match the gun to the bullet, just to be sure. And then we search for provenance.'

'It hadn't been fired in a while,' Paul continued. 'Hadn't been looked after.'

'Rust,' McFadzean explained. 'And a lack of oil.'

'Unused bullets in the other chambers,' Paul added. 'They had to be a couple of decades old.'

'From the fibres we found, it had probably been stored in a piece of cloth, just plain white cotton.'

'So they should be searching the cottage for that cloth,' Fox said.

'They have done – at our request.'

'Nothing so far,' Paul interrupted.

'Nothing so far,' McFadzean confirmed.

Fox blew air from his cheeks. 'What do you make of it?'

'I'm not really sure,' she confided. 'Paul's theory is that the gun had been taken to the cottage, used to kill the victim and then his prints pressed to it in a half-baked attempt to make it look like suicide.' She paused.

'But?' Fox prompted.

'But ... you've just given us reason to believe the gun may have been in the cottage all along.'

'Alan Carter might have had cause to be fearful,' Fox stated. 'Maybe he kept the revolver close by.'

'That doesn't work,' Paul said, rising from his chair and pouring himself more coffee. 'Victim was seated at the table. From the spray pattern, we know that's where he was when he was shot. If someone's taken your gun from you and is pointing it at you ...'

'You're not likely to stay seated with your back to them,' Fox agreed. He thought for a moment. 'What if someone has the gun pointed at you and tells you to sit down? They want something from you, something that's already on the table?'

Paul considered this and nodded slowly. 'You find it for them, and they then shoot you?'

'Or you refuse, and they shoot you anyway,' McFadzean added. The room was silent for a moment.

'So,' Fox asked, 'was the revolver there all along, or did someone bring it with them?'

'I know CID are looking at the victim's nephew,' McFadzean commented. 'He would have known the cottage, and might have known where the revolver was kept.'

'The two men weren't exactly close,' Fox argued. 'If there *was* a gun on the premises, Carter kept it secret even from his oldest and closest friend. And what about the missing cloth?'

'Killer took it with him,' Paul suggested.

'If there *was* a killer,' McFadzean cautioned.

'*If* there was a killer,' her assistant agreed. Then he turned towards Fox. 'One other thing ... Fiona's quite right when she says not many guns go astray – these days, I'd say none at all.'

'But back then?' Fox prompted.

'A few of the guns that turned up in police custody began life with the army. Back in the seventies, a lot of stuff – explosives included – went AWOL from barracks up and down the land, most of it destined for the Troubles.'

'Northern Ireland?'

'The paramilitaries needed weapons. They were being stolen to order.'

'What's your point?'

Paul shrugged. 'That revolver could have been destined for Belfast.'

'Ulster wasn't the only place with terrorists,' Fox informed

him. 'We had our fair share on the mainland, too.' He was thinking of the Scottish National Liberation Army and letter bombs in
Downing Street, the Dark Harvest Commando with their anthrax
spores ...

And their possible paymaster, Francis Vernal.

'You've got a point,' Paul said. He went to a filing cabinet,
pulled open a drawer and started searching. McFadzean gave
Fox an indulgent smile. He nodded his agreement: Paul was good
at his job. A minute later, he'd found the relevant file and was
handing a photograph to Fox. It showed a desk in a police station.
Laid out for the media's attention was an array of firearms. The
dozen or so rifles were tagged; the pistols, revolvers and ammuni-
tion were in sealed evidence bags. Fox read the label on the back
– '1980, Scottish Republican Socialist League trial'. He nodded at
Paul.

'Another splinter group to add to the list,' he commented. 'Some
of these would have come from the army?'

'From "break-ins" at barracks.'

Fox looked at him. 'Inside jobs?'

'All it takes is a few sympathisers, a blind eye turned, a key
handed over ...'

'I'm seeing shotgun cartridges but no shotguns,' Fox said, handing the photograph to McFadzean.

'Par for the course,' she explained. 'No one's saying these groups
had high IQs.'

'Not even the leadership?'

'We caught them, didn't we?' She brandished the photo as
proof.

While Paul placed the photograph back in its file, Fox rubbed at
his jaw with the palm of his hand.

'Can I ask you something else?'

'Fire away, if you'll pardon the expression.'

He gave her a smile. 'Do you have a theory about these explosions?'

McFadzean gestured towards Paul's computer. 'Paul's been
doing a bit of work on that. Plastic containers filled with bits
of metal – screws, washers, stuff you can find in any DIY store.
Detonation sent the whole lot flying a distance of thirty metres.'

'Probably not kids, then?'

'Not unless they've been reading *The Anarchist Cookbook*,' Paul
said.

'They've not perfected it yet, though,' McFadzean added, folding her arms.

'But they're getting better,' her colleague cautioned.

McFadzean nodded her agreement, looking pensive.

'They're getting better,' she said.

'And once they're satisfied?' Fox asked.

'Then it won't be trees they'll be targeting,' McFadzean said.

Fox thought long and hard about a detour to Kirkcaldy, maybe a snack at the Pancake Place with Kaye and Naysmith, but weighed up the risks and decided against it. Instead he drove back to Edinburgh, stopping for petrol and a burger. He had called ahead, but Charles Mangold was busy until two. At half past one, Fox was parked outside the New Town headquarters of Mangold Bain. The offices were on the ground floor of a steep-sloping Georgian terrace, looking directly on to Queen Street Gardens. The receptionist smiled and asked him to take a seat. There was a copy of the *Financial Times* on the coffee table, along with the latest property guides and a golfing magazine.

When a taxi drew up outside, Fox got to his feet and watched Mangold get out. His face was reddened by alcohol. As he came inside, he spotted Fox immediately and offered his hand.

'Good weekend, Inspector?'

'I did a lot of reading.'

'Anything interesting?'

'Actually, a bit of a page-turner.'

Mangold seemed satisfied by this answer. 'Coffee, please, Marianne – good and strong,' he barked to the receptionist. Fox shook his head to let her know he wouldn't be needing any. Mangold was already leading the way through the door to the right of reception. They entered what would have been the hallway of a private house at one time. There was an unused fireplace, and a grand staircase leading up. Another door at the foot of the stairs took them into what Fox guessed would have been a sitting room. Fireplace with antique mirror above it; intricate cornicing and ceiling rose. Mangold switched on some lights.

'Marianne said it was urgent,' he began, resting his hand against an electric radiator, then stooping to turn it on. 'Should warm the place up,' he said, rubbing his hands together.

'Good lunch?' Fox inquired. 'New Club, was it?'

'Ondine,' Mangold corrected him.

'The other night ... you were waiting for guests ...?'

'Yes?'

'Did Colin Cardonald happen to be one of them?'

Mangold shook his head. 'Though I did spot him in the club that evening – dozing in his chair with the crossword half-finished.' He checked his watch. 'Did Marianne say?'

'She told me I could only have fifteen minutes.' Fox followed Mangold's lead and seated himself at the polished oval table. 'But that only holds if I'm working for you – which I'm not. I'm a police officer and this is a police matter, which means I take as long as I need.'

There was a knock and the coffee arrived, along with a bottle of water and two glasses. The receptionist asked Mangold if he wanted her to pour.

'Yes please, Marianne.'

They waited until she'd gone, closing the door behind her. Mangold was gulping at the coffee, eyes closed.

'Can't drink like I used to,' he explained. 'And I *do* have a very full afternoon.'

'Then I'll get to the point – two points actually.'

'Fire away.'

'I want to talk to Imogen Vernal.'

'Impossible,' Mangold said with a flutter of one hand. 'Next point, please.'

'If I don't see her, I'll drop off those two box files at the front desk and that's the last you'll hear from me.'

Mangold stared hard at Fox, pushing out his bottom lip. 'What is it you need from her?' he asked.

'What is it *you* think you're protecting her from?'

'I've already told you – she's very sick. I don't want her to be made to feel even less comfortable.' Mangold paused. 'Second point,' he commanded, reaching into his pocket for a voluminous handkerchief.

'Not until we've dealt with the first.'

'It *has* been dealt with,' Mangold stated, wiping around the sides of his mouth.

'I want her take on things,' Fox decided to explain. 'I want to hear her talk about her husband.'

'*I* can tell you about Francis!'

'You weren't married to him, though.'

147

'I knew him as well as Imogen did.'

Fox didn't bother responding to this. Instead, he moved to item two.

'All these groups of the time ... the SRSL, SNLA, Dark Harvest Commando ... I forget the Gaelic one ...'

'Siol Nan Gaidtheal.'

'That's it.'

'Seed of the Gael.'

'How close was Vernal to them? I only know what I've read.'

'Imogen can't help you there. None of those rumours ever reached her.'

'But *you* heard them?'

'Of course.'

'And believed them?'

'I asked Francis a few times. He would just dismiss the suggestion with one of his looks.'

'What's your feeling, though?'

Mangold took a sip of coffee while he considered the question. 'Was he an active paramilitary? No, I doubt that. But there are ways in which he could have helped.'

'Legal advice?'

'Possibly.'

'What else?'

'Money had to be raised, and then kept safe. Frank would have known what to do with it.'

Fox nodded. 'He was their banker?'

'I have absolutely no proof.'

'Would he have kept the money on him?'

Mangold offered a shrug.

'How much are we talking about?'

'Thousands,' Mangold speculated. 'There were a few bank robberies early in the decade; a couple of security-van hold-ups.'

'Claimed by the SNLA?'

'Those were the stories at the time.'

'All the years you worked with him – dodgy visitors ... locked-door meetings ... odd phone calls ...?'

'No more than any other lawyer,' Mangold replied with a lop-sided smile. He stared into the bottom of his cup. 'I really do need to stop drinking at lunchtime. I'll feel bloody awful later on.' He glanced up at Fox. 'Are we finished here, Inspector?'

'Not quite. Did you ever hear names?'

'Names?'

'Members of these various groups.'

'MI5 would know more about that than me.'

'But they're not here right now ...'

Mangold conceded the point and furrowed his brow in thought. 'No, no names,' he said at last.

'Any of Vernal's friends seem a bit out of place?'

'We met all sorts, Inspector. You'd visit a couple of pubs and end up in the company of vagabonds and cut-throats. Never knew if you were going to wake up with a tattoo or an infection – or not wake up at all.'

Fox managed the smile he felt was expected of him. 'How about your own politics, Mr Mangold?'

'Unionist now ...'

'But back then?'

'Broadly the same.'

'Funny you were such good friends with a dyed-in-the-tweed nationalist.' Fox paused. 'Or is that where *Mrs* Vernal comes in?'

'I'd rather she didn't come into it at all,' Mangold said quietly.

'But she must,' Fox insisted, dropping his own voice a little. Mangold looked suddenly tired and defeated. He held up his hands in surrender, then slapped them down against the table.

'I'll see what I can do.' He paused, staring down at his cup again. 'More coffee, I think.'

'Thank you for your time.' Fox started to get up. 'But just re-member – *you* came to me.'

'Yes,' Mangold said, with almost a trace of regret.

'Oh, one other thing ...'

Mangold had risen and was facing Fox.

'Did Alan Carter ever mention the car to you?'

Mangold seemed confused. 'What car?'

'Francis Vernal's Volvo.'

'No, I don't think so – why do you ask?'

'No reason really,' Fox said with a shrug. But inside he was thinking: *What else did he keep from you ... and why?*

Mangold stayed in the room, Fox insisting that he could see himself out. He stopped at the receptionist's desk. She looked up from her work and smiled.

'Marianne, isn't it?' Fox enquired. She added a nod to her smile. 'Something I've always meant to ask Charles and somehow keep forgetting ...'

'Yes?'

'The firm's name – Mangold Bain: is there still a Bain?'

'It was Vernal Mangold,' she explained.

'Ah yes, until poor Francis died ...' He tried his best to sound like one of Mangold's oldest clients. 'You're too young to have known him, of course?'

'Of course,' she agreed, looking slightly put out that he could mistake her for someone of *that* vintage.

'So Mr Bain ...?' he prompted.

'There's never been a Mr Bain. It's a maiden name.'

'Mr Vernal's widow Imogen?' Fox guessed. 'She's a partner of some sort?'

'Not that, no. Mr Mangold meant it as a ... well, a kind of memorial, I suppose.'

'Wouldn't it have been more of a memorial if he'd just kept the name Vernal on the stationery?' Fox asked. Marianne seemed never to have considered this. 'Thanks for your help,' Fox told her, bowing his head slightly and taking his leave.

21

Fox sat at his desk in the Complaints office, staring at the blank screen of his computer. Bob McEwan was taking a phone call. As ever, it seemed to concern the upcoming reorganisation. The Complaints would be swallowed up by 'Standards and Values'. They would go, in the words of McEwan, from 'micro' to 'macro'.

'Just don't ask me what that means.'

Fox had sent texts to both Tony Kaye and Joe Naysmith and was waiting to hear back from them. He had thought about visiting the Central Library, digging into its newspaper archive. He had cuttings from the *Scotsman*, but not from the *Herald* or any other Scottish paper of the time. He doubted he would find anything. The media had soon lost whatever interest it had had in the story.

When the office door opened, Fox saw that the Chief Constable was leading a visitor inside. The Chief's name was Jim Byars. He was in full uniform, peaked cap included, which meant he was on his way to a meeting or else was out to impress someone. The visitor was a man in his late forties with a tanned face, square jaw and greying hair. He wore a three-piece suit and what looked like a silk tie. A handkerchief was visible in his breast pocket.

'Ah, Malcolm,' the Chief Constable said. Then, for the guest's benefit: 'This is Professional Standards – PSU.'

'The "rubber heels"?' the visitor said with a slight smile. His accent was English. The hand he held out for Fox to shake bore no rings. Fox had glanced in McEwan's direction. He could see that his boss was torn. It would be polite to end the call and greet the visitor, but he wanted Byars to know that he was earning his keep.

He gave the Chief a wave, then motioned that he would wrap up the call. Byars' gesture let him know this wasn't necessary.

'Just giving DCI Jackson the tour,' the Chief explained to Fox. Then, to Jackson: 'Malcolm Fox is an inspector – detective rank, but we don't use the term.'

'How's your workload?' Jackson asked Fox.

'Manageable,' Fox replied, wishing he had turned on his computer. His desk looked bare; half an inch of paperwork in the in-tray. Was Jackson something to do with the coming reorganisation? Was he seeking posts that could be cut? He had that look to him – a brisk, hard-nosed bean-counter.

'Working in Fife, aren't you?' the Chief asked, frowning as he realised how stupid the question sounded.

'Not today, sir. Rest of my team are.' Fox swallowed. There was no reason to suppose the Chief Constable would know he'd been kicked into touch. Even if he *did* know, it wasn't the sort of thing you wanted to advertise to a visitor. 'What brings you here?' Fox asked Jackson instead. Byars got in first with the answer.

'DCI Jackson is based at Special Branch – anti-terrorism.'

'Didn't know we had much of that in Edinburgh,' Fox felt obliged to state.

Jackson gave the same brief smile. 'The blast in the forest outside Peebles?' he offered. 'And Lockerbie before that?'

Fox nodded to let him know he'd heard.

'We're thinking they may have been a trial run, Inspector.'

'Why Peebles?'

'Anywhere would have done.' Jackson paused. 'Remember Glasgow Airport? The perpetrators lived quietly in the suburbs.'

'And as Peebles is part of Lothian and Borders,' Byars explained, 'we're assisting DCI Jackson and his team.'

Not quite a bean-counter, then.

Jackson was looking around the office, as if filing every detail of it away. Bob McEwan was trying desperately to wind up his conversation. 'What's happening in Fife?' the Englishman asked.

'Not much,' Fox said.

'CID officer,' Byars told Jackson. 'In court for overstepping the line. We've been asked to check whether his colleagues covered up for him.'

Jackson looked at Fox, and Fox knew what he was thinking: *I'm with you, chum – never give away more than you have to.*

McEwan had ended the call and was coming towards them.

Byars made the fresh round of introductions and explanations.

'Interesting,' McEwan said, folding his arms. 'Never goes away, does it?'

'How do you mean?' Jackson asked him.

'Domestic terrorism. Malcolm's latest case has an angle ...'

'Really?' Jackson sounded suddenly interested.

It had to be Naysmith. Had to be Joe Naysmith who'd let it slip to McEwan.

Fox made show of shrugging it off. 'A very *slight* connection,' he mooted.

But Jackson was not to be deflected. 'As in?' he prompted.

'Someone Malcolm interviewed,' McEwan obliged. 'He was doing some research into a lawyer who got himself involved with Scottish separatists.'

'Quarter of a century back,' Fox stressed.

The Chief Constable looked at Jackson. 'Not quite the same as your Peebleshire bombers.'

'Not quite,' Jackson admitted. His next question was aimed at Fox: 'What happened to the lawyer?'

'Died in a car crash,' Fox stated.

'Unlike the researcher,' McEwan added. '*He* put a revolver to his head.'

'Dearie me,' Jackson said. Then he gave Fox that same unnerving smile again.

When Naysmith called Fox's mobile an hour or so later, Fox was alone in the office, McEwan having left for yet another meeting elsewhere in the building. Before Naysmith could say anything, Fox thanked him for telling McEwan all about Alan Carter and Francis Vernal.

'He just asked me what I was up to,' Naysmith responded.

'Well, thanks anyway. Now we've got Special Branch interested.' Fox went on to explain the circumstances.

'Could be a bonus,' Naysmith argued. 'Can't you ask him if there's anything in the files on Vernal? Whether he really *was* being spied on?'

'You think he'd tell me, even if he knew? This was twenty-odd years ago – reckon the spooks have instant access?'

'Maybe not,' Naysmith conceded. 'But how else are we going to find out if they were keeping tabs on him?'

'We aren't,' Fox said eventually. There was silence on the line for a moment.

'Want to hear what I've got?' Naysmith asked.

'What have you got?'

'Barron's Wrecking.'

'You spoke to him?'

'He's a good age now, but what a memory. When I said as much, he joked that it was because so much of his business was kept off the books. Told me I could grass him up to the taxman if I liked ...'

'But you got round to asking about the car eventually?'

'He remembered it well. Tow-truck brought it in, but it was there hardly any time at all before someone came asking for it to be taken elsewhere.'

'Gavin Willis?' Fox guessed.

'The very same,' Naysmith confirmed. 'They got it as far as the cottage, but it took four of them to push it up the slope into the garage.'

'Did he tell them why he wanted it?'

'I don't think anybody asked. He paid Barron in cash and that was that.'

'And no one came to the scrapyard asking for it?'

'Willis slipped Mr Barron an extra twenty and told him to say it had gone into the crusher.'

'And Barron never bothered asking why?'

'The way he put it was, when a cop tells you to do something, you do it.'

'I'm not sure that's so true these days.' Fox thought for a moment. 'Willis worked the firearms detail,' he informed Naysmith. 'Could have pocketed the revolver that was used on Alan Carter.'

'Why, though?'

'I'm still not sure. Did Barron remember anything else about the car? He didn't swipe anything from it?'

'Nothing he's admitting to.'

'Then that's that,' Fox said, pacing the empty office.

'What do you want me to do next, Malcolm?'

'Gavin Willis – I wouldn't mind knowing how and when he died. Maybe he's got some family left ...'

'I can check.' Naysmith sounded as if he was writing himself a note to that effect.

'Have you seen Tony?' Fox asked.

'Told me he was taking Billie and Bekkah out for coffee.'

'The hairdressers?' Fox stopped by the window. He had a view towards the car park, with Fettes College behind it. The pupils seemed to be heading home, a line of parental cars waiting to collect most of them. 'What's his thinking?'

'Hormonal?' Naysmith guessed.

Fox saw DCI Jackson being escorted to his car by the Chief Constable. Jackson had his own driver; nice executive saloon, too. He got into the back, Byars closing the door for him. As the car pulled away, a window slid down. Jackson was staring up towards the Complaints office. There was no way he could see Fox standing there, but Fox backed away all the same, though he wasn't exactly sure why.

22

Francis Vernal's widow lived in a detached Victorian mansion house in the Grange district of the city. The narrow streets were devoid of traffic and pedestrians. Almost no homes were visible. They remained hidden, like their owners and those owners' wealth, behind high stone walls and solid wooden gates. Charles Mangold had been adamant that Fox could only visit if Mangold accompanied him. Fox had been just as adamant that this was a non-starter. Nevertheless, Mangold was waiting in an idling black taxi as Fox approached the driveway. As Fox got out of the car to announce his arrival at the intercom, Mangold emerged from the back of the cab.

'I have to insist,' the lawyer was saying.

'Insist all you like.'

'What if Imogen wants me there?'

'She can tell me that to my face. But you stay *this* side of the gates until she does.'

Mangold looked furious but said nothing. He spluttered his way back to the taxi, slamming the door after him. Fox told the intercom he had an appointment. The gates swung back on themselves with a motorised hum, and he returned to his car. It was a long, winding driveway, with thick shrubbery to either side. Fox emerged into a gravelled parking area in front of the two-storey gabled house. It was dusk, birds roosting in the well-established trees. He locked his car from habit only. The front door to the house was open, a woman in her thirties standing there. She introduced herself as Eileen Carpenter.

'I look after Mrs Vernal.'

'Her nurse, you mean?'

'And other things besides.'

The hall smelled musty, but had been dusted. Carpenter asked him if he wanted some tea.

'Please,' he answered, following her into the drawing room. It boasted a huge bay window. Imogen Vernal's chair had been placed so that it faced the garden to the side of the property.

'You'll forgive me if I don't get up,' she said. Fox introduced himself and shook her hand. Her ash-blonde hair was thin and wispy, and there were lesions on her cheeks and forehead. Her skin was almost transparent, the veins showing. Fox reckoned she couldn't weigh more than seven and a half stone. But her eyes, though tired, were lively enough, the pupils dilated by recent medication.

There was a dining-room chair to one side of her, and Fox seated himself. A book was open on the floor – a hardback copy of a Charles Dickens novel. Fox presumed one of Eileen Carpenter's tasks was to read to her employer.

'Quite a house,' Fox said.

'Yes.'

'Did you live here with your husband?'

'My parents bought it for us – a wedding gift.'

'Great parents.'

'*Rich* parents,' she corrected him with a smile.

There were framed photographs of her husband on the mantelpiece. One looked familiar: the orator in full flow, fist clenched as he addressed his audience.

'I wish I'd heard him speak,' Fox said truthfully.

'I think I have some recordings.' She paused and raised a finger. 'No,' she corrected herself, 'I donated them to the National Library – along with his books and papers. People have done their PhDs on him, you know. When he died, an American senator wrote an obituary for the *Washington Post*.' She nodded at the memory.

'He was quite a character,' Fox agreed. 'In public.'

Her eyes narrowed a little. 'Charles told me about you, Inspector. Such a pity about the other man, the one who passed away ...' She paused. 'Is Charles outside the gates?'

'Yes.'

'He's very protective.'

'Was he one of your lovers?'

She took her time answering, as if wondering how to respond.

'You make me sound like a Jezebel.' Her voice was becoming more noticeably Scottish.

'It's just that he seems to have a great deal of affection for you.'

'He does,' she agreed.

'And there were always the rumours that your marriage had been stormy.'

'Stormy?' She considered the word. 'Not a bad description.'

'How did the two of you meet?'

'Manning the barricades.'

'Not literally?'

'Almost – a sit-in at the university. I think we were protesting against Vietnam.' She seemed to be thinking back. 'Although it could have been apartheid, or Rhodesia. He was already a lawyer; I was a student. We hit it off ...'

'Despite the age gap?'

'My parents didn't approve at first,' she conceded.

'Was Mr Vernal a nationalist back then?'

'He was a communist in his youth. Then it was the Labour Party. Nationalism came later.'

'You shared his politics?'

She studied him. 'I'm not sure what it is you want from me, Inspector.'

'I just felt we should meet.'

She was still mulling this over when Eileen Carpenter arrived with a tray. The teapot was small, and there was just the one bone-china cup and saucer. It was loose-leaf tea, accompanied by a silver strainer. Fox thanked her. She asked her employer if anything else was needed.

'We're fine, I think,' Imogen Vernal replied. 'You might want to let Charles know.' Then, for Fox's benefit: 'He'll be waiting for her to send him a message.'

A little colour was rising to Carpenter's cheeks as she left the room.

'She's not a spy, exactly,' Imogen Vernal told Fox. 'But Charles *will* keep fussing ...'

Fox poured tea for himself. 'You know why he hired Alan Carter?' he asked.

'To clear up my husband's murder.'

'You're sure in your own mind that it *was* murder?'

'Pretty sure.'

'Did you say as much at the time? I don't recall the newspapers mentioning it.'

'To be quite honest with you, I was a little bit afraid.'

Fox accepted this. 'But all you have are suspicions – no actual evidence?'

'No more than you'll have gleaned,' she conceded, placing her hands on her lap.

'And suicide ...?'

'Not an option: Francis was too much of a coward. It's something I've been thinking about recently. I told them I was coming off the chemo and everything else – it was too, too much. There's morphine for the pain, but you can still feel it, just beyond the cotton wool. Suicide had to be considered, but that particular course of action takes a certain bravery. I'm not brave, and neither was Francis.'

'He wasn't ill, was he?'

'Strong as an ox.'

'Despite the cigarettes?'

'Yes.'

'Had there been a falling-out?'

'No more so than usual.'

'That stormy relationship again?'

'Stormy rather than rocky. Has anyone used the word "firebrand" in connection with him?' She watched as Fox nodded his reply. 'I'd be disappointed had they not – that was Francis, you see: in his life, his work, his politics. He didn't care if you were for him or against him, so long as you had fire in your belly.'

'There's a cairn near where he died ...'

'Charles had it placed there.'

'And the yearly bouquet?'

'From me.'

Fox leaned forward a little. 'Who do you think killed him, Mrs Vernal?'

'I don't know.'

'The period leading up to his death ... had he been worried about anything?'

'No.'

'He thought he was being watched.'

'That pleased him: it meant he was "getting to them".'

'Who?'

'The establishment, I suppose.'

159

'And how was he getting to them?'

'His speeches. His power to change people's minds.'

'The polls suggest he wasn't changing *too* many minds.'

She dismissed this with a toss of her head. 'Everyone he met ... he had an effect on them.'

She paused and watched Fox bring out the photograph of her husband with Chris Fox.

'Do you know this man?' he asked her.

'No.'

'His name's Chris Fox. He died in a motorbike crash, a few years before your husband. It happened near Burntisland.'

She considered this. 'Not so far from where they killed Francis. You think there's a connection?'

'Not really.'

'He shares your surname.'

'He was my father's cousin.'

She looked at him. 'Did he know Francis well?'

'I've no idea.' Fox studied the picture again before returning it to his pocket. He took another sip of tea. 'I've heard break-ins mentioned ...'

'Yes – here and at the office. Two in as many weeks.'

'Reported to the police?'

She nodded. 'No one was ever caught.'

'Was much taken?'

'Money and jewellery.'

'None of your husband's papers?'

'No.'

'Did Francis ever discuss breaking the law himself?'

'How do you mean?' She seemed to be focusing on the view from the window, even though it was now dark and the garden was invisible.

'He was said to be close to certain groups ...'

'He never spoke about it.'

'But it's not exactly news to you?'

'He knew a lot of people, Inspector – I dare say one or two wanted to take the struggle that bit further than the law of the time would allow.'

'And he would have supported that view?'

'Perhaps.'

'Do any names come to mind?'

She shook her head. 'You're thinking,' she said, 'that political friends sometimes turn into foes. But if Francis had enemies – *real* enemies, I mean – he kept them to himself.'

'But you know he supported paramilitary groups? Mr Mangold seems to think you'd no inkling.'

'Charles doesn't know *everything*.'

Fox took another sip of tea and placed the cup and saucer back on the tray. The room was silent for the best part of a minute. He got the feeling that when she was left alone, this was how she sat – calm and still and waiting for death, staring at her reflection in the window, the rest of the world lost somewhere beyond. He was reminded of his father: *I don't sleep ... I just lie here ...*

Eventually, he cleared his throat. 'What do you think he was doing on that particular road?' he asked.

'Politically, you mean?'

He smiled at the error. 'No, the road between Anstruther and St Andrews.'

'It was the weekend,' she said, her voice fading a little. 'He often spent weekends in Fife.'

'On his own?'

'Not with me.'

He knew from her tone what she meant. 'Other women?' he suggested. She gave the slightest of nods. 'Many?'

'I've no idea.'

'He used the weekend house?'

'I suppose so.' She looked down at her lap and brushed something from it, something Fox couldn't see.

'And Anstruther ...?' he prompted, waiting her out. Eventually she gave a sigh and took a deep breath.

'That's where *she* lived.' She fixed him with a stare. 'I was quite a catch when Francis met me, but maybe you know what it's like.'

'A little,' he offered, since she had waited for his response.

'She was a student too. Alice Watts – that was the name.'

'He told you?'

She shook her head. 'Letters from her. Hidden in his office desk. It was months before I came across them – there was so much to be gone through.'

'She lived in Anstruther?'

Imogen Vernal was staring at the window again. 'She was studying politics and philosophy at St Andrews. He gave a talk to the students and she met him afterwards. I suppose you'd call her

161

a groupie.' Her voice dropped almost to a whisper. 'I've not told anyone about her.'

'Charles Mangold?'

She shook her head.

'So Alan Carter wouldn't have known either?'

'I suppose Charles might have known,' she said. 'He was Francis's friend, after all. Men sometimes talk to one another, don't they? When they're out drinking.'

Fox conceded that they did. The temperature in the room had dropped a few degrees – the thick floor-length curtains should be closed and the gas fire turned on.

'I want to thank you for seeing me and for being so open,' Fox said. 'Maybe we can talk again?'

But Vernal's widow wasn't finished with him. 'I went looking for her, you know. I felt I needed to see her – not talk to her, just *see* her. I had her address from the letters. But when I went there, she'd packed up and left. The university told me she'd quit her course.' She paused. 'So I suppose it's just possible she may have loved him.'

'Do you still have those letters, Mrs Vernal?'

She nodded. 'I wondered whether you would ask.' She reached down the side of her chair and produced them, still in their envelopes. They bore neither addresses nor stamps. Hand-delivered, then.

Fox turned them over in his hands without opening them. 'You were prepared,' he stated. 'Why am I the first person you've told?'

She smiled at him. 'You insisted on coming here alone,' she explained. 'You stood up to Charles. That speaks to me of a certain something ... a quality.'

'You know some of the rumours of the time?' he felt able to ask. 'The papers hinted that you'd had a string of lovers, and maybe one of them had ...'

'You don't believe that,' she stated. 'Francis was the only man I loved – and I still do. Goodbye, Inspector. Thank you for coming.' She broke off, and thought of something else. 'You asked me earlier who killed him. In a sense, I think we all did. But if I were to place a wager, I'd say the odds favoured your own kind.'

'Meaning the police?'

'Police, Secret Service – you'll know better than I do. But take heed, Inspector: the man Charles employed ended up dead. You'd best be careful.'

'Why do you think Mangold hired him in the first place?'

'I thought I'd already answered that. Why do *you* think he did?'

'To solve the mystery while you're both still alive to hear it.'

She considered this, then shook her head slowly. 'Perhaps.'

'What other reason?'

'Charles wants me to think less of Francis, so I'll think more of *him*.'

'He wants to prove that your husband consorted with bombers as well as women?'

She gave a thin smile. 'Leading to my deathbed conversion. I recant and clasp Charles to my bosom – metaphorically speaking or otherwise.'

'That sounds unlikely to me.'

'Please don't misunderstand: Charles has been a good friend, loving and loyal.'

'But not as reciprocal as he would like?'

'No.'

'And adding your maiden name to his law firm ...?'

'Part of the wooing,' she agreed. 'Should I feel flattered, do you think?'

Fox had no answer to that. As he left the vast and underfurnished drawing room, he could see her reflection in the window, just as she could see his.

Fox lay in bed that night thinking of Imogen Vernal. She had given up on the chemo, but hadn't given up on life. She still loved her husband. She was loved, in turn, by Charles Mangold. He wondered whether the widow was rich – an inheritance from her parents; money left by her husband – or whether Mangold was paying for Eileen Carpenter and everything else. He thought of his own father, fighting hard against dementia, regular visits from son and daughter, trips to the seafront at Portobello, ice cream on his chin until a handkerchief could be produced ...

The letters from Alice Watts to Francis Vernal were more like essays – lengthy, discursive, political. There were moments of emotion too, but no purple prose, no drawings of hearts pierced by arrows – and no rows of kisses at the end. Fox couldn't tell if Vernal had ever written her letters of his own. It was obvious he was a regular visitor to Anstruther, but the letters were not dated.

Judging by the few contemporary events she mentioned, they had to be from 1984 and '85.

His phone was charging on the bedside cabinet. When it rang, he had to unplug it before answering. It was Evelyn Mills, calling him at eleven p.m.

'Evelyn?'

'Did I wake you?'

'What's up?'

There was silence on the line for a moment. 'Funny, isn't it?' she eventually answered, her voice slightly nasal. 'You coming into my life again. Coming into my life right now, I mean.' Fox realised she had been drinking.

'Things are a bit shaky at home?'

'No ... not really.' She seemed to recall the lateness of the hour. 'I should have waited till morning.'

'It's fine.'

'Freddie's a lovely man, you know.'

'I'm sure he is.'

'If you met him, the two of you would hit it off. Everybody likes Freddie.'

'That's good.'

There was more silence on the line. 'I've forgotten why I was calling you,' she admitted.

'Maybe just for a chat.'

'No, hang on, I remember now. Paul Carter's been talking to Scholes.'

'Oh?'

'He seems scared, and not sure who to trust. He as good as asked Scholes if *he'd* had something to do with the uncle's death.'

'What did Scholes say?'

'Told him he was off his head.'

'They seemed to be talking freely?'

'Nothing to suggest they think there might be a tap.'

'Have you told this to Kaye and Naysmith?'

'Not yet. Should I be giving them the recording?'

'They're the ones on the ground.' He paused. 'Any news from the Alan Carter inquiry?'

'The wheels are turning.'

'How close are they to charging the nephew?'

'Nobody knows if we're even calling it a murder.'

'"The death is being treated as suspicious"?' Fox said, quoting the exact words the media would have been given.

'Advice is being taken from the Procurator Fiscal,' Mills commented. 'Everything all right at your end?'

'Feet up, relaxing.'

'Lucky you.'

'Lucky me,' Fox echoed.

'I should go.'

'Any time you want a chat, Evelyn ...'

'Thanks, Malcolm.' She paused again. 'As you know from bitter experience, a few glasses of wine and my defences begin to crumble.'

'I blame myself.'

'For what?'

'I was the sober one that night.'

'It's not like you took advantage of me.'

'But all the same ...'

She started to sing a slurred snatch of Edith Piaf, then broke into a tired laugh.

'Maybe a glass or two of water before bed,' Fox advised.

'That's what Freddie always says.' The sigh she gave translated into a crackling on the line.

'Good night, Evelyn.'

'Night-night, Malcolm.'

He plugged the phone back into its charger and lay down again, head against the pillow, eyes closed. The bedside lamp was on, but he liked it that way. When he got up in the morning, he would switch it off before opening the curtains. He placed his hands behind his head and opened his eyes to stare at the ceiling. He would drift off to sleep eventually.

He always did.

But first, he had some more thinking to do.

Seven

Seven

23

The morning was blustery. Fox parked on the esplanade and got into the back seat of the car next to his.

'Coffee,' Joe Naysmith said, handing him a takeaway. Fox thanked him and removed the lid. The liquid was tepid but drinkable.

'Keeping our seats warm for us at Fettes?' Tony Kaye asked.

'Little visit yesterday from Special Branch,' Fox informed him. 'They've got their eye on those explosions.'

'Kids with fireworks,' Kaye said. 'I'd bet the house on it. Suits the spooks to act as though it's serious – keeps punters worried and them in their cushy little jobs.'

'Since when did kids put together nail bombs?' Fox countered.

'You saying we've got to start watching out for a tartan jihad?' Kaye rolled his eyes. 'As if we didn't have enough on our plates.'

'Maybe the Dark Harvest Commando are back,' Naysmith added.

'Aye, you and Malcolm should paddle out to Anthrax Island, see if they're digging it up again.' Kaye shook his head slowly.

'But in the meantime ...' Fox prompted.

'Got a call from your pal Mills this morning,' Kaye obliged. 'I was hardly out of the shower – she's a keen one, isn't she?'

'What did she say?'

'A little present would be waiting for us in reception.'

'And?'

Naysmith held up a memory stick. He then reached down and produced his laptop from the floor between his feet. The three men finished their drinks as they listened to the telephone recording. It had been logged at eight ten the previous evening, and the quality was variable.

'That's me just home,' Paul Carter complained. 'Ten hours of questions.'

'Harsh,' Ray Scholes offered.

'Harsh is right. Someone's knifing me in the gonads here.'

'I know.'

'Any ideas?'

'You remember the Shafiqs? I've been wondering if one of the sons maybe held a grudge.'

'That was last year.'

'Well, I've offered it to Cash anyway.'

Naysmith turned in his seat. 'I did a quick check: the Shafiqs own a range of businesses all across Fife.'

Fox nodded and continued listening.

'Your uncle had a few headcases on his books,' Scholes was saying. 'Tosh Garioch, Mel Stuart ...'

'I know them,' Carter said.

'Then you'll know they've both done time. Short-fuse merchants pumped up from bodybuilding and illegal supplements.'

'Uncle Alan had them working as doormen.'

'That's right.'

'And you're thinking they might've had a grievance?'

'Not really,' Scholes eventually admitted.

'CID seem to think the only one around here with a motive is yours truly.'

'I'm doing my best, mate.'

'Look, Ray,' Carter responded, 'I can appreciate you might've thought you were doing me a favour—'

'Let me stop you right there, Paul. No way I had anything to do with this, so let's get that clear in our minds.'

'What about Gary or Mark?' Meaning Michaelson and Haldane.

'You're grasping at the wrong straws.'

'Sounds to me like you think I did it.'

'Nothing's for certain yet – the crime scene might look a bit wonky, but it's suicide until proven otherwise.'

'I didn't kill him, Ray.'

'That's what I'm saying – maybe nobody did.' There was the sound of a door opening and a woman's voice. 'I've got to go, Paul,' Scholes said, sounding relieved rather than apologetic. 'Stay strong, eh?'

'Can I come over?'

'Not tonight, mate.'

'I'm ... sorry. About everything.'

'You'll beat this, Paul – you're Mr Non-Stick, remember?'

'Non-Stick,' Paul Carter echoed, sounding tired and not nearly convinced.

Naysmith closed the laptop. 'End of,' he stated.

'Carter said he was sorry,' Kaye stated. 'Presumably for all the shite he's put Scholes through – including perjuring himself.'

'Bit of detail would have been nice,' Naysmith argued. 'What do you think, Malcolm?'

'He's pretty adamant he didn't top his uncle.'

'Aye,' Kaye retorted, 'like he was adamant in court he didn't do anything to those women.'

'Speaking of which ...' Fox prompted.

'I spoke to Billie and Bekkah again,' Kaye obliged. 'Interesting that Scholes mentioned those two knuckle-draggers: Tosh Garioch happens to be Billie's current squeeze.' Kaye turned in his seat so he was facing Fox. 'It was when you mentioned that Alan Carter's company employed doormen ...'

'You thought you'd see if the two connected?' Fox nodded slowly. 'And they do.'

'Coincidence, eh?' Kaye said with a twitch of the mouth. 'Alan Carter doesn't get on with his nephew ... makes a complaint about him ... nothing much comes of it until Teresa Collins changes her mind and Billie and Bekkah come forward.'

'And Billie's boyfriend,' Naysmith added, 'happens to work for the uncle.'

'So what's your thinking?'

'Bit more digging required,' Kaye answered. 'But I'm just beginning to see a glimmer of light.'

'Paul Carter was set up by his uncle?'

'If so,' Naysmith argued, 'even more reason to hold that grudge.'

'Which puts him back in the frame for the murder.'

'If it *was* murder.' It was Naysmith's turn to twist in his seat so he could make eye contact with Fox. 'What if Alan Carter wanted to get his nephew in even deeper shit? He's already decided to do away with himself. He phones Paul so it'll be on record as the last call he made – knowing Paul will then have some awkward questions to answer.'

171

'Been watching *Midsomer Murders*, Joe?' Kaye asked with a snort.

'It's a scenario,' Fox conceded. Having finished his coffee, he pushed the plastic lid into the crushed cup. 'Have you got anything for me about Gavin Willis?'

'Not yet.'

'You could try asking Alec Robinson.'

'Who's he?'

'The desk sergeant.'

'He looks at me like I've just nicked all his pens,' Naysmith complained.

'Other person who might help is Superintendent Hendryson – he ran the show before Pitkethly was brought in.'

'Steady on, Foxy,' Kaye said. 'The lad'll start thinking he's a proper grown-up detective.'

'How about you, Tony? Enjoying being your own boss?'

'I like it fine.'

'But you're starting to think maybe the case against Paul Carter was flawed?'

'Maybe.'

'Don't be so sure. I had Carter on the phone on Friday, just after they lifted him. He admitted that he'd "pulled a few stunts" down the years.'

'His exact words?'

Fox confirmed as much with a nod.

'Why did he phone you?' Naysmith asked.

'He's not sure who he can trust.'

Kaye seemed to ponder this. 'I was going to try talking to Teresa Collins again,' he confided. 'Neutral territory – maybe a café or a pub. You know she's out of hospital?'

'The shrink gave her the all-clear?'

'All I know is, she's back home.'

'You'll be sure to go easy on her?'

'I can do the empathy thing,' Kaye stated.

'A nation rejoices,' Malcolm Fox said.

The geography of St Andrews defeated Fox.

On paper it looked fine. A road led you into the town, after which there were a couple of main shopping streets parallel to one another. But he had an hour to explore the place on foot, and kept finding new angles. Golf course – yes, there was a golf course, naturally enough. Two beaches, one at either end of it. But there was also a ruined castle. A tower. And tucked between venerable college buildings, he caught glimpses of new architecture: glass and steel. And a harbour – St Andrews had a harbour, too, not far from its sea pool. There were no bathers brave enough today. Cliffs ... with signs warning the unwary, and regular jet-fighters screaming across the sky, reminding him that there was an RAF base not too far away.

Plenty of students seemed perfectly at ease, running around this maze without getting lost. Elderly residents shared relaxed pavement gossip. Smiling tourists sought cream teas, tartan travel rugs and whisky miniatures shaped like golf balls. But having parked his car on what he thought was the main drag, it took Fox several goes to find it again, by which time he was flustered and annoyed with himself. Two main streets: how hard could it be?

He was kicking his heels because, having eventually found the right person at the university, they had then informed him that it might take an hour or two to come up with anything. The assistant in the registry and admissions office had made it sound like Fox only had himself to blame. She had jotted down what details he had – Alice Watts/Politics and Phil/1985.

'Date of birth?'

He'd shaken his head.

'Home address?'

Another shake. 'Term-time, she stayed in Anstruther.'

'Year of entry?'

'I'm not sure. Sorry.'

So there he was, exploring the town and finding himself intrigued by the way its disparate elements somehow didn't drive everyone slightly mad. He compared it to Edinburgh: students, tourists and residents, all finding space and creating the place in their own image. He had passed up an elegant glass box of a restaurant on the seafront for a tuna-melt panini in the café attached to the Byre Theatre. He had jotted down some notes based on his morning conversation with Kaye and Naysmith. He had forgotten to take a contact number from the assistant, so couldn't check whether enough time had elapsed. Buying a newspaper for company, he headed back to her office but she was nowhere to be seen. A young man was there instead. He wore a sleeveless jumper and a bow tie, and asked Fox to take a seat. While Fox skimmed the *Independent*, he was aware of the man studying him surreptitiously. No doubt he had been warned that Fox was a police officer. Whenever Fox tried meeting his stare, he would go back to his computer screen, his fingers busy with keyboard and mouse.

'Sorry,' the female assistant said, entering briskly by the same door as Fox. She returned to her own side of the desk, removing her coat and hanging it on a peg, then patting her hair back into place. 'Took *quite* a bit of digging.' She had been carrying a large brown envelope. As Fox approached the counter, she pulled a few A4 sheets from it.

'This is what we have,' she said.

Alice Watts had been born in Glasgow in March 1965, making her twenty at the time of Vernal's death. She had enrolled at St Andrews in September 1983. There were two passport-sized matriculation photos of her, one from 1983 and the other from '84. She had changed dramatically inside a year – mousy and deferential-looking in the first; tousle-haired and determined in the second. In her first year she had stayed in a hall of residence; by second year she was renting the Anstruther address.

'Bit of a hike,' Fox commented as he read.

'But Anstruther's lovely,' the female assistant argued.

Her home address was a street with a Glasgow postcode. There was a phone number too. Fox flicked to another sheet and saw that it listed her exam passes along with progress reports from relevant members of staff. He would have called these reports 'glowing' to begin with, but then tutors had started to notice that Alice was spending more time 'on demos than essays'. She was 'increasingly active in student politics, to the detriment of her studies'. Fox turned the sheets over, but they were printed on one side only.

'Nothing after second year?' he commented.

'She left.'

'Kicked out?'

The assistant shook her head and pointed to the relevant text. Alice had stopped attending St Andrews altogether. Letters had been sent to her Anstruther address and eventually to her family home. She had responded to none of them. Fox checked the relevant dates. As the widow had said, after Francis Vernal's death, Alice had wanted nothing more to do with her university.

'Never heard from again,' the assistant said. Then, leaning towards Fox and dropping her voice: 'Has she been murdered?'

Fox stared at her and shook his head.

'What then?' Her eyes had widened, eager for details. Her male colleague had stopped typing and was paying close attention.

Fox kept his counsel, holding up the sheets. 'I'm taking these with me,' he informed the assistant. 'All right?'

'The originals need to stay here,' she said, failing to hide her disappointment in him. 'I'll have to make you copies of them.'

'Will that take long?'

'A couple of minutes.'

Fox nodded his satisfaction with this, then noticed that she was holding out her hand, palm upwards.

'It's thirty pence per sheet,' she informed him. 'Unless you have a student card ...'

The Anstruther address was a flat overlooking the harbour. So many day-trippers were queuing at the fish and chip shop, they had spilled out on to the pavement. The woman who lived in the flat was an artist. She offered Fox some herbal tea but little else. She had bought the place from the previous owner, who had died of old age. Yes, it had been a rental property at one time, but she had no details. Mail sometimes arrived for people she'd never heard of, but she just threw it in the bin. She didn't recognise the name Alice Watts, and none of the old tenants had ever paid a visit. Fox made show of admiring her work – the walls were covered in vibrant paintings of fishing boats, harbours and coastlines – and left her to it, but only after she'd pressed a business card on him and informed him that she did commissions.

'I'll bear that in mind,' he said, making good his escape.

He considered a trip to Glasgow – it would take maybe ninety minutes – but made a few calls from his car instead. Eventually someone got back to him from Govan police station. The officer had driven out to the address himself.

'It's an office block,' he informed Fox.

'Offices?' Fox frowned as he stared at Alice Watts's university details. 'How long has it been like that?'

'It was a warehouse until 1982. Renovated in '83.' Nineteen eighty-three: the year Watts had arrived at St Andrews.

'I must have the wrong address.'

'Reckon so,' the officer agreed. 'No housing in that street at all. Far as I can tell, never has been.'

Fox thanked him and ended the call. He tried Alice Watts's home phone number again. The constant tone told him no such number existed. He held the two photos of Alice next to one another. A low sun had broken from behind the clouds, causing him to lower his windscreen visor. Even with the windows closed, he could smell batter and oil from the chippy.

'I've got a gun that shouldn't exist and a student who's vanished without trace,' he explained to the photographs. 'So I have to wonder, Alice – just who the hell are you?'

And where was she now?

24

'Thanks for meeting me,' Tony Kaye said.

The café was in a tired-looking shopping centre next to the bus station, all strip lighting and bargain bins. Teresa Collins had dark rings under her eyes, and he reckoned the stains on her clothes were blood from a few days earlier. He'd actually gone back to her street, sitting in the Mondeo for a time. Smears on her living-room window – blood again. He hadn't gone to see her, though. Instead he had pushed a note through her door with his phone number and request, then waited for her to get back to him.

'I'm starving,' she said, pushing the matted hair out of her eyes. There were faded home-made tattoos on the backs of her hands, and one wrist was bandaged, the other needing nothing more than a large sticking plaster. He pushed the menu towards her.

'Whatever you like,' he said.

She ordered a banana split and a mug of hot chocolate.

'I wanted to apologise about the other day,' he said, once the order had been placed.

'And it's true about Paul Carter? He's been done for murder?'

Kaye nodded, seeing little harm in the lie. 'So he won't be bothering you again.'

'Poor man,' she muttered.

'Paul, you mean?'

She shook her head. 'The one he killed.'

He could see she was itching for a cigarette. The pack was on the table in front of her, and her fingers played with a cheap plastic lighter. But when the dessert arrived, she tucked in. Three sachets of sugar were added to the accompanying drink. There was something almost childlike about the way her face softened as she ate, as though she were remembering past pleasures.

'Good?' he asked.

'Yeah.' But as soon as she'd finished, she asked if they could leave. He paid the bill, leaving his own coffee untouched, and she led him out on to the high street, lighting the needed cigarette and inhaling deeply.

'Where do you want to go?' he asked.

She shrugged and kept walking. They crossed at some lights. He knew they were headed in the vague direction of the football park.

'Town's seen better days,' he speculated.

'Seen worse ones, too.'

'You've always lived here?'

'I went to London once – hated it.'

'How long were you there for?'

'Until the money ran out. Took me nearly three days to hitch home.'

The shops thinned out, many of them looking closed permanently. A few high-rises separated them from the seafront. She walked towards one of them and in through a broken set of doors, stopping at the lift.

'Want to show you something,' she told him. The lift jolted them upwards to the top floor. When they stepped out on to the walkway, the wind hit them hard. She stretched her arms wide, facing the onslaught of air.

'Loved coming here as a kid,' she explained. 'Always expected to be lifted clean off my feet and taken somewhere else.'

Kaye stared at the drop, and felt a moment's giddiness. Instead, he focused on the view across the water towards Edinburgh.

'I had an auntie lived here,' Teresa Collins was saying. 'She wasn't really an auntie, just my mum's pal. I got to stay with her when my dad was home.' She saw that Kaye didn't quite understand. 'He was in the army – lots of time away. When he came back, there was always booze and shagging and then maybe a few slaps.'

'Your mum didn't want you to see it?'

Collins shrugged. 'Either that or she didn't want him starting on *me*.' She paused, fixing him with a look. 'All the places he went ... stories he told ... he never brought me back a present. Not once. Men are right bastards, eh? Never met one that wasn't.'

178

'That makes me a bastard, then.'

She didn't deny it, but tried lighting a fresh cigarette instead. He held his coat open to shelter the lighter's flame.

'Thanks,' she said, leaning over the wall of the walkway, exhaling a stream of smoke.

'What happened to your auntie?' he asked.

'Moved away. Then I heard she'd died.'

'Your mum and dad?'

'Mum had a stroke. Died a year later. No idea where my dad is.'

'Do you want to know?'

She shook her head.

'No man in your life at the moment, Teresa?'

'Now and again,' she admitted. 'But only when I'm short of cash.' The smile was rueful. 'You got any cash to spare?'

'I could lend you twenty.'

She looked at him. 'And why would you do that, Mr Policeman?'

He shrugged, pushing his hands deep into his coat pockets.

'What is it you want?' she asked, struggling to push the hair out of her eyes.

'I'm just curious.' She waited for him to go on. 'You didn't take your original complaint against Paul Carter very far. But then later on you did. What changed your mind?'

'I couldn't let him get away with it.'

'That line sounds rehearsed.'

'So what? I've said it often enough. You think somebody paid me – is that it?'

His eyes narrowed a little. 'Hadn't crossed my mind,' he said quietly.

She turned away from him, wrapping her arms around herself, cigarette tightly held between thumb and forefinger.

'Nobody needed to pay me,' she said. 'I did it because it had to be done.'

'But did you talk to anybody? Is that what you're getting at?' He took a step closer, remembering what she'd said back in the café – *poor man* ... 'Paul's uncle? Alan Carter?'

She was staring up at the sky. The wind had caught her hair again, wrapping it around her face, so that it seemed to be muffling her.

'Alan Carter?' Kaye persisted.

179

She pushed up on to her toes and flung out her arms again. For a second he thought she was going to launch herself into the void. He went as far as stretching out a hand towards her. She had her eyes squeezed shut, a child readying to fly.

'Teresa?' Kaye said. 'All that stuff about Paul Carter – was it true?'

'He deserved what he got,' she recited. 'He's a disgrace to the service.'

Not her words – but Kaye could imagine a fellow officer saying them; or a retired one.

'Can't let him get away with it – wouldn't just be me ... there'd be others.' Her eyes were still closed. 'Deserved what he got.' Kaye's fingers had closed around her thin forearm.

'Let's get you back to the lift,' he said.

'Can't I stay here for a bit?'

'Not on your own, no.' She opened her eyes and looked at him. 'I need you to be safe, Teresa.'

'They all say things like that,' she told him. 'They all want to look after you.' Kaye wondered if it was just the breeze forcing a tear from her eye. 'But they all change,' she said quietly, allowing him to lead her away from the dream of escape.

Joe Naysmith took one look at the desk sergeant and thought better of it. Ever since the Murder Squad had arrived, the man had looked ready to explode. *His* station, *his* fiefdom – not any more. Detectives and uniforms swarmed through reception, toting equipment or with questions and demands. They needed chairs, desks and electrical adaptors for their incident room. They hardly acknowledged him or gave him the time of day.

No, Naysmith doubted he'd get anything from Sergeant Robinson. But that didn't matter: he had another plan. The CID rooms were chaotic, but he found Cheryl Forrester in a corner, watching the activity with excited eyes. She saw him and he gestured towards the corridor. By the time she reached him, he was loading coins into the drinks machine.

'Buy you a can of something?' he offered.

'Sprite,' she said, squeezing closer to him as two detectives jogged past.

'How are you bearing up?' he asked, handing her the chilled drink.

'Great,' she said. 'Do you need me for more questions?'

'Sort of.' He realised they were going to get no peace in the corridor, so led her towards the stairwell. She asked him if he didn't want anything to drink for himself.

'I ran out of change,' he admitted. She smiled and offered him her opened can. He took a sip and handed it back.

'All very mysterious,' she said, studying her surroundings.

'I'm after a favour,' he conceded. 'You won't remember a detective called Gavin Willis?'

'I've heard the name.'

'Died a long time back,' Naysmith told her. 'But presumably you knew Superintendent Hendryson?'

'Of course.' She took a slurp from the rim of the can.

'I was wondering if there was any way of contacting him.'

'He's retired.'

'Does he never look in?'

She shook her head. 'Bit of a hike from Portugal.'

'He moved to Portugal?'

'I think it was his wife's idea. He sends us a postcard now and then – always makes sure to mention how warm the sea is.'

'Someone must have an address, then, eh?'

Forrester stared at him. 'What's this all about?'

'No idea,' he dissembled. 'I'm just running an errand for my boss.'

'I know that feeling.' She paused and tilted her head a little to the side. 'You doing anything this evening?'

'Why?'

'Just thought you could buy me a drink – dinner too, if you like. I might have something for you by then.'

Naysmith thought for a moment. 'I'm not sure, Cheryl.'

'Because you're the Complaints?'

'Yes.'

'But I'm not under investigation, am I?'

'You'll still figure in the final report.'

'So?'

'It's an ethical thing.'

'We'll be eating dinner, that's all. And I'll be giving you the address your boss needs.'

Naysmith pretended to be weighing up the options. 'Okay then,' he told her.

'If you're not too busy.' She was teasing him now.

'Somewhere local?' he guessed.

She shook her head again. 'Smashing wee place in North Queensferry.'

'Why there?'

'It's where I live.'

'Is it now?'

When she broke into a smile, he couldn't help smiling back.

'Yeah,' he said. 'Yeah, why the hell not?'

25

Professor John Martin – JDM to friends and colleagues – lived in a
chic new-build apartment block behind Edinburgh Zoo. Although
the evening temperature had dropped, he was happy to allow Fox
a few moments on the balcony.

'Can you hear them?' he asked.

Fox nodded. Animals: snuffles and bellows and squawks.

'You can smell them sometimes, too,' the professor said. 'Anyone
round here with a garden is prone to pester the zoo for manure.
Amongst other things, it has certain rebarbative qualities.'

'Meaning?'

'Scares domestic cats – stops them crapping in your flower
beds.'

The third-floor flat didn't quite have a view into the zoo itself,
but Fox could see the outline of the Pentland Hills to the south,
and hear the traffic on Corstorphine Road. Professor Martin had
moved indoors again, so Fox followed suit, sliding the door shut.
Classical music was playing, but just barely audible: it sounded
modern and minimalist. The open-plan room boasted a wall of
packed bookshelves and a cream leather suite. An archway led to
a small kitchen of shining chrome and mahogany panelling.

'Nice place,' Fox commented. 'Been here long?'

'Couple of years.' Martin had poured them both drinks – red
wine for him, sparkling water for Fox. 'We downsized when our
offspring flew the nest.' Martin swilled the wine around his glass
and tested it with his nose. 'I admit I'm intrigued – tell me how
you found me.'

Fox gave a shrug which he hoped looked modest. 'I spent the

weekend surfing online: Scottish militancy in the 1980s. Your name kept coming up. When I saw you'd written a book on the subject ...'

'Been out of print for years,' Martin stressed. 'It was my doctoral thesis.'

Fox reckoned that would be about right. Martin could only be in his mid-forties – tall, toned and handsome. Fox had spotted a tennis racquet in the hall, and a photo of Martin with some trophy he'd won. The book had been published in 1992 ...

'Written in the late eighties?' Fox speculated.

'Finished in 1990,' Martin confirmed. 'But you've still not explained how you found me.'

'Your online biography said you taught at Edinburgh University.' Fox gave another shrug. 'But before calling them, I thought I'd try the telephone directory.'

Martin chuckled. 'Easy when you know how.' He raised his glass in a toast. 'But I need to confess, I've probably forgotten a lot of that book. My specialism has shifted in the years since.'

'Scottish politics,' Fox reeled off, 'constitutional procedure, parliament and protocol ...'

Martin offered up another toast.

'Probably a wise move on your part,' Fox concluded. 'Not so many paramilitaries about these days.'

Martin smiled. 'The lesson of Northern Ireland – bring your terrorists into the fold. They end up wearing suits and running the country.'

'Does that hold for Scotland?'

Martin considered this. 'I'm not absolutely sure. The SNP polished up its act, got itself a leader with charisma to fit the rhetoric. Devolution provided a rostrum. No need for grievance.'

'Plenty of grievances in the eighties.'

'And in the seventies,' Martin added. 'With roots stretching back much further.' He paused. 'I'm sure I can find you a spare copy of the magnum opus.'

'I've already ordered one,' Fox confessed.

'Ah, the internet again?'

'I think it's a review copy.'

'That gives it a certain rarity value – my publishers didn't do much in the way of promotion.' Professor Martin paused. 'Is it to do with the bombs?'

'Sir?'

'Peebles and Lockerbie? Surely no one thinks the SNLA and its ilk are back?'

'One of my colleagues asked much the same thing. But I doubt anyone's looking in that direction. It's certainly not the reason I'm here. I want to ask you about Francis Vernal.'

Martin took a sip of wine and was thoughtful. 'A man I wish I'd met,' he eventually commented. 'His speeches read well, but to hear him was something else – a few recordings exist, you know. And some film footage, too.'

Fox gave a nod.

'Has something come to light? Some new evidence?'

'It's more in the way of a personal interest.'

'Not official, then?'

'*Semi*-official, let's say.'

Martin nodded and seemed lost in thought again. 'I had the devil of a job, you know,' he said at last. 'One morning, I got the feeling someone had been in my flat and had taken a look at a few chapters. Then, when the thesis was placed in the university library, someone stole it. It was hardly there a week ...' He shook his head. 'I was almost starting to believe the conspiracy theories.'

'Up until then you'd dismissed them?'

'Francis Vernal was a heavy drinker in a bad marriage. Nobody could be surprised at how things turned out.'

'Did you interview his widow for your book?'

'She wouldn't see me.'

'How did you do your research?'

'In what sense, Inspector?'

The music had finished playing. Martin lifted a tiny white remote-control unit from the coffee table and the same sequence of tunes started again.

'You tried talking to Mrs Vernal – that makes it sound "hands on". So I'm wondering if you managed to talk to any of the actual groups.'

'A few fellow travellers and sympathisers. I wrote to all of them.'

'And?'

'Almost none got back to me, so I tried again – same thing happened.' He paused. 'What has this got to do with Francis Vernal?'

'Wasn't he rumoured to be a banker of sorts for some of the groups?'

'Yes.'

'I'm trying to build up a picture of him.' It was Fox's turn to pause. 'Do you think he took his own life?'

'Either that, or his wife had him killed.'

'Why would she do that?'

'Maybe to protect all her lovers – or because her husband was involved with someone.'

'She says the papers made up all those stories about her being unfaithful.'

Martin's eyebrows lifted a little. 'You've spoken to her?' He sounded intrigued and impressed. Another toast was made, this time with an empty glass. He went into the kitchen for a refill. Fox waited for him to return.

'Did you turn up anything at all linking Vernal to these terrorist groups?' he asked.

'He would doubtless have called them "freedom fighters" – either that or "the resistance".' Martin went back to swirling his wine. 'Anecdotal stuff only,' he eventually admitted. 'People would mention his name. There were minutes of meetings – usually in code, but easy enough to read. I think they often referred to him as "Rumpole".'

'From the TV show?'

'A fellow lawyer, you see.'

Fox nodded his understanding. 'So he attended meetings?'

'Yes.'

'Maybe even *led* those meetings?'

'He was never mentioned as a leader. You've heard of Donald MacIver?'

Fox nodded: another name gleaned from the internet. 'He's in Carstairs these days.' Carstairs: the maximum-security psychiatric facility.

'Which is why I failed to get an interview. MacIver led the Dark Harvest Commando. He almost certainly knew Francis Vernal ...' Martin paused. 'Are you suggesting Vernal was killed by one of the groups he supported?'

'I don't know.'

'Or by some shadowy establishment conspiracy?'

Fox shrugged. 'He reckoned his home and office had been broken into – and his widow confirms it. Maybe he was being watched. And now you've just told me you think people spied on your work, too.'

'It went further, actually: my first publisher went bust; a second decided all of a sudden he didn't want the book. Had to go to a small left-wing press in the end. Pretty slapdash job they made of it too.'

'You're really whetting my appetite,' Fox joked.

'I just hope you didn't pay over the odds for your copy.'

'Worth every penny, I'm sure.'

'No guarantees, Inspector.' Martin leaned back in his chair, arms resting over either wing.

'Any other names?' Fox asked.

'One or two are probably still a bit cracked – living as hermits in the Western Isles and writing anarchist blogs. Most of them probably found that as they got older, they became the sort of person they'd previously despised.'

'The establishment, in other words?'

'These were bright people, in the main.'

'Even the ones scooping up handfuls of anthrax from Gruinard?'

'Even them,' Professor Martin said, sounding sleepy from all the wine. 'It's all changed now, though, hasn't it? Nationalism has entered the mainstream. If you ask me, they'll sweep the next election. A few years from now, we could be living in an independent European democracy. No Queen, no Westminster, no nuclear deterrent. That would have been impossible to predict a scant few years back, never mind quarter of a century.'

'Pretty much what the SNLA and all the others were fighting for,' Fox concurred.

'Pretty much.'

'Is there anyone I could try talking to about all of this, other than psychiatric patients and hermits?'

'Do you know John Elliot?'

'I don't think so.'

'He's on TV all the time. News and current affairs.'

'Never heard of him.'

'He merits a mention in my book.'

'What about Alice Watts?'

'Who?'

Fox repeated the name, but it was clear Professor Martin had never heard of her. Fox showed him the two matriculation photos anyway. Martin blinked a couple of times, as if trying to focus. 'Oh yes,' he said, suddenly animated. 'It's good to have a name for her at last.' He got to his feet quite slowly, but managed to make it

187

to the bookshelves without too much of a detour. Fox went with him, and watched as he plucked out a copy of his own book – *No Mere Parcel of Rogues: How Dissent Turned Violent in Post-War Scotland*.

'Catchy title, incidentally,' Fox commented.

'A misquote from Burns.' Martin had opened the book two thirds of the way through, at a section comprising black-and-white photographs. He pointed to one of these. It filled half a page, and looked to Fox like a CND demo.

'Coulport,' Martin confirmed. 'It was the handling and maintenance depot for Polaris warheads. Every week, a nuclear convoy would set out from there on its way by road to the Royal Ordnance factory near Reading.'

'That's a fair few hundred miles.'

'I know – and by road! An accident ... a hijacking ... It boggles the mind, the risks they took.'

Ten demonstrators had been arrested that particular day: Sunday, 7 April 1985, three weeks before Vernal's death. Martin's finger slid to the photo covering the bottom half of the page.

'Do you see your man?' he asked.

'I see him,' Fox said quietly. This second photo was of a protest outside a police station, inside which, presumably, were the ten 'martyrs'. One man, older than his neighbours, was at the centre of the shot – Francis Vernal. Next to him, in dungarees and a knitted hat, stood Alice Watts. 'Who's that she's linking arms with?' Fox asked. He meant not Vernal, but the man to Alice's left. Tall, with long black hair, a bushy black beard and sunglasses.

'I wish I knew. What did you say the young lady's name was?'

'Alice Watts,' Fox repeated.

'Watts ...' Martin broke into a huge smile. 'Bravo, Inspector – twenty years too late, but bravo anyway.'

'Enlighten me.'

'Another of the code names,' Martin explained. '"Steam".' He was still smiling.

'Steam as in James Watt,' Fox guessed.

'And from James Watt to Alice Watts.'

Fox nodded his agreement that it was entirely feasible. 'Do you still have the notes from the meetings?' he asked.

'I only have my notes of *their* notes – I was shown them; I wasn't allowed to take them away.'

'Shown them by a sympathiser?'

'Quite the opposite, actually. One of the problems with all these splinter groups was that they couldn't *stop* splintering. And when factions fell out, it got as messy as any divorce. I was shown records of the meetings so I could see how amateurish the group had become.'

Fox held up a finger to interrupt the professor's flow. 'Which particular group are we talking about?' he asked.

'The DHC.'

'Dark Harvest Commando?'

Martin nodded. 'They were extreme even by extremist standards – the paramilitary wing of the Scottish Citizen Army. You've already mentioned the anthrax ...'

'And Alice Watts was a member?' Fox studied the photograph again.

'I'd say so, yes.' Martin paused. 'Is that important, Inspector?'

'What if I told you she was also Francis Vernal's lover? And that she disappeared almost immediately after his death?'

The professor was silent for a moment. He closed the book and pressed it to his chest. 'I'd say,' he said softly, 'that a new edition of my book might be in prospect.'

'It gets better,' Fox added. 'Because as far as I can work out, Alice Watts was never alive in the first place ...'

That night, Fox watched TV with the sound muted, and ignored one call from his sister and two from Evelyn Mills. He was wondering what it would be like to live next to a zoo, hearing and smelling the animals without ever seeing them.

And what it would be like to be a student, choosing to live in a small place like Anstruther.

Or work in television news and current affairs.

Or be incarcerated in Carstairs.

Or be suspected of murder.

When the credits rolled, he realised a film had been playing. He couldn't remember the first thing about it.

Jude had sent him a text: *Go see Dad. It's YOUR turn!*

She was right, of course. And it isn't as if you've got anything better to do, Foxy, he told himself.

No Mere Parcel of Rogues ... A misquote from Burns, according to Professor Martin. Fox hadn't studied Burns since his school-days. He reached for his laptop, fount of all knowledge – some of it even dependable. He would look up the line in question. And then maybe he'd also check a couple of names – Donald MacIver; John Elliot.

Bed straight after, he promised himself.

Maybe with the window open an inch or two, allowing in the noises and scents of the night ...

Eight

Eight

26

Fox woke up early and went to see his father. There was a bench in the garden of Lauder Lodge, and Mitch fancied sitting there, so Fox got him wrapped up, and one of the staff provided a travel rug for his legs. But Mitch drew the line at a hat and scarf.

'Any more swaddling and I'll be fit for a pharaoh's tomb.'

The garden's high walls gave protection from the North Sea's gusts. The gardener looked like he'd be checking in as a guest some time soon. He nodded a greeting, then carried on with his work.

'I was never one for gardening,' Mitch told his son.

'Mum had the green fingers,' Fox agreed.

'If I'd had my way, I'd have turned the whole lot into a patio.'

'Remember that time I was hanging from the clothes-rope? It snapped and I bounced off the nearest flagstone.'

'Your mum phoned me from the hospital. Three stitches, was it?'

Fox rubbed at the crown of his head. 'Five,' he corrected his father.

Mitch smiled. 'Know what your mum said when she called? She told me she'd have a job getting the blood out.'

Fox remembered: a striped bath towel wrapped around his head to staunch the wound. He hadn't seen it again afterwards.

Mitch watched as his son tried stifling a yawn. 'Late night?'

'A bit.'

'Business or pleasure?'

'Take a guess.'

'Work's all well and good, Malcolm, but there's got to be more

193

to life. Still, it explains why I haven't seen you in a few days.'

'Jude's been visiting, though?'

'Saturday and Sunday – your absence was noted.'

'I was busy.'

'Not just avoiding us, then?'

'No.' Fox shifted on the bench. 'We always seem to end up fighting, though.'

'You and your sister?' Mitch nodded slowly. 'I think she's annoyed that the money for this place is coming out of your pocket.'

'I don't begrudge it.'

'They've hiked the fees again, though, haven't they?'

'It's not an issue.'

'Maybe Jude thinks it is.'

Fox offered nothing more than a shrug.

'How's Fife?' Mitch asked after a lull.

'I was in St Andrews.'

'Went to a caravan there once – when your mum and me were winching. Had to make sure her dad never found out.' Mitch looked at his son. 'What's so funny?'

'I just don't hear people say "winching" these days.'

'What do they say?'

'Dating, I suppose.' Fox paused. 'Did we ever go to St Andrews? As a family, I mean.'

'Maybe for a day ... Do you think you remember it?'

Fox shook his head. 'I just seem to have forgotten quite a lot.'

'Join the bloody club – I remember that the caravan was pale green, but I couldn't tell you what I had for dinner last night.' Mitch watched his son try to swallow back another yawn.

'I've got pills in the bathroom – you should sneak a few out with you.'

'I might do that,' Fox said, only half-joking.

'Jude was looking through the shoebox again. I don't know if it's for my benefit or hers.'

'Both, maybe.'

'Plenty memories in there. No photos of the caravan, though.' He paused. 'We had some good holidays. Could be that's what Jude's looking for – times when you and her were a team.'

'We're still a team: she visits; I pay the bills.'

'There are other places I could go, you know – places cheaper than this must be. It's no wonder you can't afford a new shirt or tie.'

Fox peered down towards his chest. 'What's wrong with my shirt and tie?'

'You were wearing them last time you were here.'

'Was I? I don't remember.'

His father gave a sudden smile and slapped him on the knee. 'No, me neither – I'm just winding you up.'

'Thanks for that.'

'You're more than welcome.'

They were still smiling when the tea tray arrived.

'By the way,' Mitch said, 'I'm sorry about the other day – teasing you in front of Sandy.'

'Is that what it was: teasing?'

'I could see you were hurt. But we both know you're good at your job.'

'That's not what you were saying, though. You were wondering whether I'm cut out for life outside the Complaints. I've been asking myself the same thing.'

'Well, I'm sorry I said it anyway.'

'Don't worry about it – gives me a bit of ammo next time Jude tells me I'm your favourite.'

'You are, though – you know that.'

Fox looked at his father. 'Do you say the same to Jude when I'm not around?'

'Of course I do.'

'Thought as much.'

When Mitch Fox started to laugh, his son couldn't help but join in.

The three men – Fox, Kaye and Naysmith – convened at their office at HQ. While Naysmith made coffee for all of them, stifling yawns of his own and needing a shave, Kaye told Fox about his meeting with Teresa Collins.

'Thing is,' he concluded, 'if Alan Carter *did* get her to testify against his nephew, we're stuck with the nephew as prime suspect in the murder.'

'And it *is* murder now,' Naysmith confirmed. 'Fiscal's office gave the Murder Squad the nod.'

'When did you hear that?' Kaye asked.

Naysmith hesitated. 'Last night,' he eventually admitted.

'Who's your source, Joe?' Kaye gave a wolfish smile. 'Certain young lady in CID? Keep you out late, did she?'

Naysmith kept his back to his colleagues as he finished making the drinks.

'Billie and Bekkah only knew Alan Carter through Billie's boyfriend, right?' Fox asked Kaye.

'Tosh Garioch,' Kaye confirmed. 'Do I talk to him next?'

'Can't do any harm.'

'Any reason to suppose he'd grass up his boss?'

Fox offered a shrug and took the proffered mug from Naysmith. Accepting his own drink, Kaye made a little kissing sound. Naysmith scowled, but refused to meet his eyes.

'Joe,' Fox said, 'got anything on Gavin Willis for me?'

'Not exactly.' Naysmith eased himself on to his desk, letting his legs hang over the side and placing his coffee next to him. 'Best I could do is a number for Superintendent Hendryson. He lives in Portugal. There's an address, too ...' He brandished a page torn from a notebook.

'And all it cost him was his virtue,' Tony Kaye offered.

'By the way,' Naysmith added, ignoring Kaye, 'Mark Haldane's back from sick leave – effective as from this morning.'

'That means the two of you can have a proper word with him,' Fox said. He had risen from his chair and taken the phone number from Naysmith. 'Portugal, eh?' he commented as he looked at it.

'Portugal,' Joe Naysmith confirmed.

'And you got this from Cheryl Forrester?'

'Yes.'

'Careful there, Joe.'

'No fraternising with the enemy,' Kaye added teasingly.

'She's not the enemy.' Naysmith couldn't help sounding defensive.

'Maybe not now,' Fox cautioned. 'But all the same ...'

Bob McEwan arrived just as Kaye and Naysmith were leaving. 'Off to Fife?' he guessed.

Kaye gestured in Fox's direction. 'How soon till we get our pal back?'

'Not my decision. How near are you to being able to make a comprehensive report?'

'Nobody's admitting anything,' Kaye told him.

McEwan's focus moved to Naysmith. 'Is that true, Joe?'

'Yes, sir.'

'You don't sound too sure.'

'Nobody's admitting anything,' Naysmith echoed. 'And the tap hasn't—' He stopped abruptly, winded by Kaye's elbow finding his kidneys.

'What tap?' McEwan asked quietly.

'We're about to lift it, Bob,' Fox explained, walking towards his boss.

'I didn't authorise any surveillance.'

'It was a Fife call,' Fox stated.

'I should still have been told.'

'Sorry about that.'

McEwan stabbed a finger towards Fox. 'I don't like this, Malcolm.'

'Yes, sir.'

McEwan stared at him hard, then turned his attention back to Kaye and Naysmith. 'Off you go, then.'

Kaye didn't need telling twice, steering Naysmith out of the door ahead of him.

'What's going on, Malcolm?' McEwan asked.

'Nothing.'

'Who's under surveillance?'

'Scholes,' Fox admitted. 'But with Paul Carter a murder suspect, we're pulling it.'

'This is a simple enough procedure: three interviews, three reports.'

'These things have a way of growing, Bob – you know that yourself.'

There was a finger pointing at Fox again. 'A simple enough procedure,' McEwan repeated, laying equal stress on each word. 'If that has somehow changed, I need to know the why and the what – understood?'

'Understood, sir.'

Fox knew he had only to bide his time. The two men settled at their desks and worked in silence. When Fox got up to make more coffee, McEwan refused his offer, which told Fox that he was still in the bad books. Forty-five minutes later, McEwan checked his watch and sighed, making to rise from his chair.

Another planning meeting.

'Got enough to keep you busy?' McEwan asked.

'Always,' Fox replied.

McEwan found the paperwork, but then had to come back

because he'd left his phone charging beside one of the sockets. When he'd left for a second time, Fox got up and went to the doorway, checking that the corridor was empty. He closed the door and returned to his desk, picking up the phone and placing a call to Portugal. When a woman answered, he told her he wanted to speak to Mr Hendryson.

'Is that you, Andrew?'

'My name's Fox – I'm phoning from Edinburgh.'

'Just a minute, then,' she trilled. He could hear her placing the phone on a solid surface and then calling out for her husband.

'Rab! You've a call from the old country!'

It was a few moments before anything happened. Fox was trying to visualise the scene: a view of a mirror-flat blue bay, perhaps. Wooden decking with recliner chairs. The retired superintendent in flip-flops and baggy shorts. Maybe there was a golf course nearby, and an ex-pat golfing buddy called Andrew whose voice sounded a bit like Fox's ...

'Robert Hendryson,' a voice said as the phone was picked up again.

'Mr Hendryson, my name's Malcolm Fox – I'm an Inspector at Lothian and Borders Police.'

'I know who you are.'

'Oh?'

'Pitkethly told me.'

'Did she now?'

'She used to call me a lot when she first took over. Finding her feet, but not always able to locate the key to a cupboard or some requisition form.'

'And she's still in touch?'

'She wanted to let me know about Alan Carter.'

'You knew him, then?'

'A little. He was CID and I wasn't – you'll know yourself there's a tribalism there. Plus Alan was retired before I took over at Kirkcaldy.'

'So what did Superintendent Pitkethly tell you?'

'Just that the Complaints were in town, led by someone called Fox. All that business about Paul Carter ...'

'You'd have known him better than his uncle,' Fox stated.

'Paul could be a handful, Inspector. But he got results – and I never heard a bad word about him until I was nearly retired.'

'But when the allegation was made, did you ever doubt his innocence?'

'Innocent until proven guilty,' Hendryson recited. Then: 'Is that what this is about?' He considered for a moment, and answered his own question. 'Of course it is. You want to know if CID really did cover up for Paul. Maybe you think it went beyond CID – the whole station, eh?'

'Not at all, sir.'

'I don't need to speak to you, you know.' The voice was growing irritated. 'I can put the phone down right now.'

Fox waited for Hendryson to draw breath. When he did, Fox uttered a name and waited again.

'What?' Hendryson said, bemused by the switch.

'Gavin Willis,' Fox repeated. 'I was wondering what you could tell me about him. Nothing to be afraid of – he's been dead for years.'

'Why do you want to know?'

'Simple curiosity. Alan Carter is dead, and the two of them seem to have been very close.'

'What has any of that got to do with the Complaints?'

'It's a fair question, sir. Paul Carter's looking a likely candidate for his uncle's murder. I happen to be in a minority – I don't think he did it. So I'm trying to build up a picture of Alan Carter's life, hoping it might help me understand why he died.'

Hendryson spent some time mulling this over. 'Yes,' he said at last, 'I can see that. The thing is, I barely knew the man, and never as a serving officer.'

'How, then?'

'There were get-togethers sometimes – reunions, I suppose you'd say, though it might just be a few drinks one night after work.'

'What was he like?'

'A big, no-nonsense guy – the sort of cop we used to treasure. Knew everyone in the town, and if something happened he'd have a pretty good instinct who was to blame. Graffiti on a wall or a stone through a window ... more likely than not, justice would be dispensed on the spot.'

Fox thought of a phrase Alan Carter had used: *the backlands, where things tend to get fixed on the quiet* ... 'A slap around the ear?' he guessed.

'As and when needed – and no bleeding-heart liberals to cry foul. We'd be better off if that was still the case.'

199

'Is that why you emigrated?'

'Wife wanted a bit of sun on her face,' Hendryson explained. 'But you have to admit, policing's got a lot harder.'

'We're more accountable,' Fox countered.

'Being the Complaints, you'd think that a good thing, of course.'

Fox didn't want to get into an argument, so instead he asked how close Willis had been to Alan Carter.

'Like teacher and star pupil. From the minute Alan joined CID, Gavin was there to see him right.'

'Did they work together on the Francis Vernal case?'

Hendryson took a moment to place the name. 'The lawyer? Smashed his car and topped himself?'

'That's the one.'

'What case are we talking about?'

'I just meant the crash site ... collecting evidence and what have you.'

'I've no idea.'

'Did you know anything about the deceased's car?'

'What is there to know?'

'Willis seems to have salvaged it from the scrapyard. It's been sitting in his garage all these years.'

'News to me, Inspector.'

'Now that I've told you, what do you think?'

'I'm retired – I don't think anything.'

'Bit of luck, wasn't it, sir? You leaving the force just as all this was about to break.'

'All what? Paul Carter, you mean?'

'For starters. Alan Carter came to you, and you decided to take it to your own Complaints people ...'

'Yes?'

'No thought of brushing it under the carpet?'

'Alan wouldn't hear of it. He wanted an inquiry.'

'Or?'

'Or he'd talk to the newspapers.'

'Even so, the local Complaints didn't get very far, did they?'

'Not until that woman changed her mind.'

'Teresa Collins?'

'Yes.'

'Why do you think she decided to speak up?'

'I've no idea.'

'Alan Carter can't have been too happy when the original investigation drew a blank.'

There was silence on the line, interrupted only by a crackle of static.

'Is there anything else?' Hendryson's voice eventually responded.

'When did Gavin Willis die?'

'Nineteen eighty-six. Towards the end of January. Keeled over in the street one day. Heart attack.'

'And Alan Carter snapped up the cottage?'

'What if he did?' Hendryson waited, but Fox had no answer worth giving. 'Are we done here?'

'Just you go and enjoy the sunshine while you still can,' Fox told the man, ending the conversation.

27

He had parked his Volvo on the street outside the police station. Sergeant Alec Robinson looked to left and right as he crossed the car park, and craned his neck to make sure there were no witnesses at the windows. He got into the passenger seat without ceremony.

'Drive,' he ordered.

Fox did as he was told. When they'd left the police station behind, Robinson relaxed a little. He was wearing a force-issue outerwear jacket over his uniform – not quite mufti, but as close as he could get.

'Thanks for this,' Fox acknowledged. Robinson shrugged off the show of gratitude.

'I'm not going to shit on my own kind,' he warned.

'I'm not asking you to. I'm just trying to find out a bit more about Gavin Willis. In police terms, Sergeant, you're as close to Methuselah as I'm going to get.'

Robinson looked at him. 'Not exactly buttering me up, are you?'

'Would you appreciate it if I did?' Fox watched as Robinson shook his head. 'What rank did you have, back in the mid-eighties?'

Robinson thought for a second. 'Constable,' he answered.

'So you wouldn't have had many dealings with CID?'

'Not many.'

'Probably didn't know Willis and Alan Carter too well?'

'There were times we worked together – door-to-door enquiries; scouring the area for a missing person ...'

'And nights in the pub, eh?'

'Not just nights – not back then.'

202

Fox nodded his agreement. 'Lunchtime sessions? They were being phased out by the time I signed on the line.'

Robinson was looking at him. 'How long have you been in the Complaints?'

'A few years.'

'You like it?'

'Maybe I want to make sure the force is on the side of the angels.'

'That's the answer you always give?'

Fox smiled. 'I change the wording a bit.'

'But is it the whole truth?'

'I'm not sure.' Fox paused, checking to left and right as they stopped at a junction. 'I'm also not convinced Paul Carter killed his uncle.'

'Then who did?'

'That's what I'd like to know. Got any ideas yourself?'

'How does Gavin Willis fit into it?'

'Willis and Alan were pals as well as colleagues. Alan obviously doted on the man – to the extent of buying his house when he died.' Fox glanced at Robinson. 'We found Francis Vernal's car tucked away in a garage next to the cottage.'

'Oh, aye?'

'Have you any notion why Willis would have hung on to it, let everyone think it had been scrapped?'

Robinson shook his head.

'Or why Alan Carter would have left it there?'

Another shake of the head.

'It's a mystery, then,' Fox seemed to concede. 'But here's something else – the gun used to kill Alan Carter was part of a police haul that should have been destroyed back in the eighties, when Gavin Willis was on the detail.'

'Oh, aye?' Robinson repeated.

'You knew both men – *and* you know Alan's nephew. There's something I'm not seeing here, and I was hoping you could help.'

'Gavin Willis was a tough customer,' Robinson admitted.

'That much I sense.'

'A rule-breaker too, from time to time.'

'But back then that was the norm, more or less.'

'I suppose it was. People were scared of Gavin Willis – but only if they deserved to be. If you kept your nose clean, there was no reason for him to be interested in you.'

'He was Alan Carter's mentor – you think some of that rubbed off?'

'Alan was a different generation. He wasn't just some sort of replica.'

'But there were similarities?' Fox thought for a moment. 'So maybe he made enemies?'

'In the force and out of it.'

'You mean his security firm?'

'There was a bit of trouble with the Shafiqs last year.'

'Scholes seems keen on reminding everyone about that. I also know Alan Carter hired people for their brawn rather than their brain.'

'If a fight breaks out in a club, college degrees aren't the first thing you reach for. Alan Carter knew that. He joined the force straight from school, same as me. We learned on the job, Inspector, not from textbooks.'

'Did Willis ever get into any trouble? Disciplinary hearings, that sort of thing?'

Robinson shook his head

'What about Alan Carter?'

'Nothing. Paul, on the other hand ...'

'A loose cannon from a family of cops – therefore protected.'

'Ray Scholes kept him in the right – out of respect for his dad and uncle.' Robinson had shifted a little in his seat, the better to face Malcolm Fox. 'You really think Paul didn't do it?'

'I'm fighting the tide on that one.'

'And your theory is that it all somehow ties to Gavin Willis?'

'Maybe – if Gavin Willis saved that revolver from the furnace.'

'And Francis Vernal ...?'

'I don't know what happened there – either lazy policing or pressure from upstairs. But the case should have been investigated and wasn't.'

'I doubt Gavin Willis would have reacted well if someone had told him to drop it.'

'Maybe that's why he hung on to the car – evidence on its way to being destroyed.'

'But then he didn't do anything with it.'

'And neither did Alan Carter – but Alan kept it there under the tarpaulin anyway.'

'Nineteen eighty-five, Inspector – long time back. You really think you're going to make progress now?'

'Would anyone care if I didn't?'

Robinson shook his head again. 'But they might if you *did*.' He peered through the windscreen. 'You can drop me here, I'll walk the rest.'

'You sure?'

'Better that than the pair of us being seen together.'

Fox signalled and drew to a stop by the side of the road. Robinson undid his seat belt and got out. Fox thought he might have some parting words – a helpful sentence or two – but he just closed the door and marched away, zipping up his jacket. Fox drummed his fingers against the steering wheel.

You're nowhere, he told himself. When his phone rang, he answered it with a half-hearted 'Yes?'

'Sounds like you've already heard,' Evelyn Mills said.

'Heard what?'

'My boss has ordered us to pull the surveillance. I tried fighting your corner, but with Paul Carter looking like a murder suspect …'

'Surveillance could jeopardise any trial,' Fox said, finishing the argument for her.

'Sorry, Malcolm.'

'To be honest, my own boss would have pulled it anyway.'

'You eventually owned up?'

'Someone let it slip.'

'Pissing him off in the process. Well, we gave it our best shot.'

'And I'm grateful.'

'Then you can buy me dinner some time.' She waited, but Fox stayed silent. 'To be honest, Malcolm, the tap was getting us nowhere anyway.'

'Just that one call?'

'A second one this morning – arranging a drink together tonight.'

'Carter and Scholes?'

'And the other two.'

'Haldane and Michaelson?'

'Yes.'

'Whose idea was that?'

'Paul Carter's. I think he wants reassurance that he still has a few pals. Sounded to me like the pressure's getting to him.'

'What did Scholes say?'

'He sounded pretty reluctant, but Carter kept on at him.' She paused. 'Is it important?'

'First time the four of them will have been together since the trial.'

'That we know of.'

'That we know of,' he agreed.

'You wouldn't mind being a fly on the wall?'

'Are you saying you'd steer clear?'

She gave a little laugh. 'Would it really matter what I said?'

'Where are they meeting?'

'The Wheatsheaf, at eight o'clock. Mind you don't bump into anyone from the Murder Squad.'

'Thanks, Evelyn.'

'I tried calling you last night, Malcolm ...'

'I must've been asleep.'

'Not giving me the brush-off, then?'

'No.'

'Are you sure about that?'

He assured her he was, then ended the call, punched in Tony Kaye's number and waited. When Kaye picked up, Fox asked him if he was in the middle of something.

'Wee chat with Tosh Garioch.'

'Is he giving you anything?'

'I doubt he'd give me the smell from his farts – no, tell a lie: in that one respect he's being more than generous.'

'Paul Carter's taking his mates out for a drink tonight.'

'All of them?'

'All of them.'

'How do you know?'

'It's the last thing we'll glean from the phone tap.'

'You reckon we should be there?'

'Pub's called the Wheatsheaf – why don't you check it out, see if there's any chance of us blending in.'

'They know all our faces.'

'There's always the dressing-up box.'

'Hat and scarf and a pair of glasses?' Kaye sounded doubtful.

'Joe's always been in the background – you and me have done all the talking.'

'True.'

'One guy standing at the bar ... who's to know?'

'Joe might have plans for tonight.'

'Nothing he can't cancel.'

Kaye seemed to be thinking it through. 'Can't do any harm to give the place the once-over. Soon as I've finished with Garioch.'

'Thanks, Tony.'

'Listen, one last thing ...'

'Yes?'

'Your pal Evelyn Mills.'

'What about her?'

'She phoned me. I got the feeling she was after some gen on you – relationship status and such.'

'Thanks for letting me know.'

'I'm not trying to put you off or anything – quite the opposite.'

'She's married, Tony.'

'Not always a bad thing, Malcolm.'

'I'm putting the phone down now.' He could hear Kaye chuckling as he ended the call.

Fox started driving again, not really sure where he was headed. Not for the first five minutes anyway, after which he realised he was on the Kinghorn road. He passed the filling station where Paul Carter had been spotted on the night of the murder. Signalling right, the Volvo climbed the gradient, coming to a stop at the door to the cottage. The field was empty; no vans or patrol cars. With the incident room set up in Kirkcaldy, the team had finished with Gallowhill Cottage, but not before boarding up the window of the living room to deter gawpers. Fox got out and checked, but the door was padlocked and there was no key beneath the flowerpot on the windowsill. He walked to the garage – judging by the outline under the tarpaulin, Francis Vernal's car was still there. He was starting down the slope again when he heard another vehicle approaching. Paul Carter parked his silver Astra directly behind the Volvo, blocking Fox in.

'What are you doing here?' Carter asked, slamming shut his driver's-side door.

'Just came for a look,' was all Fox could come up with.

Carter said nothing to this. He took some keys from his pocket, selected one and undid the padlock, kicking open the door.

'This all yours now?' Fox asked.

'Until they do me for his murder,' Paul Carter muttered. 'Nobody's found a will yet, and I'm next of kin.' He walked inside, and Fox followed.

'So what happens to your uncle's company?'

'Goes to the wall, I'm guessing – he's the only one that can sign cheques.' Carter was looking around the hallway. 'Hell am I supposed to do with all this?'

'There are companies who clear houses,' Fox offered.

'Bonfire might be a better bet. I could be back inside any day.'

'Sheriff Cardonald's still deliberating?'

'Bastard's taking his time.'

'Are you surprised he let you out?'

'Been better for me if he hadn't.' Carter walked into the living room. 'Place has been given a good going-over,' he commented.

'They took my prints,' Fox admitted.

'And mine.'

Fox was studying Carter's face. If he *had* killed his uncle, would it show as he stood here? Would images from the night flash before him? He looked flustered and fearful, but without remorse or obvious guilt. Fox noticed that the table had been cleared – every scrap of paper had been bagged and removed by the inquiry team. No one, however, had washed the fine spray of blood from the window. Carter opened a drawer – it, too, had been emptied of paperwork; all those neatly kept household bills and bank statements. Carter slid it shut again and stood in the middle of the room, running a hand through his hair, scratching at his scalp.

'When was the last time you were here?' Fox asked.

'Night he died – after Ray phoned me. He wanted to be the one to break the news.'

'And before that?'

'Months ... maybe a year.'

'He said you came here drunk one day, spouting off about stuff.'

'I was in court, remember?' Carter muttered. 'I heard it from his own lips.'

'But he wasn't lying?'

'I was off my tits; no idea what I said or didn't say.'

'But would that have been the last time you were here?'

'Yes.'

'When he made the accusation, you didn't come back here to ask him why?'

'What good was that going to do me?'

'So why do you think he phoned you the evening he died?'

'No idea.'

'He hadn't spoken to you since the trial?'

Carter shook his head. He walked over to the wall next to the fireplace and ran a hand down the uneven wallpaper. 'Did all this himself, you know. Top to bottom. My dad used to say he was cack-handed.' He found a join in the paper and slid a finger underneath, tearing it. 'Cack-handed's just about right.'

Without uttering another word, he left the room and started climbing the stairs. After a few moments, Fox followed. There were three rooms in the eaves – two bedrooms and a bathroom.

'Look at this,' Carter said. He was showing how wallpaper, badly fitted to the ceiling in the main bedroom, was falling off. Then he knocked against a skirting board with the heel of his shoe, showing that nails were missing. The door didn't close properly, and the knob was loose.

'Cack-handed,' he repeated.

Fox saw cracks in the plasterwork, badly fitted windows, loose floorboards. Some of the cupboards were open, showing that Alan Carter's wife had not bothered taking all her clothes with her when she left him. Had he kept them in the hope that she might come back? And then, after her death, to keep her memory alive? In the bathroom, tiles were missing from the shower, and the bath looked antiquated. Both of the handbasin's taps dripped. Fox tried not to linger on the dead man's toiletries: his wet-razor, denture cream, nail scissors.

'What would *you* do with the place?' Carter asked.

'Same thing your uncle presumably did when he got hold of it – rip it up and start again.'

'When he first bought it, my dad dragged me along a few times. Dad found it hilarious, the way Uncle Alan thought he was tarting the place up, when he was actually making it worse ...' Carter seemed caught for a moment in the memory, but shook it away. 'Maybe I should torch the place and collect on any insurance.'

'Are you sure you should be telling me that?'

Carter managed a smile. He looked washed-out – the interviews had taken their toll; maybe the whispers and stares around town had too.

'Thing is, I liked him when I was a kid – and I thought he liked me.'

'I forget, what was his wife called?'

'Aunt Jessica – you always had to get it right. If you tried "Jess" or "Jessie", she'd be quick to correct you. Turned out she'd been seeing someone behind Uncle Alan's back, and that was the end of that.'

'Did you really make your parents' lives a misery?'

'Plenty of nippers do.'

'But after you'd stopped being a nipper?'

Carter shrugged and moved from the bathroom to the small spare bedroom. This was used for storage, boxes and suitcases piled high.

'Bonfire,' he muttered again, before turning towards Fox. 'I wasn't so different from anyone else. If he told you I was some sort of monster, he was lying.'

'He grassed you up,' Fox stated quietly.

'Then maybe *he's* the monster – you ever considered that?'

'I have, actually.'

Paul Carter had not expected this. He studied Fox, eyes unblinking. Fox noted a slight nervous tremor just below one eye. Carter, conscious of it, pressed a finger to the flesh, as if this would cure it.

'Know what they do to cops in jail?' he asked quietly, before answering his own question. 'Course you do – you put cops away all the time.'

'Just the ones that deserve it.'

'You think *I* deserve it?' Carter's voice was rising. 'For asking one sad wee slut for half an hour of her oh-so-precious time?'

'Why did the other two women come forward?'

Carter banged the heel of one hand against the wall. The whole building seemed to shudder. 'I don't know!' he cried out. 'She must have told them to!'

'She didn't know them.'

'I never did anything to those two – never even tried!' This time he took a swipe at the wall with his foot, cracking the plaster.

'Remember, this is your place now,' Fox cautioned.

'I don't *want* it!' Carter ran his hand across his head again. 'I'm sick of all this. I want my life back. Any minute now, that judge could make his mind up, or Cash could charge me with murder. Some choices, eh?' He looked at Fox. 'But what's the point of telling you? You don't give a damn.'

He shouldered Fox aside and descended the stairs two steps at a time. Fox waited a moment before following. By the time he reached the hallway, Carter had started the Astra's engine and was making an awkward three-point turn. From the doorway, Fox watched the car head down the hill. The padlock hung loose. It wouldn't lock without the key. Paul Carter hadn't been bothered about that – the cottage was just another weight dragging him down. Fox closed the door as best he could, got into his own car and started the long journey home to Edinburgh.

The day's post, waiting for him inside his front door, included the copy of *No Mere Parcel of Rogues*. It was scuffed, and the section of photos had come loose, but it was still serviceable. Fox skimmed it for an hour or so. Professor Martin was sparing with names. Fox jotted a few down anyway. Then, just before the index, he saw a note stating that the names were fictitious – 'changed to protect the subjects'.

'Thanks a bunch,' Fox said.

He went back to the paperwork Charles Mangold had given him. There were trial reports from the early eighties, and this time the names would be real. There were photographs, too – taken at police stations after the suspects had been arrested. A few bruised faces, cuts on lips and noses, swollen eyes.

Donald MacIver merited a few mentions, along with John Elliot. Wikipedia had a whole page on the broadcaster. When Fox saw his photograph, he realised that he had seen him present the Scottish news a few times. His Wikipedia entry stated that he had been involved in 'fringe politics' as a student, and had faced trial for plotting the hijacking of a government minister's car. Fox compared photos – yes, the newscaster and the radical student were one and the same. The hair had been longer back then, the clothes scruffier and the skin sallower. Fox wouldn't have called the twenty-year-old Elliot handsome, but promotional shots of him these days showed a chiselled chin, gleaming eyes, and a healthy glow, the hair immaculate, the teeth pearly and the shirt crisp. Elliot employed a management company, and could be hired for 'corporate and charity functions'. Fox noted the phone number, got up to stretch his spine, and went to make some tea.

When six o'clock came, he turned on the TV, but it was someone else presenting the day's headlines. He went back to his desk for an hour, phoned his sister to tell her he'd visited Lauder Lodge, got into the usual argument with her, then ate a tin of tuna mashed with mayonnaise and mustard.

At half past eight, his phone rang. It was Tony Kaye.

'Tell me,' Fox said.

'They clocked him,' Kaye growled, meaning Joe Naysmith had not been able to blend in at the Wheatsheaf.

Fox exhaled slowly and noisily. 'Did he get *anything*?'

'Place wasn't exactly mobbed, but they were at a table and he had to stick by the bar – a good eight or ten feet away.'

'So what happened?'

'He says it was Haldane. Kept staring, then said something to the others. Scholes comes storming over and tells Joe to sod off. After that, there's silence in the bar – everybody knows who Joe is, and Joe knows he's going to get hee-haw ...'

'It was a long shot,' Fox conceded.

'I blame Joe, though.'

'Can I assume he's listening in?'

'We're in the Mondeo, fifty yards downhill from the pub.'

'Any point tailing them?'

'Not if we can't hear anything they're saying,' Tony Kaye suggested.

'Okay, then. Might as well get yourselves home – and thank Joe for trying.'

'Foxy says thanks for nothing,' Fox heard Kaye tell the hapless Naysmith.

'You're a cruel man, Tony Kaye.'

'Cruel but fair, I think you'll find.'

Fox wished his colleague good night.

Nine

28

John Elliot was filming a piece for later in the day. The up side was, Fox didn't need to drive into the centre of Glasgow. The downside: he was on a trading estate on the outskirts. For some reason, a modern black slab of a hotel had been placed there, and Elliot's crew had taken over the restaurant. Bemused guests were eating breakfast in the bar area while lights were repositioned, cameras slotted into place on their tripods.

'It's guerrilla stuff,' the segment's director told Fox. Fox had been provided with a little cafetière and a couple of miniature *pains au chocolat*. Elliot was being attended by a make-up woman in a corner of the restaurant. There was a large illuminated mirror, and something resembling a toolbox, but filled with cosmetic products rather than wrenches.

'Mad business,' Elliot commented to Fox, meeting his eyes in the mirror. His hair was being combed into place, his nose and forehead checked for sheen, a paper towel protecting his shirt collar from smudges. His eyes glittered, and Fox wondered if drops had been applied. He was dressed in an open-necked shirt, black cotton jacket, and faded denims, frayed at the bottom.

'I appreciate you seeing me at short notice.'

'When I'm done here, we'll have about fifteen minutes. After that, I have to be back in the studio.'

The director had arrived at Elliot's side. He was holding a script and looking stressed.

'Chef says the lobster's claws are taped shut, so there's no danger,' he was explaining.

'The glamour of television,' Elliot said, meeting Fox's eyes again and sand-blasting him with a smile.

There was a rehearsal, after which it took three takes to get the piece right. Then there were cutaways and changes of angle and lighting and other stuff Fox didn't quite understand. An hour and a half after starting, they had their three minutes of screen time. Elliot was rubbing a wet-wipe across his face as he crossed the room towards Fox. The gear was being packed away, tables and chairs returned to their original positions. One guest, a middle-aged woman, intercepted Elliot and asked him to sign her copy of the breakfast menu.

'A pleasure,' he said. A small tremor seemed to pass through her as she watched him write.

'Get a lot of that?' Fox asked when he was eventually able to shake the presenter's hand.

'Better a fan than the abuse I'd get on Sauchiehall Street after closing time. Let's sit here.' Elliot nodded towards a banquette in the open-plan bar. 'So,' he said, slapping his palms against his knees, 'my nefarious past catches up with me ...'

'It's no secret, is it?'

'My whole life is public property, Inspector.'

A waiter came over to ask if they needed anything. Elliot ordered mint tea, then changed his mind to sparkling water. Fox was nursing half a cup of lukewarm coffee.

'Are you still interested in politics?' he asked when the waiter had retreated.

'The question is: was I ever?'

'You nearly went to prison ...'

Elliot nodded slowly. 'But even so. How much of it was posture? I mean, students back then ... we didn't always think too clearly about the reasoning.'

'What was it, then – a way to pick up the opposite sex?'

Elliot gave a lopsided smile. 'Maybe.' He wriggled in his seat, making himself more comfortable. 'That court case ... it was ridiculous really. We were made to look like the mujahideen, but we were just kids playing games.' His eyes widened slightly, perhaps hoping Fox would share his incredulity. 'Hijack a government car? Hold the minister to ransom?' He shook his head. 'The ransom, incidentally, consisting of a referendum on Scottish self-government – how hare-brained is that?'

'You doubt it would have worked?'

'Of course it wouldn't have worked! People were *laughing* at us during the trial – they'd sit in the public gallery and their shoulders would be heaving as we explained the tactics. The prosecution went on about "planning", but as we pointed out, this amounted to a couple of nights in the pub and a few doodles on the back of a napkin.'

'Might explain why none of you went to jail.'

'Our university didn't even bother kicking us out – *that's* how seriously everyone took it.'

'Might be different today,' Fox commented.

'Almost certainly.'

'Stirling was your university?' Elliot nodded, then thanked the waiter as his water arrived. There was a bill with it, but the presenter pointed the waiter in the direction of one of the crew.

'Ever see any of your old gang?' Fox asked.

'Hardly ever.'

'None of them still active?'

'*Active?* You mean plotting the overthrow of the state? No, none of them are still "active".' He sipped the water, stifling a belch. 'We were young and foolish, Inspector.'

'Is that what you really think?'

'You've got me pegged as some sort of sleeper agent?'

Fox returned Elliot's smile. 'Not at all. But you're a public figure – it's good PR to play down a militant past, maybe make light of it, turn it into an after-dinner routine ...'

'That's probably true.'

'And they were very different times.'

'They were.'

'Plus, as far as I can tell, the Dark Harvest Commando had a seriousness of purpose. If you'd just been along for a laugh, I doubt they'd have tolerated you.'

Elliot's face darkened a little. 'The DHC was too much for me,' he confided.

'You went to a few of their meetings, though?'

'A few.'

'So you knew Donald MacIver?'

'Poor Donald. They got him eventually, even managed to have him certified after he attacked another prisoner. He's in Carstairs now.'

'Ever thought of visiting him?'

'No.' Elliot seemed surprised by the question.

'He must have been close to Francis Vernal, though ...'

'I can't believe anyone's finally paying attention to that,' Elliot said.

'In what way?'

'We all knew Francis had been assassinated – MI5 had him on their hit list. When he died, nobody seemed bothered – no police investigation, almost nothing in the papers ...' He took another sip of water. 'But it did the job all right.'

'How do you mean?'

'A lot of the groups got the message and disbanded. They didn't want to end up like Francis.'

'How well did you know him?'

'I didn't.'

'You never met him at meetings?'

'I was in the same room as him a few times, but I was a foot soldier. He was at the top table.'

'He was the money man, wasn't he?'

'Another reason the groups fell apart – when Francis went, the cash went with him. It wasn't as though anyone used bank accounts. We didn't have a chequebook with Dark Harvest Commando on it.'

'I suppose not.'

Elliot remembered something. 'There was one meeting where things got a bit heated. Hawkeye needed money for something. Francis went outside and came back in with a wedge of fivers and tenners.'

'Where was this?'

'A pub in Glasgow – we used the back room sometimes. Spit and sawdust and patriot songs ...'

'The money must have been in Vernal's car, then?'

'I suppose so.'

The car saved from the scrapyard by Gavin Willis. Had he taken it back to his garage to strip it? If so, how had he known about the money? And if there was money to be found, what did he do with it?

And why hang on to the car ...?

'Who's Hawkeye?' Fox thought to ask.

Elliot offered a shrug. 'Never knew his real name. He wasn't normally the type to attend meetings – everyone was a bit scared of Hawkeye.'

'Oh?'

'He definitely wasn't just playing at radicalism. Two or three armed robberies, I'm pretty sure he was responsible. The members liked to talk about Hawkeye when he wasn't there – he was our Robin Hood. Liked his explosives, too.'

'The bombs sent to Downing Street and Parliament?'

'More than likely.'

'Why the name Hawkeye?'

'No idea.' Elliot had finished his water. The equipment had been packed away, the crew heading for their vans. 'I need to go,' he apologised. 'You really think you can get to the truth after all this time?'

'I'm not sure.'

'Reckon anyone out there really wants to hear it, Inspector?'

Fox didn't bother answering this. He reached into his pocket instead and produced Professor Martin's book. 'Ever seen this?' he asked.

'I've heard of it,' Elliot stated, taking it from Fox and flipping through its pages.

'You've never wanted to read it?'

'Archaeology doesn't interest me.'

Fox took the book back from him, found the photo of Vernal and Alice Watts outside the police station and held it open for Elliot to see.

'Do you remember her?' he asked.

'No.'

'You don't recognise her from the meetings?'

Elliot shook his head. 'Is it important?'

'She seems to have had some sort of relationship with Mr Vernal – I'd like to talk to her about it.'

'I wish I could help.'

'Her name back then was Alice Watts ...'

Elliot tried to place it but failed. 'Back then?' he prompted.

Fox didn't say anything, but when he went to close the book, Elliot took it from, him, still open at the photograph. 'Seventh of April 1985 ...'

'Were you there that day?'

'In a manner of speaking: I was one of the ones they arrested. But we were out again by late evening.'

'But you don't recall seeing Alice Watts?'

Elliot shook his head again. 'Nice to see Hawkeye again, though.' He turned the book towards Fox. 'That's him there, arm in arm with the young lady.' Fox took the book back and studied the photo again. The man Professor Martin hadn't known, the one with long hair, beard and sunglasses.

'You're sure?'

'Fairly sure.' One of the production runners was standing in front of them, hugging her clipboard to her chest and tapping at an imaginary watch on her wrist.

'I really have to go,' Elliot apologised to Fox.

'Can you give me anything else on Hawkeye?'

'Afraid not.'

'A first name? His accent?' Fox was trying not to sound desperate.

'Scottish,' was all Elliot said, rising to his feet. And there was that smile again, the one that told the world John Elliot had moved on, that he lived for the present and not the past.

'Can we talk again?' Fox proposed.

'I really don't have anything more to say.'

'I might have more questions.'

Elliot stretched out his arms, underlining that he'd told Fox as much as he could.

'You're the first terrorist I've ever met,' Fox told him.

'I hope I've lived up to expectations.' Elliot's voice had hardened.

'We're out hunting bombers right now – wonder if they'll be hosting TV shows in a few years.'

'You'll excuse me.' He turned away and started to follow the assistant. Fox was only a step or two behind him.

'Did your side win?' he asked.

Elliot paused and seemed to give the question some consideration. The assistant started to say something, but he silenced her with a gesture.

'We're closer than ever to an independent Scotland,' he told Fox. 'Maybe that process started when the government in London *had* to acknowledge our existence.'

'Sounds to me like you've still got a few political bones left in your body, Mr Elliot.'

'I'm not allowed to take sides, Inspector.'

'Bad for the public image?'

The assistant was actually tugging at Elliot's arm. With a slight bow of the head in Fox's direction, he allowed himself to be led away to the waiting van.

Fox's phone rang. He was staring at the photograph as he answered.

'Paul Carter's dead,' Tony Kaye's voice informed him.

'What?'

'Happened some time last night. They pulled him from the harbour early this morning.'

'Drowned?'

'Body's gone for autopsy.'

'Christ on a bike, Tony ...'

'Quite so.'

'Do we know anything else?'

'Not much.'

Fox was remembering his last meeting with Carter. Remembering, too, that Joe Naysmith had seen him even more recently.

'The Wheatsheaf,' Fox commented.

'Suppose I better let someone know we were there.'

'When I saw him at the cottage, he seemed pretty wrung out.'

'Suicidal, though? I wouldn't have said he was the type.'

'Me neither.'

'You know, Malcolm, just for once I'd like a nice clear-cut death.'

'Are you in Kirkcaldy?'

'Station's a bit subdued.'

'Does the incident room know?'

'Yep.'

'What about Scholes?'

'Haven't seen any of that lot yet.'

'You better talk to DI Cash. Let him know about last night.'

'Okay.'

'Will the autopsy be at the hospital?'

'Far as I know.'

'Then I'll see you there.'

'Cash might not like it.'

'Mood I'm in, that'll suit me fine.'

'Just so long as I can have a seat ringside,' Tony Kaye said.

'Bring a pair of white gloves and I'll make you referee.' Fox ended the call and headed out to his car.

29

'Always in the basement,' Joe Naysmith commented as they walked along the windowless corridor. All three were rubbing anti-bacterial foam into their hands. 'Path labs, autopsy suites ...'

'You want them in the car park?' Tony Kaye shot back. 'So everyone can see the cadavers?'

'Time was,' Fox stated, 'the public liked a post-mortem exam.'

'That's because the public, as we all know, are sick and twisted.' Kaye pushed open another set of doors and almost wished he hadn't.

'Well, well,' DI Cash drawled. 'The gang's all here. Come to check out your handiwork?' He turned towards DS Brendan Young. 'Nothing the rubber heels like better than hounding a man to his death.'

'While all you were doing was accusing him of murder,' Fox countered. 'How long did the questioning go on – nine, ten hours at a stretch?'

Cash stabbed a finger towards Fox. 'I seem to remember sending *you* to the wilderness.'

'And I was quite happy there, but we've got a bit of news we need to share.'

Cash slid his hands into his pockets and went up on his toes. 'This'll be good,' he told Young.

'First we need to hear what the autopsy says.'

'Join the queue,' Young muttered, checking the time on his phone.

On cue, the door marked 'Examination Suite' swung open. The pathologist was suited and booted and looked impatient.

'How many of you want to watch? We only have three sets of scrubs.'

Naysmith looked relieved to hear it. Kaye stared dolefully at Fox, knowing rank was about to be pulled on him. Five minutes later, Fox, Cash and Young were inside, listening to the hum of the extractor fan and the pathologist chivvying his assistant.

'We're a man down, but it can't be helped,' he told Cash. Fox knew that Scots law required corroboration – meaning two pathologists should have been present. 'We can always put him in the fridge until tomorrow ...?'

But Cash shook his head. 'Let's get on with it.'

Paul Carter was laid out on the metal table. Water was still seeping from him, being diverted to the table's drainage channels and from there into pails beneath. Fox could see that Carter's face was swollen. There was a brackish smell in the small, already claustrophobic room. Maybe he'd misjudged this: Fox hadn't been present at many autopsies; he was hoping he wouldn't keel over. Nor was Brendan Young looking too comfortable. The pathologist spoke into a microphone as the examination got under way. He pushed down on the chest, expelling a gurgling stream of water from the corpse's mouth. Fox's own mouth was dry, his heart pounding in his ears. The body had probably been in the water eight to ten hours, putting time of death at somewhere between eleven p.m. and one a.m. Core temperature was tested, and the eyeballs checked. Once the Y-incision had been made and the ribcage prised open, the pathologist was able to examine the contents of the lungs.

'No doubt in my mind that he drowned,' he said. 'Whether he fell in or jumped ...' He made a gesture that could have been a shrug.

As the examination continued, organs removed and weighed, Brendan Young shuffled back until he was resting against the wall, eyes all but closed. Fox stood his ground, though he was concentrating with his ears rather than his eyes.

'Nose is broken,' the pathologist said, almost to himself, as he peered closely at the face.

'Maybe the body took a pounding against the sea wall,' Cash offered.

'Not much wind last night ... doubtful there was enough of a swell to cause an injury like that.' The pathologist moved to Carter's hands and arms. 'Tissue on the knuckles is scraped ... Same goes for the tips of the fingers.'

'He was in a fight?' Fox speculated.

'Or fell to the ground. Put his hands down instinctively and grazed them.' Eventually, the stomach was opened.

'Smell that?' the pathologist asked, turning his attention to his audience.

'Booze,' Cash said.

'Lager, I think. And spirits of some kind.' The man bent down over the body and sniffed. 'Whisky.'

'So he's drunk and he goes walking down by the harbour.'

'It's one scenario. Another would be a tussle of some kind.'

'But he was alive when he went in the water?' Fox asked.

'Almost definitely,' the pathologist stated.

Quarter of an hour later, they had taken off the protective clothing, splashed water on their hands and faces and were back in the corridor, leaving the pathologist and his assistant to finish up.

'Spit it out,' Cash told Fox. An unfortunate choice of words, since DS Young had just spent several minutes bent over the sink, attempting to hack some residual taste from the back of his throat. He looked pale and was still perspiring. When Naysmith offered him a stick of gum, he snatched at it.

'Carter had a meeting in a local bar last night,' Fox said. 'But before I tell you who with, I want a promise that me and my team won't be kept out in the cold.'

'No promises,' Cash said.

Fox took his time considering this. He even turned his head to make eye contact with Kaye.

'I need to know what *you* know first,' Cash went on, his tone softening a little.

'The meeting was with Scholes, Haldane and Michaelson,' Fox conceded.

Cash slid his hands into his pockets again. The habit was beginning to annoy Fox. It was as if the detective inspector had learned most of his moves from old gangster films.

'How do you know that?' he asked.

'We sent Naysmith in to eavesdrop.'

'And how did you know about the meeting in the first place?'

'Does it matter? The thing is, the four of them were out together last night. You're going to want to talk to them, and I want to hear what they've got to say.'

Cash was looking at Naysmith. 'What sort of time?'

'It was just before eight when they sat down with their drinks,' Naysmith obliged.

'And when did they leave?'

Naysmith looked towards Tony Kaye for help.

'They clocked him,' Kaye told Cash. 'By ten past the hour, we were on our way.'

Cash didn't say anything for a few moments, happy to bask in the Complaints' inefficiency.

'So your undercover surveillance lasted a maximum of fifteen minutes?' He turned his attention to Fox and offered a gloating smile.

'All right, you've had your fun,' Fox said coldly. 'The thing is, they'll know what sort of state Paul Carter was in, and what time the session broke up.'

'That they will,' Cash acknowledged with a nod.

'So we need to talk to them.'

Cash stared at him. 'No promises, remember?'

Fox had had enough. He got right into Cash's face. 'One thing you're forgetting – my report goes straight to *your* Chief Constable. That report's already going to make pretty interesting reading. The whole reason we're here is so your boss can show everyone how spick and span everything is. Last thing he wants is the media getting wind that obstacles were put in our way. Names will be named, Detective Inspector Cash.' Fox paused. 'I never did catch your first name. Better spell it out for me, just to be on the safe side.'

Cash made Fox wait – which was fine by Fox. He knew the man would climb down eventually. Eventually he held his hands up in a show of surrender.

'Cooperation has always been my byword,' he said with a humourless half-smile. 'We're all on the same side after all, aren't we?'

Fox maintained eye contact, their faces only inches apart.

'Duly noted,' he told the CID man.

There was further news waiting for them at the station – news that changed everything. Cash mulled it over and decided he wanted all three of Paul Carter's colleagues in the same room at the same time. The interview room was too cramped, so he cleared the CID office. DS Young had been sent to fetch Scholes, Haldane and Michaelson.

'We've got recording equipment,' Fox told Cash. The DI nodded his agreement and Joe Naysmith started setting everything up: video as well as audio. The three others – Cash, Fox and Kaye – started moving desks, making a decent-sized space. Eight chairs were needed: five facing three. Phones rang but went unanswered. Cash wiped sweat from his forehead with a voluminous white handkerchief.

'You three,' he explained to Fox, 'are here to listen.'

'Until advised otherwise,' Fox agreed.

The door opened and four figures trooped in. Haldane and Michaelson looked dazed, Scholes wary. DS Young pointed towards the three chairs.

'What is this?' Scholes asked.

'Got a few questions for you,' Cash stated.

Scholes took in the three Complaints officers and nodded his understanding. 'Next time you try a stunt like that,' he said, eyes on Fox but gesturing towards Naysmith, 'use someone old enough not to be asked for proof of age by the landlord.'

The colour rose to Joe Naysmith's cheeks as he checked the gear. Scholes had turned to his colleagues.

'It's because we were out with him last night,' he told them. Then he sat down. There was silence in the room, until Naysmith said, 'Okay.' Cash took a deep breath and folded his arms.

'It's pretty grim, all of this,' he said. 'Sorry you've lost a friend ...'

Scholes grunted a response.

'As you say, you were out with him last night ...'

'Few jars at the Wheatsheaf,' Michaelson stated.

'What time was that?'

'We left the back of nine, maybe half past.'

Cash kept his attention on Scholes, whether or not he was the one to answer. 'What were the four of you talking about?'

'This and that.'

'His uncle's death?'

'For a bit.'

'You all left the Wheatsheaf together?'

There wasn't an immediate answer. Haldane glanced in Scholes's direction.

'Yes, DS Haldane?' Cash prompted him.

'We'd had a few words,' Scholes admitted, pre-empting his colleague. 'Bit unsettling to find you're being tailed.' He gave Naysmith a hard stare. 'Paul was on his high horse about it.'

'And after a few drinks, he did have a bit of a temper.'

'It wasn't that,' Haldane blurted out. 'It was just such a bloody headache listening to him drone on.'

'Droning on, was he?'

'The Complaints, the court case hanging over him, then his uncle and the finger of blame.'

'Poor bastard was cracking up,' Scholes commented.

'So you had words in the pub?' Cash asked.

Scholes nodded. 'We left him to it.'

'He was still there?'

'*We* had work the next day.'

Cash nodded slowly. 'I gave the manager a bell. He reckons it was close to eleven when DC Carter staggered out of there. Manager guesses he'd had about six pints and three nips by then.' He paused, unfolding his arms and pressing his hands together. 'So how do you think he ended up in the water?'

'Does it matter?' Scholes glared at Cash. 'Makes your job that bit easier, doesn't it, now he's not here to fight his corner. Pin his uncle's murder on him; case closed. No trial necessary ... all nice and tidy.'

'Ah, but that's just what it isn't.' Cash waited for his words to sink in.

'How do you mean?' Michaelson eventually asked.

'We had a phone call earlier. Member of the public happened to be out walking his dog last night. He saw a man down on the beach. He was being chased by another man. First guy wasn't screaming or shouting or anything. Just running as best he could.' Cash broke off, waiting for a reaction.

'What makes you think it was Paul?' Scholes eventually asked.

Cash shrugged. 'Just that the witness saw him run into the sea. His only chance of getting away. Onlooker took them for a couple of drunks having a laugh.' He looked down at his lap. 'We're not long back from the autopsy. DC Carter somehow ended up with a broken nose and grazes on his hands ...'

'Wait a minute,' Haldane said, voice unsteady. He had gripped the arms of his chair and was starting to rise to his feet.

'Sit down,' Cash said.

Scholes placed a hand on Haldane's shoulder, and Haldane lowered himself back on to the chair.

'What's this got to do with us?' Scholes asked.

'You tell me.'

'I will, then – the answer is: nothing. We left Paul in the pub, went back to our cars and drove home.'

'You weren't over the limit?'

'Of course not. We're the law, aren't we?'

'And you went your separate ways – meaning none of you can vouch for the others, unless you have psychic powers.'

Michaelson snorted and shook his head. 'This is fucking unbelievable,' he announced, pointing a finger at Fox. 'That lot'll stop at nothing to see us flushed down the pan.'

'Your wife will vouch that you were home before ten?' Cash asked.

'Absolutely.'

'How about you, DS Haldane?'

'I went round to my mum's. Left her place just after eleven.'

'Night owl, is she?'

'She nodded off for a bit; the news does that to her ...'

Cash nodded. 'Which brings us to you, DI Scholes.'

'I really can't believe I'm hearing this.' Scholes looked calm enough, but he only just had his emotions under control. When he spoke, it was as if his voice was trying to rid itself of a straitjacket. 'Paul was our *mate*. Now you're saying one of us smacked him? You're saying he was so scared of us, he ran into the *sea*?' Scholes actually laughed, arching his head back.

'I'm waiting,' Cash said, sounding as if he had all the time in the world.

Scholes stopped laughing. 'You might as well lock me in the cells,' he stated. 'All I did was drive to Milnathort to see my girlfriend. She was out, so I came back to town. Didn't see or speak to anyone.' He stared at Cash. 'So I must've done it, mustn't I?'

'Only if you can't think of anybody else. DC Carter couldn't have been the most popular character in Kirkcaldy.'

Scholes seemed to give this some thought. 'You're right,' he conceded. 'And here I am in a room with the people who probably hated him the most.' He pressed his hands together in imitation of Cash and leaned in towards him. 'Going to charge me, or what?'

'Don't give them the satisfaction, Ray,' Michaelson said.

'This interview is over.' Cash got to his feet, checked the time and announced it out loud for the benefit of the recording. Scholes remained seated, eyes on Malcolm Fox.

'I'm sorry about Paul,' Fox told him.

'Fat lot of good *that* does anybody,' Scholes replied.

30

'What about a line-up?' Tony Kaye asked Cash, once Scholes, Michaelson and Haldane had departed. 'Maybe the witness got a good look.'

'That's not the message we received,' DS Young countered. 'Just two figures. He only marked them out as male because of their size and the way they moved.'

'So we're only guessing that Paul Carter was the one being chased?' Fox added.

Cash gave him a look. 'Muddying the water seems to be your particular party trick, Fox.'

'I call it "keeping an open mind".'

Cash turned back to Brendan Young. 'Let's bring the witness in anyway. Need to get a proper statement from him.'

'If Carter ran into the water and drowned,' Joe Naysmith speculated, 'what's the charge?'

'Might not be one,' Cash acknowledged. 'On the other hand, if he got himself in a fight, realised he couldn't win and legged it ...'

'And the assailant,' Young continued, 'gave chase, putting the fear of God into him ...'

'Then that assailant's guilty of something,' Kaye determined.

'That'll be for *us* to decide,' Cash cautioned. 'Meaning CID – not the Complaints.' He turned his attention back to Fox. 'So you and your merry band of fuck-ups can bugger off back across the Forth.'

'Can't do that,' Fox responded. 'Not until your Chief Constable tells us that's what he wants us to do.'

'*You're* not even supposed to be here!' Cash jabbed a finger into Fox's unyielding chest.

'We handed you those three on a plate.'

'Am I supposed to kiss your feet for that?'

'A simple "thank you" would suffice.'

'Six,' Young broke in. 'You handed us six on a plate.'

'That's right,' Cash said with a nod. 'I forgot you three were there last night.'

'Just Naysmith and me,' Kaye corrected him.

'That true?' Cash asked Fox.

'I was at home in Edinburgh.'

'Anyone with you?'

'No.'

Cash turned his attention towards Kaye and Naysmith. 'Then we'll start with the two of you.' He walked over to the video camera. 'How does this work, son?'

Naysmith looked to Fox for instruction.

'You've made your point, Cash,' Fox stated.

'The hell I have: this has got to be done by the book. Don't tell me the Complaints wouldn't agree. There's a local copper lying on a slab, and here I am with two witnesses who saw him the night he died.' Cash gestured towards DS Young. 'Know how to operate this thing, Brendan?'

'Can't be that hard,' Young suggested.

Cash turned back towards Fox. 'You still here? I might have to make a complaint, Inspector.'

Fox looked ready to stand his ground, but Kaye gave a jerk of the head towards the door.

'I'll be outside,' Fox said to nobody in particular.

'Best place for you,' Brendan Young muttered in reply.

Fox sat in his car for a while, drumming his fingers against the steering wheel and staring out of the windscreen without really seeing anything. He tried the radio but couldn't find a station he liked. There were no messages on his phone. Eventually he got out and paced the car park. He thought of Paul Carter, lying in the chill gloom of the mortuary, his last moments filled with fear and flight. Then he pictured Alan Carter, seated at his desk in Gallowhill Cottage – quite relaxed, unafraid of whoever stood behind him.

Unafraid or unaware.

Francis Vernal had driven off the road, or been shunted off it.

Shot while he was driving, maybe? It would have taken a marksman – but marksmen could be found.

Fox's last memory of Paul Carter alive: running from the cottage to his car. *I'm sick of all this ... I want my life back ...*

'Me too, pal,' Fox muttered, lifting his phone to check the incoming message.

Start the engine – we're blowing this joint!

He had just reached the station's rear door as it swung open. Kaye led the way, Joe Naysmith behind him.

'Well?' Fox asked.

'He pissed us about as long as he felt able to,' Kaye reported. 'Not sure he *quite* bought Joe's story, but then neither did I.'

'I drove to North Queensferry,' Naysmith explained to Fox.

'To see his squeeze,' Kaye added.

'Did Cash ask for her name?' Fox watched Naysmith shake his head. 'That's just as well. We can't go giving him any more ammo. Any second now, the bosses are going to decide we're more trouble than we're worth.'

'Home sweet home,' Kaye answered, rubbing his hands together. 'I can't wait.'

'We were given a job,' Fox reminded him.

Kaye rolled his eyes. 'From which you quickly absconded, dusting off the history books instead.'

'I was kicked into touch, remember?'

'Thing is, Malcolm, you're so happy there, I'd swear you'd fallen on a team of pompom girls.'

Naysmith smiled at the image. After a moment, so did Fox. Eventually Kaye joined in too.

'What if I show you?' Fox suggested.

'Show me?'

'Joe's been there; it's right and proper you should see it too.'

Naysmith nodded his understanding. 'How many cars?' he asked Fox.

'Just the one should do it. And mine seems to be closest.'

Indeed it was: he'd parked it in Superintendent Pitkethly's bay again.

The door was still unlocked; didn't look as if anyone had been there since Fox's last visit.

'So who gets it?' Kaye asked, as practical as ever. He was examining the cottage like a prospective buyer.

'Paul Carter seems to be the only family,' Fox answered, pushing open the door.

'I'd have the Land Rover,' Joe Naysmith added. 'Rather that than the house.'

'Can you imagine being shown round?' Kaye was following Fox into the living room. 'The selling agent trying to avoid the obvious ...'

'Should we even be in here?' Naysmith asked. 'It's still a crime scene, isn't it?'

'One that's been picked clean,' Fox reassured him. He was studying Tony Kaye. For all his faults, Kaye had a true cop's instinct. Fox wasn't expecting revelations: he was hoping Kaye might reinforce a few theories he himself had.

'Alan Carter was seated here,' he explained, touching the back of the solid wooden chair. Paperwork in front of him – everything he'd discovered about Francis Vernal's death.'

'Everything? You sure about that, Malcolm?'

'Everything we know about.'

'He let his killer in?'

'According to Carter's best friend, the door was usually kept locked.'

'No signs of a break-in?'

Fox shook his head.

'Someone he knew then – which brings us back to the nephew.'

'The papers had been moved – swept to the floor.'

'Deceased could have done that himself,' Kaye commented. 'Annoyed about something ... fit of temper.'

Naysmith was resting his backside against the arm of Alan Carter's fireside chair. 'Why leave the dog?' he asked.

'Good question,' Kaye replied with a nod. 'An animal-loving assassin?'

'There was no grievance against the dog,' Fox said.

'As far as they were concerned,' Naysmith added, 'Alan Carter *had* to die.'

Kaye gave a grunt that sounded like agreement. 'So what had he turned up?' he asked Fox.

'The Vernal case, you mean?' Fox considered his answer. 'Not a whole lot, as far as I can see.'

'That might be a dead end, then – and we're back to the nephew again.'

Kaye did a circuit of the room, opening drawers, studying ornaments, even crouching down in front of the fireplace and peering at the ash and dead cinders in the grate. He got to his feet, sniffed, and made for the kitchen, after which all three men climbed the stairs to the upper floor.

'Cottage used to belong to Gavin Willis,' Fox recited. 'Willis was Alan Carter's mentor – seasoned DI to his L-plate DC. When Willis died, Carter bought the place and practised his lack of DIY skills on it.'

'Should've stuck to the day job,' Kaye agreed.

'When Paul Carter was young, his dad brought him here – Uncle Alan said he didn't need any help.'

'He was lying,' Kaye stated.

'Bit of replastering ... new wallpaper ...'

Kaye looked at Fox. 'You think he was looking for something?'

'Money went missing when Vernal died – a few thousand.'

'Cash? That would make a hell of a bump in any patch of wallpaper.'

'Maybe it wasn't money, then,' Fox speculated.

Kaye had caught on by now: he knew Fox was using him as a sounding board, and acknowledged as much with a wink.

'The car?' Joe Naysmith asked. 'Much better hiding place.'

'Yes,' Fox agreed.

'But the car was in the garage, right?' Kaye said. 'So why tear the cottage to pieces?'

'Maybe Alan Carter didn't know about the car,' Naysmith replied. 'Not straight off.'

'Maybe,' Fox conceded.

'You want to come back here with some tools and start stripping the place?' Kaye offered. He watched Fox shake his head. 'Because you think if anything *was* here, Alan Carter found it?'

This time Fox shrugged.

Kaye took another of his little tours, opening drawers and cupboard doors. 'We're all cops here,' he commented. 'Where would *we* hide something?'

'In full view?' Naysmith suggested.

'That might actually work, so long as it was the likes of Cash and his stooge looking for it. How about you, Foxy?'

'Under the mattress ... maybe a loose floorboard ...'

Kaye stared at him. 'At least Joe's got a bit of imagination.'

'There are acres of farmland and hundreds of trees out there. Could be anywhere.'

Kaye considered this. 'Seems to me Paul Carter's still the obvious candidate.' He paused. 'Can we go home now?'

Fox met his colleague's stare. 'I'd like it if you took a look at the garage first,' he requested.

'And *then* we can go home?'

'Maybe,' Fox hedged.

The key to the garage's padlock was back on its hook in the kitchen. It seemed that nobody from CID had been particularly interested in the rusting wreck. Naysmith and Fox removed the tarpaulin while Kaye looked at the tools and paint cans on the cobwebbed shelves.

'Removed from the crash site before anyone could really examine it,' Fox stated.

'Willis went to the scrapyard personally,' Naysmith added. 'Had them bring it here.'

'So?' Kaye brushed dust from his palms.

'All we really know about Willis is he was old-school, he was close to Alan Carter, and he maybe pocketed firearms instead of getting rid of them.'

'None of which ties him to Francis Vernal.'

'Except that Vernal had links to radical groups, and those radical groups had weapons.'

'What do we have on the gun that killed the lawyer?'

'Next to nothing,' Fox conceded.

Kaye folded his arms. 'Okay,' he said, 'give me the wildest fucking conspiracy theory you can come up with.'

Fox hesitated for only a moment. 'Spooks,' he said. 'Vernal was being followed, office and home broken into. His friends in the Dark Harvest Commando were scaring the powers-that-be.'

'They assassinated him? Why?'

'He was a threat?' Naysmith offered.

'Was he, though?' Kaye asked Fox.

Fox considered the question. 'At most, he handled the money. Nobody seems to think he led any group.'

'Then who did?'

'Donald MacIver.'

'Have you spoken to him?'

'He's in Carstairs.' Fox paused. 'You think I should go see him?'

235

'Your call, not mine.' Kaye walked around the Volvo. 'You've checked it out?'

'I did,' Naysmith replied. 'Climbed in and had a rummage.'

'Find anything?'

'No.'

'The logbook,' Fox corrected him.

'Look in the boot?'

When Fox shook his head, Kaye lifted a chisel from the workbench and started prising at the metal. Naysmith joined in with a screwdriver. Eventually the lock gave way. There was straw inside: all that remained of a nest of some kind. The spare tyre was flat, the rubber perished. Kaye lifted it and checked beneath. When he tried moving the felt flooring, it crumbled. There was a jack, but nothing else. Fox realised he'd been holding his breath, half expecting the money to be there. Kaye made a non-committal noise and walked to the other end of the vehicle, examining the crumpled frame. 'I thought these things were built of bricks. Must have been doing a fair lick ...'

'Vernal had been visiting his lover,' Fox informed him.

'Was he in a hurry to get away?'

'Someone could have been on his tail.'

'Spooks again, eh? Reckon they'd open their files to us?'

'Doubtful.'

Kaye placed the tarpaulin on the ground and lay down on it, shuffling underneath the car. 'Doesn't look like anything's been tampered with. Hard to say, though, after all this time ...' When he emerged, he brushed himself down. 'Does the girlfriend have anything to add?'

'She did a vanishing trick soon after.'

'Which you interpret as someone putting the frighteners on her?'

'Not necessarily.'

Kaye rubbed at his jaw. 'If I'm being honest, Malcolm, I don't think you've got *anything*.'

'But is that because there's nothing there to get?'

Kaye narrowed his eyes and thought this over. 'I wouldn't go *quite* that far.'

'Would you keep at it, though?'

'Me personally?' Kaye shook his head slowly. 'Simple life's what I'm after. You, on the other hand ...' He didn't feel the need to finish the sentence.

236

Fox stared at the car, then grabbed a corner of the tarpaulin. Joe Naysmith helped him cover it up again.

Fox dropped them back at the car park behind the police station.

'What's next?' he asked.

Kaye looked at Naysmith. 'I'd say we're ready to prep a final report.'

'I might have a couple of supplementary questions,' Naysmith countered.

'And would those be for the fragrant DC Forrester?'

Naysmith tried his hardest not to let the colour rise to his face. Kaye chuckled and slapped him on the back.

'How about you?' he asked Fox.

'Cash doesn't want me anywhere near here.'

'The perfect excuse to go back to your archaeological dig?'

'Something like that.'

Kaye nodded, then slung an arm around Naysmith's shoulders. He was offering dating advice as the two of them headed for the station's rear door. Fox sat in his car with the engine idling, thinking of the smashed-up maroon 244. Willis had wanted it for a reason. He must have thought that it represented evidence of something – a little insurance policy of some kind. If he had removed the money, why hang on to the car? And how could he have known about the money in the first place? Unless he had ties to the Dark Harvest Commando. Close ties.

A member?

A sympathiser?

Fox looked down at the floor in front of the passenger seat. The 244's logbook was lying there. He reached down and picked it up. What was it Naysmith had said ...?

In full view ...

And Tony Kaye: *That might actually work ...*

A lot of the pages had stuck together. Fox tried separating them, but they tended to tear. He ran his fingers over them, feeling for anything hidden inside. At the back was the clear plastic pocket containing MOTs and service invoices. These weren't in the best of health either. The car's owner was listed as Mr F. Vernal, address in the Grange. The car had been serviced by a garage on Edinburgh's south side.

Replacement tyres ... oil changes ... brake fluid ...10,000-mile service ... new windscreen wipers ...

Fox stared at one of the sheets, trying to make sense of it. It was on the same headed paper – MJM Motors – but the handwriting was different. It looked like an invoice, but it wasn't one.

'You sneaky little bastard,' Fox said quietly to himself. Gavin Willis's work: had to be. A list of firearms supplied to someone called 'Hawk' – presumably short for Hawkeye. The sums added up to almost twelve hundred pounds. Looked to Fox as though there had been three or four different deliveries, totalling twelve weapons and numberless rounds of ammo. Two revolvers, two pistols, a shotgun and seven rifles. Fox ran a finger across the word 'Hawk'.

Whether member or sympathiser, here was evidence that Gavin Willis had definitely been a supplier, dealing with the man called Hawkeye, who would then use the guns in his armed robberies.

Willis must have told Alan Carter – and Carter didn't want his mentor's reputation sullied. Nobody could ever know, even with Willis in his grave.

'Couldn't risk it, could you?' Fox muttered aloud. 'Couldn't risk anyone buying the cottage and finding something.'

Had the revolver been there all along? Alan Carter holding on to it? In which case, someone had wrested it from him and made him sit at the table ... Fox shook his head slowly. He couldn't imagine it. Alan Carter would have stood toe-to-toe with any assailant. If told to sit, he would have refused.

Wouldn't he?

Fox went through the other invoices, but there were no other clues. He wondered if Alan Carter had known. No, because wouldn't he have destroyed it? Come to that, wouldn't he also have rid himself of any gun he found? Yes, ripping up the cottage and destroying whatever he deemed incriminating. Willis's reputation had to be upheld. Tony Kaye's words rang in his head: *I don't think you've got* anything ...

'Not strictly true, compadre,' Fox said determinedly.

Ten

31

Nothing happened for a few days.

The Complaints were back in their office in Edinburgh. Kaye and Naysmith were writing up their report for Fife Constabulary. The message had come through: with the death of Paul Carter, no further action was to be taken.

'Just give the bosses in Fife whatever you've got,' Bob McEwan had explained.

Alan Carter's body had been released, but not his nephew's. Carter's wish had been for cremation, ashes scattered on the rose beds outside the crematorium building. Fox attended the ceremony. Teddy Fraser led the tributes, and sure enough, when the minister failed to mention Alan's football prowess, Teddy put him right with mention of the twenty-nine-goal season. Jimmy Nicholl was there too, Teddy carrying the compliant dog with him to the podium, refusing offers of help.

The chapel was packed. Fox wondered if there'd be half as many at Paul Carter's funeral – somehow he doubted it. The Fife Constabulary brass might feel they had to show willing, but a lot of the townsfolk would stay away. They knew the rumours: Alan Carter's body had been released only because his killer was also deceased.

As they waited for the coffin to arrive, retired cops shook hands with each other, patted backs, slapped shoulders and reminisced. Robinson was there in his sergeant's uniform, its silver buttons gleaming. Half the town seemed to have known Alan Carter. There were scowls and mutterings concerning the presence of the Shafiq family, the ones Carter's firm had butted heads with. Father and two sons, the sons with their hair slicked back, sharply suited, Ray-Bans a fixture throughout.

Fox had asked Teddy Fraser about the history.

'Storm in a whisky glass,' he explained. 'Except that the dad's teetotal.'

Scholes, Haldane and Michaelson were in attendance too, but kept clear of Fox – and the Shafiqs. Evelyn Mills went for a drink with Fox afterwards.

'Case goes on,' she told him. 'Just because the major suspect's also dead doesn't mean we brush it under the carpet.' She paused. 'On the other hand ...'

'No one's going to be busting a gut?' Fox guessed.

He had suspected as much from the look of DI Cash and DS Young as they sat in their pew, faces relaxed, job done.

'Thing is, Evelyn, if Paul didn't do it, the killer's still out there.'

'Give me another name, then – give me something concrete.'

Charles Mangold had asked much the same of him, a night later.

'Imogen is slipping away from us, Inspector. She may not be here much longer.'

'Sorry to hear that,' Fox had said.

'Time is pressing.'

'I'm doing what I can.'

Except that he had done almost nothing. Mostly he'd been preparing to give evidence in court – a case dating back almost a year and a half had finally come to trial. Reading back through the notes, he realised there were a couple of gaps – little holes in proper procedure – which a good counsel would spot and then jab away at, like a boxer spying a nick above their opponent's eye. Fox had worked on his defence, honing two or three counter-arguments, only for the trial to be postponed at the last minute.

So now he sat in the office at Fettes, offering occasional help to Kaye and Naysmith as they prepared the report, and providing a sympathetic ear to McEwan as he muttered darkly about the latest meetings and proposals for cost-cutting.

'Are we police or accountants? If I'd wanted to spend all my time on a calculator, I'd have paid more attention during Mr Gentry's maths lessons ...'

When the phone rang on Fox's desk, it was reception, telling him he had a visitor.

Detective Chief Inspector Jackson.

Fox narrowed his eyes. 'You sure it's me he wants?' Jackson: the tourist from Special Branch in London.

'You're the only Fox we've got,' the officer on the front desk said. 'Want me to fob him off?'

'Point him in the direction of the canteen,' Fox instructed, ending the call and shrugging his arms back into the sleeves of his suit jacket.

Jackson was queuing at the counter, nothing on his tray as yet. Fox caught up with him as he stood in front of the till.

'What can I get you?' Jackson asked.

'Tea,' Fox said.

'Two teas,' Jackson told the server.

'Pot and two tea bags?' she suggested.

'Perfect,' Jackson responded with a smile.

They went to a table by the window, sitting down so that they faced one another.

'What brings you here?' Fox asked.

'Just passing.' Jackson saw the look on Fox's face and gave another smile. 'No, not really.'

'How are things going with Lockerbie and Peebles?'

'Okay.'

'Found your bombers yet?'

Jackson stared at him. 'They *are* out there, you know. I'd have thought you would understand that.'

'How do you mean?'

'The case you're working on.'

It was Fox's turn to stare. 'What about it?'

'I was curious. So I did a bit of digging. You have to admit, the internet is a real old viper's nest, isn't it? Half-truths and guesswork and theories from the outer limits ...'

'Plenty of conspiracies,' Fox made show of agreeing.

'From what I hear, though, your researcher was killed by his nephew – some sort of long-held grudge.' Jackson sipped his tea, peering at Fox above the rim of the cup.

'That's all right, then, isn't it?' Fox responded.

'Why *was* Alan Carter so interested in Francis Vernal?'

'More to the point, why are *you*?'

Jackson shrugged, as if to concede that the question was fair. 'I spoke to a detective inspector. He tells me the lawyer's car's been found.'

Thanks, Cash ...

'Supposedly went for scrap,' Jackson continued, 'but someone decided to keep it.'

Fox made a non-committal noise.

'Willis, is that the name?'

'*Was* the name,' Fox corrected him.

'Willis and the researcher were friends ... colleagues ...'

'I still don't see why any of this would concern you.'

'Or you, come to that,' Jackson countered. 'Who was Alan Carter working for?'

'What makes you think he was working for anyone?'

'The lawyer died a quarter of a century back – I'm guessing something, or more likely someone, piqued his interest.'

'What if they did?'

Jackson took another sip of tea and shifted his gaze to the world outside the windows. 'Those outer limits I was talking about ... plenty of conspiracy theorists seem to think the security services might have had a hand in Francis Vernal's demise.'

'You're here to tell me they're wrong?'

'The game's changed these days, Inspector. Lots of new ways to spread gossip and disinformation. A good number of people out there have a vested interest in seeing the security services tripped up and tarred.' He glanced back towards Fox. 'It would reassure me if I knew who had ordered the investigation into Vernal's death.'

'Nobody with a grudge against your sort,' Fox stated.

'Are you sure about that?'

'A friend of the widow. He wants her to have a sense of closure before she dies.'

'No other motive?'

Fox visualised the red-faced, rotund lawyer. 'No other motive,' he said.

Jackson gave a thoughtful pout. 'Thank you for that, Inspector.' He seemed to be considering what to say next.

'You went digging?' Fox prompted him.

Jackson nodded slowly.

'And you found something?'

'Something and nothing. Friend Vernal had been on our radar for some time.'

'Special Branch?'

'Sort of.'

'MI5?'

Jackson offered a twitch of the mouth. 'He'd been under surveillance.'

'The night he died?'

'Yes.'

'He had a tail on him? Could that be why he was speeding?'

'I'm not sure.'

'But there were ...' Fox sought the right word. 'There were agents? Tracking his car?'

Jackson nodded, but said nothing.

'But that means when he crashed ...' Fox's eyes were boring into Jackson's, 'there were people *there* ... within *seconds* ...'

'Nobody shot him, though. They checked he was breathing, then got the hell out of there.'

'To phone for an ambulance?'

Jackson shook his head. 'Afraid not.'

'Why?'

'Couldn't risk it. Any involvement, the operation would have been jeopardised.'

'They just left him there?'

'Breathing. Not looking too bad at all.'

'This is all in the files?'

'Reading between the lines.'

Fox thought for a moment. 'Reading between the lines, was he also assassinated?'

'No.'

'How can you be so sure?'

'They were watchers – not an armed detail.'

'And no orders to kill him?'

'Absolutely not.'

'But they *did* break into his house, his office ...?'

Jackson looked ready to concede as much. 'There were rogue elements on both sides back then, Inspector. Let's remember that Vernal's friends were nothing short of terrorists. Bombs, guns and bank raids – those were his creed.' He paused. 'I'm telling you this because we're on the same side, you and me ...'

Fox stared at him. 'A car crash, an injured victim – and they just walked away?' Jackson didn't respond to this. 'What?' Fox persisted.

'They took a quick look first.'

'Rifled the car, you mean?' Fox saw he was right. 'Bloody hell ...

There was stuff missing: his cigarettes, a lucky fifty-pound note ...'

'They were questioned about that. They didn't take anything.'

'Did they turn up a revolver?' Fox asked eventually.

'No. That was only found later.'

'Yes, at some distance from the car.' Fox thought for a moment 'And you got all this from the files?'

Jackson nodded.

Fox was wondering about the DHC funds, secreted somewhere in Vernal's car ... The agents hadn't found the cash, had they?

There was silence at the table for a few moments. 'Vernal and his friends wanted to bring us to our knees,' Jackson stated quietly.

'Who killed him?' Fox asked.

'We don't know.'

'Can I talk to the men who tailed him?'

'No.'

'So much for being on the same side.'

'What do you think they could add?'

'Hard to say without speaking to them.'

Jackson leaned back in his chair. 'Do I get the name of the man who employed Alan Carter?'

'Not from me you don't.'

'Many of these men went unpunished, Inspector. I dare say they're still out there, warmed by their past antics.' He paused. 'They had plenty of help at the time, too ...'

Fox wondered if Gavin Willis, supplier of guns, had been on the security service's 'radar'. There was no way to ask Jackson without giving quite a lot away, so Fox concentrated on the beverage in front of him.

Jackson's phone was switched to silent mode. It was vibrating as he lifted it from his pocket and studied the screen.

'I have to take this,' he said, rising from the table. He walked towards the entrance to the cafeteria, his back to Fox. Fox watched the man's head dip as he listened to whatever the caller was telling him. His face looked grim as he ended the call and turned back towards Fox.

'I have to go,' he said.

'Peebles?' Fox guessed.

Jackson shook his head. 'How long will it take me to drive to Stirling?'

'This time of day ... maybe an hour, a bit less if you're lucky.'

'Another explosion,' Jackson explained. His phone was vibrating again. 'I really have to go.'

He started walking away, answering the call.

'Mad buggers with bombs,' Fox muttered to himself. Why did there seem no end to them? His own phone started to ring. When he answered and the caller identified herself, he knew he had a journey of his own to make.

32

Organising this visit had taken several days and more than a few phone calls, but now Fox was driving through the gates of Carstairs State Hospital. Carstairs to many was a stop on the night train between London and Edinburgh. There wasn't much of anything there – the railway station; a village with a shop; and not far away, the home to many of Scotland's most violent and least predictable prisoners. He parked in a ring-fenced area, was buzzed through a gate, and entered the main building. A few other visitors had arrived at the same time as him. They looked inured to the security procedures. Palms were checked by a machine. It would show if the visitor had been in contact with drugs in the recent past. A positive reading meant no visit that day. Bags were checked, and there seemed to be a random sampling of mobile phones, a swab identifying traces of illicit substances. The queue shuffled forward. The faces were docile, if strained. One woman had brought her young daughter. The kid clung to her mother and sucked on a dummy she was probably a year or two too old for.

'Inspector?' A woman was pushing past the queue. She shook Fox's hand and introduced herself as Gretchen Hughes. 'It's Dutch,' she explained, as if to intercept a question she was always being asked.

'Thanks for getting back to me,' Fox said.

'No problem.' She went to a window and retrieved an ID badge for him. Fox reckoned the drill would be the same as at any prison, so handed over his phone at the same time.

'Donald doesn't get many visitors,' Hughes was telling him.

'He gets some, though?'

'Not in the past year.'

'And before that?'

She studied him. She had short blonde hair and pale-blue eyes. There was a plain gold band on her wedding finger, indicating the existence of a Mr Hughes.

'That sort of information probably requires a formal request.'

'Probably,' Fox agreed as she led him past the queue. All he had asked for was a meeting with Donald MacIver. 'But would Donald tell me?'

'I doubt you could trust his answer.'

'Is he a fantasist?'

She looked at him again and gave a wide smile. 'Have you been reading up on the subject?'

Fox was not about to admit that he had.

'No, not a fantasist,' she decided to answer. 'But he has good days and bad. The medication keeps him on a fairly even keel.'

'Any subjects I should avoid?'

'Just be sure to call him *Mr* MacIver. I worked with him almost two years before we were on first-name terms.'

'How many inmates do you have?'

She made a tutting sound. '*Patients*, Inspector – please remember that.'

'Patients usually get better and leave their hospitals,' Fox replied. 'Does that happen much here?'

Doors had been unlocked and locked again behind them. Fox wasn't sure what he had expected. It was a lot quieter than a jail. Plenty of people, but they moved slowly, cautiously. The staff were in T-shirts and looked as if they trusted this new arrival a lot less than they did their regular charges.

'Where am I seeing him?' he asked into the silence. He was trying to work out if Gretchen Hughes was a doctor of some kind. Her badge wasn't giving anything away.

'His room,' she answered. 'He likes it there.'

'Fine with me.'

A few moments later, they arrived at the open doorway. Hughes tapped on the jamb with her knuckles.

'Donald? This is the visitor I was telling you about ...'

She took a step back so that Fox could walk past her into the room. MacIver was seated at a table. There was space for a single bed and some shelves. An antique map of Scotland had been Blu-tacked to the wall. MacIver was reading a newspaper. He had a

249

stack of them on the floor next to him. He was marking words and phrases with a thick blue crayon. So far, he seemed to have underlined almost every paragraph of the page under scrutiny. There was a chair opposite him, so Fox eased himself down on to it.

'Do you want anything?' Hughes asked. Fox started to shake his head, until he realised the question had been aimed at MacIver.

'Nothing,' the man muttered, still intent on his task.

'I'll just be outside,' she said, moving away but leaving the door open. Fox studied MacIver, trying to think of him as 'patient' rather than 'inmate'. The man was tall, maybe six three or four, and broad-shouldered. He had long grey hair, reaching halfway down his back, and a grey beard that would have made a wizard proud. The eyes behind the circular spectacles were large, the spectacles themselves smeared and in need of a wipe. His short fingernails were crusted with grime, and there was a slightly sulphurous smell in the room.

'Mr MacIver, my name's Fox.' Fox could see newsprint reflected in the spectacles. Another paragraph needed to be underlined. MacIver did it with painstaking care, skipping any word he did not deem essential. As far as Fox could see, it was a story about the plans for a new road bridge across the Firth of Forth.

'They've done away with the toll, you know,' Fox said. 'The Forth Road Bridge – one of the first things the SNP did when they got into power was—'

'Call that power?' MacIver interrupted. The voice sounded as if it was being drawn from the bottom of a well. 'Power's exactly what *that* isn't.' Fox waited for more, but MacIver was back at work.

'What *is* power, then?' he decided to ask.

'It's something you hold in both hands like a weapon, something you can choose to use to strike at your enemies' hearts. When you bring light to the deserving and cold darkness to everyone else – *that's* power.'

Fox was scanning the books piled on one shelf. Some names he recognised, some he didn't. 'I remember reading MacDiarmid's poetry at school,' he commented.

'Christopher Murray Grieve – that was his real name.'

'You knew him?'

'We might have crossed paths – there were certain howffs in Edinburgh and Glasgow. Preachers and communists, gentlemen philosophers ...' His voice drifted away and he stopped his work, staring at the page without seeing it. Finally he looked up into the face of his visitor. 'Have we met before? Should I know you?'

'No.'

'Only, I forget things.'

'My name's Fox, and I'm interested in Francis Vernal.'

'He died.'

'I know.'

'A martyr to the cause.'

'You really think so?'

'When Francis spoke, he could make kings or topple them.'

'You knew him pretty well, then?'

'He was that rarest of creatures – a thinker who could *do*. A man who didn't just talk about things but worked to make them happen.'

'He was pretty active,' Fox seemed to agree.

'Which was why he had to die.'

'You think he was targeted?'

'The man was shot at point-blank range. No more than four weeks later, they came for me. They'd been busy in the interim – planting evidence in my basement. All very impressive when they kicked the door down and came in dressed in their radiation suits. I was wearing pink striped pyjamas.' He was enunciating with care. What teeth Fox could see were blackened and uneven. 'Wouldn't even let me get dressed. And they knew exactly where to look for their "evidence".'

'You went to prison at first.'

'Aye, but that wasn't enough for them. They could see I was prospering there, talking to the men, opening their eyes to the tyranny.'

'You got in a fight with another inmate ...'

'He was paid for his efforts. That's the only explanation as to why *I* was the one punished! Solitary, then Barlinnie, then Peterhead ...'

'More violence?'

'More goading and intimidation,' MacIver corrected him. 'More of everything that might break the spirit and drive a man towards the madhouse.' He wagged a finger at Fox. 'But I'm as sane as you are – take that news with you when you go.'

Fox nodded, as though in agreement. 'So what did Francis Vernal do exactly? Within the organisation, I mean?'

'Francis was our one-man brains trust. Lot of hot heads that needed cooling – he was the man for the job.'

'He looked after the finances too, didn't he?'

'He was useful in many ways.'

'The money came from hold-ups and robberies,' Fox persisted. 'You used it to buy guns and explosives?'

'A necessary evil.'

'Did Mr Vernal keep any guns in his car?'

MacIver blinked a few times, as though waking from a nap. 'What are you doing here? Why all these questions?' He looked down at the newspaper as if he had never laid eyes on it before. 'Burns said it best, you know: *bought and sold for English gold.*' He stabbed a finger against the artist's impression of the new bridge. 'That's what you're seeing here.'

'*A parcel of rogues in a nation,*' Fox said, finishing the quote while reaching into his pocket. He had the photo from Professor Martin's book, the one of Vernal with Alice Watts and Hawkeye. He placed it on top of the newspaper, along with the two matriculation photographs of Alice.

'Francis,' MacIver said, rubbing his thumb across Vernal's face. 'And Alice.' His eyes widened and he lifted one of the snaps, holding it up and studying it.

'Any idea what happened to her?' Fox asked.

The old man shook his head. He was stroking his beard with his free hand. He seemed transfixed by the picture. 'Youth, energy, beauty – everything a movement needs.'

'She was sleeping with Vernal.'

'Alice had many admirers.'

'Including yourself? Did you ever hear from her afterwards?'

'She did the right thing. They assassinated Francis and then came for me. Alice went underground.'

'And Hawkeye?' Fox leaned forward a little to tap the photograph. Hawkeye arm in arm with Alice.

'Still out there, I dare say. Somewhere in the world where there's a cause worth fighting for.'

'Did you know his real name?'

'He was always Hawkeye.'

'Does no one from the old days keep in touch?'

'Why would anyone want to come see me? I've nothing to offer.'

'I spoke with John Elliot recently. *He's* not exactly gone underground, has he?'

'I've seen him on the television.'

'He's never visited?'

MacIver shook his head.

'That photograph's from a book,' Fox went on. 'It was written by an academic called John Martin.'

'Like the singer?'

'Different spelling. He asked to speak to you and you turned him down.'

'Did I?'

'That's what he says.'

MacIver shrugged. 'I don't remember him.'

Fox thought for a moment. 'Does the name Gavin Willis mean anything to you?'

'Gavin Willis?' MacIver rolled the words around his mouth. 'Gallowhill Cottage?'

'Yes.'

'Beautiful spot. Somewhere over in Fife ...'

'Near Burntisland. Gavin was a policeman when you knew him.' MacIver nodded. 'And a sympathiser?' Fox paused. '*More* than a sympathiser?'

'Never an active member.'

'He got guns for you, though, didn't he? Maybe kept them at the cottage until you needed them. And I suppose he could get rid of them for you too, when occasion demanded.' *After a bank job, say: who was going to notice an extra handgun going into the furnace? Evidence destroyed ...* 'Gavin held on to Francis Vernal's car, Mr MacIver. Why would he do that?'

'Clever man,' MacIver said quietly. 'I always wondered ...'

'Wondered what?'

'Whether anyone found the money.'

'The money from the armed robberies? A few thousand, wasn't it?'

'That's what they said. They didn't want the public to know.'

'Know what?'

'We were good at what we did. We sent anthrax to the highest in the land, razed government buildings, held up banks and armoured cars ...' He smiled at the memory. 'We were several hundred strong, and I'm the only one they ever locked up.'

'How much money was in the car, Mr MacIver?'

253

'Thirty or forty thousand.' MacIver paused to think. 'More or less.'

'Did he keep it in the boot?'

MacIver nodded. 'Below the spare tyre.'

Fox remembered Tony Kaye crowbarring open the boot and lifting the perished tyre – nothing underneath.

'You're sure about that figure? Thirty or forty?'

'A lot of money back then.'

Fox nodded in agreement, recalling the price of an Edinburgh flat in 1985 –thirty-five thousand. Was it money worth killing for? Of course it was; people had died for far less.

'There are bombs going off right now in Scotland,' he told MacIver. 'You think the bombers are justified?'

'*Justified* is an interesting word – we could spend a year and a day debating it.' MacIver fixed Fox with a stare. 'They have a *cause*, they have passion and commitment. They have seen the systems around them fail, yet the status quo remains. Frustration turns to anger and anger to a sense of injustice.'

'That's how you felt back in the day?'

'We *all* felt it!' MacIver's voice was rising as his agitation grew. Suddenly Gretchen Hughes was in the doorway, flanked by a couple of orderlies.

'Is everything all right?' she asked.

MacIver was on his feet. He stared down at the newspaper with all its underlined paragraphs, then snatched at it and began tearing it to shreds. The orderlies moved forward, Fox making room for them.

'Betrayed and given trinkets?' MacIver was spluttering. 'Call that power? Why not call it what it is?'

Hughes's hand was on Fox's arm.

'Time for us to leave,' she said.

Fox stood his ground. 'What is it?' he asked MacIver. The hand on his arm tightened.

'I think that's quite enough, Inspector.'

'It's a kind of death,' MacIver stated, voice shaking. 'And we're paying for it. Mark my words – we're paying for it ...' He slumped down on his chair.

'You need to go now,' Hughes was telling Fox.

'I'm going,' he assured her, backing out of the room.

33

Fox had no way of getting in touch with DCI Jackson, so he started driving in the direction of Stirling. The radio news reports told him the blast had happened somewhere close to the village of Kippen. Fox's satnav advised him to take the A73 and the M80. His heartbeat was returning to something like normal as he played back the visit to Carstairs in his head. MacIver had lost little of his zeal. He wasn't an orator like Francis Vernal, perhaps, but Fox could imagine him filled with passionate argument, sounding heated but rational. He could well imagine young people hanging on his every word. He would have sounded like a man with justifiable grievances, if few answers – other than insurrection.

Fox stopped at a service station, filled the car's tank and stayed parked while he ate a sandwich and drank a bottle of Irn-Bru. When he got back on the road and started to see signs to Kippen, he found himself part of a convoy, tucking in behind a van with a satellite dish on its roof. The TV crews were on their way to cover the bomb blast. The van eventually signalled to enter a country park at the foot of a range of hills. Paths led into the woods, and there was a muddy car park, filled with police patrol cars. Fox hauled his Volvo on to the closest verge and got out. Journalists were talking into their phones or to each other. Uniformed officers were trying to stop them wandering off. Bemused ramblers were returning to their cars, only to find them blocked in. Fox could see no sign of Jackson. He showed his ID to a uniform and was pointed in the direction of the right-hand path. On another day it would have been a pleasant enough hike, though Fox would have chosen different footwear. He slipped on leaves a few times, just about staying upright. As he walked further into the forest it grew eerily quiet, and he stopped and listened, breathing deeply. He was reminded of the Hermitage of Braid, near where he'd grown up in Edinburgh. As a kid, he'd gone there with Jude, playing games of hide-and-seek and chasing sticks down the narrow, fast-flowing stream. Right up until the day she started finding other boys more interesting than her brother.

He took out his phone, tempted to call her and share the memory, but hesitated. A couple of uniformed officers emerged from the path ahead. They asked to check his ID.

'I'm not a reporter,' he assured them, but they took a good look anyway. The one who handed the warrant card back looked like he had a question to ask – *What's this got to do with the Complaints?* – but Fox moved on before he got the chance. The climb levelled out and he could see a clearing over to his left. Several figures had gathered there. Fox walked towards them, no one paying him any attention. Jackson, arms folded, was talking to a dark-haired woman. She wore a cream trench coat and green wellingtons, and she too had her arms folded. Fox stood and waited for Jackson to notice him. It was the woman who turned her head first, narrowing her eyes a little as she tried to place the new arrival. Jackson turned to see what had caught her attention. He muttered something to her and tramped in Fox's direction.

'What the hell are you doing here?' he asked, keeping his voice low.

'Sorry,' Fox apologised. 'I would've called if I'd had your number.'

Jackson was trying to lead him out of the clearing, but Fox stayed put. There was a small crater that everyone else seemed interested in. Blackened foliage and strewn earth. Fox wondered for a second why the trees were glinting, then realised their bark was studded with shrapnel – bits of nails and nuts and bolts.

'Looks like they've got the quantities about right,' he stated.

Jackson had placed himself between Fox and the scene. 'Look, I'll give you my number; we can talk later.'

'It was just the one question, really.'

Jackson didn't seem to be listening. He handed Fox his business card. The address was New Scotland Yard, London.

'Just the one question,' Fox repeated.

'Can't it wait?'

Fox stared at him. Jackson sighed and folded his arms again.

'The watcher team – is that what you called them? The ones who rifled Vernal's car while he lay injured in the front seat ...'

'What about them?'

'Did they leave their jobs soon after? Or maybe start buying flash watches and Italian suits?'

'What are you talking about?'

'I've just heard that there was thirty or forty grand in that car.'

'You think they stole it?'

Fox shrugged. 'It's a theory, and that means I may have to write it up.'

'Look, write whatever the hell you want. I've told you what I found in the vaults.'

'You've not told me their names.'

'And I'm not going to.'

'Are they still active?'

'I've no idea.'

Over by the bomb crater, the woman cleared her throat. Jackson took the hint. 'You need to go,' he told Fox.

'Who is she?'

'She's the Chief Constable of Central Scotland, and right now I'm keeping her waiting.'

'Didn't recognise her without her uniform,' Fox said. 'I'll let you get back to it, then.'

Jackson didn't need a second invitation. He strode towards the circle of investigators and mumbled some sort of apology.

Fox took his time returning along the path. Another forensics team passed him, lugging heavy boxes of equipment. The TV vans had got their satellite dishes properly positioned. One reporter was doing a piece to camera. Fox recognised the face – he worked on the same show as John Elliot. Somehow Elliot himself, one-time dabbler in terrorism, was stuck doing pieces about restaurant menus.

'No word from the authorities as yet,' the reporter was telling the audience at home, 'but a press conference will take place in an hour or so's time ...'

The sound recordist wasn't happy. A dog was barking in the back of a nearby car. The dog's owner was remonstrating that he was boxed in by the reporter's own van.

'Middle of bloody nowhere,' the cameraman complained, 'and there's still always something ...'

A few cars had arrived after Fox, and had parked behind him. Locals, it looked like, curious to see what was going on. Fox manoeuvred past them and headed in the direction of the M90. His phone let him know he'd missed a call. He checked voicemail. It was Fiona McFadzean, asking him to ring her. But the signal was dropping, so Fox decided on a detour north and east along the A91 into Fife, heading for Glenrothes. Tulliallan Police College wasn't far away at one point, and that got him thinking about Evelyn Mills again. There was a short course coming up – Bob McEwan had mentioned it in passing. Nobody in the office had shown interest, but Fox wondered if Mills might know about it. Three days and nights ... back at the scene of the crime...

'She's married,' he reminded himself out loud, then he switched the radio on, turning the music up, trying to drown out his own thoughts.

'You shouldn't have come all this way,' McFadzean said when she opened the door to him. Paul was seated at his computer and offered a wave by way of greeting. Fox nodded back.

'I was actually in the vicinity,' he lied.

'I've been hearing about Kippen – just gets grimmer and grimmer, doesn't it?'

Fox made a non-committal sound. 'What was it you wanted to tell me?'

McFadzean gestured towards Paul, who twitched his head, meaning he wanted Fox to approach the computer.

'Remember you asked about those revolvers? Specifically: provenance?'

'Yes.' Fox bent at the waist, the better to study the monitor. It was a paper trail. Paul had managed to split the screen in half, so one side showed information on the gun that had killed Alan Carter and the other the revolver found near Francis Vernal's body.

'There's a connection,' Paul stated. 'Both weapons were reported "lost or mislaid" in June 1982.'

'Stolen from an army base?'

'Good guess, but not quite right. I'm amazed they were still using revolvers in the eighties, but apparently some officers liked them.' Paul clicked the mouse again, and Fox read the details.

'The Falklands?'

'The Falklands,' the young man confirmed. 'Conflict kicked off that month. Lot of equipment was handed out but not handed back.' There was list after list to confirm this. He kept clicking on the mouse, so fast Fox couldn't keep up – but then that was the whole point.

'So how did the guns end up here?' Fox asked.

'Servicemen probably smuggled them back,' McFadzean joined in. 'Either as keepsakes, or so they could sell them on.'

'Definitely the latter in this case,' Paul added. 'A few other firearms from the conflict – pistols rather than revolvers – turned up on the streets of Britain in the mid-eighties.' The police reports appeared on the screen. 'London, Manchester, Nottingham ...'

'Birmingham, Newcastle, Glasgow,' McFadzean added.

'And Belfast,' Paul stressed. 'Mustn't forget Belfast ...'

'We even caught one of them,' McFadzean told Fox. The police photograph duly appeared on the screen.

'Name was William Benchley,' Paul said. 'Operated out of Essex. Left the army after the campaign – even picked up his medal. But stolen weaponry became his business.'

'Did he sell the revolvers?'

Paul shrugged and looked to his boss.

'No idea,' she confessed.

'Where is he now?' Fox was studying the photo of the shaven-headed, scowling Benchley.

'Died in Barbados a few years back. Drowned in his swimming pool.'

'Moved there after serving his sentence,' Paul explained. 'Bearing in mind his lifestyle, I'd say some of the arms money was waiting for him when he got out.'

'Much good it did him,' Fox said quietly, reading the news report of Benchley's death.

'Anyway,' Paul cautioned, 'we've no reason to suppose he sold those particular guns.'

'But someone did.'

'Someone did,' the young man agreed. 'The one found at the scene of the Vernal car smash – I've got nothing else for you on that.'

Fox took the hint. 'Go on,' he said.

'Took a bit of tracking down ...' Paul paused. 'The internet was no use – a lot of stuff in the Fife Constabulary vaults hasn't been digitised.'

'Paul had to actually spend time poring over something other than a screen.'

259

Paul stuck his tongue out in response to McFadzean's sarcasm. Then he handed Fox a set of stapled photocopied sheets. 'The revolver found next to Alan Carter had been handed in to police in October 1984. It was found in a hedge in Tayport.'

'Near Dundee?' Fox asked.

'The Fife side of the Tay Bridge. Police at the time wondered if it might have been used in a robbery. There'd been a bookmaker in Dundee relieved of the week's takings by a masked man toting a handgun. This was three days before the revolver was discovered.'

'So the gun had gone from the Falklands to Dundee?'

Paul shrugged. 'Could have ended up there after being passed along a chain of owners.'

'Was the gunman ever caught?'

But Fox could see well enough from the printout that the case had never been solved. The profit from a week's betting – just shy of nine hundred pounds. Would that have been enough to tempt the likes of the Dark Harvest Commando? It was hardly a bank heist ...

'Any of this useful?' McFadzean asked as Fox continued reading.

'I'm not sure,' he confessed. Then he patted Paul on the shoulder. 'But it's bloody good work, all the same ...'

Once home, Fox called Tony Kaye.

'How's the report going?'

'We're managing to make it look like it was put together by a pair of Einsteins.'

'No change there, then. What are you up to tonight?'

'Dinner with my good lady. Want to join us?'

'Can't spare the time, Tony.'

'I keep forgetting about your busy social calendar.' Kaye paused. 'Well, the offer's always there ...'

'Thanks, but I'm sorted. Any news from the kid?'

'He's headed back over to Fife. Been to the barber and everything.'

'Cheryl Forrester again?'

'He's smitten.'

'Warn him off, will you? We don't know what titbits she might be collecting for Scholes and the others.'

'You reckon her for a Mata Hari?'

'Wouldn't be the first time.' Fox was lying along the sofa, the TV remote in his free hand. He flicked to a news channel, keeping the sound muted. 'Did you hear about Stirling?'

'Sounds like a copycat to me – these nutters see it on TV and think: I could do that; stir things up a bit.'

'The brass seemed to be taking it seriously enough.'

There was silence on the line while Tony Kaye digested this. 'What were you doing there?'

'Looking for DCI Jackson.'

'The guy from Special Branch?'

'I had something I needed to ask him.'

'This is Vernal, isn't it? You're still digging?'

'And I think I'm hitting a few worms, too. According to Jackson, the spooks had nothing to do with Vernal's death. But Donald MacIver says there was a chunk of cash hidden in the car boot. Thirty to forty grand's worth.'

'Who the hell's Donald MacIver?'

'He led one of the splinter groups at the time.'

'And where is he now?'

Fox hesitated before answering. 'Carstairs.'

'You've been to Carstairs?'

'Had to be done, Tony.'

'Was he in a straitjacket?'

'Bit high-strung, but coherent with it.'

'And you believe him about the money?'

'Yes.'

Kaye seemed to think for a moment. 'Then Gavin Willis got it,' he surmised.

'And did what with it?' Fox countered. 'Plus, how would he have known it was there?' But of course there was every chance Willis might have known – guns exchanged for cash, maybe at dead of night in a deserted car park ...

'More questions than answers, Malcolm,' Tony Kaye was saying. 'Mind if I give you a word of advice?'

'You're going to tell me to drop it.'

'Something like that, yes. Hand the whole lot over to CID – not Fife necessarily; there's got to be someone in Edinburgh you can give it to.'

'Just when I'm starting to enjoy myself?'

'Is that what you're doing?' Kaye gave a sigh. 'You've not got

261

anything to prove, Malcolm. To me or the High Hiedyins or anyone else.' He paused for a moment. 'At least take a night off – go see a film or something.'

'I should visit Mitch.'

'Except *that's* not exactly a night off, is it? Bound to be a Jason Statham playing somewhere.'

'Lots of explosions and cars getting wrecked? Those'll help me feel the benefit, will they?'

'Don't just sit there stewing – that's all I'm saying.'

Fox thanked Kaye and ended the call. He didn't fancy going out for dinner, not on his own again. He looked online and saw that the Filmhouse was showing *The Maltese Falcon*. For five minutes, he told himself he would go.

Then he drove to Lauder Lodge to see his father instead.

Mitch was drowsy. There was whisky on his breath, and though seated in his chair, he was already in his pyjamas. Fox checked his watch: it wasn't even eight o'clock. He sat opposite his father for over an hour, sifting through the photographs from the shoebox, concentrating on cousin Chris, Jude as a toddler, and Fox's own mother. He would glance at his sleeping father from time to time, the mouth slightly open, chest rising and falling.

We played football, you and me: you wanted me to be a goalie – less chance of an injury, you said. And you sat with me night after night as I tried learning my times tables. You laughed at bad TV sitcoms and shouted at refereeing mistakes, as if they could hear you from behind the glass screen. On Remembrance Sunday you stood to attention for the minute's silence. You were never much good in the kitchen, but always made Mum a cup of tea before bed. She wanted two sugars but you only ever added one, telling her she was sweet enough already.

And look – there's Jude on a donkey at Blackpool beach. You're walking beside her, making sure she's safe. You've rolled the legs of your trousers up, a concession to the sunshine. You saved all year for the summer holiday, a little bit out of each week's pay packet.

Are you happy with the way we've turned out?

Will you ever stop worrying about us?

So many of the photographs showed faces Fox didn't know, none of them still alive. Moments in time captured but also flattened. You could see the beach, but not feel its salty heat. You could study the smiles and the eyes above those smiles, but not see beyond them to the hopes and fears, ambitions and betrayals.

When a member of staff opened the door, it took Fox a moment to realise anyone was there.

'We should be getting your father into bed,' she said.

Fox nodded his agreement. 'I'll give you a hand,' he said quietly.

But she shook her head. 'Regulations,' she explained. 'Got to stick to the script, or they'll have my head on a block.'

'Yes, of course,' Fox replied, starting to put the photographs away.

On his way home, he stopped at a fish-and-chip shop and bought a haggis supper. While he waited for a fresh batch of chips, he stood at the counter and stared at the TV. The Scottish news was on: the press conference from earlier. Flashes going off and the Chief Constable, Alison Pears, reading from a prepared statement, taking a couple of questions afterwards. She had tidied her hair and was wearing regulation uniform. She seemed to speak calmly and authoritatively, though he couldn't hear any of it above the sizzle of the deep-fat fryer. The report cut to the car park at Kippen and the same reporter Fox had seen earlier. *Live from the scene*, according to the on-screen banner. There were fewer vehicles now that night had fallen, and no barking dog to mess things up. The reporter held one of those big fluffy microphones in front of him. It was starting to drizzle, rainwater dotting the camera lens. The reporter was trying to look both knowledgeable and interested, but Fox could sense fatigue in his unblinking gaze. He seemed to get a question in his earpiece and nodded before starting to answer. The director cut to a blurry photo of the bomb crater. It looked to have been taken with a mobile phone, presumably snapped by a member of the public before the area could be cordoned off. A second picture followed, this time showing a close-up of one of the trees with the metal shards embedded there.

'Bloody hellish thing,' the proprietor of the chip shop said. He sounded Polish to Fox, but it could have been Bosnian, Romanian – just about anywhere really. Fox was not exactly an expert. On another night, he might have asked, just out of curiosity.

But not tonight.

Back home, he ate on the sofa, and caught the press conference again. When it cut to the studio, the presenter had some news.

'Police confirmed just a short time ago that they are working on a definite line of inquiry. And we'll keep you up to date as that story progresses. Now all the latest sport with Angela ...'

Fox must have dozed off at some point, because he woke up stretched along the sofa with his shoes still on and the half-empty plate resting on his chest. The food was cold and unappetising. He could smell sauce on his fingers, and went to the kitchen to dump the remnants of the meal into the pedal bin and wash his hands in the sink. He returned to the sofa with a mug of tea and found himself face to face with Chief Constable Pears again. They had gone to her live as she stood on what he guessed were the steps of Central Scotland Force HQ – presumably in Stirling itself. She had to push the hair out of her face as the wind gusted around her. She had no statement this time, but still sounded coolly professional. Fox was blinking the sleep out of his eyes. When she stopped speaking and listened to a journalist's question, she jutted her chin out a little. Fox tried to think who it was she reminded him of – Jude maybe; the jutting chin denoting concentration. But it wasn't Jude.

It was a photograph.

Fox hauled his laptop on to the sofa and punched her name into the search engine.

Alison Pears was one of only two female Chief Constables in Scotland. She was married to the financier Stephen Pears. Fox knew that name. Pears was in the papers a lot, pulling off deals and seemingly keeping the straitened financial sector afloat in Scotland. He found photos of the couple – had to admit, the Chief Constable scrubbed up well, and filled a little black dress with easy glamour. On the TV, however, she was fighting the elements and dressed in the same uniform as before. The rain was coming at her near-horizontally. The ticker tape along the bottom of the screen read: *Three arrests in bomb scare.*

'Fast work,' Fox said, toasting her with his mug.

Then he got to work himself, finding as much of her curriculum vitae as he could, while failing to locate any historical photos of her. Nevertheless, he was fairly sure.

Very fairly sure.

In 1985 she'd been a recent graduate of the Scottish Police College at Tulliallan. Not Pears back then – she was yet to meet her husband and take his name.

Alison Watson, born in Fraserburgh in 1962. Not such a jump, really, from Alison Watson to Alice Watts. He reached for the photo in Professor Martin's book, and the two matriculation snaps. There was the slightly jutting chin. It was evident in some of the online photos, too – at a film premiere, an awards dinner, a graduation ceremony, hand in hand with her husband. Stephen Pears glowed. Did the tan come from skiing or a salon? The hair was immaculately clipped, the teeth shiny, a chunky watch on one wrist. He was stocky, his face fattened by success. Twelve years since they'd first met, married for ten of those.

'Quite the pair, Mr and Mrs Pears,' Fox muttered to himself. But she was even better connected than that, because her brother Andrew was a Member of the Scottish Parliament. He was part of the SNP government: Andrew Watson, Minister for Justice.

Minister for Justice ...

Fox pushed the computer aside and slumped back against the sofa, head arched towards the ceiling.

What the hell do I do with this? he asked himself.

And what exactly did it mean?

Eleven

Eleven

34

'Bloody hell, Foxy, did you get any sleep at all last night?'

'Not much,' Fox admitted, as Kaye dragged out a chair and sat down across from him. It was just after nine in the morning, and the Police HQ cafeteria was doing a roaring trade in breakfast rolls and frothy cappuccinos. Fox had a half-drunk cup of tea in front of him, alongside an apple he had yet to start. Kaye's tray held a mug of coffee and a Tunnock's caramel wafer.

'Good dinner last night?' Fox asked.

'Cost enough,' Kaye grumbled. 'Did you go out like I told you to?'

Fox nodded slowly.

'Whatever film you saw,' Kaye commented, 'looks like it was downer enough for both of us.' He took a slurp of coffee, leaving a white milky mark on his top lip, and peeled the wrapper from the biscuit.

Fox started at the beginning – more or less. First sighting of Alison Pears in the flesh, then on TV. And then the connection and his findings and theories.

'Her photo's on page one of *Metro* today,' Kaye said, picking bits of caramel from between his teeth. 'Three home-grown terror suspects in custody.'

'Her brother was on the box this morning too,' Fox added. He had watched from his sofa, having spent much of the night there, some of it busy at the laptop. Andrew Watson: four years younger than his sister; short red hair, steel-framed glasses, a pudgy face with some traces of acne. *Peely-wally*, Mitch Fox would have said.

'He's only Justice Minister because everyone before him either

269

screwed up or fell out with the "Great Chieftain".' By which, Fox knew, Tony Kaye meant the First Minister.

'Handy to have him on your side, though, if you're a Chief Constable ...'

Kaye managed a rueful smile. 'You're really going to stand up and accuse her of being a terrorist?'

'No.'

'What then?'

'A spy.'

Kaye stared at him. 'A spy?' he repeated.

'Infiltrating Dark Harvest Commando and God knows who else.'

'And shagging Francis Vernal into the bargain?' Kaye took a deep breath. 'If that ever got out ...'

'Wouldn't do her reputation any good,' Fox confirmed.

'So you'll be having a *quiet* word with her?'

'I suppose so.'

'Rather you than me. She's suddenly the face of equality in the police – glass ceiling shattered; nobody's going to want *that* to change.'

'No,' Fox agreed.

'Bloody hell – look what the cat dragged in!' Kaye smiled as Joe Naysmith trudged his way towards the table, nothing in his hand but a can of some super-caffeinated energy drink. Naysmith's eyes were bleary, and he had skipped a shave.

'Yeah, yeah,' he commented, sitting down next to Kaye.

'She's too much woman for you, young Joseph,' Kaye persisted. 'Maybe I should take her in hand.'

Naysmith gulped at his drink, eyes squeezed shut. When he opened them, he looked from Kaye to Fox and then back again. 'Something I should know?' he asked.

Fox gave an almost imperceptible shake of the head in Tony Kaye's direction.

'Man talk, Joe,' Kaye went on to explain. 'Nothing for you to worry your little head about.'

'How's DC Forrester?' Fox asked.

'She's fine.'

'Any word on Paul Carter?'

Naysmith thought for a second, then nodded. 'Another witness,' he decided to confide. 'Saw a man walking along the high street some time after midnight. A man with shoes that squelched.'

Fox frowned. 'Not Carter?'

'This guy was bald. Shaved head, anyway. But he'd definitely been in some water, according to the witness. Worried look on his face. Might have had a tattoo on his neck.' Naysmith paused, eyes on Kaye. 'The side of his neck.'

'Who is it?' Fox asked.

Kaye rubbed a hand down his face. 'Sounds like someone I know,' he conceded.

'Who, though?'

'Tosh Garioch,' Kaye answered. 'Billie's boyfriend.'

Naysmith was nodding. 'Might not be, of course – but it fits the description you gave me after you interviewed him.'

'Garioch's the doorman?' Fox checked. 'The one who worked for Alan Carter's firm?'

'That's him,' Kaye confirmed. 'Big tattoo of a thistle creeping up his neck. Shaved head. Criminal record.' He turned his attention back to Naysmith. 'Did you let on to Forrester?'

Naysmith shook his head. Kaye and Fox shared a look.

'Decisions, decisions,' Kaye commented. 'But I like our choices better than yours, Foxy ...'

Stirling.

There were armed officers and security checks outside Central Scotland Police Force HQ, keeping the media at bay and on the lookout for terrorist sympathisers and demonstrators.

Inside the main building, the Alert Status had been raised to CRITICAL. In all his years as an officer, Fox had never seen that before. After CRITICAL, there was nowhere else to go.

Fox had been seated in reception for over half an hour. Around him there was a real buzz of anticipation. He got the distinct feeling this wasn't normally the case. Somewhere in the vicinity, the three suspects were being questioned. Outside, the TV broadcast vans had set up camp on the main road. Print journalists clustered in each other's cars. Foragers had been sent out, returning with pies and bridies, hot drinks and crisps. On his way in, Fox had spotted the news reporter from the previous day. He looked exhausted and exhilarated in equal measure and was rubbing his hands together to keep warm, an as-yet-unneeded earpiece draped over one shoulder. A couple of uniformed officers in visored riot helmets, body armour strapped across their chests, had been placed at the entrance to the car park and were being filmed by cameramen who lacked anything more interesting to fill the time.

Fox's request to the woman behind the reception desk had been clear and succinct. 'Need a word with the Chief Constable. My name's Fox. Professional Standards Unit, Lothian and Borders Police.' The woman had studied his warrant card.

'You know she's kind of busy?' she had asked, voice heavy with sarcasm.

'Aren't we all?' he had retorted. The look on her face told him he wasn't making a new friend.

'Take a seat, Inspector.'

'Thank you.'

After five minutes, he'd walked up to the desk again, only to be told she hadn't managed to get through to 'the Chief'.

A further ten minutes: same story.

He'd been busying himself with his phone: checking for news and e-mails; deleting old messages ... and watching the hubbub around him.

Twenty minutes: a shake of the head from the receptionist.

Same thing at the half-hour mark.

And then the journalists had arrived, camera crews in tow. They had to be allocated visitor passes and shown where the news conference was happening. Fox decided to queue up with them. The receptionist gave him a questioning look.

'Thought it might pass the time,' he explained. So he too filled in his details and was handed a pass and a laminate sleeve with a clip on the back. He fixed it to his jacket and followed the herd.

The large conference room was bursting at the seams. Fox realised there was some sort of unspoken arrangement, whereby the most senior journalists were saved seats at the front. His own TV reporter was there, next to the aisle. Chairs had been laid out in rows. Some looked to have been requisitioned from the canteen, others from offices. A young woman in plain clothes was handing out a press release. People got busy on their phones, texting the salient points to their newsrooms and studios. She gave Fox a look that told him she knew most of the media representatives but not him. He just smiled and relieved her of another copy of the release.

Three arrests, no charges as yet.

If needed, extra time in custody would be sought under the Prevention of Terrorism Act.

Material found at the scene was being examined.

Fox was still reading when the Chief Constable brushed past him and made her way down the aisle towards a table festooned with microphones. The cameras got busy and the audience switched their phones to 'record' mode. Alison Pears was flanked by her Deputy Chief Constable and a DCI who had nominally been put in charge of the case. She cleared her throat and began to read from a prepared statement. Fox could smell her perfume. It lingered where she had pushed past him. Tony Kaye would be able to place it, but Fox couldn't. He felt a hand touch his forearm. Turning, he saw DCI Jackson standing in the doorway. Jackson's eyes narrowed, his brow furrowing. The unspoken question was clear.

What the hell are you doing here?

Fox gave him a wink and turned to concentrate on Pears's closing remarks. There were questions from the seats. Again Fox saw a hierarchy at work: if a hand went up from the front row, Pears would go there first. She had been well briefed: knew what would be asked and had her answers ready.

Were the suspects local?

What nationality?

Did anything tie them to the blasts near Lockerbie and Peebles?

Pears gave away precious little, but did so while appearing open and friendly. Once or twice she batted a question to the DCI, who was gruffer and less gifted but also knew what to say and what not to say. Jackson was tugging at Fox's arm again, gesturing towards the corridor, but Fox shook his head. As the press conference broke up, Pears led her small delegation back towards the door, fending off a slew of questions with a pleasant smile and a wave of the hand.

She wasn't looking at Fox as she made to pass him, but he stepped in front of her.

'Care to make a statement about Francis Vernal?' he asked.

Her eyes drilled into him, face frozen.

'Who?'

'Nice try, Alice,' he responded. The DCI placed a hand on Fox's chest, clearing the route. Fox took a step back, apologising to the cub reporter whose toes he managed to squash. Pears was out of the room, stalking down the corridor. Jackson had caught up with her, but she was saying something to her own DCI. He peeled off and approached Fox, handing him a card.

273

'Put your mobile number on there,' he growled.

'I've already been waiting a while.'

'She'll get back to you.'

Fox scribbled down his number and the DCI snatched the card back. As the man left, it seemed to be Jackson's turn.

'What are you trying to do?' he muttered, his mouth close to Fox's ear so no one else could hear.

'You've got your case, I've got mine.'

'You're the Complaints, not some fucking Simon Schama.'

'History seems to have a funny way of repeating itself.'

Jackson glowered at him. The journalists were comparing notes, or on their phones, or preparing themselves for their pieces to camera. But they kept glancing over towards the two men, too, recognising at least one of them from the site of the Kippen explosion.

'Leave it be,' Jackson urged in a fierce undertone.

'I need some time with her.'

'Why?'

Fox shook his head slowly. 'Maybe afterwards,' he offered.

'You're a bastard, Fox. Really and truly.'

'Coming from you, I'll take that as a compliment.'

'Trust me, it's not meant as one, not in the slightest.'

Jackson turned and headed back down the corridor. The young woman who had handed out the press releases was ushering everyone from the room. She had been joined by an assistant, ensuring that no one wandered off on their own.

'Linda says she's not seen you before,' the assistant informed Fox.

'Temporary assignment,' he explained.

'Me too. I'm usually Community Liaison.' She looked around her. 'Makes a change, I suppose.'

Fox nodded his agreement, and followed everyone else back to reception.

Alison Pears had his number; all he could do was wait. He drove into Stirling, and started seeing signs pointing him towards the Wallace Monument. He could see it in the distance, a single Gothic-looking tower atop a hill. He tried to remember what he knew about Wallace. Like every other Scot, he'd watched *Braveheart*, won over by it. Stirling Bridge was the battle Wallace had won against the English invaders. Having no other plan, Fox kept following the signposts, eventually turning into a car park. A couple of single-decker buses sat idling, awaiting the return of their tour parties. Fox got out of the Volvo and wandered into the Legends café. He was recalling more snippets of information about Wallace, mostly about his life's excruciating end. There was an information desk, and the woman behind it told him it cost £7.75 to visit the monument.

'Seven seventy-five?' he queried.

'There's an audiovisual presentation – and Wallace's sword.'

'Anything else?'

'Well, you can climb to the top of the tower.'

'The hill looks pretty steep.'

'There's a free bus to the top.'

'Free if I pay seven seventy-five?' Fox pretended to be thinking about it. 'Is the statue still there? The one that looks like Mel Gibson?'

'It's been moved to Brechin,' she replied, a little coolness entering her voice.

Fox smiled to let her know he wasn't going to become a customer. Instead, he saved five pounds by settling for peppermint tea in Legends, where he had a good view of the hillside and the memorial above it. Wallace was reckoned a patriot: could the same really be said of Francis Vernal? Had he been *justified* – that word MacIver had wanted to debate – in his stance and his actions? And what would either of them make of the Scotland where Fox found himself: was this the same country they had fought for and lost their lives for? There were visitors in the shop next to the reception desk. They were debating the purchase of beach towels made to look like kilts. Theirs was probably a romantic Scotland of glens and castles, Speyside malts and eightsome reels. Other Scotlands were available if you cared to check, and at least as many people these days favoured looking forward to the longing glance back at the nation left behind. The tables around him were filling up. He didn't bother pouring a second cup from the teapot. As he was returning to his car, his phone rang. But it wasn't Alison Pears.

'Mr Fox? This is the nurse at Lauder Lodge. I'm afraid your father's been taken ill.'

He drove back to Edinburgh in a daze. It was only when he reached the Royal Infirmary that he realised the car radio had been switched on throughout. He couldn't remember listening to any of it. He'd been told to try A and E first. Mitch had been found on the floor of his room.

'Could just be a fall,' the nurse had told Fox, her tone of voice indicating that she didn't believe her own words.

'Was he conscious?'

'Not really …'

Fox parked on a double yellow line in the ambulances' drop-off zone and headed inside. Someone was being served by the receptionist, so he waited his turn. There were only two or three people seated in the waiting area. They were staring at a TV in the corner of the room. The receptionist didn't seem to be in a hurry, so Fox walked past her desk and towards the receiving area. Nobody stopped him or asked him what he was doing. Patients lay on trolleys, some in curtained cubicles. Fox did a circuit of the room. A member of staff was busy at a computer. He asked her where he might find Mitchell Fox.

'He was brought in an hour ago,' he explained, 'from Lauder Lodge nursing home.'

'Might not be in the system yet.' She walked over to a marker-board on the wall and studied it. Then asked another member of the team, who nodded and approached Fox.

'Are you a relative?'

'I'm his son.'

'Mr Fox has gone for an X-ray. After that, it'll be straight to the day ward.'

'Is he all right?'

'We'll know more in a little while. There's a waiting area just—'

'Can I see him?'

'The receptionist will let you know.'

Fox was pointed back in the direction of reception. By the time he got there, there was no queue, so he gave his name and was told to take a seat. He slumped as best he could on the hard plastic chair and stared at the ceiling. No one was watching the TV any more; they were busy peering at the screens of their phones. A woman with a bandaged arm kept walking around. When she got too close to the doors, they opened automatically, allowing in a blast of cold air from the world outside. It was a process she seemed happy to keep repeating. There was a cupboard nearby that kept being unlocked and locked again by members of staff. Fox couldn't see what they were doing in there exactly. The two toilet cubicles were being kept busy, as were the snack machines. One young man was trying to get the coin slot to accept a particular ten-pence piece. Every time it was rejected, he tried again, having studied the coin for any obvious flaws. Fox eventually went over and replaced it with a ten-pence piece of his own. This one worked, but the young man looked no happier.

'You're welcome,' Fox told him, returning to his seat.

One member of staff seemed to have the job of emptying the waste bin and removing any newspapers that had been left lying around. The bin bag wasn't even half-full when he replaced it. Ten minutes later he was back, checking to see how full the new bag was, then moving the bin across to the other side of the room. Fox managed to stop himself asking why. On the TV, a man was telling another man how little a small ornament was worth. It then went for auction, and failed to sell. Was it an heirloom? Fox wondered. When first purchased, had the buyer had any inkling that it would one day feature on a daytime programme – and sorely disappoint its current owner?

The waiting area's resident smoker returned from another cigarette break, her hacking cough heralding her arrival. Then the doors shuddered open again as the woman with the bandaged arm wandered past them. Fox turned in his seat to face her.

'Will you bloody well stop that!' he shouted. She looked surprised. So did the receptionist, who followed this with a frowned warning. Fox held up a hand in capitulation and went back to staring at the ceiling. It wasn't just his dad, he realised – it was everything else, too. The questions that seemed to whirl all around him; the characters whose lives were suddenly connected to his own; the hours of sleep he was lacking; the sense of utter, abject futility …

And then his phone interrupted with a text. It was from a number he didn't recognise, and when he opened the message it was an address, postcode and time. The postcode was FK9, the time 7.15 p.m. Fox copied the postcode into his phone's map. The highlighted area took in Stirling University. Fox guessed that he was being invited to Alison Pears's home, and that she and her husband lived practically next door to the university. He decided not to bother replying, but he added the phone number to his address book, just for future reference.

And for something to do.

After almost an hour, he asked the receptionist for a progress report, and was told his father was in Combined Assessment.

'Along there,' she explained, pointing through another set of doors. Fox nodded his thanks and followed the signs on the wall. Eventually he arrived at a nurses' station. His father seemed to have arrived only a few minutes before. Staff were still fussing around his bed. A machine was monitoring his heart rate. It gave a regular beep, creating a rhythm with the other machines nearby.

'How is he?' Fox asked.

'A doctor will be along soon.'

'But he's all right?'

'The doctor will have a word ...'

A chair was provided for Fox's use. His father's eyes were closed, the bottom half of his face covered by a translucent oxygen mask. Fox went to squeeze his hand, but saw that there was a spring-loaded clip on one finger, linking it to the machine. He touched the wrist instead, finding it warm. He looked for any signs that his father might be about to open his eyes. There was a bruise on his forehead and a bit of swelling – probably from the fall.

'Dad,' Fox said, just loud enough for his father to hear. 'It's Malcolm.'

No response. His fingers sought the pulse in Mitch's wrist. It beat a slow, steady tattoo in time to the machine.

'Dad,' he repeated.

The staff seemed to be discussing something at the nurses' station. Fox wondered where his father's clothes were. He was wearing a short-sleeved hospital gown. One of the staff had broken off from the discussion to make a phone call.

'We can't take any more admissions,' he explained. 'No spaces left.'

So it could always have been worse: Mitch could have been kept waiting on a trolley in a corridor. Fox wondered if there were some sort of hierarchy, and whether that meant things were serious.

Could just be a fall ...

'I don't believe it.' The voice came from behind him. He turned his head and saw Jude standing there, arms by her sides. Fox got to his feet.

'They say he fell,' he began to explain.

'I don't mean Dad,' she said, her voice shaking. 'I mean *you*.'

It took Fox a moment to realise what crime he had committed. 'Jude, I'm sorry ...'

'Walked into Lauder Lodge as usual. "Oh," they tell me, "did your brother not say? Your father's been rushed to hospital ..." So thanks for that, Malcolm. Thanks a bunch.'

A member of the nursing team was approaching, gesturing for them to keep the noise down.

'I plain forgot, Jude. I was up to high doh ...'

'How do you think *I've* been? All the way here in the taxi ...' She had turned her attention from Malcolm to Mitch. 'Not knowing what I was going to find.'

'Sit down,' Fox said, offering her the chair. 'I'll get you some water.'

'I don't want any of your water!'

'Look,' the nurse started to warn them, 'I know this is difficult, but you'll have to keep it down for the sake of the other patients.'

'What's wrong with him?' Jude was still studying her father.

'It might be a stroke,' the nurse said. 'But we can't know that for sure yet.'

'A stroke?' Jude lowered herself on to the chair, gripping its sides with both hands.

'He's already had an X-ray,' Fox explained to his sister.

'There'll be a doctor along in a minute,' the nurse added.

Fox nodded to let the nurse know everything was fine now. But when he made to squeeze Jude's shoulder, she shrugged him off.

'Don't touch me,' she said. So Fox stood there and watched as she leaned forward until her head was resting against the edge of the bed. Her whole body spasmed as she sobbed. Fox looked over towards the staff, but they'd seen it all before. Eventually the same nurse came with a few words of advice.

'There's a café in the main entrance. You might be better off there. Give us your number and we'll buzz you when the doctor turns up.'

But Jude shook her head. She was staying, so Fox stayed too. Another chair was found for him and he placed it next to his sister. She was squeezing their father's hand, and failing to dislodge the finger-clip.

'They found him on the floor of his room,' Fox explained quietly. 'He hit his head when he fell.' He paused, realising there was nothing else to add, apart from yet another apology. Jude wouldn't look at him. When she did lift her face from the bed, she focused on the machine instead.

When the doctor arrived, he seemed impossibly young to Fox –

barely out of his teens, surely. No white coat or stethoscope; just a shirt and tie and rolled-up sleeves.

'No bones broken, no fractures,' he recited, flicking through the notes he'd been handed. 'Might just do a scan. We'll keep him in a day or so ...'

'Someone mentioned a stroke,' Fox said.

'Mmm, it's one possibility.' Fox had been expecting the doctor to shine a light in Mitch's eyes, or take his blood pressure and pulse ... something like that. But the young man just glanced at the patient. The notes were telling him what he needed to know. 'We'll start to get a better idea when he comes round.'

'Should we try rousing him?' Fox asked.

'Best leave it.' The doctor had come to the end of his reading. 'Scan later today or maybe tomorrow. After that, we'll hopefully have some firmer news.'

And with that he was gone, moving to a patient on the other side of the room.

Jude didn't say anything, and neither did Fox. He'd seldom felt as useless. When someone from the nurses' station asked if they'd like a cup of tea, he nodded and felt pathetically grateful. Jude wanted water, and both drinks duly arrived. Fox said sorry again, and this time Jude looked at him.

'You never think of me – either of you,' she said.

'Not now, Jude. Leave it for later.' Fox nodded towards Mitch. 'He might be able to hear.'

'Maybe I *want* him to hear.'

'Even so ...'

She took a sip of water from the plastic glass, cupping it in both hands. Fox's tea was too strong. The only way to make it drinkable was to add both sachets of sugar.

'Look,' he told his sister, 'I was in the middle of something when they phoned me. I wasn't thinking straight – even when I got here.'

'No room in that head of yours for me, eh?'

'Can we cut the martyr crap, Jude, just this once?'

He managed to hold her gaze, but only for a few seconds.

'You're some piece of work, Malcolm,' she said, slowly and steadily. 'You really are.'

'Better to be something than nothing, eh?' He made the mistake of glancing at his watch.

'Somewhere you need to be?' she asked.

'Always.'

'Don't let family get in the way, will you?'

He was trying to calculate how long it would take him to get to Stirling. Would the evening rush hour slow him?

'Christ, you really *are* planning to up and leave.' Jude's mouth stayed open. 'Whatever it is, it can't be more important than this.'

'Just because you don't understand doesn't mean Dad wouldn't.'

'And I'm supposed to just sit here?'

'You'll do whatever you want to do, Jude, same as always.'

'Said the kettle to the pot.'

It was hard to disagree, so Fox didn't bother trying. He asked her if she needed money for the café. She kept him waiting for an answer before admitting that the taxi had cleaned her out. He placed a twenty-pound note on the bed, next to where she was holding Mitch's hand.

'I'll be back later,' he promised. 'You going to be all right?'

'What if I say no?'

'Then I'll feel worse than I already do.'

'Just bugger off, Malcolm.'

Which was exactly what he did, after handing one of the nurses his card with his mobile number on it.

The nurse nodded, but then looked over towards Jude. 'Is she going to throw another wobbly?'

Fox shook his head with some confidence. 'Just so long as I'm not here,' he explained.

35

It was a large, modern house down a side road opposite the university and not far from the Wallace Monument. A low brick wall separated it from its neighbours. There were fake shutters either side of each set of windows, and Palladian-style pillars flanking the front door. The gates had been left open for him, and the driveway was tarmacked. As Fox parked alongside a sleek Maserati and a small, sporty Lexus, the door opened. Fox recognised Stephen Pears from his photographs. The man beckoned towards him, as if welcoming a guest to a party.

'Alison's taking a phone call,' he said. 'She'll only be a minute.' Then he stretched out his hand for Fox to shake. He had good teeth and that tan, but was a stone or two heavier than necessary. His permanent five o'clock shadow could not disguise the double chin and jowls. Life, it seemed to Fox, was close to proving too much of a good thing for Stephen Pears.

'Find the place okay?' he asked as he led Fox into a double-height hallway.

'Yes thanks.'

A dog appeared at Pears's side, a Labrador with a glossy black coat. Fox reached down a hand to stroke its head. 'What's she called?' he asked.

'*He's* called Max.'

'Hiya, Max.'

But the dog had already lost interest in the visitor and was turning away. Fox straightened up. There were photographs lining the wall next to him. Fox recognised a number of celebrities. They were all pictured standing alongside Pears, smiling, occasionally shaking hands.

'Sean Connery,' Fox commented, nodding towards one particular photo.

'Bumped into him and just had to get a snap.'

'Looks like the New Club,' Fox commented.

Pears looked surprised. 'Are you a member?'

Fox shook his head. 'You?' he asked.

'It's nice and central when I want to impress people,' Pears explained. 'Come on through, won't you? I was just pouring Andy a drink.'

Andy being Justice Minister Andrew Watson. He rose from the sofa at Fox's approach and they shook hands.

'Malcolm Fox,' Fox said by way of introduction. No reason for Watson to be told any more than that.

'Lothian and Borders Police?' Watson commented.

Okay, so the Justice Minister knew. Fox nodded and turned down Pears's offer of a malt.

'Water's fine,' he said.

It came with ice cubes and a wedge of lime in a heavy crystal tumbler. Pears clinked glasses with his brother-in-law and sniffed the whisky before sampling it.

'Not bad, Stephen,' Watson said approvingly.

'Sit down, Inspector,' Pears commanded, hands in movement again.

Most of the ground floor seemed to be devoted to this huge open-plan space. Four or five sofas, a vast glass dining table with a dozen chairs placed around it, a fifty-inch TV screen on one wall. Spotlights picked out undersized paintings in overwrought frames. Piano music was being piped from somewhere – Fox couldn't see any speakers. The French doors to the rear of the room led out to a terrace with lawns and a tennis court beyond. The tennis court was floodlit, either in an effort to impress, or because Pears could well afford to waste the electricity.

'How's she bearing up?' Watson asked his host.

'Your sister doesn't "bear up",' Pears chided him. 'She commands, she overcomes, she triumphs.'

'And how is she "triumphing" tonight?'

Pears smiled into his glass. 'This is just the sort of thing she's been needing. Otherwise it's all meetings and number-crunching.'

Watson nodded. 'I know the feeling.'

Fox was staring at the ice cubes in his drink.

'You all right there?' Pears asked.

'Fine, yes.'

'Sure?'

'Sure.' But something made Fox change his mind. 'My dad's in hospital. Just happened this afternoon.'

'Sorry to hear that,' Pears said, while Watson made a grunting sound that could have passed for commiseration. 'Shouldn't you be there? Alison can make a bit of space in her diary tomorrow.'

Fox gave a shrug. 'I'm here now.'

Pears nodded, keeping his eyes on Fox. 'Something serious?' he enquired.

'They're doing tests ...'

Pears smiled. 'I meant your business with Alison. She's been a bit cagey, hasn't she, Andy?'

'A bit.'

'It was that Scotland Yard bloke who mentioned you're Lothian and Borders ...'

'DCI Jackson?' Fox guessed.

'Left here half an hour ago,' Pears stated. 'I think he was keen to stick around.'

The Justice Minister was loosening his tie, undoing the top button of his shirt. 'He said you've got some case in Fife.'

Fox nodded slowly. 'Started off pretty straightforwardly,' he admitted. 'Then it got complicated.'

'The opposite of my business,' Pears commented, getting up to refill his glass. He offered to do the same for Watson, but Watson shook his head. 'I like taking complex things and turning them into something that's simple to understand and communicate. That way you sell it to people. Problem with the way finance was going the past ten or so years, nobody could grasp *any* of it, so nobody questioned it. Back to basics, that's my motto.'

Watson looked as if he had heard this speech many times. He did everything short of roll his eyes. When the financier was seated again, he leaned forward towards Fox.

'Is it anything you can talk about?' Pears asked. 'I swear I won't breathe a word, though I can't vouch for the Justice Minister ...'

'There was a CID officer, misusing his position,' Fox began. He felt a crushing tiredness all of a sudden, and had to grip the tumbler for fear he would drop it. 'Then his uncle died – looked like suicide, but it wasn't. CID seem to have the nephew in the frame for it ...'

'But?' Fox had Pears's full attention.

'The nephew's dead now too. Someone chased him into the sea and he drowned.'

Pears sat back in his chair as if to think this through. Watson, however, was checking his phone for messages, apparently un-interested.

'The uncle was doing some research into the death of an SNP activist called Francis Vernal,' Fox went on.

Watson stopped what he was doing. *Now* he was interested. 'I know that name,' he said. 'He was in the news around the time I joined the party.'

'I thought you were still in a Babygro when you took the pledge,' Pears teased his brother-in-law.

'Not quite – I was in high school. One of our teachers was an SNP councillor.'

'You underwent the indoctrination process?' Pears swallowed some more whisky.

Watson grew prickly. 'We all know *your* politics, Stephen.'

'I don't,' Fox countered.

Watson looked at him. 'Take a wild guess. I'm even hearing rumblings of a peerage, now the Tories are in power down south. Cameron's stuffing them into the House of Lords like there's no tomorrow.'

Pears laughed and shook his head, while still seeming gratified. 'I'll bet you fifty quid your boss'll end up in the same place eventu-ally – maybe when he gets a drubbing at the next election.'

'That's not going to happen.'

'With the lead Labour have got?'

'We'll pick up votes from the Lib Dems – they hate what your lot have done to their party in Westminster.'

Pears seemed to think about this, then turned back to Fox. 'What's your opinion, Inspector? Are you a political animal?'

'I try to keep my head down, sir.'

'One way of avoiding the shrapnel,' Pears conceded. 'But you've got me intrigued now – what has all this stuff about drownings and activists got to do with my wife?'

'She was a student at St Andrews at the time Mr Vernal died. There's a theory she may have known him.'

'St Andrews?' Watson was shaking his head. 'Two years at Aberdeen, then she jacked it in and joined your lot instead.'

Pears was nodding. 'Someone's fed you a line, Inspector.'

Watson was holding his phone to his ear, having punched in a number. 'Rory?' he asked. 'What time's the car picking me up?' He listened, checking his watch. 'Fine,' he said, ending the call.

'Such a busy life,' Pears said, feigning sympathy. 'All of it paid for by the Inspector and me.'

'And worth every bloody penny,' Watson muttered. He glanced towards the sweeping staircase. 'Is she ever coming down? Maybe I should go up ...'

'Finish your drink, man.' Pears found to his surprise that he'd finished his own – again. He rose to his feet, and this time Fox needed his own tumbler refilling. 'One more,' Pears stated, 'and I'll call it a night.'

Watson pursed his lips, telling Fox that this might not necessarily be the case. There was the sound of a door closing upstairs. Alison Pears made an exasperated sound as she descended the staircase, phone in hand.

'Do I need to be there every minute of every day?' she complained. Then, to Fox: 'Hello again.'

'The inspector has been telling us what he's working on,' Pears said, handing her a gin and tonic. 'All very mysterious, but also a wasted trip – got you mixed up with someone who was a student at St Andrews.'

The Chief Constable toasted the room with her drink and took a slug, exhaling afterwards.

'Better?' her husband asked.

'Better,' she confirmed. Then, to Fox: 'Let's go into the study and clear this up.'

Her brother got to his feet. 'I need a word first, Ali – when my boss asks, what can I tell him about these bloody bombers?'

'Nothing so far to indicate they won't be charged,' she said after a moment's thought. 'The house they were renting is a gold mine – material, blueprints and manuals, even a list of targets.'

'Glasgow Airport again?' her husband guessed.

'RAF Leuchars,' she corrected him. 'And the naval dockyard. And our ex-prime minister.'

'Whoever caught them should get a medal,' Pears said, staring with purpose at the Justice Minister.

'They might at that,' Watson conceded.

'Come on then,' Alison Pears said to Fox. 'Let's hear this story of yours – might take my mind off things.'

'Be gentle with the inspector,' her husband suggested. 'He's had some bad news ...'

She led him to a door in the corner of the room. It opened on to a study with wood-panelled walls and a fake bookcase. A small brass telescope stood on a tripod by the window. There was a two-seater brown hide sofa, and a swivel chair in front of the desk. Pears took the chair and signalled that Fox should take the sofa. The leather creaked as he settled.

She was dressed casually – baggy pink T-shirt, black joggers, Nike trainers. Fox wondered if there was a gym somewhere on the property.

'Bad news?' she said, echoing her husband's words. Fox shrugged the question aside, ready with one of his own.

'He doesn't know?'

She considered the range of answers and evasions open to her. 'Know what?'

Fox gave her a look that said: *let's not do this.* 'Neither of them do?' he persisted, bringing out the matriculation photographs. 'Wonder what they'll say when I show them these. You've changed, but not quite enough to be unrecognisable.'

She studied the photos, saying nothing for a moment. 'Andy knows I did some undercover work in my early years on the force,' she eventually conceded.

'But not that you posed as a St Andrews University student for two years?'

'No,' she admitted. 'Though he may be wondering about it now.' She was using her feet against the floor to swivel gently in the chair. There was a slice of lime in her glass, and she extracted it, placing it on a corner of the desk.

'DCI Jackson filled you in?' Fox surmised.

'Some; maybe not all.' She squeezed the bridge of her nose, as if trying to ward off a headache. 'What's this bad news you've had?'

'Never mind,' Fox said. 'Let's concentrate on your affair with Francis Vernal.' He ignored the glower she gave him. 'It was a way of infiltrating the Dark Harvest Commando?'

She was still giving him the same hard stare.

'I know what you're thinking,' Fox went on. 'It was a long time ago, you were a different person. And this isn't the best time for it all to come bobbing up again.' He paused, placing the photos back in his pocket.

'I'll tell you what it was,' she eventually said, keeping her voice low in case anyone outside the door might be listening. 'It was two years down the pan.'

'Because of the car crash?'

She nodded slowly. 'The whole bloody edifice just crumbled after that. Some were too scared to go on – they thought MI5 were out to assassinate the lot of them.'

'And were they?'

'I wasn't MI5.'

'You were recruited by Special Branch?'

'They needed someone on the inside – a pretty face usually does the trick. But it couldn't be a pretty face from south of the border, could it? The English were supposed to be the enemy.'

'While you were fresh out of Tulliallan and looked younger than your years. So Special Branch managed to get you into St Andrews, where you could become political, burrow ever deeper and feed information back?'

'If you know so much, why do you need me?'

'I need you because a man was murdered, and no one at the time or since has done anything about it.' He watched her for a moment; it was impossible to read her face. 'The home address in Glasgow ...?'

'Short-term office let,' she explained. 'Used for mail drops.'

'And all the time you were edging closer to Francis Vernal?'

'Francis was the conduit. He was supposed to lead to the people we were *really* interested in.'

Fox was thoughtful for a moment. 'He was with you that evening, the night he died?'

'Yes.'

'And you knew he was being tailed?'

She gave a slow nod.

'Did you know about the money he kept in the car?'

'He usually had some. Every meeting the DHC held, someone needed a bit of cash.'

'For buying weapons?'

'All sorts of reasons.'

'According to Donald MacIver, there could have been as much as forty grand hidden in the boot – that was a chunk of money back then.'

'Donald MacIver?' She gave a wistful smile. 'He lives in a fantasy world, Inspector; he always did.'

'He remembers you fondly.'

'It's *Alice* he remembers,' she corrected him.

'How about John Elliot?'

'I see him on TV sometimes.'

'He's never gleaned that you're Alice Watts?'

'We didn't know one another back then – John was only interested in women who were on heat.' She stared at him. 'As far as I know, you're the first to make the connection, so well done you.' Her voice dripped sarcasm.

'Alan Carter never got in touch?'

'He's the ex-detective?' She watched Fox nod. 'I didn't know anything about that until Jackson mentioned it.'

'Do you know the name Charles Mangold?'

She gave a heavy sigh. 'This really can't wait a week or two?'

'It really can't,' Fox stated. 'Charles Mangold?' he repeated.

'Francis's partner in the law firm. He had a thing for *Mrs* Vernal, I seem to remember. Francis thought so, anyway.'

'Mangold was paying Alan Carter to look into Vernal's death. He wanted to prove something to the widow.'

'What?'

Fox shrugged. 'Either that her husband was a political assassination ...'

'Or?'

'Or that he was a terrorist and sleazebag she's been a fool to idolise all these years.'

'You sound like you favour the latter theory.'

'I think I do. You never met the wife?'

She shook her head. 'I'd no interest in her. All I wanted was whatever information Francis could provide.'

'Did you get any?'

'Not much.'

'But you went to quite a lot of trouble to seek it out.'

The glower was back. 'Meaning?'

'Sleeping with him.'

'Who says I did?'

'You're telling me you didn't?'

'I'm telling you it's none of your business.'

He let the silence sit between them for a moment, then mentioned that he had the letters.

'What letters?' She failed to stop a spot of colour appearing on either cheek.

'The letters you sent him. Imogen Vernal found them and hung on to them.' He waited for her to take this in. 'You're telling me you never loved him?'

She squeezed shut her eyes, then blinked them open again. 'I'm telling you it's ancient history – and also none of your business. You're a *Complaints* officer. This is not a Complaints matter.'

'You're right. Maybe I should just hand everything over to CID …'

'Don't be crass.'

Fox waited a beat before continuing. 'There was a cop called Gavin Willis. He led the inquiry – such as it was – when Vernal died. But you'd vanished by then.'

'Special Branch didn't want me sticking around – the questions could have been awkward. Besides, the DHC had scattered …'

'So you said. For some reason, Willis held on to Vernal's car.'

Her eyes widened a little. 'Why did he do that?'

'I'm not sure. One thing I do know: he was selling guns to groups like the DHC. Specifically to a man called "Hawkeye".' Fox handed her the photograph. She took her time studying it.

'I haven't seen this in years.'

'The man you've linked arms with?' Fox prompted.

'Hawkeye, yes. He looks a bit awkward, doesn't he? The arm thing would have been my idea. He wasn't much of one for social-ising … or for the ladies. Never went to the pub after meetings – most people, that was what they looked forward to: not the political theory but the booze-up.'

'After Vernal's death, you never spoke to any of them again?'

She shook her head and folded her arms across her chest, as if suddenly chilled. 'I was another person,' she stated quietly.

'How do you think Francis Vernal died?'

'I think he shot himself.'

'Why?'

'The drink, his marriage, the fear of discovery. He knew we were monitoring him.'

'The two of you didn't argue that night?'

'Not really. I think it annoyed him that all I ever wanted to talk about was the group. He said it was a madness in me.' She unfolded her arms, and studied the photograph again.

'He never twigged you were undercover?'

'I don't think so.'

'If he had ...?'

'It might have led him to do something, I suppose.'

'Did you ever see a gun in his car?'

'Doesn't mean one wasn't there.'

'That's a no, then?' Fox paused for a moment. 'DCI Jackson doesn't know?'

'About Francis and me?' She considered this. 'I don't think so. Why should he?'

'He's been digging in the files.'

'Why?'

'Wondering why I was interested. He told me something ...'

'What?'

'The agents tailing Francis Vernal took a look at him after the crash.' Fox was studying her reaction. 'He was still alive. No head shot at that point.'

'What did they do?' The blood had drained from her face. Her voice was pitched just above a whisper.

'If Jackson's to be believed, they didn't kill him. They just walked away and left him there. No call to the emergency services. Nothing.'

She seemed to wrap her arms more closely around herself. 'That's awful,' she said.

'I'm glad we agree.'

There was silence in the room for almost a full minute.

'They could have shot him,' Alison Pears eventually conceded. 'Shot him and taken the money.'

'They could,' Fox agreed. 'Tell me, was Vernal really just a job to you?'

Her look hardened a little. 'How often do I need to say it? That's something I'm not willing to discuss.'

'It might be the one thing I can take back to Charles Mangold for him to give to the widow.'

'I think this has gone far enough.'

'Alan Carter really never contacted you? Never connected you to Alice Watts?'

'I've already told you, Inspector – you're the first.' She stood up, indicating that the meeting was over. Reluctantly, Fox got to his feet. 'I need to know how far you're going to take this,' she asked.

'I can't answer that.'

'It would put my mind at rest,' she persevered. 'There's a job I should be focusing on.'

He nodded his understanding. 'Thank you for seeing me.' He was holding out his hand for the photograph.

'I'd like to keep it,' she said.

Fox kept his hand held out. Her phone rang and she answered it, relinquishing the photo at the same time. 'Speak to me,' she said. As she listened, Fox watched her turn into a Chief Constable again. It was as if her talk with him had been slotted into a filing cabinet somewhere.

'No,' she was stating, 'Govan can't bloody well have them. They're *my* suspects.'

Govan: the high-security police station in Glasgow. It was where terrorist suspects usually ended up, but Pears was fighting her corner. As the argument continued, Fox realised she craved the media attention because it gave her the chance to shine. What was it her husband had said? Something about her 'needing' this case. By the time she ended the call, she had made her determination clear to the other participant. She looked at Fox, and he knew what she was telling him: *I'm a fighter. I'm used to winning. Just remember that* ... He nodded and opened the door for her. She marched out ahead of him, making for the stairs again. Stephen Pears was watching TV, but rose to greet Fox.

'Everything cleared up?' he asked, watching his wife disappear from view.

'I'm fairly satisfied,' Fox decided to answer. He noted that Andrew Watson seemed to have left. The lights by the tennis court had been switched off.

'A case of mistaken identity, then,' the financier was stating.

'It happens,' Fox concurred.

Pears patted him on the back and said he would show him out. 'In fact, it's such a lovely evening, I might take Max for a walk.'

'Thank you again, Mr Pears,' Fox said, shaking the man's hand. Pears applied his free hand to Fox's wrist.

'Sorry again about your father. I hope he's all right.' He paused, still grasping Fox's wrist. 'And if you ever need anything, Inspector...'

Fox could see he meant nothing by it – it was just something the self-made millionaire had grown used to saying. But he thanked him again anyway.

*

Jude was asleep on her chair. The nurse said she hadn't moved from the spot.

'We told her to go stretch her legs, but she wouldn't. I brought her tea and biscuits but she left them.'

They were standing at the nurses' station, keeping their voices low. Almost all the patients were asleep. 'My dad's not woken up?' Fox asked.

'Not yet.'

'What about the scan?'

'CT's a bit backed up. It'll be tomorrow now.'

'What's the drip for?' Fox nodded towards the tube inserted into his father's arm.

'Need to keep his fluids up,' the nurse explained. 'Do you want to rouse your sister, or will I do it?'

Fox had been informed on his arrival that there was a bed ready for his father on a proper ward. Orderlies would be coming to wheel the bed along to its new berth.

'I'll do it,' he said. He walked up behind Jude and rested a hand against her neck. Her skin was cool. She inhaled, twitched and jolted awake, giving a moan of complaint.

'They're putting him on a ward,' Fox explained. 'Nothing we can do till tomorrow. Let me give you a lift home.'

'I can manage.' Sleepily, she pushed the hair out of her eyes. 'There's buses and a taxi rank outside.'

'Be a lot quicker if I did it.' He paused. 'Please, Jude.'

She focused on him, and saw something in his eyes. For whatever reason, he needed to do this for her. She was giving a little nod of acquiescence as the orderlies arrived for their patient.

The nurse made sure brother and sister had the ward details and a contact number. Fox thanked her and walked with Jude back along the corridor past the A and E desk. He didn't recognise any of the people waiting. The doors swung open, Jude sucking in lungfuls of the cold night air.

'Better?' he asked her. She made a non-committal sound and followed him to his car.

They didn't say much during the drive. Fox was thinking back to the house in Stirling, the Chief Constable and her politician brother. And the money man making sure everyone got what they needed.

Fox was wondering if *he* had got what he needed. It took him a moment to realise that Jude was crying. He assured her that everything would be fine.

'What if it isn't, though?'

Then it isn't.

But he found himself saying 'It will be' instead.

He dropped her at her terraced house. She had a neighbour called Pettifer and Fox said she should knock on her door.

'I'll do it for you, if you like,' he offered.

But Jude shook her head. 'I'll just go to bed,' she countered. 'Bit of a lie-down.'

Fox could only nod. 'I'll pick you up tomorrow – we'll go see him together.'

'Don't put yourself out on my account.'

'Let's not do this, Jude.'

She rubbed at her eyes. 'What time, then?'

'I'll phone you.'

'Something might come up,' she warned him.

'I won't let it.'

'Didn't stop you tonight, did it?' She studied his face, then gave a sigh. 'All right,' she conceded. 'I'll see you in the morning.' She closed the passenger-side door and began walking up the path towards her house with its curtainless front window and unkempt garden. Fox remembered a promise he'd made three or four months back – *I'll help you tidy it; only take us a couple of hours.* A couple of hours he had never quite found. Jude didn't glance back over her shoulder towards the car, didn't turn and wave. Once indoors, her lights went on but she didn't come to the window. Fox put the car into gear and drove off.

Twenty minutes later, he was sitting outside another house – nicer, more modern. No front garden for Tony Kaye, just lots of lovely monoblock so he could park his Mondeo off-road. Fox had just ended the call. He watched shadows moving behind the living-room curtains. Then the curtains parted and Kaye gestured towards him. But Fox shook his head. The door opened and Kaye padded out in what looked like a pair of leather carpet-slippers. His shirt was untucked, open at the neck.

'My place not good enough for you?' he said, yanking open the passenger-side door and getting in.

'Didn't want to disturb you. How's Hannah?'

'She was fine till five minutes ago. Now she's wondering what she's done to offend you.' Kaye peered towards the house, as if expecting to see his wife scowling at a window.

'I've had a hell of a day and I need to dump it on someone,' Fox confided.

'Think *you've* had it hard? I spent about three hours on the phone to Cash, trying to persuade him to bring Tosh Garioch in for an interview.'

'And?'

'Tomorrow morning first thing.' Kaye sounded proud of the achievement.

'What about the report?'

'On your desk. McEwan likes it well enough.'

'Has it gone to Fife Constabulary?'

'Not without your say-so, Foxy.'

'Then I'll look at it in the morning.'

Kaye nodded, then fixed his eyes on Fox. 'Is it Evelyn Mills?' he asked.

'What?'

'Throwing herself at you, and you need my advice?'

'I haven't heard a cheep from her.'

'Is that a good thing or a bad thing?'

'Give it a rest, Tony.'

Kaye gave a low chuckle and patted Fox's leg, then shifted a little in the passenger seat, the better to face his friend. 'Okay,' he said, 'small talk done and dusted – time for you to spit it out. And I want every single gory detail.'

So Fox gave him the lot.

Twelve

Twelve

36

Fox's alarm woke him at seven. His thinking: go to HQ, grab the report and take it to the hospital with him. He poured All-Bran into a bowl, then found that the inch of milk left in the carton had turned to yoghurt. He used cold water from the kitchen tap instead, and wrote out a shopping list while he ate. Driving to Fettes Avenue, he felt that his breakfast had formed a solid mass in his stomach. The canteen was just opening, so he took a coffee to the Complaints office and unlocked the door. As Kaye had promised, Fox's copy of the report was waiting on his desk. Kaye had added a yellow Post-it note: 'Affix gold star here'. Fox peeled it off and binned it. He couldn't help flicking to the last page. The summary was four lines long and suggested that 'concrete evidence' against the three officers would be hard to find, leaving only 'legitimate concerns about the level of competence and compliance'.

He smiled to himself, knowing that given a freer hand, Tony Kaye's language would have been altogether more colourful. What the investigators were saying to the brass in Glenrothes was: there's a problem, but it's up to you if you want to pursue it.

And the best of British luck.

There were another twenty-three pages of text, but they could wait. Fox rolled the report into a tube he could fit in his jacket pocket. He looked around the office. Naysmith had left a note on Tony Kaye's desk reminding him that he now owed the best part of a tenner in 'Tea n Coffee Kitty' arrears. Naysmith had broken the figure down like any accountant of repute, though Fox doubted it would do him much good. He checked his office phone for messages, but there weren't any. No mail, either. Bob McEwan's desk was strewn with reports and other paperwork. Fox knew that when it got too messy, it would be stuffed into one of the drawers.

When he left the office, he locked the door again after him. No one except the Complaints had access to the room – not even the cleaner. Once a week, Naysmith shredded the contents of the various waste-paper baskets and sent it off for recycling. Fox stared at the sign on the door: Professional Standards Unit. How professional was *he* being? By rights, he should be writing his own report – laying down everything he knew and suspected about the deaths of Alan Carter and Francis Vernal. The report could then go to CID: *there's a problem ... up to you if you want to pursue it.*

'The very man,' a voice barked from behind him. He turned to see the Chief Constable, Jim Byars, striding towards him in almost military fashion, arms swinging. The Chief stopped a couple of inches from Fox's face. 'What in the name of the Holy Father is going on?' he demanded.

'Sir?'

'How have you managed to get up Andrew Watson's nose?'

'I needed to discuss something with his sister.'

Byars glared at him. 'I take it you mean Alison Pears, Chief Constable of Central Scotland Constabulary?'

'That's the one.'

'Who happens to be a personal friend of mine, and who is also currently leading the highest-profile inquiry of her career.'

'So she probably doesn't need me sticking my oar in?' Fox nodded slowly. 'Well, she answered my questions, so that's that.'

'What was it you were asking in the first place?'

'Just a tenuous link to the death of Alan Carter.'

Byars rolled his eyes. 'As tenuous as *your* connection to the whole bloody thing.'

'Hard to disagree, sir,' Fox conceded.

'Well then ...'

Fox removed the report from his pocket. 'I've got our conclusions right here. Just need to check a few details before it goes to Fife Constabulary.'

'And that'll be the end of it?'

'That'll be the end of it,' Fox stated.

'I can put Andrew Watson's mind at rest?'

'Absolutely.' Fox paused. 'You can also remind him that his job title includes the word "Justice".'

'What's that supposed to mean?' the Chief Constable was asking, as Fox began to walk away.

He drove to Jude's house. She wasn't answering her phone. He wondered if she'd maybe knocked herself out with some tablets or a few slugs of vodka. When he rang her doorbell, there was no response. He put his face to the living-room window but the place seemed deserted. He bent down at the letter box and yelled her name. Nothing. No sign of life at her neighbour's house either, so he got back in his car and headed for the hospital. He was hitting the rush hour, and the traffic crawled. Then it took him a few minutes to find a bay in the car park. He entered the main concourse. The café and shop were doing good business – not just staff and visitors, but patients, too, identifiable by name tags on their wrists. Fox was gasping for a coffee, but took one look at the queue and kept walking.

As he'd suspected, Jude was seated by Mitch's bedside.

'Thought I was collecting you,' he complained.

'Woke up early.' She was holding her father's hand again.

'He's still not come round?'

She shook her head. There were three other beds in the ward, one of them vacant, elderly patients in the other two. 'Shouldn't you be at work?' she asked.

'I've already been.' He pulled the report from his pocket. 'I was going to sit here and read this.'

'Fine.'

Chairs were stacked against a nearby wall. He lifted one down and carried it to his father's bedside. He didn't know if it was a conscious decision on her part or not, but Jude's chair was angled so that if he were to sit next to her, his own chair would be sticking out into the room, posing a possible obstacle to the staff. Instead of asking her to slide over a bit, he seated himself on the other side of the bed from her.

'Have they given you a time for the scan?'

She shook her head again. She was stroking their father's hair. There was grey stubble on his cheeks and chin, and a line of dried saliva at the side of his mouth. A nurse stopped to check the readout on the machine and enter the findings on a chart at the bottom of the bed. Fox asked her about the scan.

'Hopefully before lunchtime,' she told him. 'He had a peaceful night.' She smiled, as if to reassure him.

He's not peaceful, Fox wanted to correct her, *he's comatose.* But

301

he just returned her smile and thanked her. As the nurse moved away, Fox saw that his sister was scowling at him.

'What?' he asked.

'Can't you throw some weight around?' she hissed.

'What sort of weight?'

'You're a cop, aren't you? Have a word with them – see if there's any way of jumping the queue.'

'They're not the enemy, Jude.'

'Not exactly putting themselves out either, though, are they?'

She had barely finished when two attendants arrived. The nurse brought them over to the bed.

'CT scan,' she announced.

'Thank you,' Fox said again.

'Can we go with him?' Jude asked, getting to her feet.

'Best stay here,' one attendant stated. 'We'll have him back in no time.' The man had tattoos on his arms. He was broad-shouldered and sported a couple of scars on his face. He seemed to have placed Fox as a policeman, just as Fox would have bet money on the man having served time. Jude was reluctant to let go of her father's hand. She leaned over him to plant a kiss on his forehead, then burst into tears.

'Nothing to worry about,' the nurse stressed. Then, to Fox: 'Maybe take her for a cup of tea ...?'

Jude didn't want a cup of tea, but Fox managed to navigate her down the corridor towards the café. She pulled herself away and told him she was going outside for a cigarette.

'Thought you'd stopped,' he said.

'Someone'll give me one,' she replied, walking towards the automatic doors. Fox bought a paper at the shop, then queued for coffee and a bacon roll. He ordered the same for Jude and sat at a table. His phone buzzed. Caller ID: Tony Kaye.

'Morning, Tony.'

'How's your old man doing?'

'Just gone for a scan.'

'You at the Infirmary?'

'Yes.'

'We're just heading across the bridge. Back to sunny Fife.'

'I've not had a chance to look at the report yet.'

'No rush.'

'Conclusion looks sound, though.' Fox had made the mistake of opening the bacon roll. The meat was as grey as the faces around him. He pushed it away.

'I had a text from Cash first thing,' Kaye was saying. 'Joe and me both get to sit in on the interview. We're supposed to keep our traps shut, but if there's something we think he's missed, we give him a sign and discuss it outside the door.'

'You okay with that?'

'You know me, Malcolm.'

Fox smiled to himself. 'That's why I'm asking.'

'Nothing I like better than obeying an order, especially when there's a complete prick on the other end of it.'

Naysmith made a comment from the car's passenger seat.

'What's Joe saying?' Fox asked.

'He's accusing me of getting too close to the Beamer in front.'

'Outside lane?' Fox guessed. 'Seventy-five, eighty ...?'

'And?'

'And making a phone call.'

'Just jump-starting young Joe's heart, so he's on his mettle in Kirkcaldy.'

'Let me know how it goes.'

'Just you focus on your old man.' Kaye paused. 'How's Jude coping?'

'Not brilliantly.'

'What about you?'

'I'm all right.'

'Nothing's more important than family, Malcolm.'

'So you told me last night.'

'Because it's true. Paul Carter and his uncle ... Francis Vernal ... none of them are coming back. Flesh and blood sometimes has to take priority.'

Fox watched Jude re-enter the building. She saw him, and he gestured towards the roll and coffee waiting for her. She shook her head and pointed in the direction of the ward, then moved off that way, quickly disappearing from view.

'Let me know how it goes,' Fox repeated into the phone. Then: 'Are you playing Alex Harvey again?'

'Got to keep reminding Joe that there's more to life than Lady Gaga,' Kaye explained, ending the call.

*

Tosh Garioch's lawyer wasn't sure about the presence of Kaye and Naysmith.

'They are here to observe,' DI Cash told him.

The interview was being recorded, and Naysmith cast a jaundiced eye over DS Young's efforts to set up the apparatus, even sighing once or twice, to Young's obvious annoyance.

Tosh Garioch had pushed his chair back from the desk, the better to splay his legs. He was stocky and muscular, bald dome shining and the thistle tattoo wending its way up the side of his neck.

'You know why you're here, Mr Garioch?' Cash asked, poising a pen above his notebook. Across the table, the lawyer also had a pen. He kept clicking it, until Cash asked him to stop – 'Anyone listening might think I was firing staples at you,' Cash explained. Then he repeated the question.

'Yeah,' Garioch agreed, hand cupping his crotch as he repositioned everything down there. 'I suppose I do.'

'So what were you doing last Wednesday night?'

'I was at home. Normally I'd have been working.'

'As a doorman? For Alan Carter's company?'

'Not so easy now he's dead.'

'You could always ask the Shafiqs for a job.' Cash paused, eyes fixed on Garioch. 'Or maybe not, after you wrangled with them on your employer's behalf.'

Kaye was standing against the far wall, hands behind his back. Garioch gave a glance in his direction. He was wondering where Cash had got that info.

'The Shafiqs were business,' the doorman stated. 'It all got cleared up.'

'Is any of this relevant?' the lawyer interrupted, doodling on a sheet of paper.

'Just warming up,' Cash informed him with a cold smile. Then, to Garioch: 'Mind me asking who was at home with you?'

'Yes.'

Classic mistake – Cash admitted as much with a twitch of his mouth: never ask a question where the answer gets you no further forward.

'Were you on your own?'

'I was with my girlfriend.'

'Ah.' Cash dug a scrap of paper out of his pocket and studied it. 'Billie Donnelly, yes?'

Garioch couldn't help looking in Tony Kaye's direction again. Kaye responded with a wink.

'Is this going anywhere, DI Cash?' the lawyer asked, feigning boredom.

'We've got a witness description fitting your client to a T,' Cash explained. 'Walking down the high street in wet clothes not too long after Paul Carter was beaten up and chased into the sea. Another witness saw the actual chase. Looks to me like a line-up has to be the next order of business.'

'No way,' Garioch said, turning to his lawyer for confirmation. The lawyer slid his thick-rimmed spectacles back up his nose. Cash leaned across the desk towards the pair of them.

'Two witnesses, Tosh. And talk about a motive! You're on the dole because your boss has been topped, and the whole town knows who did it – now you see him staggering out of the Wheatsheaf. None of his CID mates are there to help him. A few angry words, and it begins to turn nasty. We all know Paul Carter's rep – fair old temper on him. I'm not saying he didn't throw the first punch.' Cash made show of studying Garioch's face for injuries. 'On the other hand, he definitely came off worse. He knew it wasn't going to get any better, so he ran. And you went after him. Along the promenade, then down on to the shore itself. You're a big man, but not in the best of shape. Maybe you were never going to catch him, but he was so scared he ran into the surf anyway. Or you *did* catch him ...' Cash's voice drifted off. 'Maybe you did at that.'

'Do I have to listen to this?' Garioch asked his lawyer.

'I think DI Cash would be foolish to think of charging you at this altogether shoddy juncture,' the lawyer speculated.

'There'll be other witnesses,' Cash warned them. 'We haven't even put the description out yet. Huge bald brute of a man with a tattoo on his neck, stumbling through the streets in drenched trousers? Think back, Tosh – you know yourself you were spotted. Nice line-up we'll put together ... but only after we've brought Billie in. Give her a good hard session.' Kaye found himself moving forward half a pace, ready to step in: looked to him as though Garioch was gearing up to go for his tormentor's throat. Cash seemed to realise it too, but it only made him lean a little further across the table towards the man. 'She might perjure herself for you – but that'll count against her in court. She'll end up going down, same as you. You know that old thing they say on TV

305

movies – motive, means, opportunity?' Cash held up three fingers. 'My scratchcard's showing three gold bars, Tosh.'

He eased back in his chair, clasping his hands together. Garioch leaned his knuckles against the edge of the desk, then rose slowly to his feet.

'Did I say you could leave?' Cash asked, not unpleasantly.

'I can go when I want?' Garioch checked with his lawyer. The lawyer nodded.

'Then I'm out of here.'

'Harder you make it for me, the more I'm going to enjoy it,' Cash warned both men.

Garioch glared at him but said nothing. Then he noticed that Tony Kaye was standing between him and the door.

'There's a deal to be done,' Kaye stated. 'If Paul Carter was being set up by his uncle and you had anything to do with it … They're both dead, what's it going to matter?'

'Did I give you permission to speak?' Cash said, his voice almost too calm. Kaye ignored him and kept his eyes locked on Garioch's.

'There's a deal to be done,' he repeated quietly, holding out a business card.

Garioch looked from Kaye to Cash, and from Cash to everyone else in the room.

'Fuck the lot of you,' he growled, pushing past Tony Kaye and hauling open the door.

But only after snatching the business card from Kaye's hand.

37

At lunchtime, Fox drove home. The tests on his father had so far proved inconclusive. It still looked like a stroke, but they wouldn't know more until Mitch regained consciousness.

'Can't you make him?' Jude had asked. 'A shot of adrenaline or something?'

There had been some more tears, and the consultant had suggested that a break from the hospital might be an idea. Fox had offered to drive her, but she'd insisted she would take the bus.

'This is just stupid,' he had made the mistake of telling her. 'Are you going to be like this the rest of your days?' She'd aimed a swipe at his face and stormed off. He had passed her in his car, standing in the bus shelter, arms folded, angry at the whole world.

He made good time and parked outside his house just before one. As he was getting out of the car, his phone rang: Tony Kaye.

'How did it go?' Fox asked him.

'I think DI Cash may be in the huff with me.'

'Excellent work.' Fox pushed his thumb down on the key fob, locking the Volvo. 'I take it you couldn't keep your gob shut?'

'I might have accidentally offered Tosh Garioch a deal.'

'What sort of deal?'

'Go easy on him over the drowning if he talks to us about his boss.'

'Cash wasn't keen on that?'

'Not overly. I'd say he's close to running us out of town.'

'The club has room for two more,' Fox conceded. He was standing at his front door, staring at it.

'Any word on your dad?'

'I'm going to have to ring you back.' Fox ended the call and walked to the living-room window, peering into the house. No sign of movement. Back at the front door, he noted the damage to the jamb. There wasn't much of it. A crowbar or some sort of chisel had been enough. He couldn't help thinking of the damage to the door of Gallowhill Cottage. He studied the neighbouring properties. It was a quiet street –people kept themselves to themselves. It had probably taken the thief half a minute to effect entry. Could have made it look like he was ringing the doorbell or pushing a delivery through the letter box. Fox edged the door open with his foot and stepped into the hall.

It didn't look as though any of the papers on his dining table were missing. Maybe they'd been looked at; it was hard to say. His laptop was gone, along with its cable and charger, though the TV and DVD player hadn't been touched. In the kitchen, the radio had vanished from its spot next to the kettle. Upstairs: bedroom drawers spilling out their contents. His good watch was missing, but his passport remained. Contents of the wardrobe tipped out on to the floor. He sat on the bed and rested his chin on his hands.

Worth calling it in? Yes, but only so he could get a reference number to pass on to the insurers. He doubted there'd be prints. A joiner would put the door right. Whoever had been there had left without taking the spare set of keys. They weren't coming back. It had been made to look like a regular break-in, but Fox wasn't convinced. He went downstairs again and stared at the paperwork on the table. Charles Mangold's name stared back at him from the topmost sheet, written there in capitals. He'd jotted down other names, too, along with dates and queries ...

If I'd been here, he wondered, would I have been made to look like a suicide ...?

'Get a grip, Malcolm,' he muttered to himself.

He tried to think how much information was to be found on the laptop. More of his thoughts, in more detailed sequence than the written notes. He hadn't got round to adding Alison and Stephen Pears and Andrew Watson to the mix. Had he made mention of Francis Vernal's logbook? The connection between Gavin Willis and the Dark Harvest Commando, specifically the man called Hawkeye? He thought so. Nothing had been printed off, but he'd copied the contents of the folder on to a memory stick.

A memory stick now missing.

And Professor Martin's book with it.

A four-quid memory stick and a tatty old book – no self-respecting housebreaker would have bothered with either. Spooks? Special Branch? Was this the same warning intended for Alan Carter, only that time things had gone wrong? Fox took out his phone and reported the break-in, then went outdoors again and checked that Vernal's logbook was still in the glove box of the car. It was. He tried the bungalows either side of his, but no one was home. Across the street, Mr Anderson, elderly and hard of hearing, had seen nothing unusual.

'A car or van?' Fox persisted, but Anderson just shook his head and offered to make a pot of tea for them both.

'Another time,' Fox told him.

He tried two more neighbours, but no one had seen or heard a vehicle. No strangers noticed.

Quiet, as usual.

When the patrol car arrived, Fox showed them his warrant card, then pointed to the damage. One of the officers had a handheld electronic device into which he tapped the details.

'Serial number for the laptop?' he asked.

Fox went to fetch the guarantee. He could have said *it won't turn up*, but then they would have wanted to know why he was so sure.

'Not Lothian and Borders issue, is it?' the other officer enquired. Fox shook his head. 'Nothing work-related on it, then?'

'No,' he lied.

'At least you won't face a disciplinary,' the officer commented.

'Bit of a blessing,' his colleague added.

'Does the sarcasm come at no extra charge?' Fox asked. 'And a disciplinary's only if you've been negligent – I don't think break-ins count.'

They'd had their fun at the Complaints' expense, so stopped smirking and suggested getting a team in to dust for prints, Fox argued it wasn't worth the bother.

'Not so sure about that, Inspector,' the elder of the two countered. 'Been a few homes broken into round here in the past six months. Might be able to tie yours to them.'

'Then when we catch the wee bastards ...' the younger officer said.

'Fine, then,' Fox said.

It took an hour for a forensic car to arrive. A young woman brought her box of tricks into the house and got to work. Fox had got the bedroom back to normal. He watched her as she brushed powder on to the front door.

'Didn't take much,' she commented.

'No.'

'Not even your telly. Means they were probably on foot.'

'Yes.'

She paused in her work. 'I'm not getting much here,' she admitted. A few minutes later she was in the living room. He asked her to dust the surface of the dining table. She came up with a few prints.

'Probably mine,' Fox conceded.

She lifted a few samples anyway, then took his prints to check them against. Fox was reminded of the scene outside Alan Carter's cottage. He was still wondering if he was lucky to have been out of the house.

But if they'd really wanted him there, they could have chosen their moment. Relatively easy to find his home address – a word in the right ear, maybe even a bit of computer hacking. He wasn't in the phone book, though Jude was. Hell, he could even have been tailed from Police HQ. They had either watched him leave the house, or they'd known he was on his way to the hospital after his brief trip to the office.

Were they listening to his phone calls?

Had someone planted bugs in his house, office or car?

He tried to snort the thought away, but knew it would bother him for the rest of the day.

'The woolly-suits gave you a reference number?' the forensics officer was asking, having finished with the upstairs bedroom.

'Woolly-suits?'

'Uniforms,' she explained with a smile. 'There was a DI who used to call them that.'

'They gave me a reference number, yes.'

'All you can do is put in a claim, then – and get a stronger door for next time.'

Fox nodded.

'Could have been worse, eh?' she said with a smile.

He seemed to agree with her that it could.

The same meeting room as before at Mangold Bain. And as expected, Charles Mangold could spare only a few minutes. There was no offer of a drink – time, as Mangold himself put it, did not permit. He pressed his hands together, lips brushing the tips of his fingers, and listened to what Fox had to say.

'My home's been broken into. The stuff you gave me got left behind, but they took my laptop. Some of my own work on the Vernal case was on it. They'll have your name now ...'

Mangold waved this aside. 'Who do you think is responsible?'

'I'm not sure. I've had a few run-ins with someone from Special Branch ...'

'Ah.'

'And last night I went to see Alice Watts.'

Mangold didn't bother trying to conceal his surprise. 'The girl Francis was seeing? You found her?'

'Yes.'

'Where is she? What's she doing?' He watched Fox shake his head slowly. 'Why not?'

'I have my reasons.'

Mangold seemed to be considering pressing the point, but Fox's look told him it would be futile. 'Did she talk to you about Francis?' he asked instead.

Fox nodded.

'Well?' the lawyer demanded.

'She didn't love him.'

Mangold stared at him. 'You're sure of that?' He watched Fox nod again. 'Why did she disappear off the face of the earth? Did she have something to do with his death?'

'I don't think so.' *Not directly.* 'But you can put Imogen Vernal's mind at rest.' Fox paused. 'Though I'm not sure that's ever been your intention.' The two men locked eyes. 'I think what you really want is for the scales to fall from her eyes.'

'Is that so?'

'It galls you that all these years she's held fast to an image of her husband – the crusader, the patriot. No matter what you've done for her – including adding her name to the law firm – she's never given you your due, has she?'

'I don't see that this outburst serves any purpose, Inspector.'

Fox shrugged the complaint aside. 'Why did you choose Alan Carter to be your bloodhound? You'd had years to look into Vernal's death, and my guess is, that's what you did. It didn't get you very far. But you knew Gavin Willis led the original inquiry, and you probably discovered that he'd been a mentor to

Alan Carter.' Fox's eyes narrowed. 'You weren't interested in what he *found*. You wondered how much he would try to conceal. That way you'd have a better understanding of the role Gavin Willis played. And you had a point – Carter didn't tell you about Vernal's car, for example, tucked away all these years in a garage behind Gallowhill Cottage. See, it works both ways: there was stuff he didn't want *you* to know. That's probably why he took the job on – he could control the investigation and make sure no mud stuck to Gavin Willis's name.'

'I don't see,' Mangold repeated, his voice quiet but trembling with anger, 'that this gets us any further.'

Fox sat in silence for a few seconds, then shrugged. 'A couple more names have come up,' he stated. 'Andrew Watson, for one.'

'Our current Justice Minister?'

'The same. Do you know him?'

'No.'

'He was a lawyer, though, before becoming an MSP?'

'A different generation from me. And he practised in Aberdeen.'

'Criminal law?'

It was Mangold's turn to nod. 'What has he got to do with Francis's death?' An eyebrow shot up. 'You're after him to reopen the investigation?'

'Would you like that?'

'It would be a nightmare for Imogen.'

'She might reach out for someone to hold her hand ...'

The look Mangold gave told Fox the lawyer reckoned this a very cheap shot. 'What's the other name?' Mangold asked.

Fox shook his head slowly, as if to indicate that it wasn't at all important. 'Just that I saw a photo of his brother-in-law.'

'Stephen Pears?'

'Taken in the New Club.'

'He's a member.'

'I thought it was mostly lawyers and judges.'

'A fairly wide spectrum,' Mangold corrected him.

'Is the Justice Minister a member too?'

Mangold thought for a moment. 'Do you know, I don't think he is.'

'Would Vernal have known Andrew Watson?' Fox asked. 'Both lawyers ... both keen nationalists ...'

'Wouldn't Watson still have been at school when Frank died?'

Mangold did the arithmetic in his head. 'Couldn't have been much more than sixteen or seventeen.'

'The age of idealism,' Fox stated. 'Sort of age when you're open to ideas, too.'

Though not, perhaps, the idea that your sister was sleeping with a man twice her age, a married man, a man called Francis Vernal ...

Lacking a computer at home, Fox returned to Fettes, hoping he wouldn't bump into the Chief Constable. The car radio news told him that the three Kippen suspects were likely to be charged by the end of the day, but would remain in custody in any event, extra time for questioning having been granted. Fox knew that after the Megrahi case, the Scottish government would feel the spotlight was on them – and on the justice system.

Next to the reception desk, the status was still CRITICAL.

'Even with the bad guys detained?' Fox asked the desk officer.

'We don't know how many more are out there,' the man replied, 'and maybe wanting revenge ...'

Fear: Fox had noticed the same thing when skimming the news reports from 1985. Fear was ever-present. When you'd stopped needing to fear a US–Soviet conflagration or an impending ice age, something else came along in its place. Fear of crime always seemed to outpace the actual statistics. Right now, people were fearing for their jobs and pensions, fearing global warming and dwindling resources. If these problems were ever resolved, new worries would fill the vacuum. He stared at the word CRITICAL, then moved past the sign and headed for the stairs.

Joe Naysmith was in the Complaints office. He gave Fox a wave.

'Done and dusted in Fife?' Fox asked him. Naysmith nodded. 'So where's Tony?'

Naysmith shrugged and asked Fox if he wanted a coffee.

'Sure,' Fox said, sitting down at his computer. He took a twenty-pound note from his pocket, folded it to make a paper plane, and launched it in Naysmith's direction. The young man looked at him.

'I'm paying off the kitty debts,' Fox explained. 'Does that cover it?'

'With room to spare.'

'Good,' Fox said. Then he got to work, doing a search on Andrew Watson. As Mangold had suggested, the current Justice Minister would just have been starting at Aberdeen University when Francis Vernal died. Fox looked carefully, but could see no sign that Watson had ever been a hardliner or especially radical. He'd graduated with a first in law, then joined a practice. SNP councillor by the age of twenty-seven and an MSP at thirty-one. The party leader seemed to like and respect him. As a 'back-room boy', Watson was credited with helping the SNP canvass its way into government.

The twenty-pound note seemed to have cheered Joe Naysmith up. He sat with Fox and let Fox bounce ideas off him, then got up and made more coffee while Fox texted Tony Kaye to ask him where he was. When his phone rang, he reckoned it would be Kaye, but it was Jude, phoning from the hospital.

'He's awake,' she said. 'But he's not right ...'

Fox drove out to the Infirmary and found himself entering the car park just behind a slow-moving Rover. He sounded his horn in irritation and gestured for the driver to put his foot down. After a couple of circuits he found an empty bay. It was at the very furthest corner, and he had to walk past the Rover as he made for the hospital entrance. The driver was Fox's father's age and looked fearful as Fox stalked towards him. The CRITICAL sign flashed in Fox's head and he paused for a moment, muttering the word 'sorry' before carrying on.

When he reached his father's bedside, Mitch's eyes were closed, hands clasped on his chest. Jude was talking to a woman who introduced herself as Mae Ross.

'Mrs Ross works at Lauder Lodge,' Jude explained.

'We were just wondering how he's doing,' Mrs Ross added.

'And I was apologising for not getting in touch sooner.'

Fox just nodded. 'You said he was awake,' he commented.

'He is ... sort of.'

Fox leaned over his father and watched the eyelids flutter, then open. The eyes took a moment to focus.

'Chris?' his father said, voice slurred.

'It's Malcolm.' Fox laid a palm against his father's hands.

'Malcolm?' The word was barely recognisable.

'Strokes do that,' Mrs Ross stated. Then, to the patient, in the sort of sing-song voice usually reserved for children: 'We're all look-ing forward to seeing our favourite client back at Lauder Lodge!'

Her wide smile disappeared as Fox turned to face her. 'He's not a "client",' he growled. 'He's *my* father!'

She looked shocked. 'I didn't mean anything, Mr Fox ...'

Jude seemed stunned by the outburst. She placed a hand on Fox's forearm.

'Chris,' Mitch Fox was repeating.

'Not Chris – Malcolm,' his son informed him.

'Cousin Chris?' Jude guessed. 'Burntisland Chris?'

'Chris is dead,' Fox was telling his father. 'He fell off his motorbike, remember?'

Fox took the photograph from his pocket – the one showing Chris Fox cheering Francis Vernal. He unfolded it and thrust it into his father's face.

'See?' he said. 'That's Chris.' He pointed to the face. 'That's Chris and I'm Malcolm.'

'It's okay, Malcolm,' Jude was telling him, while Mrs Ross looked at him as if he were mad. The hospital staff were taking an interest too. Fox lowered the photograph and watched his father's face clear.

'Chris was always so careful on that bike of his,' Mitch Fox said.

'Not careful enough, though.' But a question was starting to form in Fox's mind, a question only one person could answer. He turned towards Jude, who was still gripping him by his forearm.

'There's somewhere I need to go,' he told her. 'Will you be all right here?'

She nodded slowly, looking a little fearful. Fox freed himself from her grasp and ran his hand down the side of her head. 'But if anything changes ...'

'I'll call you,' she said.

'I shouldn't be too long.'

'Just come back to us when you're ready,' Jude told him. She even managed a smile of sorts, as if keen to bolster him. Fox did something he hadn't done in a while: leaned in towards her and kissed her on the cheek. She lifted herself a little, making it easier for him.

And then he was gone.

38

When Fox got to Police HQ in Stirling, the media presence had not lessened, and armed officers still gave his warrant card a thorough inspection. He texted the Chief Constable's mobile with a message: *Tell Jackson I'm downstairs.*

Ten minutes later, the Special Branch man was standing in front of him. Fox took his time getting up from the same seat he'd used on his previous visit.

'What the hell do you want?' Jackson snarled.

'Charged them yet?' Fox asked casually.

Jackson folded his arms and said nothing.

'I had a good chat with the Chief Constable last night,' Fox went on. 'Sorry she felt the need to keep you out of it.'

Jackson exhaled noisily through his nostrils. His phone sounded and he checked the message on his screen. Fox waited until he had the man's attention again, then started to speak.

'Chris Fox – does the name mean anything to you?'

Jackson stared at him, then gave the slightest of nods. 'Wondered when you'd get round to that,' he muttered. 'Come on ...'

Fox was given a visitor's pass by the same receptionist as the previous day. He followed Jackson along a corridor and down a flight of stairs. Another corridor, but this time with an armed officer checking IDs. Two interview rooms, facing one another across the corridor. Kevlar-vested officers standing guard outside both of them. Jackson pushed open one of the doors.

'Take a look,' he said.

Standing in the doorway, Fox saw that a man was seated at a table. He was handcuffed and refused to look up. Light-brown skin, thick wavy hair, dark rings under his eyes, the left eye swollen shut. Jackson closed the door again and stared at Fox.

'Military and political targets first, then civilian – supermarkets, football fixtures, even hospitals. He didn't care who got killed as long as we took notice.'

'What's your point?' Fox asked.

'My point is, there's a real and current threat and we'd be foolish to dwell on the past.' Jackson could tell that the guards were listening. He paced further down the corridor, past shirtsleeved detectives who nodded a greeting at him. There was a small empty office next to a further set of doors, and Jackson walked in, waiting for Fox to follow.

'Close the door,' he ordered. Fox did so, and the two men faced one another. 'A real and current threat,' the Special Branch man repeated quietly. 'We do what is necessary to stop it becoming a reality.'

'I was asking about Chris Fox.'

'I thought that's what this was all about. When I saw that surname in the vaults – had to be a connection.'

'When we spoke at the cafeteria?'

'I already knew,' Jackson confirmed. 'Made me wonder why you didn't bring it up. I was beginning to think maybe you had something to hide.'

'Such as?'

Jackson gave a shrug. 'He's a relative of some kind?'

'Cousin. How come he's in the Special Branch vaults?'

'You don't know?' Jackson sounded genuinely surprised. Fox watched him calculate how much to say.

'Strictly between us,' Fox offered.

Jackson took a few moments more to make up his mind. 'He was a shop steward – a *radical* shop steward. Liked nothing better than a violent picket or stirring things up. Card-carrying member of the Communist Party – plenty of them in Fife. But he switched to separatism. He was a good friend to Francis Vernal in the early years. The two of them hatched plans for marches and demos against visiting royals. It would only have taken one hothead with a gun ...' Jackson paused. 'It was the same back then as it is now – a real and current threat ...'

'With Special Branch doing everything necessary to stop it becoming a reality?'

Jackson fixed Fox with a look. 'We did not kill Chris Fox.'

'How do you know?'

'It was a motorbike accident, pure and simple. So if that's what all this is about ...'

'It's not.'

'What, then?'

'I don't like the idea of people getting away with murder.'

'We can agree on that, at least.' Jackson paused. 'What did the Chief Constable say to you last night?'

'Nothing she wants you to know, or she'd have said.'

'Her brother's furious with you.'

'I can live with that.'

Jackson stared down at his feet, as if studying his shoes. 'He looks quite normal, doesn't he?'

'Who?'

Jackson gestured towards the corridor. 'They always seem so ordinary. Just that bit more ... *driven*.'

'And what is it that drives them?'

Jackson could only shrug.

'What happened to him?' Fox asked. 'The black eye, I mean.'

'Punched himself in the face. That way, when the media eventually get their photo, it looks as if he's been roughed up.' Jackson looked at Fox again. 'Don't worry – local Complaints have been informed, statements taken.'

'That's all right, then.'

'Your cousin Chris ... we were keeping tabs on him, but nothing serious. We didn't see him as the real threat.'

'Who *was* the real threat? Vernal? Donald MacIver? Or the foot soldiers like Hawkeye?'

'Who's Hawkeye when he's at home?'

'You didn't come across his name?' Fox watched Jackson shake his head. 'Maybe you need another trip to the vaults, then.'

'Easier just to ask you.'

'I've no idea who he is.'

'Hardly matters,' Jackson speculated. 'Whatever threat there was, we dealt with it at the time.'

Fox glowered at him. 'I want to speak to the men who were tailing Vernal that night.'

'It's not going to happen.'

'It'll have to – if you want me off your back.'

'All they'd tell you is what I've already said – they had nothing to do with his death.'

318

'I need to hear it from them.'

'Why?'

'I just do.'

Jackson seemed to consider this, before shaking his head slowly. 'Not good enough, Inspector,' he said, pulling open the door and indicating that it was time to leave.

'My house was broken into,' Fox informed him. 'Reckon if someone goes into your precious vaults in a couple of decades' time they'll find mention of it?'

'No shortage of criminals out there.'

'At least we agree on that,' Fox replied.

They walked back down the corridor, past the interview rooms and the guards.

'I hope your father improves,' Jackson said, while Fox handed his pass back at reception.

'Thanks.'

Jackson held out his hand for Fox to shake. 'We really *are* on the same side,' he stressed. 'Don't forget that.'

'When do you head back south?'

'Next day or two. But you always know where to find me if you need me.'

'To be honest,' Fox said, 'I'm hoping I never see you again.'

At eight that evening, Fox was seated by his father's hospital bed. Jude had been persuaded to go home for a few hours' sleep. Mitch was asleep too. Fox had stopped off at Lauder Lodge for some bits and pieces, and had ended up bringing the shoebox full of photographs with him. He had looked at every single one of them, wondering what sort of story they were trying to tell him. A twentieth-century family, not very different from any other. A roof over their heads and food in their bellies. Trips to the sea-side and Christmas mornings. There was Malcolm, dressed in his favourite T-shirt, hair longer than his father liked, tearing the wrapping from a present. Jude, posing with her mother in a theatre auditorium. It would have been a musical: their mother had a passion for them. Father and son would always stay home to watch American cop shows on TV.

Burntisland again: Chris Fox, with Jude up on his shoulders. And one of him showing off his motorbike, a polishing rag in one hand. *Radical ... violent picket ... stirrer ...* Fox would have liked

319

to have known the man. If his father wasn't sleeping, he'd maybe have tried asking a few questions. Mitch's breathing was ragged. Every now and then he would seem to choke, coughing a few times without waking. His cheeks seemed sunken to Malcolm. The drip was still feeding him. Awake, he'd not been able to swallow food. Fox tried to ignore the catheter's tubing as it snaked from beneath the sheets towards the bag hanging from the bed's metal frame.

Proper detective work, that's what I'm doing, he wanted to tell his father. *For better or worse, that's what I'm doing …*

When his phone started to vibrate, he checked the screen. The caller's identity was blocked. He stood up and answered, walking past the nurses' station towards the corridor.

'Hello?'

'Is that Malcolm Fox?' The voice sounded distinctly irritated.

'Yes.'

'They told me I had to talk to you.'

'Oh?'

There was the sound of a throat clearing. Fox got the feeling the caller was a man in his sixties.

'I was there that night. They said you needed to hear about it.'

'Francis Vernal?' Fox stopped walking. 'You were tailing him?'

'Surveillance, yes.'

'I need to call you back. Let me take down your number …'

'I might be retired, but I'm not senile.'

'A name, then.'

'How about Colin? Or James? Or Fred?'

'No names?' Fox guessed.

'No names,' the voice confirmed. 'I've been out of the service for a long time, and I certainly don't owe them anything, so listen – you get to hear this once and once only.' He paused, as if expecting Fox to respond in some way.

'Okay,' Fox obliged.

'Vernal was driving like a maniac. He'd had more than a few drinks before setting out from Anstruther.'

'He'd been there all weekend?'

'With his lover,' the voice confirmed. 'If there'd been any traffic at all on that road, it could have been a lot worse. We heard the crash before we saw it. Straight into a tree he'd gone. Front end crumpled, and him with a few teeth missing in the driver's seat.'

'Unconscious?'

'But breathing ... pulse steady. If another car had stopped and seen us ... well, we didn't want that.'

'But you hung around long enough to give the car the once-over.'

'Too good a chance to miss.'

'You didn't take his money and cigarettes, though?'

'We were asked about that at the time.'

'Maybe your partner ...?'

'No.'

'Any chance of him confirming that for himself?'

'Died a year back. Natural causes, in case you're wondering.'

'Sorry to hear it. What do you think happened to Vernal's cigarettes and his lucky fifty-pound note?'

'No idea.'

'And there wasn't a gun in the car when you searched it?'

'Plenty of places he could have hidden one.'

'He'd also hidden thirty or forty thousand in cash.'

'I was told you'd mention that.'

'Kept in the boot, apparently.'

'We didn't open the boot.'

'You sure about that?'

'We didn't know anything about any money.'

'You'd been tailing Vernal. You must have seen him at DHC meetings – coming out to the car and disappearing back inside again?'

'We never saw any money.'

'Your mole didn't mention it?'

The man paused again before answering. 'I've told you what I know,' he said.

'Prove to me you were there.'

'What?'

'How am I supposed to know, otherwise?'

There was another long silence on the line. 'The reason we hightailed it,' the voice said eventually, 'is that he started coming round. The first word out of his mouth was "Imogen". We hadn't been expecting that.'

'You knew who Imogen was?'

'She was his wife. He was obviously in a bit of pain, and she was the one he wanted to see. Not Alice – Imogen.'

'But you just left him there – no thought of calling for help...'

'We were called the Watcher Service, Fox. That's what we did –

321

and a phone call to a doctor wasn't going to save him anyway, was it?' Fox didn't answer. 'Are we done?'

'Was someone called Hawkeye ever on your radar?'

'He was a DHC member. Slippery little bastard.'

'Slippery how?'

'Few times the watchers tried a follow, he either did a Houdini act or else clocked them.' The caller paused, then repeated his previous question: 'We done?'

'I don't know how you can live with it,' Fox commented.

'We're done,' the voice stated. The line went dead. Fox found that he was leaning with his back against the corridor's wall. He rested his head against its cool surface and stared at the framed print on the wall opposite. Then he looked up Alison Pears's number and punched it in.

'What?' she snapped.

'Wanted to thank you for getting Jackson to talk to me.'

'It doesn't seem to have stopped you pestering me.'

'I've just had a call from one of the two agents who were tailing Vernal that night.'

'Yes?'

'I just wondered – I'm assuming you met them?'

'No.'

'You didn't know them?'

'We never had any direct contact. They were spooks, I was a junior police officer. Is that all you needed to know?'

'Well, since I've got you ...'

'Yes?'

'Bit of a coincidence – I come to your house, and not long afterwards, someone breaks into mine.'

'I'm sorry to hear that. Was anything taken?'

'Laptop, memory stick, Professor Martin's book ...'

'I see.'

'Am I being paranoid?'

'Who do you think did it?'

'I've no idea. Have you maybe mentioned me to your handlers at Special Branch?'

'Handlers? This isn't John le Carré, Fox.'

'You've not spoken to anyone?'

'Believe it or not, I've had more important things on my plate.'

There was silence on the line for a moment, then she asked him how his father was doing.

322

'Thanks, but that's none of your business.'

Fox heard a doorbell and guessed Alison Pears was at home. 'That'll be my brother,' she said by way of confirmation. 'He's here for an update. Do we end this conversation before I open the door to him?'

'That's up to you.'

'I don't think there's anything else to say, is there? Hang on, though …' He heard her unlock her door and tell the Justice Minister: 'Him again; that makes twice today …'

The telephone changed hands. Fox listened as Andrew Watson began his tirade. Eight or nine words in, Fox ended the call and went back to his father's bedside.

39

Tony Kaye met Tosh Garioch at the door of the Dakota Hotel in South Queensferry. Neutral territory, just the Edinburgh side of the Forth Road Bridge. The hotel itself was a modern black box with its name picked out in neon, in a retail park boasting a late-night supermarket and not much else.

'Thanks for coming,' Kaye said, hand held out. Garioch hesitated for a moment before pressing his own hand against Kaye's. It didn't quite turn into a test of strength, but it was close. 'Thought we could have a drink,' Kaye added with a thin smile. Garioch nodded and they went in. The main restaurant to the rear of the bar was doing a good trade: businessmen eating alone; couples whispering over the seafood platters. There were some bar stools, but Kaye opted for a sofa. Garioch took the squishy chair opposite, the low wooden table separating them.

'It's good you kept my number,' Kaye said.

'I had to dig in the bin to find it.' Garioch held up Kaye's business card. It had been torn in half. The waiter arrived and they both ordered pints. The young man couldn't help staring at Garioch's thistle tattoo. A bowl of nuts was placed on the table and Garioch dug a paw into it, filling his mouth.

'So what's this deal?' he said.

Kaye leaned forward. 'Way I see it, we can go easy on you. You had every right to be angry with Paul Carter. Came to blows and he took off. You ran after him but gave up when he went into the water.' Kaye shrugged. 'We don't ask how far you followed him; we don't mention the wet trouser-legs. He drowned – not your fault he was stupid enough to go swimming.'

Kaye gave the man time to think this over. The drinks arrived and he paid for them, took a mouthful and began again.

'If we want to go a bit harder on you, it comes out in a different light – beating up a cop and hounding him to his doom ... wading into the water until you could be sure he wasn't coming out again.' He paused, swirling the contents of his glass. 'But for the deal to work, we'll need to know about Alan Carter and Paul.'

'You're not even CID,' Garioch countered. 'It'll be Cash giving evidence in court, not you.'

'Cash will listen to me. He'll have to.' Kaye paused. 'I blame myself anyway. You were there when I took the call from my colleague, talked to him about Paul Carter. I jotted it down in my notebook, didn't I? "Paul Carter ... Wheatsheaf ..."' Kaye produced the notebook and showed Garioch the relevant page. 'Problem with that is, if I tell Cash about it, then suddenly there's an element of premeditation. See what I mean, Tosh? You didn't just stumble across Paul Carter – you were lying in wait for him.'

Kaye left it at that, concentrating on his drink again. Garioch was right: he had no power. And as for Cash doing what he told him ... No matter: he just needed to sound confident here and now.

Garioch slouched a little in his chair, and Kaye knew he had him.

'Alan was good to me,' Garioch said quietly. 'Gave me a job and everything. Not so easy when you've done time.'

'When he asked a wee favour, you weren't going to say no?'

Garioch nodded his agreement with this. 'Paul usually went to that club on a Friday night. Couple of times we'd had to drag him off some woman he was drooling over. Billie and Bekkah were supposed to follow him out when he left, get chatting to him, then make a complaint.'

'Whether he'd done anything or not?'

Garioch nodded again. His head had fallen between his massive shoulders. 'A woman had already complained about him, but she'd been scared off. Alan got me and Mel to have a quiet word with her.'

'Mel Stuart?' Kaye checked. 'Mel's done a bit of time too, hasn't he? Didn't it feel a bit strange, the pair of you taking a wage from an ex-cop?'

'Alan was all right. You knew where you stood with him.'

'So he'd had you put a bit of pressure on Teresa Collins ...' Kaye prompted.

'Billie and Bekkah were by way of an insurance policy,' Garioch acknowledged. 'But when they left the club they couldn't see him. After a bit, Bekkah needed to pee, and that's when he drew up in his car. We didn't know he would have them lifted, but it worked out okay for us.'

'Your boss was happy?'

'He hated his nephew. Never quite understood it myself, but that's families for you – grievances get nursed.'

'You never asked him why he was doing it?'

Garioch shook his head.

'And getting the girls involved – that was Alan Carter's idea?'

'Yes.'

'Did Paul try anything with Billie and Bekkah?'

'Just like they told it.'

'Another reason for you to be furious with him.'

Garioch stared at Tony Kaye. 'It was for what he did to Alan,' he stated.

'Actually, Tosh, we're not so sure he killed your boss,' Kaye commented. 'Meaning he might have died for nothing. If you had a conscience, I dare say that fact could end up troubling it.'

Kaye rose slowly to his feet. 'We'll get a statement from you,' he said. 'Best if you talk to DI Cash direct – tell him everything you've told me.'

'I thought *you* were going to talk to him?'

'And I will. But best if it looks like you've made up your own mind. Take your lawyer with you.' Kaye was buttoning his coat. He nodded towards Garioch's empty glass. 'And no more of those tonight – don't want to add drink-driving to the list, do we?'

Fox was asleep fully dressed on his sofa when the doorbell went. He had an ache in his neck, and rubbed at his eyes before checking the time: five minutes shy of midnight. The TV news was playing, but just barely audible. He got up and stretched his spine. The bell went again. He opened the living-room curtains and peered out, then went into the hall and opened the door.

'Bit late to be canvassing,' he told Andrew Watson.

'I need a word with you,' the politician replied. A car was parked outside Fox's gate, engine idling and a driver at the wheel.

'Better come in, then,' he said.

'Bit of trouble?' Watson had noticed the damage to the door.

326

'Break-in.'

Watson didn't seem interested. He followed Fox into the house. 'I'm not used to people hanging up on me,' he said, as if reading from a script. But Fox wasn't about to apologise. Instead, he was pouring the dregs from a bottle of fruit juice into a glass and gulping it down. There was no offer of anything for the Justice Minister. Fox sat down on the sofa and switched the TV sound to mute. Watson stayed on his feet.

'I need to know what's going on,' he said.

'Ask your sister.'

'She won't tell me.'

'Then I can't help.'

'Why are the Complaints so interested?'

'That's between her and me.'

'I could make it my business.'

'I dare say you could.'

Watson glared at him. 'She's running the highest-profile case we've seen in this country for several years.'

'Maybe even since Megrahi,' Fox agreed.

The SNP man's eyes did everything short of glowing red. 'I intend to see to it that you don't come within ten miles of her.'

Fox was rubbing at his eyes again. He blinked them back into focus, sighed, and motioned for Watson to sit down.

'I prefer to stand.'

'Sit down and listen to what I have to tell you.'

Watson sat down, pressing his palms together as if to aid his concentration.

'Remember at the house?' Fox began. 'I mentioned Francis Vernal ...'

'Yes.'

'Your sister was fresh out of Tulliallan – first job she got was deep cover, posing as a student at St Andrews. Matriculation, tutorials, the lot. Student politics got her closer and closer to some of the groups on the fringes. She was feeding back any information she could get.'

'Are you quite sure about that, Inspector?'

Fox showed him the two matriculation photographs. 'Look familiar?'

Watson studied them without emotion.

'What of it?' he eventually commented.

'She started seeing Vernal – spending a *lot* of time with him.

327

He'd been with her that weekend, had just left her when his car went off the road. *That's* what I needed to talk to her about.' Fox was staring at the politician, gauging his reactions.

'I never knew,' Watson said quietly.

'Those groups tended to be separatists – not so far from your own politics.'

'I remember. It was a bad time for the SNP. Some of us were a bit desperate, a bit frustrated. We were being marginalised – that won't ever happen again, believe me.'

'But back then ...'

'Tough times,' Watson agreed.

'Did you know any of these groups? Seed of the Gael? Dark Harvest Commando?'

'Only by reputation.'

'You never met Donald MacIver?'

'No.'

'Or Francis Vernal?'

'No.'

'And you'd no idea what your sister was up to?'

'No idea,' Watson echoed.

'Now I've told you, what do you think?'

Watson turned this over in his mind for the best part of a minute, then shrugged and shook his head. 'I'm really not sure,' he said.

'All those activists must have gone someplace,' Fox commented. 'Maybe into government, even.'

'No place for hotheads and racists in the modern party, Inspector.' Watson seemed to study Fox. 'Can I take it you're a unionist?'

'It's irrelevant what I am.'

'Are you sure about that? Dusting off old enmities and conspiracies, hoping some mud might stick ...'

'Does the name Hawkeye mean anything to you?'

The question appeared to puzzle Watson. He thought for a moment. 'Just the character from *MASH*,' he concluded.

'And *Last of the Mohicans*,' Fox added.

'That too,' Watson agreed. He seemed tired, all his energy and anger used up. 'It's working, you know,' he said at last, his eyes meeting Fox's. 'The administration, I mean. A quarter of a century back, few would have said they'd see the SNP in power in their lifetime – and that includes a lot of us in the party. But we got there.' He nodded to himself. 'We got there,' he repeated. Then he stiffened. 'But we can't afford another Megrahi. These bomb-blasts ... Alison needs all her concentration, meaning no sideshows.'

'I'd hardly call murder a sideshow.'

'Murder?'

'Alan Carter – the man investigating Vernal's death. Made to look like suicide but actually an execution.'

'You can't think Alison had anything to do with that!'

'Why not? If Carter knew about her and was about to blow the whistle ...'

'Never.' Watson shook his head. 'You really can't go bandying that sort of—'

'It seems to be the only way of getting anyone's attention,' Fox countered. 'After all, it got yours.'

'She can't have this hanging over her,' Watson pressed. 'Alison's worked hard to get where she is.'

'I dare say you think you've worked hard too.'

'Of course.'

Fox narrowed his eyes. 'Is it her you're worried about or yourself? The job of Justice Minister seems to have a curse hanging over it, doesn't it? Bit of a fillip to have a Chief Constable you can depend on, especially if she can also deliver a few extra column inches ...'

'What do you mean?'

'How about if I hang fire – do nothing till after your terrorists are sentenced? You get your moment of glory ... and afterwards I start asking my questions again?'

Watson stared at him. 'What would you want in return?' he asked, his tone softening.

'Nothing.' Fox paused. 'Because it's not going to happen – I just wanted to see if you'd bite.'

Watson flew to his feet. 'For Christ's sake!' he spluttered.

Fox ignored the outburst. 'By the way, I meant to ask – how did you get my address?'

'What?'

'My address.'

'Jackson,' Watson snapped.

Fox nodded to himself: so the Special Branch man knew where he lived ...

Watson had paced to the window and back again. 'Is there any point trying to reason with you?'

Fox shrugged.

'Then I'll have to take this up with your Chief Constable.'

'What will you do – have me suspended? Remember to fill him in on your sister's history.'

'What is it you think she's done wrong exactly?'

'I'm still trying to figure that out.' Fox met Watson's gaze. 'Care to help me?'

'Help you?'

'By reopening the Vernal investigation – properly this time. Set up a public inquiry. He was being spied on by MI5 and an undercover police officer. Did that play any part in his death? Was there a cover-up afterwards? And does it connect to the murder of Alan Carter?' Fox rose slowly to his feet, keeping his eyes fixed on Watson. 'Could be a real feather in your cap if you started to get some answers to those questions.'

But the Justice Minister was shaking his head. 'Dark Harvest Commando ... the SNLA – nobody wants those corpses resurrected.'

'Nobody in your party,' Fox corrected him.

'Nobody, period.'

'You might be surprised.'

Watson kept on shaking his head.

'Just me, then?' The question was rhetorical, but Watson answered it anyway.

'Just you.'

Three minutes later, Fox was watching from his window as the car pulled away. The interior light was on, the minister mulling over documents. Fox's phone let him know he had a text. It was from Jude.

You awake?

He called her back. 'What's wrong?' he asked.

'Nothing. Didn't want to bother you if you were asleep.'

'Speaking of which ...'

'I can't stop tossing and turning,' she confessed with a sigh. 'I keep thinking about Dad – what are we going to do with him, Malcolm?'

'I'm not sure.'

'He can't stay in hospital for ever.'

'No.'

'But unless he improves ...'

'Lauder Lodge isn't much use to him either,' he agreed, finishing the thought for her. 'I'll put my thinking cap on, Jude.'

'Me too.' He listened to her shift positions, guessed she was lying in bed.

'Remember when we were kids?' he said. 'I'd sneak into your room and we'd sing songs together under the sheets?'

'Our own *Top of the Pops*, until Mum or Dad heard us. I haven't thought of that for years ...'

'I was in some woods a few days back,' Fox began, settling himself on the sofa again. 'It took me back to the Hermitage and the walks we used to take. That was in the days when you still preferred me to other boys.'

'I *never* preferred you to other boys,' Jude teased.

Fox smiled and they continued chatting. He had the TV remote in his hand and flicked through the available channels. Late-night shopping, astrology, phone-in quizzes. There was news, but he didn't linger on it. He settled on a comedy channel instead. An old episode of *MASH* was just starting. Hawkeye and Trapper John and Hot Lips and Radar. The actor Alan Alda played Hawkeye, all floppy fringe, loping walk and wisecracks. Jude was talking about a den they'd made one time at a secret spot in the Hermitage. But Fox wasn't sitting so comfortably now. His grip had tightened on the remote. He pretended to yawn, apologising to his sister.

'I should let you sleep,' she told him.

'I'm really enjoying talking, but I can hardly keep my eyes open.'

'Tomorrow at the hospital?'

'What time do you think you'll be there?' he asked.

'After breakfast. You?'

'Later, probably.'

'Things to do?' she guessed.

'Night, sis.'

'Night, bro.'

Fox ended the call and wandered into the kitchen, boiling the kettle and making himself some strong tea. On another night, he might have spent time reflecting on the thawing in his relationship with his sister – but that would have to wait. He took the mug back through to the living room and tried using his mobile phone to access the internet. It was hopeless, though – slow, and the screen too small. After peering at it for a while, he decided he needed to go to Fettes and use one of the computers in the

Complaints office. As he was readying to leave, his phone trilled. According to the display, it was Evelyn Mills. He let it keep ringing. Two minutes later there was a text: *Need someone to talk to.* He stared at the message, undecided. He had his jacket on, car key in his free hand. The phone went again and he answered.

'Evelyn?'

But it was a man's voice. 'Whoever you are, just bugger off. She doesn't need you.'

The line went dead. Fox stared at the handset. Her partner Freddie, presumably.

'Fine then,' Fox said to himself, heading for the door.

40

'It's Stephen Pears,' Fox repeated.

It was just shy of five a.m. and he was seated at the breakfast bar in Tony Kaye's kitchen. He had spent the best part of an hour trying to persuade his friend of the truth of it, the two men keeping their voices low so as not to wake Kaye's wife. Eventually Kaye had sighed, scratched his nose and suggested food.

As the toast was placed in front of Fox, he knew he wouldn't eat it.

'And this is all because of a late-night repeat on the Comedy Channel?' Kaye said, pouring more coffee.

'Yes.'

'See when you took that trip to Carstairs – madness isn't catching, is it?'

'I've told you – Hawkeye Pierce … Hawkeye Pears. He was on the archery team in high school. It was the obvious nickname for him. After university he's supposed to have spent a couple of years "drifting" – he's always been vague about it. Says he did a variety of jobs all over the world and came back to Scotland with a chunk of money. First anyone heard of him in the finance sector was mid-1986, and he had almost thirty K to invest. Split it between two start-ups, and a year later he's quadrupled his stake.'

'And you got all this from a journalist?'

Fox nodded. 'I drove to the *Scotsman* offices. Night shift comprised one staffer. He phoned the business editor for me.'

'Did either of them wonder why you were interested?'

'I told him I was the Media Unit.'

'What Media Unit?'

Fox shrugged. 'Putting together a press pack about Chief Constable Alison Pears ...'

'And to do that, you needed to ask the media for help?' Kaye shook his head slowly and brushed toast crumbs from the corners of his mouth. 'In the middle of the night?'

'It was all I had,' Fox reasoned. 'And I got what I needed, didn't I?'

'It's not enough. The guy in that photo looks nothing like Stephen Pears.'

'I can ask him.' Fox had taken the photo from his pocket, the one showing Vernal, Alice and Hawkeye. It was scuffed from so much handling.

'What if he denies it? That's all he's got to do, Malcolm.'

Fox picked up his replenished mug, but put it down again without drinking. He knew his friend was right. The photo wasn't enough. The theories weren't enough.

Kaye swallowed some coffee and stifled a belch. 'If it *is* him,' he speculated, 'the wife's got to know.'

'I'm not so sure,' Fox countered. 'They met twelve years ago and have been married for ten. That makes it thirteen years since she'd laid eyes on Hawkeye. Beard gone, hair short and dyed a lighter colour, a bit heavier around the waist and the face ....'

'She's got to have known,' Kaye persisted, wiping at his mouth again.

Fox didn't say anything. He stared at the toast on his plate, with its layer of pale yellow butter. The very thought of it was making him queasy. He slid the photograph back into his pocket as Kaye spoke.

'Even supposing – just for argument's sake – that you're right, it doesn't mean you can tie Pears to anything. Are you saying he killed Francis Vernal and Alan Carter?'

'He'd have had motive enough.'

'Because his wife's risen through the ranks and he doesn't want anyone pooping her party?'

'There's that,' Fox agreed. 'Plus he's on course for the House of Lords – a terrorist past might not sit too well with a Tory peerage. He's a donor to the party, too.'

Kaye was staring at him. 'You can't go saying any of this, Malcolm. Not without at least a few shreds of evidence.'

'I went on the internet. Pears spoke at a conference a few years back in Barbados, same time an arms dealer called William

Benchley drowned in his swimming pool. Benchley had been selling guns smuggled home by soldiers from the Falklands.'

Kaye's stare intensified. 'Malcolm ...'

Fox held up a hand. 'I know, I know – maybe I *should* check myself into Carstairs.' He paused. 'But what if at least some of it is true?'

Kaye pushed his empty plate aside and lifted his coffee mug. 'I still don't see you're in a position to do anything about it,' he said.

'Maybe not,' Fox conceded.

'But since it's a night for storytelling, I can offer you one of my own.'

Fox tried hard to concentrate on Tony Kaye's account of his meeting with Tosh Garioch.

'So Paul Carter *was* being set up by his uncle,' he stated at the conclusion.

'Not exactly,' Kaye argued. 'Garioch says Paul did try it on with Billie and Bekkah. And Alan Carter *did* put a bit of pressure on Teresa Collins, but only *after* she made her original complaint.'

Fox was thoughtful. 'Uncle Alan wanted to make sure the mud stuck.'

'He really did hate his nephew, didn't he?'

'So why phone him that night? Phone him but not speak to him?' Fox's eyes were on Kaye. 'The address book with Paul's number in it ... it was left open for anyone to find.'

'So?'

'Any check of calls made, and Paul's name would pop up. But say it wasn't Alan who did the calling ...'

'The murderer?'

Fox was nodding slowly. 'Paul's been found guilty but suddenly he's not on remand any more. The judge at his trial is no friend of the police, yet he lets him out, pending sentencing.' Fox gave a little smile.

'What is it?' Kaye asked.

'Sheriff Cardonald is a member of the New Club. I saw him there that time I met with Charles Mangold.'

'So?'

'So Stephen Pears is a member, too.'

'Pears gets his friend the sheriff to release Paul Carter?'

'Paul was the perfect fall guy,' Fox argued. 'The court case had made it clear uncle and nephew loathed one another.'

'But it only worked if Paul was back on the street.' Kaye was actually sounding half-convinced.

'It's all conjecture,' Fox admitted. 'You said so yourself – where's the proof?'

'Don't always need proof to flush someone out,' Kaye stated. 'We know that from experience.'

'Do you still think I'm mad?'

'Maybe not so much.' Tony Kaye drained his coffee. 'The thing is, though – what do you do about it?'

'I'll have to think about that.'

Having showered, shaved and changed his clothes, Fox was parked outside Mangold Bain at nine thirty. He watched the receptionist arrive but failed to bring her name to mind. He knew he needed sleep.

Straight after this, he promised himself.

Mangold arrived on foot. He turned his head at the sound of the car door opening.

'Good morning, Inspector,' he said. 'Did we have an appointment?'

'Just curious about something,' Fox explained. 'Does Colin Cardonald know Stephen Pears?'

'Sheriff Cardonald? What's that got to do with anything?'

'It's a simple enough question,' Fox reasoned.

'I've seen them together,' Mangold conceded.

'At the New Club?'

'Yes.'

'Friends, then?'

'Colin Cardonald likes to dabble.'

'Dabble?'

'Stocks and shares.'

'Handy to have someone like Pears to offer advice,' Fox surmised.

'I'd say so.' Mangold paused. 'Does this have something to do with Francis?'

'Not at all,' Fox lied. 'Like I say, I was just curious.'

'Curious enough to ambush me outside my office.'

Fox couldn't deny it.

'You're close, aren't you?' Mangold's voice had dropped, though there was no one nearby to overhear. He took a step towards Fox. 'There's a sort of fever in your eyes.'

'She won't like it, you know,' Fox responded.

'Who?'

'The widow. If I'm right, and it becomes public knowledge, she'll blame you. She might very well end up hating your guts.'

The lawyer reached out and gripped Fox's forearm. 'What is it?' he hissed. 'Tell me what it is you've found!'

But Fox shook his head slowly and got back into the car. Mangold stood by the driver's-side window, peering in. When Fox turned the key in the ignition, the lawyer thumped on the Volvo's roof with both hands. He was still standing in the road as Fox drove away, decreasing in size and importance in the rear-view mirror.

Thirteen

41

It took a few days to arrange, but that was fine. In the meantime, the terror suspects had been charged, remanded and moved into Edinburgh's Saughton Prison. The Justice Minister had enjoyed giving interviews and had praised 'my big sister', much to the delight of the tabloids. The alert level at Fettes remained CRITICAL, but would soon be downgraded. Fife Constabulary had written a letter to Lothian and Borders congratulating the Complaints team on its 'exemplary' report. Whether the media were informed or not, Fox and his team didn't know – nothing seemed to appear in the press. Reprimands would be issued to Scholes, Haldane and Michaelson, and that would be that.

Mitchell Fox had left hospital, not for Lauder Lodge but for his son's living room. Fox had bought a single bed from IKEA, Tony Kaye helping him put it together. The only toilet in the house was upstairs, so Fox tracked down a commode. Jude was promising to act as nurse for a short while – 'not for ever and a day, mind'. Mitch was slow and occasionally confused, and his speech was slurred, but he was able to eat and drink with just a little bit of help. Lauder Lodge warned Fox that they couldn't keep his father's room unoccupied for long, but he had paid them until the end of the month, which gave a bit of breathing space. At night, he sat and watched TV – him on the sofa, his dad propped up in bed. The old boy could get up during the day, though it was proving a challenge getting him dressed. More often, they left him in his pyjamas and a towelling robe.

Mitch's old drinking buddy Sandy Cameron had visited and approved of the effort brother and sister were making: *Your old man's proud of you – I can see it in his eyes.* They cooked dinner on alternate nights and pretended everything was quite normal. Afterwards, whatever the weather, Jude would disappear into the back garden for a cigarette – she was already up to ten a day – and Fox would settle down on the sofa with the TV remote and the evening paper. The room had become cramped, bed and commode taking up space. Mitch's clothes had been relegated to a suitcase and bin liner in the hall. The coffee table was covered with his paraphernalia, and the dining table had been folded closed, meaning all Fox's paperwork was now spread across his bedroom floor.

A physio was due to pay a visit once a week to work with Mitch. A speech therapist had even been mooted. They'd given him a rubber ball he was supposed to squeeze twenty times per hand three or four times a day. The shoebox of photographs sat untouched on the coffee table. Jude made a shopping list: furniture polish, fabric conditioner, vacuum-cleaner bags and dusters. Plus an iron and ironing board. She asked her brother how he'd coped all these years.

'Dry-cleaning,' was his unconvincing answer.

Stephen Pears was due to address shareholders at a meeting in Edinburgh on the Tuesday at ten in the morning. The venue was the ballroom of a venerable city-centre hotel. Fox's contact on the *Scotsman*'s business desk had proffered the information, and had also asked if Pears was in any trouble.

'Because whatever this is about, Inspector, it's not a profile of his sister.'

Fox had asked if there were any rumours flying around. As far as the journalist was concerned, their apparent lack was no great comfort.

'These days, seems anybody can go bust at an hour's notice.'

'If I get anything,' Fox assured the man, 'you'll be the first to know.'

The shareholders piling into the ballroom looked quietly prosperous. They carried their copies of the annual report and muttered about the levels of remuneration the board seemed keen on divvying up. Most appeared to be well into their twilight years. They were the prudent, cautious types who hadn't lost too much so far in the recession but would welcome good news from Stephen Pears and his team. There was to be a reception afterwards, drinks and canapés served. Names were ticked off and shiny brochures handed out. On the front of the brochure a smiling couple held hands across a restaurant table. *Future-Proofing Your Dreams*, the headline announced. Fox took a copy, then admitted that his name wasn't on the acceptance list. He showed the staff behind the makeshift desk his warrant card, then pointed to the three men behind him.

'They're with me,' he announced.

The attendants from Carstairs stood either side of Donald MacIver. Fox had picked them up at quarter past eight. Gretchen Hughes had repeated that MacIver shouldn't get too much stimulus. Fox had signed his name to the paperwork, knowing that if his bosses at Fettes HQ ever got wind of this, he would be on a charge. He had lied and lied again in order to convince Hughes and her colleagues that he was fully authorised in his actions and that a murder inquiry might be stymied without Donald MacIver's help. MacIver himself looked presentable, as though making an effort for the occasion. Fox asked him when he'd last set foot outside the compound.

'A hospital visit,' he eventually remembered. 'Suspected appendicitis. That was probably four or five years back.'

They'd all decided that restraints would not be needed in the first instance. The attendants looked like they worked out in what spare time they had, and could probably handle their charge whatever happened. During the drive, they'd kept up a dialogue about various martial arts and dietary supplements, while MacIver stared at the passing scenery, answering Fox's questions with a series of grunts, punctuated by the occasional yes and no.

'Not too many changes,' he'd muttered as they entered the city. 'A few new roads and buildings.'

'I could take a detour past the parliament,' Fox had offered.

'Why bother?' had been MacIver's response.

'"Bought and sold for English gold"?' Fox had quoted, receiving a slow, determined nod of the head in return.

So they'd headed for George Street instead, parking on a meter and entering the hotel.

The ballroom was larger than necessary. There were eighty or ninety chairs, laid out in rows of ten. Pears's team seemed to comprise sharply dressed young men and women who scanned the room for possible dissenters and handed out notepads and pens to anyone who needed them. It didn't take them long to spot Fox and his guests. They remained standing at the back of the room, and wouldn't budge when offered seats. MacIver seemed slightly agitated, but the attendants didn't look worried. His facial colouring was what Fox would call 'prison grey', but he didn't suppose his own was much better. He hadn't slept well the past few nights – and not just because of his father's presence in the house.

The stage beyond the front row of seats didn't look permanent. It supported a long table with a blue velvet cloth draped over it. Four place cards with names on them, but too far away for Fox to make out the actual names themselves. Carafes of water and pre-filled tumblers. Microphones. There were loudspeakers stage-right and left. People in the audience greeted each other with curt nods. A young man stopped in front of Fox, but Fox was ready for him. He held his warrant card an inch from the lackey's nose and identified himself as a police officer.

'I can say it louder, if you want everyone else to hear,' he offered. MacIver gave a little growl and the young man took a step back, then turned and fled. He went into a confab with others in the team. Someone punched a number into their phone and started a whispered conversation, holding their hand over their mouth as if fearing lip-readers.

Good: Fox hoped the news would get backstage.

Maybe the call had come too late, though, for now four men were arriving by way of a side door. They strode purposefully towards the stage, climbed the steps and settled themselves behind the table. Stephen Pears tugged at the cuffs of his shirt and checked the straightness of his tie. When introduced, he nodded and smiled, taking in the whole room. There were others standing at the back now – not just Fox, MacIver and the two attendants, but the team working for Pears, plus some latecomers. One person in the third row started having a coughing fit, and a staffer was quick to take them some water. The four men on the stage tried not to let this distract them. A statement of the company's achievements during the previous twelve months was being recited. Fox had eyes only for Stephen Pears, though Pears appeared focused on the rows of seats – these were his constituents. He had brought no papers with him. When a phone chirruped in the room and went unanswered, he tried not to look annoyed.

The attendant next to Fox nudged him, letting him know it was *his* phone that was the culprit. It stopped, but half a minute later started ringing again. The ringtone had been set to maximum volume. When Fox lifted the device from his pocket and checked the screen, he saw that it was Tony Kaye, right on cue. The man reading out the report had come to a stop, reminding the room that all phones should be switched off. People were turning their heads to look at Fox. He did eventually cancel the ringing, but only when he was satisfied that he had at last gained Stephen Pears's attention.

Fox stared back at him, nodding an acknowledgement. The report was in full flow again, but Pears's body language had changed. He was stiffer, less sure of himself. When he looked towards the back of the room a second time, Fox leaned past the attendant and touched MacIver's arm, whispering something to him.

'You all right there, Mr MacIver?'

An innocent enough question, to which MacIver responded with the nod Fox had wanted from him.

'Sure?'

Another nod. Fox turned his attention back to the stage and gave Pears a little smile, hoping it looked satisfied enough. Pears ran a hand through his hair, leaned back in his seat, gave the ceiling his full attention, then the tabletop. The report was winding to its conclusion. He was being invited to say a few words about the future. When people clapped, Fox clapped with them. The noise didn't agree with MacIver. He pressed his hands over his ears and gave a low moan. As Pears stood up and the applause ended, that moan could still be heard. Pears had taken hold of the microphone, but he didn't say anything. The attendants were trying to calm MacIver.

'No,' he said, repeating the word a few times.

'Better take him out,' the attendant nearer to Fox said. Fox nodded his agreement.

'I'll be there in a minute,' he replied.

The whole room watched as MacIver was led away. Then they turned back to Pears, expecting the usual poised performance, the noteless tour de force. Pears had finished all the water in his glass. More was being poured. After fifteen or twenty seconds, he started his speech.

And it was fine. Fox doubted anyone who had heard him before would notice anything different about the delivery.

Quite the actor, he thought to himself.

But then he knew that already. Five minutes in, he caught Pears's eye again, and offered a mimed handclap, along with a slow nod. Then he headed for the doors, taking out his phone as if to make a call.

MacIver was seated in the hotel's reception area, running a finger along the stories on the front of a morning paper.

'Back to normal,' one of the attendants assured Fox. Fox settled himself next to MacIver and asked if he'd recognised anyone on the stage. MacIver shook his head.

'You sure?' Fox persisted.

'Sure,' MacIver echoed.

Fox held out his copy of *Future-Proofing Your Dreams*. Its back cover consisted of smiling portrait photographs of the main players. 'Him?' Fox asked, dabbing a finger against Stephen Pears.

'He was in the room.'

'Yes, he was.'

'I don't know him.'

'He's been on TV and in the newspapers. His name's Stephen Pears. I'm pretty sure you'd have known him as Hawkeye.'

MacIver stared at him. 'You're wrong,' he stated.

'The war's over,' Fox persisted. 'No need to lie for a cause that's won.'

But MacIver was shaking his head slowly and defiantly. 'Can I go back?'

'Back?' Fox thought he meant to the ballroom.

'Home,' MacIver corrected him.

'He means Carstairs,' one of the attendants clarified. 'Isn't that right, Donald?'

'That's right,' MacIver confirmed. 'I don't like it here.' He glared at the attendant. 'And it's *Mr MacIver* to you until you know me better.'

'I've known you almost two years.'

'You're still on probation.'

'What if we went back to the hall for a minute,' Fox suggested, 'just so you could hear him speak?'

MacIver was shaking his head again.

'We don't want to make things worse,' the other attendant cautioned.

Fox considered his options. Hadn't he got what he wanted? MacIver was back to his reading, asking the attendants if they had a crayon.

'I've got a pen,' Fox offered.

'Has to be a crayon,' the same attendant told him. 'And not too sharp.'

Fox nodded his understanding. His phone bleeped a message. It was Tony Kaye, asking if it had worked.

More or less, Fox texted back. MacIver was studying the portraits on the back of the annual report. But then he seemed to dismiss it and went back to his newspaper.

'Ready when you are, Mr MacIver,' Fox announced. 'And I want to thank you for everything.'

MacIver got to his feet and took a last look at his plush surroundings. 'Russians or Arabs?' he asked.

'I'm not sure I understand.'

'Who owns this place? It'll be one or the other, mark my words. And next year or the year after, it'll be sold on to China. A nation bought and sold ...'

The attendants shared a look. One rolled his eyes. 'Here we go again,' he said.

MacIver's grievances were growing louder as they accompanied him to the door.

Having dropped the three men back at Carstairs, Fox was halfway to Edinburgh when his phone started ringing. He had a good idea who it might be and was content not to answer – not straight away. Eventually there was a sign pointing to a lay-by, so he signalled and pulled to a stop. The number wasn't one he recognised, and no message had been left. He took a hand-held digital recorder from his pocket. Joe Naysmith had assured him the batteries were brand new and it would be good for eight hours of continuous use. Fox switched it on, then called the number and engaged the speakerphone mode.

'Hello?'

It wasn't the voice he'd expected. Female. Sounds of chattering all around.

'Stephen Pears, please. He just phoned me from this number.'

'Hold on ...'

The phone changed hands. It was a man's voice this time.

'Yes?' Stephen Pears asked.

'Enjoying the canapés?' Fox commented. 'Managed to get all those juicy directors' bonuses past the shareholders?'

'Where are you?'

'I'm driving. Had to drop Donald MacIver off.'

'The man who was with you?' Pears pretended to guess.

'Your old pal.' Fox paused, watching a lorry hurtle past. 'Not much wrong with his memory ...'

'What exactly is it that you think you're doing?'

'A bit of future-proofing,' Fox stated.

There was silence on the line for a moment. 'Are we talking about money?'

'We could be – or else your own future might not be too bright.'

Pears gave a little laugh. 'I don't think I believe you.'

'Oh?'

'Nothing about you strikes me as the type.'

'The type?'

'To be bought off.'

'How much *do* you know about me, though? You've got my phone number – but then I gave that to your wife. Did your little break-in provide any clues? I wouldn't mind my laptop back, by the way – if you're done with it. And the watch. You can hang on to Professor Martin's book. What did you think of his thesis? All that political energy wasted ...'

'I don't know what you're talking about.'

'Of course you don't. And you were never known as Hawkeye when you were part of the Dark Harvest Commando. You never held up banks and post offices, never sent poison and letter bombs to London. Never stole all that money from Francis Vernal's car after putting a bullet in his head.'

'These sound like ravings, Inspector.'

'You tell your version, I'll tell mine.'

'You'll end up in a room next to your friend in Carstairs.'

Fox tutted. 'I didn't say anything about Carstairs, Mr Pears. But you've got me wondering now – would John Elliot recognise you, given a nudge? Maybe there'll be others who'll come out of the woodwork. The police can do wonders these days. We'll take a recent photo and change the hair colour and length, give you a beard ... reverse the ageing process. Then we'll start to see.'

'See what?'

'See Hawkeye staring back at us. The man who wanted to bring down the government, the man with anarchy in his veins.' Fox paused. 'Until greed got the better of him ...'

'You're making a mistake.'

'I really don't think so.'

'I do.' It was Pears's turn to pause. 'Now if you'll excuse me, I've got more important things to attend to.'

'You do that, Mr Pears. I'll just give *Mrs* Pears a call. Alice Watts, as was. Have you seen that picture of the two of you, arm in arm at the cop-shop demo?'

'Do what you have to do, Inspector.'

'Fine by me. Just need to toss a coin to decide which murder we charge you with first. Or were there more than two? My arithmetic's not what it was.'

Fox ended the call, checked the quality of the recording, then sat for a few minutes, his hands resting against the steering wheel. He hadn't got much; nothing that would begin to stand up in court. Hawkeye had learned caution somewhere along the way. Fox was about to head back on to the road when his phone rang again. Same number as before. He switched the recorder back on.

'I seem to have hit a nerve,' he commented.

'I'm a man who likes a deal, Inspector. If there's any sort of deal to be done here, I'm willing to consider it.'

'It's only when you don't get your way that the killer instinct takes over?' Fox speculated.

'Business requires a touch of ruthlessness,' Pears seemed to agree. 'But accommodation is always preferable.'

'And you're a reasonable man?'

'Unless pushed too far.'

Fox stayed silent, pretending to weigh things up.

'We need to meet face to face,' he eventually stated.

'Why?'

'We just do.'

'I'm not sure that's a good idea.'

'The Wallace Monument. Five this evening.'

'I have plans for this evening.'

'Five o'clock, Mr Pears.' Fox ended the call and stared at his phone. He found that his heart was pounding, the blood whistling in his ears, and there was a slight tremor in his hands.

Other than that, he felt fine.

42

'I don't like this,' Joe Naysmith said. 'It's too quiet.'

Fox had to agree. He was seated in his Volvo, phone pressed to his ear, listening to his colleague. He looked out at the car park. The last time he'd been here, it had been the middle of the day and there had been a few tourists about. Now the place was almost deserted. Two other cars – belonging to the staff, most probably – plus, at the far end of the car park, the unmarked white van with Naysmith and Tony Kaye hidden in the back. It was their surveillance hub, filled with listening and monitoring equipment. Mostly, it didn't stand out from the crowd, but there was no crowd here.

'Could we park further away?' Fox heard Tony Kaye ask.

'Signal's not brilliant as it is,' Naysmith answered.

Fox pressed his free hand to his chest. Beneath his shirt, a sticking plaster fixed the tiny microphone to his skin. Naysmith preferred plasters to ordinary tape – sweat was less likely to affect them. The microphone wire ran to the battery pack in Fox's back trouser-pocket.

'Is he sitting on the aerial?' Kaye was asking.

'Tell him I'll strap it to my head if that'll help,' Fox commented. Joe Naysmith passed the message along.

It had taken an hour's paperwork before they were okayed use of the van and its contents, but that was fine – just a matter of box-ticking. Fox was adept at box-ticking. At some point, someone further up the ladder would see the completed form and maybe wonder about it, but that was for later. The van's fuel tank was nearly empty. Fox had handed Naysmith fifty quid and told him to stop at the garage on Queensferry Road.

'Your own shilling?' Kaye had asked.

'That's the way I want it,' Fox had confirmed.

'Why here?' Kaye was now asking. Meaning: why the Wallace Monument?

'Resonance,' Fox responded. His rear-view mirror showed him that the tables were being wiped down in Legends, the lights turned off at the end of another working day. It was ten minutes to the top of the hour. They'd been in position since half past four. Fox was trying to guess which car Pears would arrive in – the Maserati or the Lexus. He had his answer a couple of minutes later, the black Maserati emitting a low growl as it entered the car park.

'He's early,' he said, ending the call. He watched as Pears passed the van without seeming to pause. The two other cars were empty, so he drew to a halt next to Fox's Volvo, but left the engine idling. He lowered his window, so Fox did the same.

'Get in,' Pears ordered.

'Why not my car?'

Pears shook his head. 'I know mine better.' Fox could hear music from the Maserati's stereo: jazz piano. Something similar had been playing at the house in Stirling the night he'd visited.

'This is a deal-breaker, Inspector,' the financier added.

Fox hesitated, then slid the window shut, pulled the key from the ignition and got out. He walked towards the Maserati, his eyes fixed on its driver. Pears was studying the car park in his mirrors. Fox opened the passenger-side door and got in. Pears was wearing leather driving gloves, old-fashioned-looking things with stud fasteners. The moment Fox was in his seat, Pears put the car into reverse. Once out of the parking bay, he started forward, engine roaring. As they made to pass the white surveillance van, he slammed on the brakes.

'Want to say goodbye to your friends?' he asked, sounding the horn. Then they were off again, careering towards the main road. As the engine noise increased, Pears pumped up the volume on the stereo.

'Think I'm that stupid?' he yelled, baring his teeth as he pulled out to overtake traffic.

'Stupid enough to get us killed,' Fox retorted, reaching for his seat belt. The car was already up to eighty, and Pears showed no sign of easing off. He kept glancing in his rear-view mirror, until satisfied that no tail could have stayed with him while remaining unseen.

'You've made your point,' Fox conceded. He unbuttoned his shirt and started to tug at the wiring, hauling the battery pack from its hiding place. 'See?' He removed the batteries and tossed everything on to the back seat, then started doing the buttons of his shirt up again.

'No gun?' Pears asked.

'No gun.'

'And just that old van for back-up?'

'I wasn't expecting *Wacky Races*.'

Pears took the hint and eased his foot a little from the accelerator, checking again in the rear-view. Eventually, he turned the music down.

'Are we headed anywhere nice?' Fox asked. He didn't recognise the road at all.

'We're just driving,' Pears said. 'Driving and talking.' He glanced at Fox. 'I want you to understand why it's all turned out like this.'

'Do I need to know?'

'Maybe you'll see things in a different light.'

'So you're going to tell me why you killed Francis Vernal?'

'You have to go back further. You have to understand how things were in the eighties.'

'I was there,' Fox said.

'Were you, though? Or did you sleepwalk through it? All those newspaper stories you looked at – did you remember half of it happening at the time? The marches and protests, the fear?' Pears glanced towards Fox. 'Be honest now.'

'Maybe I was too busy getting on with life.'

'You and a few million others. But some of us wanted to change the world, and we knew politicians weren't going to be much help to us ... unless we prodded them.'

'With letter bombs and anthrax?'

'You don't think terrorism works? Have you looked at Northern Ireland lately?'

'Okay, so you wanted to smash the system – right up until the minute you saw all that cash in Vernal's car.'

'Francis was becoming a problem. He was drinking too much, shooting his mouth off. MI5 were all over him.'

'You were following him that night?'

'I was watching the house in Anstruther. Two minutes after he

352

turned up, so did another car. Pretty obvious who they were. If Francis had drunk a bit less, he'd have been wise to them.'

Fox thought for a moment. 'When he left, you started to follow them – Vernal and the spooks both?'

'By the time I caught up, the crash had already happened. I saw them searching his car. They weren't especially good at it.' Pears paused. 'When they'd gone, I went over. Maybe Francis thought I was one of them. He was coming round, and pointing a bloody gun at me. I made a grab for it and it went off. There wasn't much I could do after that.'

'Except empty the boot of the DHC kitty.'

'Okay, so I took the money.'

'You did a lot more than that. Those two agents swear there was no gun in the car. That's because the gun was *yours*, not Vernal's. And it was no accident – it was a clean shot to the side of the head, identical to the way Alan Carter was killed. You assassinated Francis Vernal and I've only just realised why.' Fox paused, waiting to see if Pears would say anything, but Pears seemed to be concentrating on the road ahead. 'You said it yourself – you were watching the house in Anstruther. Meaning it was Alice Watts you were interested in. Either because you suspected her, or you had a thing for her. I'm guessing the latter. You had a thing for her, yet for some reason she preferred going to bed with the overweight drunken lawyer. I can see how that would rankle – you in your leather jacket and sunglasses, Mr Outlaw, losing out to Francis Vernal. Put a bullet in his head and Alice would think MI5 had done it. Maybe she'd want *your* shoulder to cry on.'

As Fox spoke, he couldn't help thinking of Charles Mangold and Imogen Vernal – another case of never-quite-requited love.

'But before any of that could happen,' he went on, 'she had disappeared. You had the money to tide you over and a murder everyone was calling suicide. The group was in tatters, so you walked away from it all and fell in love with the system you used to hate.'

Pears still had nothing to say, so Fox kept talking.

'I saw something on the internet during a trawl: the qualities you need to succeed in business are the same ones cold-blooded killers have. No empathy, no emotion ... whatever it takes to get the result you want.'

Pears responded to this with nothing more than a half-smile.

'Did you realise Alice was working undercover?' Fox went on.

Pears's smile faded. 'No,' he conceded.

'So how did you meet up again?'

'A charity dinner. She was being fast-tracked through CID.'

'You recognised her?'

'Almost immediately.'

'But she didn't remember you?'

'I'd changed more than she had.'

'You managed to keep it from her?' Fox waited for an answer, but none came. 'You must have worked out that she was spying on you and your friends back then.'

Pears nodded slowly. 'It didn't matter so much. Later, it didn't matter at all.' Pears glanced at Fox again. 'I'd fallen in love.'

'Again,' Fox commented.

'Properly,' Pears corrected him. 'For the first time.'

'You must have known someone would eventually place you.'

Pears gave a shrug. 'Did MacIver really recognise me on that stage?'

'Yes.'

'I don't think I believe you.'

'He wasn't sure where he knew you from,' Fox lied glibly. 'That's what got him upset. But on the way back to Carstairs ...'

'With some prodding from you?'

'Maybe a bit.'

'He's not going to make the most reliable witness in court.'

'Not that you think this is going to court ...'

'You're right.' Pears paused. 'I'm not even sure that's what *you* want.'

'Then what *do* I want?'

'You want the truth known more widely, destroying my life and Alison's reputation in the process. You think I'm a cold-blooded assassin who has been trying to protect his own back.'

'When in fact you've been your wife's shining knight?'

'That's right.'

'Alan Carter had nothing on you?'

'It was Alison's name he had. His colleague had been put in charge of the Vernal "suicide".'

'That was Gavin Willis – the man who'd had a nice little sideline selling guns to you and your kind.'

'MI5 got to him pretty damned sharp and said he had to keep the name of Alice Watts out of it. They told him she was actually a police officer, not long out of college and working undercover. If they'd bothered to give her an alias that wasn't so bloody similar to her *real* name ...' Pears shook his head, the mistake annoying him even now. 'Carter found some stuff hidden in Willis's cottage – a little insurance policy of a confession, including the name Alice Watts and the information that she'd been an undercover cop as well as Vernal's lover.'

'He put two and two together and tried blackmailing you?' Fox guessed.

'I'm the one with the money. He knew what the tabloids would do with the story. Nasty little man – not the sort that can be reasoned with.'

'I thought he was all right when I met him.'

'You saw what he wanted you to see.'

'He invited you to Gallowhill Cottage, so you could pay him for his silence?'

'Yes.'

'The door was unlocked, so you just walked in. He was seated at the table. A sitting duck, as it were. You didn't kill the dog, though – it's humans you have trouble with.' Fox paused. 'Francis Vernal might have been a spur-of-the-moment thing, but Alan Carter took a bit of preparation. First you asked a favour of your friend Sheriff Cardonald. You'd checked up on the blackmailer and you knew his history with the nephew. With Paul Carter out, you just had to set the scene – phoning his mobile a couple of times, luring him to the cottage. Then you went back home and snuggled up next to your wife.' Fox paused. 'How am I doing?'

'Does it matter? I'm not hearing anything a court would consider damning.'

'That's because you're good.' Fox paused again. 'Cardonald must have been livid when the prisoner he'd just released from custody was suddenly in the frame for murder. Won't do *his* reputation any favours.'

'Cardonald knows his place. I've made him a bit of money down the years.'

'Plus I'd guess you can be persuasive when the occasion demands it. What about the arms dealer in Barbados? Was he proving troublesome too?'

'You're not seriously suggesting ...?'

'His name was Benchley.'

'I know – he drowned in his pool.'

'And that's just coincidence?'

'Of course it is.'

Fox thought for a second. 'Cigarettes and a fifty-pound note went AWOL from Vernal's car.'

'Then someone must have taken them – maybe one of your own kind, Inspector.' Pears allowed himself another little half-smile and signalled on to a new road.

'Seems to me you've a destination in mind,' Fox commented.

'Maybe I do.' Pears was checking in his mirror again – no sign of any headlights behind him. His mobile rang, and he checked the display without answering.

'Chief Constable wondering where you've got to?' Fox guessed.

'I'm beginning to wonder if you're jealous.'

'Jealous?'

'It's a normal enough emotion,' Pears said, 'when you see someone with something you've not got and probably can't get. It's what drove Alan Carter – doesn't matter if it's money, status or love, it can make you a bit crazy.' Pears paused. 'How's your father doing?'

Fox glared at him.

'I know your own marriage didn't last long,' Pears continued. 'You've got a sister who's seen some trouble in the past. And now your father's been in hospital. He's home, though, right? Not at that care home – but home with you?'

Fox was still staring. Without looking, Pears knew it.

'Private care costs money,' he went on. 'A sister with no job can be a bit of a drain. Then you look at what Alison and I have got – not that we didn't work hard for it, but sometimes there's luck involved too.' He paused again. 'I *know* you're not after money, but that doesn't mean you can't feel bitterness at others' good fortune.' Pears gave Fox a good long look. 'How am *I* doing, Inspector?' he asked, throwing Fox's question back at him. 'The world's missing one alcoholic womaniser and one blackmailer. Three cheers for the world ...'

'I think I know where we are,' Fox said quietly, gazing out of the passenger-side window.

'Where else would we be?' Pears pulled into the lay-by, braking hard. There was a churning of gravel. He switched off the engine and turned to face Fox.

'A walk in the woods?' he suggested.

'I'm fine here, thanks,' Fox replied.

But Pears had reached beneath him and brought out another

handgun. A pistol this time. 'Kept a few souvenirs of the old days,' he explained, aiming the barrel at Fox's chest.

'You're forgetting the witnesses,' Fox stated. 'The surveillance van, for one thing.'

'As plans go, it's by no means perfect,' Pears allowed.

'So am I shooting myself in the head, or what?'

'You're going to hang yourself.'

'Am I?'

'At the scene of your obsession. I saw proof enough of it at your house – all those papers, a computer filled with guesswork. Francis Vernal got beneath your skin. Add that to your recent problems at work, and an ailing parent ...'

'I decide to end it all?' Fox watched Pears nod. 'And what are you doing all this time?'

'We drove here together. You proposed some crazy theories. You directed me to this place, thinking it would mean something to me. Then madness got the better of you and you ran into the woods. I left you to it and drove home.'

'It'll all still come out – you and Alice, Vernal and Alan Carter ...'

'There'll be hearsay,' Pears agreed. 'But I doubt the media will make much of it.' He paused. 'I have a battery of lawyers at my disposal, and I believe injunctions are all the rage. Trust me, precious little will be allowed to emerge. Why not toss your mobile phone on to the back seat? You won't be needing it.'

Fox hesitated, and Pears dug the tip of the gun into his ribs. He winced and removed his phone, threw it into the gap between the two seats.

'Out,' Pears ordered. He had opened his own door, keeping the pistol pointed at Fox. Fox undid his seat belt and got out of the car. The air was cold and clear: country air. They were next to the small cairn commemorating Francis Vernal's life.

A patriot.

It was a silent rural road. There would maybe be another car passing in half an hour or so. Plenty of time for Pears to carry out the execution – and no witnesses. There was a barking in the distance – a farm dog, or maybe a fox. Fox wished he was more like his animal namesake: swift and lean and nimble.

Cunning, though: there was always cunning ...

Pears had closed the driver's-side door and come around to Fox's side of the Maserati. He slammed shut the passenger door.

'Not often you see an expensive sports car parked here,' Fox speculated. 'Sure you don't want to leave it somewhere less visible?'

'I'll just have to risk it,' Pears responded. 'Let's get going.'

'No rope,' Fox told him.

'It's waiting for us.' Pears waved the gun in the general direction.

'Bit more planning than I gave you credit for.'

'I read about it a while back. A man walked into a forest somewhere. He was too old to get the noose over a high branch, so he just tied it to a lower one, placed his neck in it, and leaned all the way forward ...'

'That's what I'm going to do, is it? Sounds like I'd be better off refusing and taking a bullet. At least that way you'll be in the frame.'

Pears shrugged. 'My word against yours, except you won't have any words. A body could lie out here for years without anyone finding it.' He gestured towards the forest again. 'Let's not think about all that yet, though. Let's just walk ...'

Fox took a few steps forward, until he was within touching distance of the first line of trees. 'Something nobody seemed to know ...' He tried to sound beaten, resigned to his fate.

'What?'

'But you will, I suppose.'

Intrigued, Pears repeated his question.

'The actual tree Vernal's car collided with.'

Pears considered for a moment. 'Probably that one,' he answered, gesturing with the pistol. The moment it was pointed away from him, Fox made his move, grabbing Pears's wrist and twisting it. Pears gasped, his fingers splaying involuntarily. As the gun dropped to the ground, Fox scuffed it away with his foot. But Pears was the stronger of the two – he got in a few heavy blows as Fox wrestled with him. It took Fox only a few seconds to realise he was not going to win this fight, not at close quarters. He couldn't see the gun, so he gave Pears a shove backwards and ran for it.

Pears didn't follow, not straight away, which gave Fox a bit of time to dart between the trees. He was a good twenty or thirty feet away, the gloom working to his advantage, when a bullet shattered some bark inches from his left shoulder. A splinter penetrated his cheek, stinging like hell. He left it where it was and kept weaving as best he could.

He didn't know how deep the woods were. How soon would it be till he reached open ground, where he'd be an easy target? There was a half-moon in the sky above, obscured by a thin layer of shifting cloud. Enough light to see by. More than enough for Stephen Pears.

A bullet lodged in a tree: evidence waiting to be found. But would anyone find it? Though times had changed, the police could still be sloppy. He patted his pockets. If he started to discard credit cards and the like, he would be leaving a trail for Pears as much as for any investigators. Another bullet zinged past him and thumped into bark. Pears was heavyset; probably didn't get much use of the gym at the house – did Fox have half a chance of outpacing him?

Didn't matter: it was the bullets he had to outpace, and that wasn't going to happen.

Outmanoeuvre him, then – but how? The road was his best chance. It would depend on an elusive passing car, but his run of luck could change for the better, couldn't it? Another option: double back to the Maserati. Pears hadn't locked it, but Fox couldn't remember if he'd left the key. His phone was on the back seat. So was the little recorder he'd borrowed from Joe Naysmith. He'd thrown it there along with the battery pack, having switched it on first. Everything said in the car would, he hoped, be on it – and audible.

But only useful to him if Pears didn't find it …

Another shot, another miss. Would a farmer maybe hear? A poacher? Sweat was running down Fox's back. He could remove his jacket, but it was darker than his shirt and he didn't want to give his pursuer a more inviting target. His chest was hurting. He remembered the stitch when he'd run across the Forth Road Bridge. Stitch or not, this time he had to keep moving.

The fourth shot, however, found its target. He felt the impact against his left shoulder. It went in and out again, numbing him for a moment. His legs almost buckled, but he wouldn't let them. A burning sensation, and then pain shooting down his arm all the way to his fingertips.

He gritted his teeth. Knew he couldn't stop, not even for a second. Warm blood, oozing and running. He gripped his left hand in his right, cradling it against his chest.

And ran.

Risked a glance behind him but could see no sign of Pears. He realised he was being stalked. Pears wasn't panicking. He was being his usual methodical self. He was watching, listening and calculating. He was wearing his quarry down. Let Fox run in circles, then pick him off. Fox cursed his own stupidity and kept moving. Images flashed into his mind: Mitch and Jude; Imogen Vernal and Charles Mangold. Mangold getting him into this in the first place.

No, who was he kidding – he only had himself to blame.

Paul and Alan Carter ...

Scholes and Haldane and Michaelson ...

Evelyn Mills and Fiona McFadzean ...

Players in the drama of his life and death.

Alice Watts morphing into Alison Watson.

Hawkeye hiding behind the eyes of Stephen Pears.

DCI Jackson, caretaker of state secrets.

Chris Fox.

And back to Mitch and Jude again.

They swirled around him as he headed up a noticeable incline. Moss and leaves mulched beneath him. Every breath he drew into his tired lungs tasted of loam.

'Fox!'

The yelp from Pears told Fox that the man was maybe thirty or forty yards away. It also hinted at irritation, and this gave him a glimmer of hope. He tried to smile but couldn't. He licked his lips instead, his saliva as sticky as wallpaper paste.

And he ran.

'Fox!'

Keep shouting, pal: means I know where you are.

Every movement he made sent another jolt of pain through his shoulder. Blood was dripping on to his trousers and shoes. Thinking about it made him nauseous. He swallowed hard, tasting iron and bile. Emerging into a small clearing, he paused for only a moment to stare at the noose hanging from a tree branch, almost exactly in line with his eyes, one end wrapped around the trunk and knotted fast.

Move, Malcolm.

A steeper bank, a single line of trees and then a gap. He knew it had to be the road. He was forced to claw at the ground with his right hand as he climbed. When he stood up again, he was inches from the tarmac. He looked to left and right. The boot of the Maserati was just visible, the rest of the vehicle hidden around the curve of the road. Fox headed in the other direction. He was out in the open now. Couldn't hear any traffic or spot headlights in the distance. His eyes stung and he wiped the perspiration from them. He could always dive into the woods on the opposite side of the road. Safer there, but more isolated, too.

Wait ...

The sky was brightening. He could make out the treeline, silhouetted against the night. And now he could hear the faint roar of an engine. He remembered the local boy racers, their names scored into the memorial cairn. Would they stop for him? Were their brakes equal to their reaction time? It would be so bloody typical: escape a gunman just to be mown down by a spotty teen in a super-tuned Cosworth.

The roar was definitely getting louder. He was on a nice straight stretch. He started to remove his jacket – the lighter shirt might now be an advantage.

'Fox!'

Fox turned. Pears looked mightily pissed off. The pistol hung at his side as he emerged from the trees. Seemed to Fox that he had tripped and fallen. A definite limp, clothes and face smeared with dirt.

He took a few deep breaths, straightened up, and started to raise the gun. Fox was barely thirty feet away. But the car was approaching. Fox was waving with his working arm. Pears was aiming at him as the car came into view, headlights flashing from full beam to dipped and back again, horn blaring. A small car with a big engine. Fox was trying to shield his eyes. A half-glance back told him Pears was doing the same. The car skidded to a stop, ending up side-on to the direction of travel. The passenger-side door flew open.

'You trying to get yourself killed, pal?'

Just a kid, maybe not sixteen yet. Bass booming from inside the car. The driver leaving the engine idling as he too emerged, another car arriving behind him. More kids getting out. More thumping music.

Fox was staring at Pears. The gun was no longer visible, hidden behind him. He was making to retreat, backing away.

'Is that blood?' someone was asking Fox. 'You crashed your motor or something?'

Pears was no longer visible. Fox asked the passenger if he could borrow his phone.

'Aye, sure.'

But Fox's hand was shaking too hard, his fingers slippery with blood. So he recited the number instead, the teenager punching it in and holding the phone towards his ear as he started to talk to Tony Kaye.

The Mondeo turned up a couple of minutes after the Armed Response Unit. Fox had given the four officers the lowdown: type of weapon; rounds already fired; direction taken by assailant. The teenagers had stuck around, slightly nervous that there might be some hidden agenda, despite Fox's assurances. They leaned against their cars, smoking cigarettes and staring at the weaponry. When one tried to take a photo, a wagged finger was enough to deter him.

Tony Kaye was first out of the Mondeo, followed by Joe Naysmith. The last of the armed officers was disappearing into the woods as they walked towards Fox.

'Does it hurt?' Naysmith asked, nodding towards the wound.

'Like blazes,' Fox informed him.

'Called an ambulance yet?'

Fox shook his head.

'You've lost a bit of blood.'

'It's a graze,' Kaye stated, giving Fox's shoulder a cursory glance. 'Think we should see what they're up to?' He gestured towards the woods.

After a moment's hesitation, Fox nodded his agreement. 'You lot stay here,' he ordered the teenagers. 'And no phones or texting – got that?'

It was quiet in the woods: no voices, no gunfire. Just the crackling of twigs underfoot.

'You got here quick,' Fox said.

'Maniac at the wheel,' Naysmith responded.

'What did he have in mind for you?' Kaye asked, pushing his way past the encroaching branches.

'Suicide by hanging.'

Kaye shook his head. 'I thought this guy was supposed to be a pro.'

'He's got away with it in the past.'

'Overconfidence?' Naysmith guessed. Then: 'What if we get to him before the ARU?'

'There's three of us,' Kaye growled. 'Mood I'm in, shooter or no shooter he's getting a doing.'

'You sure you're all right?' Naysmith asked, noticing that Fox was faltering.

'Just a bit dizzy.' Naysmith steadied him. 'I'll be fine, Joe, honest.' Fox wiped sweat from his face with his unbloodied sleeve.

When Kaye looked to Fox for guidance on the direction they should be taking, Fox started to shrug with his one good shoulder, but then stopped as a yell rang out. Sounded like the ARU giving due warning.

'Maybe that way,' he suggested.

The three men pushed on at a brisker pace. More voices ahead of them, but appearing to be in movement. It felt to Fox as though he were retracing his steps almost exactly. Part of his brain was telling him to stop, but he kept going, the sweat pouring from him.

They all heard the car engine when it kicked into life. A low growl turning into a roar.

'Maserati?' Naysmith guessed.

Sure enough, the Armed Response Unit stood with pistols trained on the car's windscreen. Not that this was enough to dissuade the figure in the driving seat. The Maserati skidded backwards on to the road, spun, and started to speed away, its headlights switched off.

'Back to the patrol car!' one of the ARU men barked to his colleagues. 'Ronnie, call it in!'

'What do you reckon?' Kaye was asking Fox. 'Mondeo might be up to the job.'

'Malcolm needs patching up,' Naysmith warned.

Kaye ignored him, awaiting Fox's decision. Then came the sound of squealing tyres, followed by the thump of impact.

43

The Victoria Hospital again.

Fox didn't doubt that the reporter Brian Jamieson would be on the prowl somewhere in the vicinity. Fox's wound had been cleaned and stitched. Painkillers were swooshing around inside him, and he had a prescription for more in his pocket. His shoulder was strapped and there was a dull ache if he tried moving his left hand. His jacket and shirt had been bagged as evidence. Forensics would head to the scene once it was light, seeking out bullet casings and the pistol and the noose.

No weapon had been found in the car. Pears must have tossed it. Fox was standing in the injured man's room right now. His was the only bed in there. One of the medics had listed his injuries: a couple of broken ribs, two damaged knees and facial bruising.

'Why you should wear a seat belt,' the medic had stated.

A wire cage beneath the bedclothes was keeping pressure off the patient's legs. He had opened his eyes when Fox stepped into the room. There was a police officer on duty outside. He had noted Fox's name and taken a good look at his warrant card. Fox didn't blame him: the borrowed hooded top and baggy jogging bottoms were hardly standard issue for a cop.

'I think he's asleep,' the officer had said.

But Stephen Pears was awake for Fox.

'We'll find the gun,' Fox told him.

'And what will that prove? That I was so scared of you, I felt the need of it?'

'Scared of me, were you?'

'You and your outlandish theories.' Pears tried to clear his throat, his mouth parched. He looked at the water jug next to his bed, but Fox wasn't about to oblige.

'You don't seriously think that's going to work?' he asked instead.

'You'd just accused me of murder,' Pears went on. 'You'd told me to drive to the spot where Francis Vernal died. I panicked, thinking you had a similar fate in mind for me.' He was staring hard at Fox.

'And that's all you've got to play with?'

'It's all you're going to get from me.'

Fox watched as Pears slowly turned his head away from him. There was just the tiniest gasp of pain as he did so. Fox bided his time, knowing another visitor would be arriving soon. On cue, the door behind him flew open. Alison Pears ignored Fox and strode towards the bed.

'Stephen!' She leaned over her husband, planting a hard kiss on his cheek. 'What in God's name happened?'

'Can you believe they left me here alone with that madman?' Pears replied. She straightened up and turned towards Fox.

'Your husband had plans to kill me,' Fox informed her. 'Same as Francis Vernal and Alan Carter. When a noose wouldn't do the job, he tried using a gun instead.'

'Get out,' she commanded.

Fox shook his head slowly. Alison Pears's eyes narrowed. 'That's an order, Inspector.'

Fox held her stare. 'I'm wondering how long you've known. You *do* know, don't you?'

'Know what?'

'That you married Hawkeye. Did you work it out before the wedding or after? I'm not entirely sure the pair of you have ever talked about it. Ancient history, after all – you were both other people. No need to dredge up the past. Happy, healthy, wealthy and going places ...'

'I'm telling you to leave.' Her voice was almost a snarl, both rows of teeth bared.

'So you can start to get your stories straight?' Fox surmised. 'Can't have this huge, talented edifice crumble – is that your thinking?'

'I told you he's insane,' Stephen Pears complained. 'The man's completely obsessed.'

'Yes, I'd say so,' his wife agreed, her voice dropping a little. 'Obsessed and paranoid – seeing conspiracies everywhere.'

'Everywhere,' her husband echoed.

Silence descended on the room. Fox stood his ground, then nodded slowly.

'You're going to fight this?' he asked.

'Whatever it takes,' Alison Pears replied.

Fox nodded again and reached into his pocket, removing the little digital recorder and pressing the 'play' button. The speaker was tiny, but with the volume all the way up, the conversation was clear enough.

So you're going to tell me why you killed Francis Vernal?

You have to go back further. You have to understand how things were …

Fox fast-forwarded a little and hit 'play' again.

Okay, so I took the money …

It was Alice Watts you were interested in.

His eyes fixed on those of Alison Pears, he moved the recording forward a little further.

Alan Carter had nothing on you?

It was Alison's name he had.

And forward again.

Nasty little man – not the sort that can be reasoned with.

Fox switched the machine off and held it between thumb and forefinger. Alison Pears seemed frozen for a moment, then inhaled and exhaled before turning towards the bed.

'You're a fool, Stephen, and it's beginning to look like you always were.'

Pears had squeezed shut his eyes, as if every word was a fresh affliction. She loomed over him, hands gripping the metal side-rail as she started to get her breathing back under control. Blood had risen to her cheeks, and she rubbed her fingers down them, as if to erase the colouring. She ran her tongue across her lips and faced Fox again.

'I knew nothing about any of this,' she declared. 'It's all come as a complete and utter shock.' She straightened her jacket and brushed a few stray strands of hair back into place. Fox was reminded of the transformation that had taken place in her study, when she'd answered her telephone.

'The pair of you are well matched,' he commented. 'Hard to know which one is the colder, actually.' He gave a twitch of the mouth, maintaining eye contact with Alison Pears. 'Fine, then – you'll tell your story and I'll tell mine. Whichever way it works out, you've ended up married to a killer, and I doubt that'll sit too well with the position of Chief Constable. I'm guessing it might even be a matter for the Complaints ...' The recorder was back in his pocket. He used his good hand to open the door. The officer on duty was trying not to look too interested in the commotion he'd just heard. As Fox stepped into the corridor, he turned his head towards Stephen Pears. But Pears's eyes were still closed, so Fox let the door swing shut, leaving him to his fate.

Fourteen

44

It wasn't much of a homecoming.

Fox's father was asleep on the bed in the living room. Jude hadn't got round to tidying the place. Plates and mugs needed taking to the kitchen; magazines put into a bag for recycling. She gave him a peck on the cheek and said it was good to see him.

'How long will you be off work?' she asked.

'I'll be able to look after Dad, if that's what you're asking.'

'It wasn't,' she said, not meeting his eyes. His legs were stiff from all that running, and there was still a residual burning sensation in his lungs. Every few minutes he seemed to relive part of it, but to everyone who asked him how he was, he gave the same answer: 'I'm fine.'

He had so far avoided seeing any TV coverage. There had been phone messages from Evelyn Mills, Fiona McFadzean, and Charles Mangold. He had listened to them but not replied. The same went for texts – what was he supposed to say to any of them? He felt bad about ignoring Evelyn Mills in particular, but didn't know what else to do. Too many relationships had gone sour around him; he didn't want to add any more fuel to the general misery.

Jude made him tea while he sat on the sofa, watching his father. The chest rose and fell. The mouth was slightly open. Mitch's hair needed washing, and the room smelled faintly of talcum powder.

'Anything been happening?' he asked Jude as she handed him his mug.

'A lot of phone calls, but that's about it. And one of the neighbours came to the door to ask after you. Some old boy from across the street.'

'Mr Anderson,' Fox informed her.

She nodded, without really taking the information in. 'Anyway,' she said, 'I'm glad you're here, because I need to nip out for some ciggies.'

'Ten a day still?'

'Am I about to get a lecture?'

Fox shook his head. 'On you go,' he told her.

She wasted no time fetching her coat, then asked him if he wanted anything. He shook his head again. When she hesitated, he knew she needed money, so dug a twenty out of his pocket.

'Thanks,' she said. 'Sure you don't want tomato juice or something?'

'No.'

The door closed after her, leaving Fox alone with his father. He cleared some odds and ends from the chair next to the bed and sat down, taking Mitch's hand in his. The eyelids fluttered and the breathing changed, but he didn't wake up. Fox removed the photo from his pocket, the one showing Chris as he cheered on Francis Vernal. He wrote both their names on the back and added it to the shoebox. He spotted a half-bottle of whisky on the mantelpiece, and another half-bottle of vodka next to it. The vodka – Jude's drink of choice – was almost empty, the whisky almost full. Fox stared at both bottles, then got up and walked towards them. He unscrewed the cap from the whisky and put his nose to the open neck, inhaling and exhaling. He knew it would be so easy to tip a measure into his mouth, savouring before swallowing. But instead he walked back to the bed and dipped a finger into the liquid, dabbing his father's lips with it. The eyelids fluttered again.

'That's some bedside manner you've got,' Mitch Fox said, opening his eyes and smiling at his son. 'Now pour me a proper one, will you?'

Fox didn't argue. He fetched a couple of clean glasses, filling one with tap water for himself.

'None of that for me, mind,' his father cautioned.

Fox poured an inch of whisky into the tumbler and handed it over. His father managed to sit up unaided and raised the drink in a toast.

'Here's tae us,' he said, 'wha's like us?'

'Gey few,' Fox recited, lifting his own glass. 'And they're a' deid ...'

372

He watched as his father sipped the whisky. 'I can be a detective when I want to be,' he said quietly. 'Just so you know.'

'Can't be that good at it or you wouldn't have a bullet hole in you.' Mitch held out the empty glass, his eyes demanding a refill.

'Jude'll kill me if I get you drunk.'

'Then you won't have died in vain.'

'True enough, I suppose.' So Fox twisted the cap from the whisky bottle and poured again.